WITHDRAWN

The Collected Stories of Peter Taylor

Books by Peter Taylor

The Collected Stories of

PETER TAYLOR

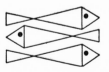

Farrar, Straus and Giroux

NEW YORK

Acknowledgment is made to the editors of *The New Yorker* for the following stories that first appeared in their pages: "Reservations," "The Other Times," "Their Losses," "Two Pilgrims," "What You Hear from 'Em?," "A Wife of Nashville," "Cookie" (originally "Middle Age"), "1939" (originally "A Sentimental Journey"), "Guests," "Heads of Houses," "Mrs. Billingsby's Wine," *"Je Suis Perdu"* (originally "A Pair of Bright-Blue Eyes") and "Miss Leonora When Last Seen"; to *McCall's* for "The Elect"; *Shenandoah* for "First Heat"; *Sewanee Review* for "At the Drug Store"; *Southern Review* for "A Spinster's Tale" and "The Fancy Woman"; *Kenyon Review* for "Venus, Cupid, Folly and Time" and "There"; and *Virginia Quarterly Review* for "Dean of Men."

For my Mother
KATHERINE TAYLOR TAYLOR
who was the best teller of tales I know
and from whose lips I first heard many
of the stories in this book.

Contents

[vii]

CONTENTS

The Collected Stories of Peter Taylor

Dean of Men

I am not unsympathetic, Jack, to your views on the war. I am not unsympathetic to your views on the state of the world in general. From the way you wear your hair and from the way you dress I do find it difficult to decide whether you or that young girl you say you are about to marry is going to play the male role in your marriage— or the female role. But even that I don't find offensive. And I am not trying to make crude jokes at your expense. You must pardon me, though, if my remarks seem too personal. I confess I don't know you as well as a father *ought* to know his son, and I may seem to take liberties.

However, Jack, I do believe that I understand the direction in which you—all of you—think you are going. I have not observed college students during the past thirty years for nothing. And I must try to warn you that I don't think even your wonderful generation will succeed in going very far along the road you are on. In this connection, Jack, I want to tell you a story. I can tell you this story because even its most recent chapters took place a very long time ago and because the events of the story don't matter to anybody any more—neither to me nor even to your mother. When you see your mother next, and if you repeat what I am about to tell you, she may give you a somewhat different version. But that doesn't matter. It is not really a story about your mother and me or about our divorce. Perhaps it is a story about you and me—about men.

I think I know the very moment to begin: I was fitting the key into the lock of my office door on a Sunday morning. I was in such a temper I could hardly get the key into the keyhole or turn the lock after it was in. There had been a scene at our breakfast table at home; I had left the house. It was a strangely upsetting scene for me, though commonplace enough on the surface. Your sister Susie, who was no more than nine or ten then—she couldn't have been more, since *you* were still in a high chair, Jack—Susie had interrupted what I was saying across my Sunday morning grapefruit to your mother. And I had fired away at her, "Don't interrupt grown-up talk, Susie!"

That sounds commonplace enough, I know. But Susie persisted. "Why don't you go up to the trustees, Daddy," said she, advising me on how to behave in the professional crisis I was then in, which I had been discoursing upon across my grapefruit. "Why don't you go up to them and tell them how the president of the college is being unfair to you?"

Somehow I found her little remark enraging. I fairly shouted across the table, "For God's sake, Susie, shut up. Don't try to talk about things you don't understand or know a damned thing about!"

I blush now to think that I ever spoke so to a child, but I remember it too well to try to deny it. You see, Jack, I had actually already resigned my appointment at that college where I was then teaching, which was the very college where, a dozen years before, I had been an undergraduate. I had resigned just three weeks before, in protest against an injustice done me, and I had not yet received a definite commitment from the place where I was going next year. (I did receive the commitment the following day, as I recall, but that is not really significant.) Anyhow, I was feeling like a fool, I suppose, to have brought into the world three children for whom I might not be able to provide—only two children, actually, though little Maisie was on the way by then. And I was feeling like a fool, I suppose, to have risked their welfare—*your* welfare, if you please—over a principle of honest administration in a small Midwestern college. I was a very unhappy man, Jack, and there before me was my little ten-year-old daughter seeming to reproach me for my foolishness . . . At any rate, after my second blast at her, Susie had burst into tears and had run from the dining room and out into the yard. Your mother got up from her chair at the end of the table and said to me, "I would be ashamed of myself if I were you."

I made no reply except to say through my teeth: "This is too much."

Your mother's words were still in my ears when I shoved open the door to my office at the college. (Marie's words have a way of lingering in your ears for a very long time, Jack.) Anyhow, I had left the table without finishing breakfast, and left the dining room without any idea of where I was going. And then suddenly I had known. What drove me from the table, of course, were those words of Marie's that were still in my ears. For, Jack, those were the very words I had once heard my mother speak to my father, and, moreover, had heard her speak to Father at a Sunday breakfast table when *he* had teased my own sister Margaret till she cried and left the room. "I would be ashamed of myself if I were you," my mother had said, rising from the table in just the same way that my own wife was destined to do twenty years later. My father bolted from the table, left the house, and went downtown to his office, where he spent the whole of that Sunday. It seemed almost impossible that the incident should be repeating itself in my life. And yet to a remarkable degree it was so, and the memory of where it was my father had taken himself off to told me to what place I must take myself that Sunday morning.

It struck me, just as the door to my office came open, that I had never before seen my office at that early hour on Sunday. I had never, in fact, been in that building where my office was on a Sunday morning—or on the college campus itself, for that matter. It was a lovely campus, on a hill and with trees and with a little river at the foot of the hill, and it was a quite handsome neo-Gothic building I was in. I altogether liked that place, I can assure you. And in addition to my liking the other people on the faculty there, I had my old associations with the place from my undergraduate days. The truth is, I had thought I would settle down there for life, to do my teaching and my writing. It was the third teaching appointment I had had, but in my profession many people have to move around even more than I before they find a congenial spot, Jack. I was not yet thirty-five. I had considered myself lucky to find an agreeable place so early in my career, a small college where I had memories of my youth and where I would be allowed to do my mature work in peace . . .

But I knew by that Sunday morning that I was going to move on. I knew that by the next fall I would be in some other, almost identical office on some other campus and that your mother and I, with our three children, would be established in another house in another college town somewhere. But when I shoved open my office door, somehow it was not as though it were the door to just any little cubbyhole of an office. It was as if it were the door to my ancestral keep—my castle, so to speak; and I burst in upon my papers, my books, my pictures that morning as if expecting to catch them, my kinsmen—my cousins germane—in some conspiratorial act against me—yes, as though it were my books, my papers, my pictures who had betrayed me. But of course the room was just as I had left it. It was the same, and yet at that hour on Sunday morning it did seem different, too.

I can see myself there now, especially as I was during the first quarter hour of that long day. I didn't knock things about or tear up the place as it was my first impulse to do. Instead, after I had slammed the door and latched it, the first thing I did was to go quickly to my desk and turn down the photographs of your mother and Susie and even the one of yourself, Jack. I took the pages of my manuscript and of my typescript which had been in little stacks all over my desk top and quietly stuffed them inside the desk drawers. The books I had been reading recently—my own and those from the library—I removed from the table by my leather chair, putting them out of sight or at least placing them where they would not catch my eye, on the lowest shelf of my bookcase. Then I took down from the walls the four or five prints that hung there, reproductions I had brought back from my Fulbright in Italy, and I set them on the floor with their faces against the wall. If I handled these familiar objects gently, I believe it was just because I had not, after all, found them in active conspiracy against me.

There was no conspiracy among my books and papers and pictures; but what was perhaps worse, I seemingly had found them all dead—murdered. I felt they were strewn about the room like corpses in the last scene of an Elizabethan tragedy. Dead and murdered, that is, so far as I was concerned. Dead and wanting burial. And so, bending over them, I tenderly tucked them away as if to their last rest. Then I went and half sat, half leaned against the sill of the room's only window. The venetian blind there was lowered and the louvers were only half open. I leaned against the sill with my arms folded on my chest and observed the crepuscular light in the room, and I was aware of the Sunday morning stillness. Once again I heard Marie's voice, and after a moment once again heard my

mother's voice. Presently I recalled my father's voice too, speaking
not through his teeth as I had done that morning, but growling out
of one corner of his mouth. I remembered how, as a younger man, I
would sometimes wonder about that outburst of Father's temper on
that other Sunday morning. It had seemed to me so unlike him. I
used to speculate even, in the most literal-minded way, on how he
had managed to occupy himself during the long hours he had spent
alone in *his* office on that Sunday. The scene he had made at his
breakfast table—or that my sister Margaret, or my mother had
made—suddenly now became very easy for me to understand.
Everything fell so easily into place that I felt I had always understood it. My father was a lawyer and a businessman who had lost
most of what he had as a consequence of the '29 Crash. My sister
Margaret was already a young lady at the time. She was no little girl
like Susie when she sat down to breakfast with Father that other
Sunday. She was a good-looking blond girl with wide green eyes,
and she had a lovely disposition. She was always cheerful, always
saying something clever or making you feel that you had said
something clever. Margaret was the oldest child in the family, and I
the youngest. But we were very close to each other, and I believe she
confided her most serious thoughts to me more often than to anyone
else, though surely it was Father she loved best. There was frequently a great deal of banter between her and Father at the table.
She was such a well-behaved girl, so puritanical really, that Father
would tease her sometimes about leading a wild life and keeping
late hours. Mother would say she thought it in bad taste for Father
to tease his own daughter about such things and that perhaps he
would be putting ideas into her head. But Margaret would laugh at
Mother and say that Father's evil mind made it all the more fun to
deceive him. Then she and Father would laugh together in a sort of
duet of laughter.

Margaret was popular with boys and always had a number of

serious admirers. But the more serious the admirers were, the more she and Father seemed to delight in making fun of them. I don't believe Margaret ever imagined she was in love with any of those young men, until the time when Paul Kirkpatrick came along. Paul's family was one that nearly everybody knew about. They were such very rich people that even the Crash and the Depression hardly affected them at all. But it worried Margaret how rich the Kirkpatrick family was. It worried her, that is, that Paul would some day be rich, that she knew he would be rich, and that he was the only young man she found herself able to love. "I know I really love him for himself," she would say to me when we were walking in the park together or if we were in her room with the door shut, "but sometimes there seems to be an ugly, suspicious side of me—another person (old, nasty-minded Mag, I call her)—who laughs and cackles at me like a witch and says, '*I* know why you love him so, dear Miss Margaret! You don't deceive me!'" Then Margaret and I would laugh together, rather the way she and Father did. But she was serious, and was worried.

Perhaps Father worried about it, too—more than I guessed, more than Margaret guessed. Naturally, he would have liked for her to marry a rich man, but there had been so much talk at our house about how hard times were for us that Father may have been afraid Margaret was going to marry into a rich family for *his* sake. At any rate, he was harder on Paul Kirkpatrick in his fun-making than he had been on any of the other young men. And Margaret went right along with him. They made fun of Paul's teeth—Margaret called them stalactites and stalagmites; made fun of his too lofty way of speaking, of the way he walked—they said he waddled; even made fun of his baby-smooth complexion.

Yet, after one of those sessions with Father, when she and I were alone, Margaret smiled at me and said, "You know something? I really think Paul's very good-looking, don't you?"

I told her that yes, I did think so. And it was true. Paul Kirk-patrick was quite handsome. He was an attractive and intelligent young man. But Margaret and Father kept on telling each other how ridiculous he was. It was the summer of 1930. Father was under great tension that summer. It was a year when he suffered one financial blow after another. And he never seemed more tense than when he and Margaret got on the subject of Paul. Sometimes it was very clear that he was prodding and trying to make her come to Paul's defense. But she never gave an inch. I was certain sometimes, however, from the way she sat smiling at Father that she was on the verge of blurting out that she loved Paul and was going to marry him. For I think my sister Margaret intended to marry Paul Kirkpatrick and would have done so had it not been for the family scene that Sunday morning. I had witnessed Paul's and Margaret's embraces and kisses at the side door more than once that summer. And once I saw—or just possibly imagined I saw—a ring with a large stone in Margaret's purse. Anyway, I remember she came down to breakfast later than the rest of us on that Sunday, and she was fully dressed, which was unusual for anyone at our breakfast table on Sunday. It seems to me that Father had not spoken at the table—he was often silent and abstracted then, though it was not in his nature to be so—he had not spoken until he looked up and saw Margaret sitting, fully dressed, at her place. "Well, you must have a church date with our toothy young friend," he said to her.

"He's coming over this morning," Margaret said with a smile. "I don't know about church." I am quite sure now that she was trying to prepare Father and that Paul was going to "speak" to him that day.

I saw Mother look at Father, and it seems to me that I heard him swallow, though his mouth and throat were empty. Then, lifting a fork heaped with scrambled eggs, he said, "Why not? It's just as easy to love a rich one as a poor one, isn't it, Margaret?"

I saw the first patches of red appear under Margaret's ears and then the same red suffuse her entire face. And I saw the tears fill her eyes before the first sob came. When she pushed herself back from the table, Father was still holding the fork with the eggs on it. He put his fork down on his plate without spilling a morsel. But he was as white as the big napkin which his left hand then drew from his lap and threw out upon the table. "My God. My God," he growled from the corner of his mouth as Margaret ran, weeping aloud, through the living room and then through the hall and on upstairs. And my mother rose at her place and said, "I would be ashamed of myself if I were you."

How Father occupied himself and what he thought about when he reached his office that Sunday were questions that occurred to me during the very hours he was there, occurred to me even though I was just a boy of twelve at the time. My father was known as "a devoted family man," he almost never went to his office at night, and if some piece of business called him there on a Saturday afternoon or a Sunday, he groaned and complained endlessly. We knew he had gone to his office that morning, however, because Mother telephoned him after about an hour, to make sure he was all right. She knew about the money worries he had then, of course, and so she was quick to blame his behavior on that. In fact, she went to Margaret's room and reminded her of "the tensions Father was under" and told her that *she* must forgive him, too. I suspect that Margaret had already forgiven him. I know that she had telephoned Paul Kirkpatrick and told him not to come that day. Her romance with Paul did not last long after that. The next year she married a "struggling young lawyer" and with him, as my mother would have said, "she has had a good life."

No doubt my father wrote a few letters at his office desk, as I did during the course of my Sunday at my office. But probably it wasn't easy for him to concentrate on letters. I recall that even while I remained leaning against the sill of my office window it came to me that what my father might have thought about in his office, twenty years before, was his own father. For yes, there *was* a story in the family about a scene that my grandfather had made at *his* breakfast table, too. I cannot give so many details about it, though possibly my father could have. There are many obscurities about the old story that I can't possibly clear up and won't try to. In fact, I don't know anything definite about the immediate circumstances that led to the scene. Perhaps I never knew them. People in my grandfather's day disliked admitting they did wretched things to each other at home or that there *were* family scenes in their families. All of the incident that has come down is that my grandfather, no longer a young man—a man past middle age, standing in the doorway to his dining room with his broad-brimmed felt hat on, hurled a silver dollar at my grandmother, who was still seated at the breakfast table, and that the silver dollar landed in the sugar bowl. There is just the additional detail that my grandmother would allow no one to remove the coin and that that sugar bowl, with the silver dollar buried in the sugar, remained on her pantry shelf as long as the old lady lived.

I have always imagined that there had been a quarrel between my grandparents about housekeeping money; perhaps my grandfather, who was not much of a family man in the beginning and who lived a big part of his life away from home, among men, and who was known by all men for his quick temper, perhaps he lost his head momentarily. He forgot he was not among men and he hurled the piece of money at his wife as he would have at some man to whom he had lost a bet. He and my grandmother may have had other difficulties between them over money or over other matters. Perhaps it was really a symbolic gesture on his part, as refusing to remove the coin was on hers. He was not a rich man, but then he was

certainly not a poor man either, and actually in his day he was quite
a well-known public figure. He was in politics, as his father and his
father's father before him were . . . I must tell you something
about their politics. They were not exactly small-time politicians.
Each one of them, at one time or another during his lifetime, represented our district in Congress. For nearly a hundred years, "we"
more or less occupied that seat in Congress. But my grandfather was
the most successful and best known of the line and in middle age
was elected to the U.S. Senate to complete the unexpired term of an
incumbent who had died in office.

Probably my grandfather brought the special type of politician
they all three were to its highest possible point of development, a
kind of frontiersman-gentleman politician with just the right mixture of realism and idealism to appeal to their constituents. Today
people would no doubt call him a pragmatist. He was known for
his elegant oratory on the platform and in public debate and known
also for the coarseness of his speech in private debate or in private
confrontation with his opponents. (My grandfather's grandfather
had once horsewhipped an opponent on the public square, and his
own father had fought a duel.) It was Grandfather's beautiful
oratory and his beautiful voice that got him elected to the Senate.
People didn't care what his stand on tariff or on the silver or gold
issue was. They believed he was an honest man and they knew he
was a spellbinder. He too believed he was an honest man and he
didn't understand the new kind of urban politician who was coming
to power in our state at the time. It may be he was actually betrayed
and ruined by the new politicians simply because they were "low-
born rascals." Or it may be he was inevitably betrayed and ruined by
them because once a human type is perfected—or almost perfected—
it immediately becomes an anachronism and has no place in society.
Who can say? He was, at any rate, betrayed and ruined by a low-

born man named Lon Lucas, and he never held political office again
after that brief term in the Senate.

And now, Jack, I come to the part of the story that I believe it is
essential for you to hear. If you have not understood why I have told
you all that went before, you will, anyhow, understand why I wish
to recount the three episodes that follow.

What happened to my grandfather's political career can be briefly
summarized. The unexpired term in the Senate, which he was
filling out, lasted but two years. When the time came for him to
make his race for a full term, he was persuaded by Lon Lucas and
others that instead of making that race it was his duty to his party to
come home and run for governor of the state. The Lucas faction
comprised a group of young men whom my grandfather considered
more or less his protégés. In earlier days they had asked countless
small favors of him, and no doubt they had done so in order to
create that relationship to him. Now they pointed out to him that
from another faction in the party there was a man who, though
loathsome to them all, was a strong candidate for the party's
nomination for governor, and pointed out that only he, my grandfather, could block the nomination and election of that man. It
would be a disgrace to the state and to the party to have such a man
in the governor's chair, they said. Yet the senator could easily come
home and win the nomination and the election for himself and
could just as easily regain his seat in the Senate at a later time.

You may well wonder that an experienced politician could be so
naïve as to accept that line of reasoning or to entrust his fate to the
hands of those ambitious younger men. Neither his father nor his
grandfather would surely, under any circumstances, have relin-
quished that prize of prizes for a politician, a seat in the U.S. Senate.
I cannot pretend to explain it. I knew my grandfather only as an
embittered old man who didn't care to have children crawling all

over him. But I have to tell you that, within a few weeks after he came home and began his campaign for governor, Lon Lucas and his faction turned on him. Some sort of deal was made with the other faction. No doubt the deal was made long beforehand. Lucas came out in support of the "loathsome man" for governor, and one of the Lucas faction was put up for the seat in the Senate. Very likely there were other considerations also, remunerative to Lon Lucas and company if not to the candidates themselves. Such details are not important here, and I never knew them anyway. But my grandfather was defeated, and he retired from public life to the bosom of his family, where, alas, I cannot say he was greatly loved and cherished.

He withdrew almost entirely from all male company, seeing men only as his rather limited law practice required him to do. He lived out his life in a household of women and children, a household consisting for many years of his wife, his wife's mother and maiden aunt, his own mother, who lived to be ninety-seven, five daughters, and three sons. He never allowed himself to be addressed as senator and forbade all political talk in his presence. The members of his household were destined to retain in their minds and to hand down to future generations their picture of him not as a statesman of high principle or even as a silver-tongued orator but as the coarse-tongued old tyrant of their little world. His three sons always feared him mightily and took from his life only the one lesson: an anathema on politics. My father was the only son who would consent to study law and become a member of the old gentleman's firm, but even he made it clear from the outset that he would not let his profession lead him astray, made it clear to everyone that his interest was not in government but solely in corporation law.

My father's guiding principle in life was that he must at all costs avoid the terrible pitfall of politics. He gave himself to making money and to becoming the family man his father had never been.

What finally happened to him I must present in a more dramatic form than the summary I have given of Grandfather's affairs. It would be as difficult for me to summarize the story of Father's betrayal as it would have been for me to imagine and re-create the precise circumstances under which Grandfather first learned of Lon Lucas's double-dealing.

When I had opened the venetian blind at my office window that Sunday morning, I stared out at May's fresh green grass on the campus for a while and down at the small river, swollen by spring rains, at the bottom of the hill. Then I went to my desk and managed to write two letters to men who had published books on the subject—in "the field"—I was doing my work in. They were perfunctory, polite letters, requesting permission to quote from the work of those men in my own book. When I had sealed and stamped those two letters, I took out another sheet of departmental paper; but it lay on my desk untouched for I don't know how long, a blinding white sheet that I sat staring at impatiently as one does at a movie screen before the film begins. Finally, I put away my pen but left the piece of paper lying there as if meaning to project upon it the images taking shape in my mind. I saw my father stepping out of the family limousine in front of the Union Station in bright winter sunlight. My mother and I were already out of the car and waiting under the canopy. The Negro chauffeur stood holding the car door open and listening to some piece of instruction Father gave him in passing. Since this was in the earliest days of the Depression, we still lived in the world of limousines and chauffeurs, a world that my father's business career had lifted us into. A number of years before this he had ceased altogether to practice law, in order to accept the presidency of a large, "nationally known" insurance company for which he had formerly been the chief attorney and which maintained its head office locally. The insurance company was now in serious difficulties, however. The company's investments were under question. It began to appear that funds had been invested in various business enterprises that seemed hardly to have existed except on paper. Many of these investments had been made before my father's incumbency, but not all of them. Anyway, the man who had most influenced the company's investment of funds was a stockholder in the company and a member of the board of directors, Mr. Lewis Barksdale. He was an old school friend of my father's and had of course been instrumental in electing my father president of the company. It was he alone who would be able to explain the seemingly fraudulent use of moneys—explain it, that is, to the other members of the board—and he alone who could straighten out the snarl that the company's affairs seemed to be in. And it was this Lewis Barksdale whom we had come to the Union Station to meet at four o'clock on a remarkably bright winter afternoon.

The Negro chauffeur threw back his head and laughed at something my father said to him, and then Father advanced toward us, wearing a pleased smile. I remember remarking to Mother at just that moment what a fine day it was and reproaching her for having made me wear my heavy coat, in which I was uncomfortably warm. The truth was, I was still irked by Father's having made me leave a game with a group of boys to come with them to meet Mr. Barksdale's train, and I was taking out my resentment on Mother. Without looking at me, she replied that it was due to turn colder very shortly and, squeezing my hand, she said, "Why can't you have an agreeable disposition like your father's? Don't be an old sourpuss like me." Father was still smiling when he came up to us, and Mother asked him, "What is it that's so funny?"

"Oh," he explained, taking Mother's elbow and escorting us on into the lobby of the station, "when I just now told Irwin not to come inside and fetch Lewis's bag but to wait right there with the car, he said he couldn't keep the car in that spot but fifteen minutes and that he was afraid the train might be late. I said to him that if he knew Lewis Barksdale as well as I do, he'd know that the engineer and the fireman would somehow understand that they *had* to get Lewis's train out here on time."

In the lobby, Father read the track number off the board and then marched us confidently down the concourse to the great iron gate at Track No. 6. Just as he predicted, the train rolled in on time. Father spoke to the uniformed gatekeeper, who let us go through the gateway along with the redcaps, so we could see Mr. Barksdale when he stepped off the train. Father trotted along ahead of us, peering up into the windows of the observation car and then into the windows of the next Pullman. Mother called after him that he had better wait there beside the first Pullman or we might miss Mr. Barksdale. And Father did stop there. But he told me to run on ahead and see if I could get a glimpse of him in the entry of any of the other cars. I said I was not certain I would recognize Mr. Barksdale, but Father said, "You can know him by his derby. Besides, *he*'ll recognize *you*."

I did run on ahead, looking up into the cars, watching the people who came down the steps from each car to the metal stool that the porter had set out for them. Mr. Barksdale, being a man who had no children of his own, was said to be extremely fond of all his friends' children. That was why, as the youngest child in the family—and the only boy—I was taken along to meet the train that day. I could vaguely recall earlier visits he had made to us and seemed to remember a sense of his paying special attention to me. Momentarily, I was persuaded that I *would* remember him if we came face to face. But no man wearing a derby got off the train, and I made out no remotely familiar face in the cars or in the crowded entry ways. Moreover, no passenger climbing down off that train showed any sign of recognizing me.

When I followed the crowd of passengers and redcaps back toward the iron gate, I found Mother still standing beside the observation car. She said that Father had climbed aboard and was going through all the cars in search of Mr. Barksdale. At last we saw Father step off the first of the day coaches, away down the track. He looked very small down there, and when he waved to us and climbed back on the train I felt a sudden ache in the pit of my stomach. "Mr. Barksdale's not on the train," I said to Mother.

"No, I guess not," she said. "I was afraid he mightn't be."

Finally, Father reappeared in the entry between the observation car and the next Pullman. "Lewis must have missed the train somehow," he said as he came down the steps and swung out onto the platform. "Let's go inside the station. I'm going to telephone New York and see if he's still there."

We found a telephone booth on the concourse just beyond Gate No. 6, but Father had to go inside the station lobby to get enough change to make the call. Mother and I stood beside the booth a long time. "He ought to have waited till we got home to make the call," she said at last. "I suppose, though, he couldn't bear to wait." She and I had just agreed to go into the lobby and look for him when we saw him coming toward us. He was all smiles and was holding up two fistfuls of coins.

"I got enough quarters to call China," he said, and seemed to be elated by the feel of the coins in his hands. When he stepped into the booth to make his call, Mother and I moved away some twenty or thirty feet. He must have talked for ten minutes or more. When he came out again, his smile was bigger than before, and he began calling out as he hurried toward us, "Lewis *did* miss the train! And it was so busy in New York today he couldn't get a line to call me.

He's coming on an earlier train tonight and will be here by noon tomorrow!"

By noon of the next day, which was Saturday, it was very much colder, and so I didn't complain about having to wear my coat. I did complain somewhat, however, about having to give up several hours of a Saturday to meeting Mr. Barksdale's train. Father seemed to understand and was not so insistent upon my going, but in private Mother was insistent and said it was little enough for me to do if it was what my father wished. As we were leaving the house, Father stopped a moment to telephone the station and ask if the train was going to be on time. He had heard a report on the radio that the weather up East had turned bad. But the dispatcher's office reported that the train was scheduled to arrive exactly on time. In the car, Father said he hoped the dispatcher's office knew what it was talking about. "Trains on the weekend are often late," he said suspiciously. When we got to the station, he told Irwin that since the train might, after all, be late, he had better take the car to the parking lot, and that we would come and find him there.

As we were passing through the lobby, we all three read the gate number aloud from the blackboard, and we laughed at ourselves for it—rather nervously, I suppose. Father had kept silent most of the way down to the station in the car and had left the talking mostly to Mother and me. He began to look more cheerful once we were in the big lobby, and as we passed out onto the concourse he said to Mother under his breath, "Keep your fingers crossed." As soon as we came out onto the concourse, we could see that the train was already backing up to the gate. "Thar she be!" Father exclaimed with sudden gaiety, and he put an arm around each of us to hurry us along. But at the gate he didn't ask the gatekeeper to let us go beyond. We waited outside, and through the bars of the grating we watched the passengers stepping down onto the platform. After a few minutes Father said, "I won't be surprised if Lewis is the last to get off. He hates crowds." We kept watching until it was obvious that no more passengers were going to leave the train and come through the gate. In what was almost a whisper, Father said to Mother, "He didn't come. What do you suppose could have happened?" And as we were passing the telephone booth on the way out, he said, "I'll call him from home."

We had been at home about half an hour when I heard him speaking to Mother from the foot of the stairs. She was leaning over the banisters in the upstairs hall. "There have been a lot of complications. Lewis has been getting together papers to bring with him. He says he can clear everything up. He's coming in on the same train tomorrow."

"Wonderful," Mother said.

"But I'm not going to ask you all to traipse down to the depot again."

"Nonsense. The third time's the charm," said my mother.

At about eleven the next morning Father telephoned the station to ask if the train was scheduled to come in on time. He was told that it would be three hours late. There were heavy snowstorms all over the East now. When Mother came into the big sun room where my sister Margaret and my two other sisters and I were all reading the Sunday paper and told us that snow had delayed Mr. Barksdale's train for three hours, she glanced out the sun-room windows at the darkly overcast sky and said, "There will be snow here before night, I think." None of my sisters even looked up from the paper. I imagine I looked up from the funny paper only because I wished to know whether or not I was going to be taken to the station again. Mother saw me look up and said, "Father says you needn't go with us today, and I suppose he's right."

"I'll go," I said. It had occurred to me suddenly that the snow might be falling by that time and that I would like to see how the old gray stone Union Station looked with snow on all of its turrets and crenelations and how the train would look backing into Gate No. 6 with snow it brought in from the East piled all over its top.

"Well, we'll see," Mother said.

Sometime after two, Mother and Father were in the front hall getting into their coats. I was there too, still undecided as to whether or not I would go along. No snow had begun to fall yet. Father seemed unconcerned about my going or not going. When Mother asked him if he thought he might call the station again, he replied casually that he already had, that the train would arrive as predicted, at three o'clock. He had already buttoned up his heavy, double-breasted overcoat when he added suddenly, "But there's another call I believe I'll make before we set out. It might take a few minutes . . . You had better take off your coat," he said to Mother.

When he was gone, I asked, "Who do you think he's calling?"

"I imagine he's calling Mr. Barksdale in New York," Mother said. She didn't remove her coat, though. She and I said nothing more. We went and looked out at the sky through the sidelights at the front door. After a few minutes we heard Father's footsteps. When we turned around, he was standing there in the hall, smiling wearily and beginning to unbutton his coat.

"Lewis is still in New York," he said.

"Why in the world?" Mother exclaimed. "What in the world did he say this time?" she asked.

"He didn't say anything. I didn't give him a chance to. As soon as I definitely heard his voice on the wire, I put down the receiver."

"What are you going to do?" Mother asked him.

"There's nothing I can do. He's not coming, that's all. I'll just have to take it however it turns out now."

We didn't go to the station, of course. And Father didn't go off to his room to be by himself, either, as one might have expected. He spent the rest of the afternoon with the family in the sun room, reading the paper, listening to the radio, and playing cards. The way he was with us that afternoon, you wouldn't have suspected anything was wrong. At just about twilight it began to snow outside. And we all went about from window to window with a certain relief, I suppose, watching the big flakes come down and, from the snug safety of our sun room, watching the outside world change.

Father didn't telephone Mr. Barksdale again. They had been close friends since boyhood, but I believe they didn't communicate again for more than twenty-five years. When they were very old men and most of their other contemporaries were dead, Mr. Barksdale took to calling Father over long-distance and they would sometimes talk for an hour at a time about their boyhood friends or about business friends they had had when they were starting out in business. We were glad whenever Mr. Barksdale called Father, because it cheered him and made him seem livelier than anything else did during those last years. He often seemed very lonely during those years, though he continued to have a reasonably cheerful disposition. After the legal difficulties and the embarrassing publicity that followed his being abandoned by his trusted friend, Father led a quiet, uneventful life. He returned to his law practice, and he was a respected member of his firm. But he made no real life for himself in his practice—that is, he seldom saw other members of the firm away from the office, and I don't remember his ever mentioning the name of a client at home. His real life was all at home, where, as he would point out, it had always been. He and Mother sometimes played bridge with neighbors, and whatever other social life they had was there in the neighborhood where we lived after we lost the old house and could no longer afford a staff of servants. He was an affectionate father, and I rarely saw him in what I would call depressed spirits. Yet how often one had the feeling that he was lonely and bored. I remember sometimes, even when the family was on a vacation together—when we had taken a cottage at the shore or were camping and fishing in the mountains—the look would come in his eye. And one was tempted to ask oneself, What's wrong? What's missing?

I don't honestly know when I decided to go into college teaching, Jack. I considered doing other things—a career in the army or the navy. Yes, I might have gone to Annapolis or West Point. Those appointments were much to be desired in the Depression years, and my family did still have a few political connections. One thing was certain, though. Business was just as much out of the question for me as politics had been for my father. An honest man, I was to understand, had too much to suffer there. Yes, considering our family history, an ivory tower didn't sound like a bad thing at all for an honest man and a serious man . . . A dozen years after gradua-tion I found myself back teaching in that college where I had been an undergraduate. Physically, it was a beautiful spot and, as I have already said, I thought I would settle down there for life, to do my teaching and my writing.

After my second year of teaching there I was awarded a research Fulbright to Italy, and so was on leave for a year. You were a babe in arms that year, Jack. I saw the ancient world for the first time with you on my shoulder, and with your mother usually following behind, leading Susie by the hand. Well, while we were in Italy, the old president of the college died of a stroke. He had been president of the college when I was an undergraduate, and I suppose it was he, most of all, who made me feel that my talents were appreciated there. By the time I returned to the campus from Italy, the follow-ing fall, the dean of men had been made acting president. Your mother and I smiled over the appointment but made no comment on it to anyone—not even to each other. You see, Jack, although Marie and I still thought of ourselves as being ideally suited to each other then, and still believed ourselves to be very happy together, there were already subjects she and I had had to agree to keep off. One of these—and by far the most important—was my professional career itself, including how I conducted my classes, my role in the department, my stand on various academic questions, and even my possible advancement in rank. We had been in graduate school together—your mother and I—and during the first years of our marriage, before Susie was born, we both had taught at the same institution. It was understandably difficult for her to refrain from advising and criticizing me in matters she considered she knew as much about as I did. When I first began ruling out that subject as a topic for discussion, she became emotional about it. She had wanted to have a career herself, and she had had to give it up temporarily. I had not realized how much her plans for a career had meant to her. But now she accused me of being an antifeminist, accused me of trying to isolate her in the kitchen, even of trying to cut her off from all intellectual life. In time, however, she came to see the matter differently—or seemed to. I think perhaps she tired of hearing other faculty wives talk about their husbands' professional problems and didn't want to be like them. At any rate, she and I merely smiled over the news of the dean's promotion to acting president. His qualifications for such a high place seemed hardly to exist. He was formerly the chairman of the Department of Athletics—that is, the college's head coach.

But since I knew that certain trustees and certain senior members of the faculty were on a committee to select a permanent president, I was careful to mention my amusement to no one. When a group of younger members of the faculty came to me, however, and told me that it was generally understood that the committee was going to recommend that the dean be made permanent president, I could not keep myself from bursting into laughter.

It was on an evening in the middle of the week that that group of young professors came to my house for the very purpose of report-

ing the information to me. How well I can see them on my front
porch, in the bright porch light I had switched on. They were a very
attractive and intelligent-looking bunch of men. With their bright,
intelligent eyes, with their pipes and tweed jackets, and with a
neatly trimmed mustache or two among them, they gave one a
feeling that here were men one would gladly and proudly be
associated with, the feeling that one had found the right niche in
life, that one had made the right choice of career. I remember that,
before they came inside, two of them—there were six in the party—
stepped back and knocked the ashes out of their pipes on the porch
banisters, and that they looked with interest at the porch banisters
and then looked up and noticed what the porch pillars were like. As
a matter of fact, as they trooped into the hallway and then over into
my study, they all of them were making comments of one kind or
another on the house . . . This was not so rude of them as it might
seem, or I thought it wasn't. You see, they had telephoned me in
advance that they wished to come over and talk to me about a
matter. And I understood, of course, that they were too polite and
too civilized to come to my house and dive right into a matter of
business without making some small talk first. That was not their
style, not their tone. Moreover, talk about people's houses used to be
a fair and favorite topic at such a college as that one was, because
there one didn't really own—or even rent—one's house. All houses
occupied by the faculty belonged to the college. The good thing
about the system was that the house was provided in addition to
your salary, and so one didn't have to pay income tax on that
portion of one's income. But by and large it was an invidious
arrangement. The elderly professors, when they retired, often had no
place to go. Further, since the senior professors and the adminis-
trators naturally occupied the best houses and one's rank could
generally be deduced from the quality of one's house, the younger
men (and their wives) eyed the houses of their seniors and thought

of the circumstances that would make them available. When someone near the top died or retired, practically the entire faculty would
move up a house.

My house was not of course one of the best houses. I was still an
assistant professor, whereas most of those young professors who had
come to see me were a grade above me in rank. My house, when we
moved into it, had in fact been one of the most ramshackle-looking
places in the village—one that nobody else would have. I had spent a
lot of time and work putting it into the reasonably good condition it
was now in. It was upon this fact that my guests were commenting
as they came in from the porch that night. And when we had seated
ourselves in my study and I had started the coffee brewing, they
went on to say that it had been a real advantage to me to have been
an undergraduate there, that I had joined the faculty with a
knowledge of which houses were basically good houses, that I *knew*
(what no one else could have guessed) how recently the run-down-
looking house I moved into had been in relatively good condition.
There was some truth in what they said, but they were not of course
really serious about it. And I saw of course that they were teasing. I
replied that my disadvantage was that the old president knew me
and knew I was the only person on the staff who was fool enough to
accept such a house.

They went on from that to speak of how I had known the late
president longer and better than they had, and to ask if it was not
true that the newest and youngest member of the board of trustees
had once been a classmate and a rather good friend of mine. They
were speaking of Morgan Heartwell, who had been the richest boy
in my graduating class, and who had during the brief years since
our graduation gone on to add several million to the millions he
inherited. Though I had seen him only two or three times since
college, we had become rather good friends during the last term of
our senior year and we still exchanged Christmas cards and even

brief letters now and then when there was special occasion. Morgan had been elected to the board during the previous year, when I was in Italy. I had written him one of those brief letters, from Florence, saying that I wished to congratulate the other members of the board on the wisdom of their choice. And Morgan had replied briefly that he looked forward to our spending some time together whenever the trustees met at the college.

The young professors who came to see me were overjoyed when I confirmed the rumor that Morgan Heartwell and I were friends. They immediately revealed the purport of their visit. There was a certain amount of caution in the way they brought forth the information about the dean's candidacy, but after my explosive fit of laughter they had thrown caution to the wind. Morgan Heartwell was on the committee. They wanted me to speak to him. They wanted me to let him know that only the handful of aging senior professors on the committee thought the dean a possible candidate; that those men thought so primarily because they were conservative men getting along in years and because the dean represented to them a known quantity; that, except for them, the entire faculty regarded his proposed candidacy as a piece of lunacy. They insisted at once that I was the only feasible channel they had to the trustees, that if I could let Morgan Heartwell know unofficially how the overwhelming majority of the faculty felt, then the trustees would come to see for themselves what the situation was. As a result, there would be no ugly rift and contest between the older and the younger members of the faculty. They were thinking of the good of the college. They did not believe that under such a man as the former head coach the college could maintain its academic excellence. They were taking the only course that their collective conscience and professional ethics permitted them to take.

Here was precisely the sort of meddling, the sort of involvement I had long since determined to avoid. I had even managed to keep out of most committee work, on the grounds that it interfered with the more serious work I had to do and on the very legitimate grounds that there were people aplenty who liked nothing better than committee work. I used to say that when I received more than one notice of committee meetings in the morning mail, I had heard the sound of my neighbor's ax, and that it was time for me to move on. My first impulse was to laugh as heartily at the role they were now asking me to play as I had at the notion of the dean's being a college president. And yet, with their talk of academic excellence and professional ethics, they really left me no choice. I agreed on the spot to perform the mission.

And it turned out just as they predicted. Morgan Heartwell had entertained doubts even before I came to him, and so had the other trustees he subsequently spoke to. The night that the group of young professors came to my house was in November. By March, another man had been chosen for the presidency. The acting president would serve till the end of the current academic year, and then the new president would take office.

But by March of that year there had been other developments. One of the senior professors in the college had died. The faculty was once again playing a game of musical chairs with houses. There were days when the community held its breath, waiting to know whether or not Professor So-and-So was going to take such-and-such a house. By March also, Marie had learned definitely that she was pregnant once again. (Maisie was born the following November.) Marie began to think that with the new baby the inconveniences of the old house we were in would become quite intolerable. Moreover, I had come to realize that upon the arrival of the baby my study would have to be converted into a nursery. And so we began to take an interest in the houses which, one after another, became available.

The rule was that each house, as it became available, was offered first to the senior member of the faculty—no matter if he had moved the month before, no matter if the house had five bedrooms and he was childless or even wifeless—and then, if it were refused, the house was offered down through the ranks till it found a taker. We could hardly believe our luck—Marie and I—when no full professor and no associate professor spoke for the Dodson house, which was offered around during the first two weeks of March. It was a charming house with four bedrooms, a modern kitchen, a study. We knew that I stood first on the list of assistant professors. We waited for the customary mimeographed notice to appear in my mailbox at the college.

Days passed. Two weeks passed. Still no notice. On the first of April, I went to the office of the acting president and made inquiry. I was told by the acting president's secretary, Mrs. Eason, that the acting president had decided that since no full or associate professor had taken the Dodson house it would be removed from the list and offered to the new chaplain, who was scheduled to be appointed within the next two years. Meanwhile, the house would stand empty. Meanwhile, Marie would continue to scrub our splintery old floors and would wash diapers in a tub in the cellar. Meanwhile, I would give up my study to the new baby . . . I lost my temper. I went to my office and wrote a letter to the acting president, saying that I wished my present house to be put on the available list and that I expected to be offered the Dodson house. I received no reply to my letter. But two days later my house was offered to another assistant professor and was accepted. After a further two days, I did receive a reply to my letter. The acting president had consulted the members of his committee on houses (whose membership coincided precisely with that of the now defunct Faculty Committee for Selecting a President) and they agreed with him that the Dodson house should not at this time be offered to anyone below the rank of associate professor.

Fortunately—or so I thought of it at the time—I had in my

possession a letter from the late president, written to me in Italy only a few days before his stroke, promising that I would be promoted to the rank of associate professor on my return. Marie had urged me to present that letter to the administration as soon as we got home, but I felt certain that a copy of the letter was in the president's files and that some action would be taken on it in due time. It seemed unbecoming of me to go at once on my return and demand that action be taken on my dead benefactor's promise. And after I had waited six months, I felt that I hardly knew how best to introduce the subject. But now I did bring forth the letter from my file. If I was entitled to promotion, then we were entitled to the Dodson house. And only by presenting my just claims to the faculty would I be able to determine for certain whether or not the dean, having heard of my role in checking his ambitions, had taken his personal revenge upon me.

With my letter in my pocket, I went to call on all six of the young professors who had sent me on my mission to Morgan Heartwell. I pointed out to them, one by one, just how the business of the house had developed, and I received the impression from each of them that he was already well aware of the developments. With each of them, I then brought out my letter from the late president and insisted upon his reading it. And finally I asked each one of them if he would be willing to present my case, in its entirety, at the next faculty meeting. There was not one of them who did not indicate that he was convinced the acting president knew of the part I had played in blocking his permanent appointment. There was not one of them who expressed any doubt that the removal of the Dodson house from the list had been an act of reprisal against me. But they were a very responsible, discreet, and judicious group of young men. Each of them asserted that he was thoroughly sympathetic to my claim, but asked to be allowed to give the matter more thought before deciding what action ought to be taken. My supposition was that there would be a general consultation among the six of them and that some sort of presentation would be made at the April meeting.

I shall never forget walking alone from my house to the administration building for that April meeting—at four o'clock in the afternoon, on the first Monday in the month. I arrived earlier than I usually did at those meetings, and so was able to choose a seat at the back of the president's assembly room. Faculty meetings there, as in most places, usually filled the room from the rear forward, in just the same way that students ordinarily fill a college classroom. I sat in the next-to-last row and watched my colleagues strolling in from their afternoon classes, some in earnest conversation, others making jokes and tapping each other firmly on the forearm or even patting each other on the back, and some few peering into notes on reports they would give that afternoon. I kept my eye out, of course, for the arrival of my six friends. Unconsciously, I had invented an image of their arriving as a group, perhaps still consulting among themselves in whispers, and taking their places together on the first row squarely in front of the president's lectern. Instead, I saw them arrive one by one, seemingly unaware of my presence and certainly unaware of one another's. Before the meeting began, all six had arrived, but they were scattered over the room. I watched them in their tweed jackets and blue or striped shirts chatting casually and amiably with various black-suited, bow-tied senior members of the faculty. At the moment when the meeting was called to order, I was struck suddenly by the notion that I had not taken these men's character and style into account. They would never be so obvious as my fantasy had suggested. They *would* enter the room separately, having decided earlier on the strategy. One of them would rise at the proper time and bring up the question of the Dodson house. And then, with seeming spontaneity and from all corners of the room, the others would join in the attack, one of them finally—if the chair adamantly refused to offer the Dodson house to the lower rank—one of them finally making direct reference to the promise of promotion made me by the revered late president.

Following the minutes from the last meeting, pieces of old business occupied the first half hour of the meeting. I sat through the minutes and through the old business with patience, anticipating what I believed was to follow. When the question, "Any new business?" came, I closed my eyes and listened for the familiar voice. Unless my ears deceived me, it was the young biologist in my group who was speaking. He was one of those with a neat little mustache on his upper lip. With my eyes closed, I could see him, could see him self-consciously patting the bowl of his pipe on the palm of his left hand as he began to speak. "Mr. President—" I opened my eyes, and then for a moment I was convinced my ears did deceive me. It was the young biologist all right, standing near the front of the room and patting the bowl of his dark pipe on the palm of his left hand, but the piece of new business he was introducing was a matter of next year's curriculum. I sat through his remarks and through other remarks that followed on the subject. In fact, I sat through two other new pieces of business, even through a count of hands on one piece that came to a motion and a vote. But when a fourth piece, relating to the awarding of honorary degrees was introduced, I rose from my chair, moved down the row I was sitting in, saying, "Excuse me. Excuse me. Excuse me," marched down the center aisle and out of the meeting.

I went home, and behind the closed door of my study I began composing my letter of resignation. Marie, who was in the kitchen, had heard me come in. But she waited fifteen minutes or so before she came and knocked on my door.

When I opened the door, she looked at me questioningly. She was white with anger. "He refused to offer us the house?" she said.

"Not exactly," I replied. "The subject was not introduced. The six of them came to the meeting and spoke at length—about other things."

Her face turned from white to crimson. Her eyes, still on me, melted. She burst into tears and threw herself into my arms. Or, rather, she drew me into her arms, for as she wept I felt her two arms go around me and felt her hands patting me consolingly high on the back between the shoulder blades. As she held me there, it was all I could do to keep from weeping myself. And somehow, for all her tenderness at that moment and despite all the need I had of it, it came over me that this was the beginning of the end for us, that our marriage would not survive it. Perhaps that was nonsense. The thoughts that cross one's mind at such times cannot always be accounted for. But the life we had lived since graduate school—beginning in graduate school—was the life most couples live who take refuge in the Groves of Academe. We had lived with each other, had lived *together* in the most literal sense. We had shared intellectual interests, had shared domestic duties, had breakfasted together, lunched together, dined together. We had slept together, too, but that had come to seem only one, not too significant facet of our—our "togetherness." I had no right to complain against this life, because this life was the life I had chosen. But I could see that the future would mean a narrowing of my activities among my colleagues wherever I might go, and that things relating to my profession, which had for some time been ruled out of our talk at home, must now inevitably become the very center of it.

When, after dinner that night, I received a telephone call from my friend the biologist, saying that he and one other of the group would like to come by and talk to me, Marie, who was sitting close by my side with her arm about my waist, indicated with a shake of her head that I should not let them come. But I was not yet ready for that. I told them to come ahead, and then I went and switched on the front-porch light.

When they arrived, I led them to my study, and we sat down on three straight chairs in a triangle, facing each other. They told me that, before that afternoon's meeting, there *had* been a general consultation among the six men I went to see and that they had decided that to bring up my "problem" at this meeting would not be a wise move, could, in fact, create a very bad situation. "It would be most impolitic," one of them said. "Strategically speaking, it would be a very bad move," said the other. "It would be a bad business." And they proceeded to explain to me that though the dean would no longer be acting president, he would continue to be a very important part of the college's administration. A head-on collision with him just before the arrival of the new president might be a very disruptive thing for the college. After all, we were all going to have to continue to live with the dean. "Even you are," they said to me. And all of this was said with the same voice that had said we must avoid any ugly rift and contest with the senior members of the faculty. Before they finished speaking, I saw once and for all what a foolish man I had been. But I did not make myself a bigger fool by losing my temper and telling them that I saw what a fool they had made of me. As we went to the front door, I agreed with them that probably my house could be reassigned to me—as no doubt it could have been—especially if one of them went to the dean and explained that I had written my letter to him in a moment of anger and that I now wished to remain where I was. But when they were gone, I put out the porch light, went back to my study, and typed up the final version of my letter of resignation.

Marie and I were in perfect agreement about the resignation. During the months that followed, which was naturally a very trying period, her understanding, her sympathy, her tenderness—her indulgence, really—were my great support. When I returned from my office late that Sunday afternoon, depressed and with a crick in my neck after a long sleep in my leather chair (I have since decided that that was most probably the way my father had spent *his* Sunday in *his* office), Marie greeted me cheerfully, and little Susie almost smothered me with kisses. But somehow the vision I had had of our future, after the fateful faculty meeting, stuck with me. I never for a moment believed our marriage could weather this new turn my life had taken. I don't know why. As my mother would have said, the Old Nick himself seemed to have got in me. I *wouldn't* be consoled, I *wouldn't* be comforted, though I consistently made an effort to seem so. I had never before been so much help in a move as I was in packing up our possessions and unpacking them again when we arrived at our new place. My new appointment was at an enormous state university, situated in a middle-sized Midwestern city. I felt it would be possible to pass unnoticed for years, in the university and in the city. I met my classes, I attended department meetings, I made revisions on the galley proofs of my book. It seems to me I spent a large part of every day taking Susie back and forth to school on the bus. And I spent hours in the park with you, Jack. I don't suppose you remember the little boy there who kept purposely interfering with your play on the jungle gym until one day I caught him and spanked him. His mother threatened to call the police. I'll never forget the satisfaction I took in laughing in her face and threatening to give her the same spanking I had given her little boy. And little Maisie, of course, was born in November after we arrived there. I never changed so many diapers for you and Susie put together as I did for Maisie, or gave so many bottles at predawn hours . . . No, I did not become the tyrant of my household, and I did not, like my father, disturb my wife with long looks and long silences. But I began to feel that with my talk about my book and my talk about the courses I was teaching I was almost intentionally boring Marie to death, boring my students to death, boring myself to death. Before the first semester was half over, Marie was helping me grade my papers and was reading all the books I had to read for my courses. By the time the second semester came round, she had made application to the department and was taken on as a part-time instructor.

It was almost a year to the day after my difficulties about the Dodson house began that two letters, which would altogether change everything for me, were put into my mailbox at the university. One letter came from my predecessor at the college where I have since made my most important contribution to the education of American youth. This letter stated that they were looking for a new dean of men at that college, and asked if I would be willing to come and be interviewed for the appointment. The other letter was from Morgan Heartwell. It was he who had recommended me for the appointment, and he wrote me that he had been able to do so because he had observed that I behaved with such discretion in my altercation with the acting president, putting the welfare of that institution above my personal interests. He also urged me to accept the new appointment, saying that this was a college that had recently been given a handsome endowment, a college with a growing academic reputation. He was not, himself, on the board of trustees there, but close associates of his were and they had happened to mention the opening there.

When Marie read the first letter, she broke into laughter. Then, giving me a serious glance, she read through Morgan's letter. "How dare Morgan Heartwell write you such a letter!" she said. "How dare he suggest such an appointment for you!" She and I were facing each other across the little carrel that we shared in the university library. When I remained silent, she put the letters down on the table and asked, "You are not seriously thinking of going for that interview?"

"I am going to take the job," I said, "if it's offered me."

Folding the letters and replacing them in their envelopes, she said, "Well, you may take it. But I'm staying on here."

"It has already occurred to me that you might say that," I told her directly. "I am not entirely surprised." She sat with her eyes lowered and she blushed so deeply that a new thought now occurred to me. "Is there someone else?" I asked.

"No, I don't think so," she said, looking up at me. "Is there for you?"

"I don't think so," I said.

Of course, the fact is we were both married again within two years to persons we did already know at that state university. But still, it is true that neither of us had been having a real love affair. Perhaps the persons we married, the persons we very soon afterward allowed ourselves to fall in love with, represented for us the only possibilities of happiness either of us had been able to imagine during that bleak year. I suppose it's significant that we both married people who shared none of our professional interests.

After I had been dean of men for two years, I was made academic dean of the college. In two more years, I was president of the college. Even with as little time as you have spent with me through the years, Jack, you have seen what a successful marriage my second marriage has been, and what a happy, active life I have had. One sacrifices something. One sacrifices, for instance, the books one might have written after that first one. More important, one may sacrifice the love, even the acquaintance of one's children. One loses something of one's self even. But at least I am not tyrannizing over old women and small children. At least I don't sit gazing into space while my wife or perhaps some kindly neighbor woman waits patiently to see whether or not I will risk a two-heart bid. A man must somehow go on living among men, Jack. A part of him must. It is important to broaden one's humanity, but it is important to remain a mere man, too. But it is a strange world, Jack, in which an old man must tell a young man this.

First Heat

He turned up the air conditioning and lay across the bed, wearing only his jockey shorts. But it didn't stop. Two showers already since he came in from the afternoon session! Showers had done no good. Still, he might take another presently if it continued. The flow of perspiration was quite extraordinary. Perhaps it was the extra sleeping pill he took last night. He had never been one to sweat so. It was rather alarming. It really was. And with the air conditioner going full blast he was apt to give himself pneumonia.

What he needed of course was a drink, and that was impossible. He was not going to have a single drink before she arrived. He was determined to be cold sober. She would telephone up from the desk—or from one of the house phones nearby. He always thought of her as telephoning directly from the desk. Somehow that made the warning more official. But she did always telephone, did so out of fear he might not have his regular room. So she said. He knew better, of course. Married for nearly fifteen years, and at home she still knocked on doors—on the door to his study, on the door to the bathroom, even on the door to their bedroom. She even had the children trained to knock on doors, even each other's doors. Couldn't she assume that since he knew she was on the way, knew she was by now wheeling along the Interstate—doing seventy-five and more in her old station wagon—couldn't she assume that whatever kind of fool, whatever kind of philanderer she might suspect him of being, he would have the sense to have set matters right by the time she got there? But what rot! As if he didn't *have* a problem, as if he needed to make one up!

He could hear his own voice in the Senate Chamber that afternoon. Not his words, just his guilty voice. Suddenly he got up off the bed, pulled back the spread, the blanket, the top sheet. He threw himself down on his back, stuck his legs in the air, and pulled off his shorts. They were wringing wet with his damnable perspiration! He wadded them into a ball and, still lying on his back, still holding his legs in the air, he hurled the underwear at the ceiling, where it made a faintly damp spot before falling to the carpeted floor. And she—she would already know what his voice in the Senate Chamber had said. (His legs still in the air.) And knowing how the voting went, know who betrayed whom, who let whom down, who let what bill that was supposed to go through intact be amended. It would all have been reported on the local six o'clock state news, perhaps even with his taped voice uttering the words of betrayal. She would have picked it up on the radio in the station wagon just after she set out, with her evening dress in a suitbox beside her. Maybe she would even have turned back, feeling she just couldn't face certain people at the mansion reception tonight . . . or couldn't face him.

Now—only now—he let his legs drop to the bed, his feet coming down wide apart on the firm, first-rate-hotel mattress. And he threw out his arms, one hand palm upward landing on each pillow of the double bed. He *would* relax, *would* catch a quick nap. But a new charge of sweat pressed out through every pore of his skin, on his forehead, on his neck, in the soft area just above his collarbone, from the exposed inner sides of his thighs and his ankles, from the exposed armpits and upper arms and forearms, from the palms of his hands and the soles of his feet. He felt he was aware of every infinitesimal modicum of sweat that was passing through every pore of every area of his body. Somehow it made him feel more utterly, thoroughly naked than he had ever before felt in his entire life. Yes, and this time the sweat came before the thought—just a little before the thought this time. The thought of what he had done and left undone concerning the amendment, said and left unsaid concerning the amendment, the thought of the discrepancy between his previously announced position and the position he finally took on the floor, all thought of *that* seemed something secondary and consequential to the sweat. Perhaps he was ill, really ill! Perhaps it was only a coincidence that this sickening sweat had come over his body. But no, he was not that sort—to claim illness. One thing for certain, though, the sweat was already like ice water on his skin.

Now he would have to get up and dry himself off again. There was a scratching sensation in his throat. He even coughed once. He would have to turn *down* the air conditioner. And he would have to find something else to focus his mind on. After all, he had not betrayed his country or his family. And not, God knew, his constituents. Was it only old man Nat Haley he was worrying about? He had agreed to support Nat Haley's waterways bill, had been quite outspoken in favor of it. The newspapers all over the state had quoted him. And then, yesterday, he had received promises from other sources, promises so much to the interest of his constituents that he could not resist. By God, it was the sort of thing he—*and* she—had known he would have to do if he stood for the legislature and got elected, the sort of thing he would have to face up to if he went into politics, where everybody had said *he* ought not to go. He and she had looked each other in the eye one day—before he ever announced—and said as much . . . Well, at the last minute he had agreed to support the very amendment which Nat Haley had said would be ruinous, would take all the bite out of his bill. But Nat Haley was, himself, the damnedest kind of double-dealer. Even *he* had observed that. Ah, he was beginning to know politics. And he was beginning to understand what "everybody" had meant. Old Nat Haley was well known for the deals he arranged and didn't live up to. Everyone knew about Nat Haley. Nat Haley wouldn't have hesitated to fight this bill itself if he had discovered, even at the last minute, that that was to his advantage.

Who, then, was he betraying? And it wasn't a bill of any great import, either.

He sat up and swung his feet over the side of the bed. His hand came down briefly on the moisture his body had left on the otherwise starchy hotel sheet. He glanced backward and saw the wet shadow of himself that his perspiration had left there, and he turned away from it. But as he turned away from his silhouette on the sheet, there he was, in all his nakedness, in the large rectangular mirror above the dresser. And there he was in the mirror on the open bathroom door. He reached to the floor and took up a bath towel he had dropped there earlier and began drying himself—and hiding himself. He stood up and went over his body roughly with the towel; then, his eyes lighting on the mirror on the bathroom door, he wadded up the towel, just as he had the jockey shorts, and hurled it at the door. It came right up against his face there! And when it had fallen, he realized that this time it wasn't—as so often—his face in the mirror that offended him. He didn't care about the face. He knew it too well and what its every line and look meant. The body interested him as never before, or as it had not in years. For a moment, it was like meeting someone from the past, someone he had almost forgotten—an old friend, and old enemy. It was—almost—a young man's body still; he was not forty yet and he exercised as much as he ever had and ate and drank with moderation. The body in the door mirror and in the large mirror over the dresser had good tone, was only a little heavier about the hips than it had once been, and the arm muscles were really better developed than when he was twenty. Taking in the different views he had of the body in the two mirrors he recalled that as late as his college days he had sometimes shadow-boxed before mirrors, usually wearing his ordinary boxer shorts and imagining they were made of silk, with his name, or some title, like *The Killer,* embroidered on them in purple or orange letters. He didn't smile over the recollection. But neither did he take any such stance before the mirrors now. The body in the mirrors was tense, as if prepared to receive a blow; and he looked at it objectively as a painter or a sculptor might, as a physician might. He observed features that particularized it: the modest island of dark hair on the chest, which narrowed into a peninsula pointing down below the navel and over the slightly rounded belly, almost joining the pubic hair above the too-innocent-looking penis; the elongated thighs; the muscular calves; the almost hairless arms; the shoulders, heavy and slightly stooped. Presently, his interest in himself seemed entirely anatomical. And all at once it was as though his eyes were equipped with X-rays. He could see beneath the skin and under the flesh to the veins and tendons and the ropelike muscles, the heart and lungs, the liver, the intestines, the testicles, as well as every bone and joint of the skeleton. And now it was as though a klieg light—no, a supernatural light—shone from behind him and through him. Only when at last he moved one foot, shifting his weight from one leg to the other, did the flesh and the covering skin return. Had it been a dream? A vision? It seemed to him now that he was not naked at all, or that this was not the nakedness he had sought when he removed his clothes. At any rate, his body had ceased to sweat.

He stepped back to the bed and lay down on his side, his back to the mirrors. He experienced momentary relief. It was as though he had seen beyond mere nakedness of body and spirit, had looked beyond all that which particularized him and made his body and his life meaningful, human. Was that the ultimate nakedness? Why, it could just as well have been old Nat Haley's insides he had seen. And he did relax now. He closed his eyes . . . But then it came on again. Only this time there was no sweat. There was just the explicit dread of that moment—soon now, soon—when he would open the door to her. And he thought of how other, older politicians would laugh at his agonizing over so small a matter. *They* would know what a mistake politics was for him. Or perhaps they would know that, like them, he was *made* for politics. Wasn't this merely his baptism—in betrayal? In politics the ends were what mattered, had to matter. In politics that was the only absolute. If you were loyal to other men, you were apt to betray your constituency. Or did he have it all backward? No, he had it right, he was quite sure. And for that very reason, wasn't the state Senate as far as he would go and farther than he should have gone? Friends had warned him against state politics especially. His father had said to him: "You are the unlikeliest-looking political candidate I have ever seen." But it was a decision she and he had made together, and together they had agreed that one's political morality could not always coincide with one's private morality. They had read that somewhere, hadn't they? At any rate, one had to be prepared to face up to that morality . . . And now, though he felt chilled to the bone, the sweat came on again. He rolled over and reached for the towel on the floor, forgetting he had thrown it at the mirror. As he got off the bed, the same hand that had reached for the towel reached out to the wall and turned down the air conditioner. He went into the bathroom and got a dry towel and came back drying himself—or those two hands were drying him. He stopped before the long mirror on the bathroom door, the hands still drying him.

He remembered something else his father had said to him once when they were on a fishing trip at Tellico Plains. He had gone for a swim in the river and stood on a rocky slab beside the water afterward, first rubbing his chest and his head with a towel and then fanning his body with it before and aft. His father, watching the way he was fanning himself with the towel, said, "You do cherish that body of yours, don't y'?" But what mistaken notions his father had always had about him. Or perhaps it was only wishful thinking on his father's part. Perhaps he had only *wished* that kind of concern for him. Ah, if only his body *had* been his great care and concern in life—his problem! And no doubt that's what his sweating meant! He *wished* it were only a bodily ill!

He wasn't, as a matter of fact, a man who was given to lolling about this way with no clothes on—either at home or in a hotel room. And it occurred to him now that it wasn't the sweat alone that had made him do so today. As soon as he had walked into the room and closed the door after him he had begun pulling off his clothes. It seemed to him almost that the sweat began *after* he had stripped off his clothes. But he couldn't definitely recall now whether it had begun before or after he got to the room. At any rate, he wasn't *sure* it had begun before. Had it? Else, why had he undressed at once? . . . He lay down on the bed again and his eye lit on the black telephone beside the bed. The first thing some men did when alone in a hotel room, he knew, was to take up the telephone and try to arrange for a woman to come up. Or that was what he always understood they did. The point was, he should have *known*. But he—he would hardly know nowadays how to behave with such a woman. He would hardly know what to say or do if one of those hotel creatures came into the room. Or would he know very well, indeed! Yes, how simple it all would be. What a great satisfaction, and how shameful it would seem afterward. How sinful—how clearly sinful—he would know himself to be. There the two of them are, in bed. But suddenly there comes a knock on the door! He will have to hide her. His wife is out there in the passage. The baby-sitter came a little early. And the traffic was not as bad as she had anticipated. With the new Interstate, a forty-mile drive is nothing. He has no choice. There isn't anything else he can do: he will have to hide the creature. She will have to stand naked, her clothes clutched in her arms, behind the drapery or in the closet, while he and his wife dress for the reception at the governor's mansion. If only—But the telephone, the real, black telephone was ringing now, there on the real bedside table.

He let it ring for thirty seconds or so. Finally, he took up the instrument. He said nothing, only lay on his side breathing into the mouthpiece.

"Hello," she said on the house phone. He could hear other voices laughing and talking in the lobby.

"Hello," he managed.

"I'm downstairs," she said, as she always said, waiting for him to invite her to come up. He invited her now, and she replied, "Is everything all right? You sound funny."

"Everything's fine. Come on up," he said. "You've heard the news?"

"I listened in the car, on the way over."

"I changed my mind about the bill," he said.

"Is Mr. Haley pretty angry?"

"He cut me cold on the Capitol steps afterward."

"I thought so," she said. "He was icy to me when I passed him in the lobby just now. Or I imagined he was."

"Do you still want to go to the reception?"

She laughed. "Of course I do. I'm sure you had good reasons."

"Oh, yes, I had good reasons."

"Then, shall I come on up?"

"Do," he said. But then he caught her before she hung up. "Wait," he said. He sat on the bed, pulling the sheet up about his hips. "Why don't you wait down there? Why don't we go somewhere and have a drink and something to eat before we dress for the reception? I'm starved."

"I'm starved, too," she said. "I had only a very small snack with the children at four-thirty."

"I'll be right down," he said.

"Well—" She hesitated and then said, "No, I have my dress with me in a box—my dress for tonight. I want to put it on a hanger. I'll be right up—that is, if you don't mind."

"Good," he said.

"And why don't we have our drink up there? It might be easier."

"Good," he said.

As soon as he had put down the telephone, he sprang from the bed, ran to pick up his sweaty shorts and the sweaty hotel towels. He began straightening the room and pulling on his clothes at the same time, with desperate speed. She must not find him undressed, this way. It would seem too odd. And if he should begin the sweating again, he was lost, he told himself. He would have to try to ignore it, but she would notice, and she would know . . . She would be on the elevator now, riding up with other members of the legislature and their wives, wives who had also come to town for the reception at the mansion. He felt utterly empty, as though not even those veins and tendons and bones and organs were inside him. Wearing only his shirt and fresh shorts and his black socks and supporters, he stopped dressing long enough to give the bed a haphazard making up. He yanked the sheet and blanket and spread about. Fluffed the pillows. But if only there were something besides his body, something else tangible to hide. Catching a glimpse of himself in the mirror, he blushed bashfully and began pulling on his trousers to cover his naked legs. While slipping his tie under his collar, he was also pushing his feet into his shoes. As he tied the necktie and then tied the shoe strings, he was listening for her footsteps in the passage. Oh, if only, if only—if only there were a woman, herself covered with sweat, and still—still panting, for him to hide. What an innocent, simple thing it would be. But there was only himself . . . When the knock came at the door, he was pulling on his jacket. "Just a second," he called. And for no reason at all, before opening the door he went to the glass-topped desk on which lay his open briefcase and closed the lid to the case, giving a quick snap to the lock. Then he threw open the door.

It was as though only a pair of blue eyes—bodiless, even lidless—hung there in the open doorway, suspended by invisible wires from the lintel. He read the eyes as he had not been able to read the voice on the telephone. They were not accusing. They had done their accusing in the car, no doubt, while listening to the radio. Now they were understanding and forgiving . . . He bent forward and kissed the inevitable mouth beneath the eyes. It too was understanding and forgiving. But if only the mouth and eyes would not forgive, not yet. He wanted their censure, first. She entered the room, with the suitbox under her arm, and went straight over to the closet. He held his breath, his eyes fixed on the closet door. She paused with her hand on the doorknob and looked back at him. Suddenly he understood the kind of sympathy she felt for him. Is it the lady or the tiger? her hesitation seemed to say. If only, she seemed to say with him, if only it *were* the lady, naked and clutching her bundle of clothing to her bosom. But he knew of course, as did she, it would be the tiger, the tiger whose teeth they had drawn beforehand, whose claws they had filed with their talk about the difference between things private and things political. The tiger was that very difference, that very discrepancy, and the worst of it was that they could never admit to each other again that the discrepancy existed. They stood facing each other well and fully clothed. When, finally, she would open the closet door, they would see only his formal evening clothes hanging there, waiting to be worn to the governor's mansion tonight. And while he looked over her shoulder, she would open the cardboard box and hang her full-length white evening gown beside his tuxedo. And after a while the tuxedo and the evening gown would leave the hotel room together and go down the elevator to the lobby and ride in a cab across town to the governor's mansion. And there was no denying that when the tuxedo and the evening gown got out of the taxi and went up the steps to the mansion and then moved slowly along in the receiving line, he and she, for better or for worse, would be inside them. But when the reception was over and the gown and the tuxedo came down the steps from the mansion, got into another taxi, and rode back across town to their empty hotel room, who was it that would be in them then? Who?

Reservations

A LOVE STORY

It was arranged, of all things, that the bride and groom should make their escape from the country club through the little boys' locker room! But this was very reasonable, really. At nine o'clock on a night in January, the exit from the little boys' locker room to the swimming-pool terrace was the exit least likely to be congested. It was the exit also most likely to be overlooked by mischievous members of the wedding party. Every precaution had to be taken! No one was to be trusted!

In the lounge of the women's locker room, the bride got out of her gown in exactly thirty seconds. (She had taken an hour, more or less, to get into it.) She pushed the wedding dress into the hands of one of the club's maids and from the hands of another accepted the tweed traveling suit—puce-brown tweed trimmed with black velvet. Because it was imperative that no suspicion of her departure be roused among the guests, the bride was not attended by her mother or by her maid of honor. Her mother and all the bridal attendants remained upstairs at the party, where there was dancing, and where waiters moved about balancing trays of stemmed glasses. At two minutes to nine, the bride ran on tiptoe along a service passageway that connected most of the rooms on the ground floor. She was accompanied now by the elder of the two maids who had assisted in the change from white satin to tweed. This woman was one of the club's veteran maids, a large, rather middle-aged person who, though she dyed her hair a lemon yellow and rouged her cheeks excessively, was known for her stalwart character and her incorruptibility. In the passageway, the bride chattered nervously to this companion who had been assigned to her. She told how she had written her name in the club's brides' book as "Franny Crowell," having forgotten momentarily that she was now Mrs. Miles Miller. The maid was not a very responsive sort, and said nothing. But this didn't bother Franny; she went on to say, sometimes laughing while she spoke, that somehow she could not shake off the feeling that it was a pity and a shame to be slipping away from a party given in your own honor.

In one hand the maid held the key to a door down the passageway that would let the bride into the little boys' locker room. In the other hand she carried a pair of fur-trimmed galoshes. As they approached the locked door, the maid interrupted Franny's chatter: "Your father said tell you your fur coat's in the car, with your corsage pinned to it. He said be careful you don't sit on it." Simultaneously the maid held out the galoshes, giving them a little shake that indicated Franny should take them.

"What are those?" Franny chirped. "They're not mine."

"No, they're not yours, Mrs. Miller," said the maid, still pressing them on her.

"Well, I don't believe I'll want them," Franny said politely.

"Yes, your mother said so. It's snowing outside now—a nasty, wet snow, Mrs. Miller."

"But they're not mine, and they're not Mother's either . . . How long has it been snowing?" She hoped to change the subject.

"Two hours off and on, Mrs. Miller. Ever since you got here from the church. It's not sticking, but there'll be slush underfoot."

"Well, whose are they?"

"Your mother snitched them from one of the guests—out of the cloakroom. She told me, 'Something borrowed.' "

Franny burst into laughter and took the galoshes. But she resolved not to put on the ugly things until after Miles had seen her and got the effect of her outfit.

While the maid fitted the key into the lock, Franny stood with her eyes lifted to the low basement ceiling. She heard the sound of the dancing overhead, and she speculated about which of the dancers upstairs these boots might belong to and thought of the pleasure it was sure to give some childhood friend of hers, or possibly some aunt or some woman friend of her parents, to learn that *she* had provided the bride with the one item that had been overlooked—the something borrowed.

Presently the door before her stood open. But Franny's eyes and thoughts were still directed toward the ceiling. "There you are," said the maid, obviously provoked by the bride's inattention.

Franny lowered her eyes. She looked at the woman beside her with a startled expression. Then she glanced briefly into the shadows of the unlighted locker room. And in the next moment she was clutching frantically at the starched sleeve of the maid's uniform. "But he is not here!" she exclaimed. Her tone was accusing; she eyed the maid suspiciously. Then, as if on further reflection, she spoke in a bewailing whisper: "He isn't hee-er!" According to the plan, he was to have been admitted to the little boys' locker room through a door from the adjoining men's locker room. But had he ever intended to be there? *He was gone! Of course he was! How else would it be?* Already Franny was thinking of what kind of poison she would administer to herself, of how she would manage to obtain the poison, of how she would look when they found her.

"What do you mean 'not here'?" said the maid, jerking her sleeve free.

Franny smiled coolly. She knew how she must carry it off. "Maybe I'll stay on for the party, after all," she said.

"What do you mean 'not here'?" the maid repeated. "He's standing there before your eyes."

Franny looked again, and of course there her bridegroom stood. "I didn't see him, it's so dark," she stammered.

But, instead of going to the bridegroom, suddenly the bride threw her arms about the woman with the lemon-yellow hair who had delivered her to him. This trustworthy woman had been known to Franny during most of her young life, but she was by no means a favorite of Franny's. And almost certainly Franny had never been a favorite of the woman's, either . . . But still it seemed the thing to do. Somehow it was like embracing the whole wedding party or even the whole club membership, or possibly just simply her own mother. And, no doubt, in that moment this woman forgave Franny many an old score—forgave a little girl's criticism of sandwiches served toasted when they had been ordered untoasted, complaints about a bathing suit's not having been hung out to dry, and many another complaint besides. At any rate, the woman responded and returned the warm embrace. Then for an instant the two of them smiled at each other through the general mist of tears.

"Goodbye, little Miss 'Franny Crowell,'" the woman said.

"Goodbye, Bernice," said Franny, "and thanks for everything." Yes, the woman's name was Bernice. What a bother it had always been, trying to remember it, but now it had come out without Franny's having to try to think of it even.

Bernice took several steps backward, as if quitting a royal presence. At a respectful distance she turned her back, and in her white gum-soled shoes she retreated silently down the long service passageway.

While waiting for the bride to come through the doorway to him, the bridegroom had literally stood dangling his little narrow-brimmed hat, shifting it from one hand to the other. He did not know what to make of that blank look she had given him at first, didn't know what to make of her saying "He is not here," didn't know what to make of her throwing herself into the arms of the hired help instead of into his own . . . The embrace perhaps he understood better than the look. But anyway, she had come to him at last, which was what he wanted most in the world at the moment. Presently he had seated her on one of the rough wooden benches in the locker room and, on his knees before her, he was struggling to push her feet into the borrowed galoshes. Franny had held on to the galoshes through both her embraces, and as soon as she had handed them to Miles and was seated on the bench, she began to chatter again—about the galoshes now, about how her mother had positively stolen "the ugly things" from somebody upstairs.

It wasn't easy getting the galoshes on. They were a near-perfect fit, but Franny seemed incapable of being any help. Her little ankles had gone limp, like an absent-minded child's. But finally Miles managed to force both galoshes on. He zipped them up neatly, and then lifted his face to Franny and smiled. Franny extended one of her tiny gloved hands to him, as if she were going to pull him to his feet. Miles seized it, but he remained on one knee before her, pressing the hand firmly between the two of his. While he knelt there, Franny made a vague gesture with her free hand, a gesture that indicated the whole of the dark locker room. "I've never been in here before, Miles," she said.

"Neither have I, you know," Miles said playfully.

"Oh," Franny breathed, thoughtfully. "No, you probably haven't, have you."

Now she felt she understood . . . *That* was why she had not been able to see him there at first. She had never *imagined* him there. It was because Miles Miller was not one of the local boys she had grown up with, wasn't one of that familiar group from whose number she had always assumed she would some day accept a husband. He was better than any of *those,* of course; he was her own, beloved, blue-eyed, black-haired, fascinating Miles Miller, whom she had recognized the first moment she ever saw him as the best-looking man she had ever laid eyes on (or ever would), as the man she must have for *hers*—and the very same Miles, of course, that at least half a dozen other girls of her year had thought they must have for *theirs*. Moreover, he was the young man who doesn't turn up in *every*body's year: the young bachelor from out of town, brought in from a distant region by one of the big corporations to fill a place in its local office, a young man without any local history of teen-age romances to annoy and perhaps worry the bride. And in Miles's case the circumstances were enhanced still further. He was an only child, and his parents had died while he was still in college. For his bride there would be no parents or brothers and sisters to be visited and adjusted to, and, since he had lived always on the West Coast and gone to Stanford, no prep-school friends, not even—at such a distance—a college roommate to be won over. Once they were married, Franny's family would be *their* family, her friends *their* friends. Besides all this, her Miles was at once the most modest and most self-assured human being imaginable. With one gentle look—gentle and yet reasonable and terribly penetrating—he could make her aware of the utter absurdity of something she said or did, and make her simultaneously aware of how little such absurdities mattered to someone who loved you.

Franny bent forward and kissed her husband gently on his smiling lips. He came up beside her on the bench, no longer smiling, and took Franny in his arms. For Franny it was as it had always been before—every time he had ever held her in his tender, confident way. It was as though she possessed at last, or was about to possess at last, what she had always wanted above everything else and had never dreamed she wanted—or, that is, never dreamed she wanted in quite the same way she wanted everything else. That was what seemed so incredible to her about it: *this* desire and *this* happiness differed only in degree from the other longings and other satisfactions one experienced. There was nothing at all unreal about it. And somehow the most miraculous part was that the man she was going to marry was not the man she had ever imagined herself marrying. On the contrary, he was the frightening stranger of her girlish daydreams—the dark, handsome man she was always going to meet on a train coming home from boarding school at Christmas or during the summer at Lake Michigan. In her daydreams she sometimes even bore that man a child, but there had always had to be a barrier to their marrying. The man was already married (perhaps to an invalid!), or he was a Jew, he was a Catholic—a French Canadian—or he was the foreign agent of a country committed to the destruction of her own country, or (when she was still younger) there was insanity or even a strain of Negro blood in his family! Yet the stranger had turned up after all—after she had almost forgotten him—and there was no barrier.

Still holding Franny close to him, Miles got to his feet and for a moment lifted his bride completely off the floor. "Franny, oh, 'little Miss Franny,' let's go!" he said. Franny laughed aloud. And to Miles she sounded for all the world like a delighted little girl of four or five. "Let's be on our way," he said, still holding her there. "Let's get out of here."

"Carry me to the car, Miles," she whispered.

"I will," he said. "You bet I will. Not this way, though. I'll set you down and get a good hold and then we'll dash."

But just as Franny's feet touched the floor, there came a great rattling sound from over toward the door to the terrace. Franny gave a little shriek that came out almost "Aha!" And then, in a quiet voice, in a tone of utter resignation, she said, "They've found us." She meant, of course, that the mischiefmakers had found them. "We'll *never* get away."

"No, they haven't, darling," Miles said impatiently.

Franny turned away from him. At the far end of the room she saw a man's figure silhouetted against the glass door to the terrace. She realized at once that the man must be one of the club's waiters. It was he, she surmised, who had let Miles in from the men's locker room. He had been present all the while, and actually he was now holding the terrace door a little way open. The rattling noise had, plainly, come from the long venetian blind on that door. But the source of the rattling no longer interested Franny; she was too angry with Miles for not having told her they weren't alone.

Suddenly her impulse was to turn back and deliver Miles a slap across the face. His inference that the waiter's presence hadn't mattered was insulting both to herself and to this man who had so faithfully performed the duties assigned him. But before she could turn or speak, Miles had seized her by the hand and the waiter had thrown open the door. Hand in hand, the bride and groom ran the length of the little boys' locker room. In the excitement of the moment, Miles had forgotten that he was going to carry Franny to the car. It was well for him that he had. Franny consented to let him hold her hand only in order to keep from embarrassing the waiter. Halfway to the door she made out just which of the club's waiters he was, and she could easily have called him by name. But instead she dropped her eyes, and she kept them lowered even when Miles paused in the doorway to slip a bill into the hand at the end of the white sleeve. In her pique with Miles, she wondered if the bill was of as large a denomination as it ought to be.

Outside, they ran along the edge of the gaping swimming pool and on in the direction of the tennis courts. Beyond the courts,

Miles's new car was hidden. The wet snow was falling heavily, and it was beginning to stick now. It seemed to Franny that the snow might fill the empty swimming pool before the night was over. They went through the gate into the area of the tennis courts. From there Franny glanced back once at the lighted windows of the low, sprawling clubhouse. Through the snow it seemed miles away. They ran across the courts and through the white shrubbery. Neither of them spoke until they were in the car. By then their rendezvous in the locker room seemed like something that happened too long ago to mention. As Miles was helping her into her coat, and she was carefully protecting the big white orchid that she knew her father had pinned on the coat with his own hands, Franny said, "What are we going to do, Miles? I'm terrified. I hate snow. We can't get even as far as Bardstown tonight."

"Of course we can't, honey," he said. He had switched on the car lights and was starting the motor. "We'll have to stay here in town tonight. I telephoned the hotel a while ago. We'll have to stay there."

They had planned to spend the first night at Bardstown, which in good weather was only a few hours away, down in Kentucky, and where there was an attractive old inn. They had planned to make it to Natchez by the second night, and to be at the Gulf Coast by the third. Franny's father had urged them to fly down, or to take a train. But they were able to think only of what fun it would be to have their own car once they got to Biloxi. It had been silly of them, they acknowledged now, driving into town through the snow, but they did have the satisfaction of knowing that all planes would be grounded on such a night, anyway. And to both of them the idea of spending their wedding night in a Pullman berth seemed grotesque.

It took Miles three quarters of an hour to get them through the snow and the traffic to the downtown hotel where he had managed to make reservations. Along the way, he apologized to Franny for putting them up at this particular hotel—the hotel, that is, where he had himself been living during the past year and a half. "As luck would have it," he explained, "there are two big conventions in town this week. I was lucky to find a room anywhere at all. I hope you don't mind too much."

"Why in the world should I mind?" Franny laughed. "We're a bona fide married couple now."

Yet the moment she had passed through the revolving door into the marble-pillared lobby of the hotel, Franny rested a gloved hand on the sleeve of Miles's overcoat and said, "I *do* feel a little funny about it, after all."

"I was afraid you might feel funny about it," Miles said. They stood there a moment waiting for the boy with their luggage to follow them through the revolving door, and Miles began to apologize all over again. "The other hotels were all full up," he said. "It's only because I happen to hit it off so well with Bill Carlisle that I was able to get a room here. It wasn't easy for him even; he's just the assistant manager. Your father, or almost any of the guys in the wedding, might have found us something better. But it seemed worse, somehow, to have any of them—even your father—know exactly where we're spending the night, since we can't get out of town. I guessed you would feel the same way about it."

But Franny was not listening to Miles. She had become aware that she was the only woman in the lobby, and the mention of the assistant manager's name had further distracted her. Bill Carlisle had been invited to the wedding—she recalled addressing his invitation—but he had not been invited to the reception and supper dance. As for her own acquaintance with him, it was very slight. She had known him for a long time, however, and she knew that he knew just about everyone that she did. She interrupted Miles's apologies to say, "Do we have to see Bill Collier?"

"Who?" asked Miles.

"You know—the assistant manager."

"Of course we don't, darling," he said. "We don't even have to register. That's all set."

The boy with their luggage had joined them now. Another boy had appeared with their key and was beckoning them to follow him to the elevator. As they crossed the lobby, Franny began laughing to herself. Miles noticed, and asked what was funny.

"I was wondering," she said, "do you think he'll have put us in your room?"

"Will who have?"

"You know, your friend Bill—the assistant manager."

"At least it won't be that," said Miles. "There was someone waiting to take it over when I got the last of my possessions out this morning."

"What a shame," Franny whispered. "It would have been kind of interesting, and no one but Bill Cook need ever have known."

"Bill Carlisle's his name," Miles said rather petulantly. Then he added, "He's a pretty nice fellow, in case you don't know."

"Certainly he is," Franny said with a wink. "I've known him for years."

Franny stepped into the elevator, followed by Miles. Then the boy with the luggage got in, then the one with the key. Franny observed that both the boys were mature men, and the key boy was even bald-headed. They kept their heads bowed, very courteously, not even looking up when presently they had occasion to speak to each other.

"Where's Jack?" the luggage boy asked quietly.

"He's coming," said the key boy.

"Who's Jack?" Franny asked Miles.

Thinking the question directed to him, the luggage boy replied, "He's the elevator boy." As he spoke, he glanced up at Franny. Probably he thought it was demanded of him. Unlike the key boy, he had a heavy head of hair, as dark and thick as Miles's own, and the face he lifted was youthful, almost handsome even, with a broad jaw and black, rather cruel eyes that seemed brimming with energy. As soon as he looked up he realized his mistake and bent his head again. But he had reminded Franny of someone—someone she didn't like. Or *did* like. Which was it? She couldn't think who it was, and felt vaguely that she didn't want to. And what would Jack, the elevator operator, be like, she wondered, when he turned up? Somehow she was sure he would be a redhead. Presently he would come running; he would hop into the elevator, close the door, push the button, and there she would be, locked in the elevator with Miles and with the three men in their dark-green livery and with the heap of luggage, and the elevator would shoot them up to their floor and stop with a sickening little bounce. She wished Miles would *say* something!

"Jack seems to have gotten lost," Miles said. Franny burst out laughing.

Immediately, Jack appeared, as if from nowhere. He was a Negro boy, but with light skin and a reddish tint to his hair.

Franny was conscious of Jack's arrival, and conscious of the color of his hair, but at the same time her real attention had been caught by a figure out in the lobby. It was the figure of a woman, and she was moving swiftly across the lobby toward this elevator, making her way between the heavier figures of the conventioners in their tweed overcoats and gray fedoras. (Most of them, it seemed to Franny, were smoking cigars, the way conventioners were supposed to.) The woman was wearing a navy-blue topcoat and hat, and carried an oversize handbag. "Wait!" Franny said to the elevator boy.

"What do you mean, 'Wait'?" Miles asked.

"Don't you see who that is trying to catch us?" Franny said, rising on her toes.

"I see who it is, but you don't know her, and I can promise you I don't either."

One of the hotel boys snorted, but he cut it off so short Franny couldn't tell for sure which of them it was. She suspected the bald-headed one.

"It's Bernice! The maid from the club!" Franny tried to recall whether she had forgotten anything essential. No, the woman must have an urgent message for her. Her father or her mother had been taken ill, or there had been some disaster at the club—a fire perhaps. She remembered distinctly having left a cigarette burning in the women's lounge.

"It's no such thing," Miles was saying. "Let's go, Jack!"

The woman was close enough now for Franny to see it was not Bernice. The long stride and the yellow hair sticking out from under the hat had deceived her. But she should have known, shouldn't she, that Bernice could not have worn such heels.

The elevator door was closing right in the woman's face, and even if the woman wasn't Bernice, this was more than Franny could bear. "Stop it!" she commanded, utterly outraged by the ungallant behavior of these men. "There's room for another person, easily!"

The boys looked at Miles. "Let the lady in," Miles thundered.

Jack slid the door open. But the woman hesitated. With a swift glance she seemed to have taken in every aspect of the situation—that it was a bride and groom she was intruding upon, that the bride had insisted upon holding the car for her, that the groom had protested. She now signaled Jack to go on without her, but with Miles's thundering command still in his ears Jack made no move to do so. Miles kept silent. And so did Franny, who in a last-minute glance as swift as the woman's had taken in *her* total situation—that she was a middle-aged prostitute late for an engagement. There was but one solution to the awful silence and to the irresolution of the elevator boy. The woman stepped into the elevator and abruptly turned her back to the other passengers.

As the car shot upward, Jack asked with easy nonchalance, "Your floor, please?"

Again there was silence. Finally Miles said, "What's our floor?"

The key boy looked up, showing his full face for the first time— eyes set close together, a small, puffy nose, ears flat against the bald head. Franny thought it the stupidest, most brutal face she had ever set eyes on. "*Your* floor is eight, Mr. Miller," he said, barely opening his swollen lips when he spoke.

After a moment Jack repeated, "Your floor, please?"

The woman now turned her face toward the elevator boy so that Franny saw her profile. Her face was plain—neither homely nor otherwise, really—and seemed devoid of expression. Only the fact that she had turned her face toward him showed that she knew the boy expected an answer from her. It occurred to Franny that in her agitation this poor creature had forgotten what floor she was going to. At last, and as if with great effort, she did speak. "Seven for me," she said.

With a long, bony forefinger Jack stabbed the seventh-floor button. The elevator stopped almost at once, and the door slid open. The woman stepped out into the hallway, where there was a broad mirror facing her between two metal cigarette urns. Instead of turning to left or right she stopped here just outside the elevator, and for one instant her pale eyes met Franny's in the glass. Then the door closed quietly between them.

Franny had not been aware of a bouncing sensation when the elevator stopped at that floor. But when it stopped at the floor above, the sensation so upset her equilibrium that she felt positively faint. Her two feet in their fur-trimmed galoshes seemed chilled to numbness. She felt that if she tried to take one step down the hallway in the direction of the bridal chamber her knees might buckle underneath her. She wondered how she would ever manage it.

To Miles Miller, his bride had seemed not herself at all, from the time they met in the shadows of the locker room at the country club until at last they were alone in the hotel room. But her confusion and nervousness were very understandable, he reasoned, in view of the upsetting change in their plans. And once they were alone in the room, she was indeed very much herself again. She was once again the vivacious, unaffected, ingenuous little being he had decided to marry after talking to her for five minutes during an intermission at a big debut party last year. From the beginning, Miles had felt that he appreciated her special brand of innocence and even artlessness as no one else ever before had. One thing he had determined when he left college and entered upon his career in business was that he would not be the sort—the type—to marry the boss's daughter and further his career that way. He detested that type. He extended this pledge to himself even to include the daughters of prominent and influential men who might indirectly help him in his career. He extended it even to cover all the debutantes he had ever met or would ever meet. He had had no definite ideas about where he *would* find his wife, except one idea that was so childish he laughed at it himself: He had thought of meeting a perfectly unspoiled girl while vacationing in an unspoiled countryside—perhaps in the highland South, perhaps even somewhere in Europe. He had thought particularly of Switzerland. But when thinking more realistically, Miles told himself simply that he would not marry for the sake of his business or social advancement. His marriage and his family life must be something altogether apart from his career.

And then, in his twenty-sixth year, he had met Franny Crowell and had had a wonderful insight. Franny was, in a most important sense, as beautifully innocent and provincial as any little mountain girl might have been. She delighted in her surroundings, accepted her relation to them without question, and would be content to remain where she was and as she was for the rest of her life. She had been practically nowhere away from home. For two years she went to boarding school in Virginia but hated dormitory life and thought it silly of girls to go East to college when they could be so much more comfortable staying at home. She had herself attended the local city university for two years and had relished meeting different kinds of people from her own home town. True, she had spent most of her summers at a resort on Lake Michigan, but even there most of her companions had been the same people she went to school with at home during the winter. Miles Miller recognized in Franny Crowell the flaxen-haired mountain girl of his childish imaginings. Her outward appearance might deceive the world but never him. She arranged her golden-brown hair always in the very latest, most sophisticated fashions. Last summer she had even let the beauty parlor put a blond streak in her hair. She plucked her eyebrows, even penciled them. The shade of her lipstick paled or darkened according to whatever was newest. But Miles perceived that all of this was as innocent and natural in his Franny as plaiting flaxen pigtails might have been.

Miles and Franny had agreed in advance that they should each have only one glass of champagne at the club on their wedding night. But among the bags that they had had brought into the hotel was Miles's genuine Gucci liquor case—a present from the men at his office. Packed with ice in the plastic compartment of the elaborate leather case were two bottles of champagne of a somewhat earlier and better year than that offered the guests by the bride's father. And into Franny's make-up bag she had managed to fit two of their very own champagne glasses. Together they had thought of everything.

In their hotel room, they spent the first half hour making toasts.

They drank to Betty Manville's debut ball, where they had met, drank to their first date, to their first kiss, to the night he first proposed, to the night she accepted, to the night of the announcement party. Each toast had to be followed by a kiss. Each kiss inspired and motivated another reminiscence. Finally, they turned to toasting people whom they associated with events of their courtship. Since Franny was a talented and tireless mimic, Miles encouraged her to "do" each of these people. She "did" Betty Manville's mother, her own father, and then one of her bridesmaids, who had once upon a time imagined *she* was going to have Miles Miller for herself. This last was the funniest of all to Miles. He was seated on the side of the bed, leaning on one elbow, and when he had witnessed Franny's version of that poor, misguided girl, he set his champagne glass on the floor and fell back on the bed in a spasm of laughter. He threshed about, still laughing aloud, and all the while wiping tears from his eyes and begging Franny to stop.

When Franny promised to stop, Miles got control of himself and sat up in the center of the bed. Wiping his eyes with his handkerchief, he looked up again and found Franny sitting on the side of the bed with her thumb pressed against her nose so hard that her little nose was flattened on her face. Her eyes were squinted up and her mouth, which was normally small and tight, was stretched and spread into a wide ribbon across her face. "You know who this is?" she asked, barely moving her lips.

"I'm glad to say I don't," Miles said, as if offended by her ugliness.

"Oh, you do," Franny insisted.

"I don't, and it's not very attractive."

"Of course it's not attractive," said Franny, keeping the thumb pressed against her nose. "It's that bald-headed bellboy, the one with the key."

"What's wrong with him?" Miles said, swinging his feet around

to the other side of the bed and thus momentarily turning his back
to Franny.

"You don't have to turn your back," Franny said. "See, it's still
only me."

Miles looked around and smiled apologetically. Franny's face was
her own again, and she was looking down at her hands very seriously. "Weren't all three of those bellboys grotesque?" she said.

"I don't think so," Miles said. "They're perfectly normal-looking
human beings. I see them every day."

"Normal-looking!" Franny exclaimed, lifting her eyes to his.
"How can you say so? The bald-headed one was really monstrous.
And the one with the mop of hair had a really mad look in his eyes.
And that pale Negro boy with the kinky red hair! How blind you
are to people, Miles. You don't really *see* them."

"Maybe not," said Miles, meaning to dismiss the subject, since
Franny seemed so emotional about it. Turning now, he let himself
fall across the bed toward her, and again he took one of her hands
between the two of his. But before he could speak the endearment
he intended, something else occurred to him that he felt must be
said first. It was in defense of his vision, or—he couldn't define
it—in defense of something even more specially his own that had
been disparaged. "Anyway," he said, "you must admit that not one
of those bellhops was half as weird-looking as that painted-up
creature you had your hug fest with when we were leaving the club.
After the elevator ride, I don't have to tell you what *she* looked
like." Though they had been in the room for more than half an
hour, this was the first reference either of them had made to the
woman in the elevator.

Franny withdrew her hand and stood up.

Miles said, "We're not going to quarrel about something so silly
on our wedding night, are we?"

Franny was silent for a moment. Her eyes moved about the room as if taking it in for the first time. Then she bent over and kissed Miles on the top of his head. "We aren't *ever* going to quarrel again, are we, Miles?"

"Never," he said. He reached out a hand, but she pulled away. "Come back," he said in a whisper.

"Not until I've slipped into something more—more right." She smiled vaguely.

Miles lay with his head propped on one hand and watched her go to her little overnight bag and take out the folds of lace and peach silk that were her negligee and gown. Suddenly he leaped from the bed with outstretched arms. But the bride dashed through the open doorway to the bathroom and closed the door.

Miles had long since changed into his blue silk pajamas with the white monogram on the pocket when he saw the first turning and twisting of the doorknob. When Franny failed to appear at once— that is, when the knob ceased its twisting and the bathroom door didn't open—his vexation showed itself momentarily in one little horizontal crease in his smooth forehead. But the moment was so brief that even his eyes didn't reflect it, and soon a sly little smile came to his lips . . . He would give her a signal that all was ready and waiting, and at the same time give her motivation and courage. Stepping over to the dresser he uncorked the second bottle of champagne. He managed it very expertly, taking satisfaction in his expertness. The pop was loud enough for Franny to hear and comprehend, yet there was not one bubble of wasteful overflow. The tiny golden bubbles came just to the mouth of the champagne bottle and no farther. Miles had not even taken the precaution of having the two glasses handy. He was expert and he was confident of his expertness.

He watched the first bubbles appear and then shot a glance across the room at the doorknob. It was turning again. He stepped over to where the two glasses were, on the bedside table, filled them, and then returned the bottle to its ice. Still no Franny. But the doorknob was now turning back and forth rather rapidly. Miles watched it as if hypnotized. Finally he uttered a tentative "Franny?" There was no response except in the acceleration of the knob's turning. "Franny?" he repeated, striding toward the door. "What's the matter?" Still no answer. The turning was frenzied now. "Franny, do you hear me? What are you doing?"

"Of course I hear you!" Franny exclaimed through the door. "I'm trying to get out of here, you fool!"

Miles seized the knob and gave it a forceful twist.

"That's not going to help," said Franny, resentful of the overpowering yank to the knob she had been holding on to.

"The thing must be locked," Miles said, astonished. "Why did you lock it?"

Franny was silent. Then said, *"I* didn't lock it."

"Well, *I* didn't." Miles laughed. "Anyway, try unlocking it."

"Do you think I haven't already?"

"What kind of lock is it? Is there a key?"

"No. It's one of those damned little eggs you turn."

"But why on earth would you have locked it?"

"If I did it, Miles, I did it without thinking."

Miles was now trying to see the bolt through the crack of the door. "But why would you?" he said absently.

"Why would I what?"

"Lock it without thinking."

"All decent people lock bathroom doors," she said with conviction.

"We didn't at our house," Miles said. He could definitely see the bolt through the crack. "My father used to throw away the key to the bathroom door as soon as we moved into a place."

"Don't start on your father *now*, Miles."

"My father was all right."

"Who said he wasn't? *Do* something, Miles, for God's sake."

"There's nothing to do but call the desk and have them take down the door."

Franny, who had for a moment been leaning against the rim of the washbowl, now straightened and grasped the doorknob again. "Miles, you *wouldn't!*"

"Don't go to pieces, Franny."

"You'd let them send up those three stooges—"

Miles burst into laughter.

"How coarse you are, Miles," Franny said, her voice deepening.

"Oh, honey, there's a regular maintenance crew, and—"

"Maybe so," she broke in, her voice climbing the scale till it was much higher than Miles had ever heard it before. "But don't you know, Miles, that Bill Carlisle would certainly know about it? Oh, God, everybody in this town would know about it before tomorrow morning!"

"In God's name, Franny, what do you propose I do?"

"What kind of man are you, Miles? Take the door down yourself. You've been living in this hotel so long you depend on them for everything. You seem to think the world's just one big hotel and that you call in the maintenance crew for any and every thing."

"O.K., Franny, I'll try," Miles said amiably. "But have you ever tried taking down a locked door?"

"Why did you have to bring me to this dump?" Franny wailed.

"And why did you have to lock the door?" he countered.

Now they were both silent as Miles went to the closet door where his Valpak hung, and dug out a small gold pocketknife. His first effort to remove the pin in the upper door hinge was fruitless. The pin wouldn't budge. Neither would the pin in the lower hinge. He decided he needed a hammer to drive the knife blade upward against the heads of the pins, and he was just turning to go and fetch his shoe for that purpose when Franny spoke again.

"Miles," she began, speaking very slowly and in a tone so grave that it stopped him, "do you remember that night at Cousin Jane Thompson's party?"

He listened, waiting for her to continue. Then he realized she expected some response from him. "Yes, Franny," he said.

"That night at Cousin Jane's," she now went on in the same sepulchral tone, "when you said Sue Maynard's date was drunk and that she asked you to take her home." Sue Maynard was the bridesmaid who had thought *she* would have Miles for herself. Miles had been a stag at the party that night.

"Yes, I remember."

"You were lying."

"In a way, Franny—"

"In the worst way," she said flatly. "You thought I would think it was just Sue's lie and that you didn't know better, or that you knew better but were too honorable to give her away."

"Maybe."

"That's how you *thought* I would think. But I knew even that night, Miles Miller, that you engineered it all. Her date was Puss Knowlton, and you had no trouble giving *him* the shove. And don't you think I know it's more than just necking that Sue Maynard goes in for? . . . And, Miles, the night last summer, *after* we were engaged, when you couldn't come for dinner at our house with Daddy's Aunt Caroline because of the report you had to write up— you didn't have any report to write up, Miles. You went someplace out on the South Side with a little creature named Becky Louise Johnson."

By the time Franny had finished, Miles had silently crossed the room to the bedside table and downed one of the two waiting glassfuls of champagne. He had listened intently to what she said, and the more he heard the more intent he had become on getting that damned door down. In his liquor case he found a bottle opener that he decided would work better than his knife. He returned to the door with his shoe and the bottle opener, and in no time he had the top pin out of its hinge.

"Miles—" Franny began again, still in the same tone.

"Shut up, Franny!" Miles said, and at once began hammering at the lower pin. It offered a little more resistance than the other, but was soon dislodged. The door was still firmly in place, however. Twice Miles jabbed the bottle opener into the crack on the hinge side, as though he might prize the door open. Then he laughed aloud at himself.

Franny heard him laugh, of course. "Is it funny? Is it really funny to you, Miles?" she said.

"Try giving it a push from in there, on the hinge side of the door," said Miles. Franny pushed. The door creaked, but that was all.

"Miles," Franny began once again, in a whisper now, and he could tell that she was leaning against the door and speaking into the crack. "I've thought of something else I've never confronted you with."

Miles felt the blood rush to his face. Suddenly he banged on the door with his fist. "Will you shut up, you little bitch! You know, I'm not above socking you in earnest if ever I get you out of there!"

"You would sock me just one time, Miles Miller."

"It would be the second time. Don't you forget that," he said.

They were really at it now, for he was reminding her of an occasion two days after their announcement party when he had found her kissing a college kid whose name he did not even know. He had struck her with his open hand on the back of her neck—not while she was kissing the kid but afterward, as he pushed her along the terrace there at the Polo Club. He had had too much to drink that night, and that was what saved them. Franny could claim that he had deserted her in favor of the bar. She also claimed that she had not really been kissing the boy and added that, anyway, he was an old, old, old friend and therefore meant nothing to her. They hardly spoke to each other during the week following, though of course they continued going about together. And until now they had neither of them ever referred to the incident, as if by mutual agreement.

"You're no gentleman, Miles," Franny pronounced, carefully keeping away from the door now. "As Daddy said of you to start with, you have all the outward signs of a gentleman but that's no evidence you're one inside."

"I've already settled your father's hash, Franny."

"You mean he's settled yours."

It was an unfortunate word—"settled." And both of them were aware of it immediately. It quieted both of them for some time. It referred to another incident that was assumed to be closed. Franny's father had apparently suspected Miles of being a fortune hunter, and before the engagement was announced he had asked Miles frankly what kind of "settlement" he expected. Miles had stormed out of the house, and was reconciled with Mr. Crowell only after having it hammered home to him by Franny that what her father had done was merely the conventional, old-fashioned thing for a man in Mr. Crowell's position to do. Miles had finally accepted Franny's explanation, but only a few weeks ago he had had another stormy session over a similar matter. This time it was with both the bride's parents. At that very late date he had learned about certain letters of inquiry that had been sent out concerning his "background." The letters had been written to various family friends and relatives of the Crowells who had lived for many years in Santa Barbara and Laguna Beach. When Miles learned of these letters through a remark of Franny's, it was many months after the letters had been written and replied to. The revelation sent Miles into a rage. He was in such a state that Franny feared he might do real violence to her father, or even to her mother, who had actually written the letters.

She had let the cat out of the bag inadvertently. She and he were just going out to a movie one night. Franny had come down to the living room already wearing her coat and even with her gloves on, but Miles had wanted to linger and talk awhile. Before she came down, he had wandered about the room studying some family photographs taken thirty years before. These "portraits," in their upright frames on the mantelshelf and on the various tables, had reminded him of pictures in his own family's living room when he was growing up. He commenced talking to Franny about how his mother always placed the same pictures on the same tables and bureaus no matter where they were living, and then he went on to speak, as he had on several previous occasions, of how restless his father had been after he left the service. (Miles's father had been a West Point graduate and had remained in the army until he had his first heart attack, just a few months before Pearl Harbor.) And now, as Miles had already done several times before, he began listing for Franny the towns they had lived in during and after the war. Franny, who was impatient to get on to the movie, didn't listen very carefully. When Miles hesitated, trying to think of which town it was he had omitted from his list, Franny absent-mindedly supplied "Palo Alto." But it was not Palo Alto he was trying to think of; it was San Jose.

"Palo Alto?" said Miles. "How did you know we ever lived in Palo Alto?"

"You've told me all this before," she answered.

But he had not told her about the spring in Palo Alto! It was then that his parents had quarreled so endlessly, though he—and probably they—had never known just why. At any rate, he was always careful to leave Palo Alto out of his catalogue of towns. And he was not content now until he had wrung a confession of the whole business of the letters of inquiry out of Franny. Once she had confessed, he insisted upon taking the matter up with her parents that very night; he insisted upon *seeing* the letters. For a time, Mrs. Crowell maintained that she had already thrown away the letters. But at last she broke down. She went upstairs and returned with the packet of letters, all of which Miles read, sitting there in the family circle. He had known there couldn't be anything really bad in them, because just as there was nothing very good that could be said of his parents, there was nothing very bad, either. The worst the letters said of them was that they were "rootless people and apparently of restricted means." Miles found he could not even resent one lady's description of his mother as a "harmless little woman—pleasant enough—with a vague Southern background." The letters repeated each other with phrases like "thoroughly nice" and "well bred" and "well behaved." The sole reference to Palo Alto was "I think they lived at Palo Alto for a time. John's sister Laura met them there. She thought Major Miller very handsome. He had a small black mustache, if I recall."

The memory of all this and of the "settlement" episode occupied Miles's mind as he crossed the hotel room and picked up the glass of champagne that he had poured for Franny. The champagne had gone flat already, but he relished its flatness. He sipped it slowly, as if tasting in each sip a different unpleasant incident or aspect of their courtship and engagement—tasting all they had not tasted and toasted with the first bottle. Suddenly he put down the glass, leaving still a sip or two in the bottom, and stepped quickly over to the bathroom door. "Franny," he said, "it has just occurred to me! It wasn't your father's idea to talk about a settlement with me. You put him up to it! It was you who thought I might be after your family's money! If it had been your father's idea, he wouldn't have been so meek and mild when I called his hand. And, by God, you put your mother up to writing those letters, or she never would have given in and shown them to me."

He waited for Franny's denial, but none came. "And, Franny," he went on after a moment, "there's one more thing I know that you didn't know I knew. Your father went down to my office and asked about the likelihood of my staying on here or being transferred."

"I knew he did that, Miles."

"Darn right you knew it. You put him up to that, too. You didn't even want to take a chance on my moving you away from here." But before he had finished his last sentence, Miles heard the water running full force into the bathtub. "Franny, I'm not finished!" he shouted. "What are you doing?"

"If you don't get this door down within ten minutes"—she was speaking through the crack again—"and get it down without having Bill Carlisle up here to witness it, I'm going to drown myself in the damned bathtub."

As a matter of fact, she had begun running the water to drown out Miles's accusations, but as she spoke she became convinced that suicide really had been her original intention.

"Yes," Miles boomed, "you drown yourself in the bathrub and I'll jump out our eighth-floor window! Romeo and Juliet, that's us!"

Franny shut off the water. She opened her mouth to reply, but no words came. She burst into tears. And the poor little bride could not herself have said whether her tears were brought on by the heavy irony and sarcasm of her groom or by the thought of her dear Miles and her dear self lying dead in their caskets with their love yet unfulfilled.

Almost at once Miles began pleading with her not to cry. But it seemed that his every word brought increased volume to the wailing beyond the bathroom door. It was as if she had decided she could more effectively drown out the sound of his voice with tears than with the rush of bath water. But actually it wasn't the sound of her bridegroom's voice alone that she wished not to hear. There was the sound of another voice—other voices. She had first become aware of the other voices during one of hers and Miles's silences. Which silence she couldn't have said, because for some time afterward she tried to believe that she had only imagined hearing the other voices, or at least imagined that they sounded as near to her as they did. Finally, though, the persistence of the voices drew her attention to the fact of the other door. The other door, she finally acknowledged, must certainly lead into an adjoining room. And the voices—a man's and a woman's—came to her from that room. And now the ever-increasing volume of her own wailing was meant to conceal from herself that the woman's voice was addressing her directly through that door.

"Honey, I think we can help you." The offer was unmistakable.

"No, you can't, no, you can't!" Franny wailed.

"The gentleman in here thinks he is pretty good with locks."

"No, no, please don't come in here," Franny begged, too frightened, too perplexed for more tears now.

"Franny, what's going on?" Miles seemed on the verge of tears himself. "Darling, I'll get a doctor, you'll be all right!"

"Miles, there's another door."

"Yes?"

"And there's someone over there. Oh, Miles, make them go away."

"Keep your head, Franny. What do they want?"

"It's a woman. She says there's a man in there who can get me out of here."

"You do want to get out, don't you, Franny?" It was as though he were speaking to someone on a window ledge.

"Not that way, I don't," said Franny. Now she was whispering through the door crack. "Miles, their voices sound familiar!"

"Now, Franny, cut it out!" scolded Miles, and Franny understood his full meaning. For a moment she listened to the other voices. From the start the man's voice had been no more than a low mumbling. He didn't want his voice recognized! The woman spoke more distinctly. Franny could hear them now discussing the problem. Presently the man said something and laughed. And the woman said, "Hush, the kid will hear you." Somehow this gave Franny courage. She stepped over to the other door and said bravely, *"Will* you help me?"

Hearing her, Miles gave a sigh of relief. Then he said, "Ask them to let me come around into their room—and help."

"Will you let my—my husband come around into your room?"

She heard them deliberating. The man was opposed. Finally, the woman said, "No. He can come and meet you outside our hall door if we get this one open."

She repeated this to Miles.

"Tell them O.K.," he commanded.

"O.K.," said Franny softly.

Now the man and woman were at the door. The man was still mumbling. "Is there a latch on your side?" the woman asked.

"Yes," said Franny. "A little sort of knob."

"Tell her to turn it," the man muttered.

"Turn it," said the woman.

Franny turned it. It moved easily. "I have," she said. She watched the big doorknob revolving, but the door didn't open. There was more discussion on the other side of the door.

"It's locked with a key," said the woman to Franny. "But that's how he's going to make hisself useful." Franny's deliverer was hard at work. She couldn't tell whether it was a skeleton key or some makeshift instrument he was using. Presently, she heard the click of the lock and heard the man say, "That's got it."

"Miles!" Franny called out. But Miles didn't answer. He was

already waiting at their neighbors' hall door. There was the sound of footsteps hurriedly retreating, and then the door opened. The room itself was in darkness, but in the light from the bathroom Franny could see the man's figure outlined on the bed. The sheet was pulled up over his face. Franny looked at the woman. She was fully dressed, though barefoot, and she stood smiling at the ridiculous sight in the bed and probably at the memory of the male figure's racing across the room and jumping into the bed and pulling the sheet over its head.

"You're an angel," Franny said, without having known she was going to say it.

The woman acknowledged the compliment only by allowing the smile to fade from her lips. "He'll get up from there and try to open the other door for you in a minute," she said.

Franny gave her a grateful smile, and then she turned and walked with perfect poise toward the hall door. Her peach negligee was floor-length and its little train of lace swept gracefully along the dark carpet. When her hand was on the doorknob, she turned and said simply, "Good night." She might have been at home, turning to say a casual good night to her mother.

In the hallway, Miles had waited, fully expecting to have to carry his bride back to their room in his arms. When she appeared he was stunned by her radiance and self-possession. He had never seen her so beautiful. And Franny was equally stunned by Miles's manly beauty as he stood before her in his blue silk pajamas. For a moment they stood there beaming at one another. Finally, Miles slipped his arm gently about his bride's waist and hurried her off to their room.

They found their bathroom door standing half open, and the door beyond it tightly closed. The two heavy pins still lay on the floor, but Miles quickly slipped them into the hinges. The door was now in perfect working order. Miles stood a moment gazing into the bright bathroom where Franny's clothes were heaped in one corner like a child's. "Well," he said at last, "that fellow worked fast."

"Miles," said Franny, also looking into the bathroom but with her eyes focused on the door opposite, "did you see who it was?"

"What do you mean?"

"The woman over there—she was the woman on the elevator."

"Franny, Franny! . . . She got off at the seventh floor! How could you forget?"

"And the man—" Franny began.

"Franny, Franny, Franny," Miles interrupted, already having left her side to fetch the champagne glasses and refill them. "The man in that room is one of the conventioners from out of town. You never heard his voice or saw him before in your life."

She had been going to say that the man in the bed was Bill Carlisle. But she saw it was useless. And she knew she would never say it now. Miles came toward her slowly with the two glasses filled to the brim. They sipped their champagne, looking at one another over the glasses. In their hearts, both of them were glad they had said all the things that they said through the door. As they gazed deep into each other's eyes, they believed that they had got all of that off their chests once and for all. There was nothing in the world to come between them now. They believed, really and truly, that neither of them would ever deceive or mistrust the other again. Silently they were toasting their own bliss and happiness, confident that it would never again be shadowed by the irrelevances of the different circumstances of their upbringings or by the possibly impure and selfish motives that had helped to bring them together.

The Other Times

Can anybody honestly like having a high-school civics teacher for an uncle? I doubt it. Especially not a young girl who is popular and good-looking and who is going to make her debut some day at the Chatham Golf and Country Club. Nevertheless, that's who the civics teacher was at Westside High School when we were growing up in Chatham. He was the brother of Letitia Ramsey's father, and he had all the failings you would expect of a high-school civics teacher and baseball coach. In the classroom he was a laughingstock for the way he butchered the King's English, and out of school he was known to be a hard drinker and general hell-raiser. But the worst part of it was that he was a bachelor and that the Ramseys had to have him for dinner practically every Sunday.

If you had a Sunday afternoon date with Letitia, there the civics teacher would be, out on the front lawn, playing catch with one of Letitia's narrow-eyed little brothers. Somehow, what disturbed *me* about this particular spectacle when I was having Sunday dates with Letitia was the uncle's and the little brother's concentration on the ball and the kind of real fondness they seemed to feel for the thing.

When either of them held it in his hand for a minute, he seemed to be wanting to make a pet of it. When it went back and forth between them, smacking their gloves, they seemed to hear it saying, yours, mine, yours, mine, as though nobody else had ever thrown or caught a baseball. But of course that's not the point. The point is that it was hard to think of Letitia's having this Lou Ramsey for an uncle. And I used to watch her face when we were leaving her house on a Sunday afternoon to see if she would show anything. But not Letitia!

It may not seem fair to dwell on this unfortunate uncle of a girl like Letitia Ramsey, but it was through him that I got a clearer idea of what she was like, and the whole Ramsey family, as well. They were very well-bred people, and just as well-to-do, even in the Depression. Mr. Ramsey, like my own father, was from the country, but, also like my father, he was from one of the finest country families in the state. And Mrs. Ramsey and my mother had gone through Farleigh Institute together, which was an old-fashioned school where they studied Latin so long that it made a difference in the way they spoke English all the rest of their lives.

Anyway, though I didn't take Latin, fortunately I didn't take civics, either (since I was hoping to go to college if the Depression eased up), and fortunately I didn't go out for the baseball team. This made it not too hard for me to pretend not to notice who Letitia's uncle was. Also, since Letitia didn't go to the high school but went to Miss Jordan's, a school that has more or less replaced Farleigh Institute in Chatham, it could have been as easy for her to pretend not to notice as it was for me.

It could have been, except that Letitia didn't want it that way. When she and I went across the lawn to my father's car on those Sunday afternoons and her uncle and one of her little brothers were carrying on with that baseball, she would call out something like "Have fun, you two!" or "Come see us this week, Uncle Louis!"

And her voice never sounded sweeter than it did then. After we were in the car, if I hadn't thought of something else to talk about she would sometimes begin a long spiel like "I always forget you don't really know my uncle. I wish you did. You probably know how mad he is about sports. That's why my little brothers adore him. And he's just as shy as they are. Look at him and Charlie there. When I'm dressed up like this to go out on a date, he and the boys won't even look at me."

The truth is I felt that Letitia Ramsey was just as smart as she could be—not in school, necessarily, but in the way she handled subjects like undesirable relatives. I think she was very unusual in this. There was one of her friends, named Nancy O'Connor, who had a grandmother who had once run a fruit stand at the old curb market, up on the North Side. The grandmother lived with the O'Connors and was a right funny sort of person, if you know what I mean, and Nancy was forever apologizing for her. Naturally, her apologizing did nothing but make you uncomfortable. Also, there was Trudie Hauser, whose brother Horst was a good friend of mine. The Hausers lived out in the German section of town, where my mother hadn't usually gone to parties in her day, and they still lived in the kind of castle-like house that the first one of the Hausers to get rich had built. Poor Trudie and poor Horst! They had not one but three or four peculiar relatives living with them. And they had German servants, to whom their parents were apt to speak in German, right before you, and make Trudie and Horst, who were both very blond, blush to the roots of their hair the way blonds are apt to do. Then there was also a girl named Maria Thomas. She had a much older brother who was a moron—a real one—and if he passed through the room, or even came in and sat down, she would simply pretend that he wasn't there, that he didn't even exist.

This isn't to say, of course, that all the girls in Chatham had something like that in their families. Lots of girls—and lots of the boys, too—had families like mine, with nobody in particular to be ashamed of. Nor is it to say that the girls who did have something of this kind weren't just as popular as the others and didn't have you to their houses to parties just as often. Nancy O'Connor's family, for instance, lived in a most beautiful Spanish-style house, with beamed ceilings and orange-colored tile floors downstairs, and with a huge walled-in sort of lawn out in the back, where Nancy gave a big party every June. But, I will say, at those parties you always felt that everybody was having more fun than Nancy, all because of the old grandmother. The peculiar old woman never came out into the light of the Japanese lanterns at the party, or anywhere near the tennis court, where the dancing was. She kept always in the shadows, close to the walls that enclosed the lawn. And someone said that Nancy said this was because her grandmother was afraid we would steal the green fruit off the trees she had trained to grow like vines up the walls.

Whether or not Nancy had a good time, her June party was always one of the loveliest events of the year in Chatham. Even though it was the Depression, we had many fine and really lovely parties, and Nancy O'Connor's usually surpassed all others. It was there, at one of them, two nights after we had graduated from high school, that Horst Hauser and Bob Southard and I made up our minds to do a thing that we had been considering for some time and that a lot of boys like us must have done at one time or another. We had been seniors that year, you understand, and in Chatham boys are apt to go pretty wild during their senior year in high school. That is the time when you get to know a city as you will never have a chance to again if you come from the kind of people that I do. I have lived away from Chatham quite a long while now, mostly in places which are not too different from it but about which I never kid myself into thinking I know very much. Yet, like a lot of other men, I carry in my head, even today, a sort of detailed map of the city where I first learned to drive a car and first learned to make dates with girls who were not strictly of the kind I was brought up to date. And I don't mean nice girls like Nancy and Trudie, whose parents were different from mine but who were themselves very nice girls indeed. Chatham being only a middle-sized city—that is, without a big-league baseball team, yet with almost a quarter of a million big-league fans—and being not thoroughly Midwestern and yet not thoroughly Southern either, the most definitely complimentary thing I usually find to say about it is that it was a good place to grow up in. By which I don't mean that it is a good place to come *from,* or anything hateful like that.

For I like Chatham. And I remember everything I ever knew about it. Sometimes, when I go back there for a visit, I can direct people who didn't grow up there to a street or a section of town or even to some place out in the country nearby that they wouldn't have guessed I had any knowledge of. And whenever I am there nowadays, the only change I notice and the only thing that gives me a sad feeling is that the whole city is so much more painted up and prosperous-looking than it used to be during the Depression. And in connection with this, there is something I cannot help feeling is true and cannot help saying. My father, who came from a country town thirty-five miles east of Chatham, used to tell us how sad it made him to see the run-down condition of the house where he was born, out there in the country. But my feeling is that there is something even more depressing about going back to Chatham today and finding the house where I lived till I was grown—and the whole city, too—looking in much better shape than it did when I called it home. There are moments when I almost wish I could buy up the whole town and let it run down just a little.

Of course, that's an entirely selfish feeling, and I realize it. But it shows what wonderful times we had—decent good times, and others not so decent. And it shows that while we were having those fine times we knew exactly what everything around us was like. We didn't like money's being so tight and didn't like it that everything from the schoolhouse to the country club was a little shabby and run-down. We boys certainly *minded* wearing our fathers' cut-down dinner jackets, and the girls certainly *minded* wearing their older sisters' hand-me-down evening dresses; although we knew that our party clothes looked all right, we knew, too, that our older brothers and sisters, five years before, wouldn't have put up with them for five minutes. We didn't like any of this a bit, and yet it was *ours* and the worriers among us worried even then about how it was all bound to change.

Of course, when the change came, it wasn't at all what anyone had expected. For it never occurred to us then that a war would come along and solve all the problems of the future for us, in one way or another. Instead, we heard so much talk of the Depression that we thought that times were bound to get even worse than they had been, and that all the fun would go out of life as soon as we finished high school, or, at the latest, after college. If you were a worrier, as I was, it didn't seem possible that you would ever be able to make a living of the kind your father had always made. And I sat around some nights, when I ought to have been studying, wondering how people would treat me when I showed that I couldn't make the grade and began to go to pieces. It was on those nights that I used to think about Letitia Ramsey's uncle, whom I considered the most dismal failure of my acquaintance, and then think about how he was treated by Letitia. This became a thing of such interest to me that I was never afterward sure of my own innocence in the way matters developed the night of Nancy O'Connor's party.

I don't need to describe the kind of mischief the boys in my crowd were up to that year—that is, on nights when we weren't having movie dates or going to parties with the usual "nice girls" we had always known. Our mischief doesn't need going into here, and besides it is very old hat to anyone who grew up with the freedom boys have in places like Chatham (especially at a time like the Depression, when all the boys' private schools were closed down). Also, I suppose it goes without saying that we were pretty careful not to mix the one kind of wonderful time we were having with the other. To the girls we had known longest, we did make certain jokes and references they couldn't understand, or pretended they couldn't. We would kid each other, in front of them, about jams we had been in when they weren't along, without ever making any of it very clear. But that was as far as we went until, toward the end of the year, some of the girls got so they would beg us, or dare us, to take them with us some night to one of our "points of interest," which was how we referred to the juke joints and roadhouses we went to. We talked about the possibility of this off and on for several weeks. (Five years before, it wouldn't have taken our older brothers five minutes to decide to do such a thing.) And finally, on the night of Nancy O'Connor's party, Horst Hauser and Bob Southard and I decided that the time had come.

The three of us, with our dates, slipped away from the party just after midnight, telling Nancy that we would be back in about an hour, which we knew we wouldn't. And we didn't tell her mother we were going at all. We crossed the lawn and went out through a gate in the back wall at one of the corners, just behind a sort of tool house that Nancy called "the dovecote." She had told us how to find the gate, and she told us also to watch for her grandmother. And, sure enough, just as we were unlocking the gate, there came the old grandmother running along the side wall opposite us, and sticking close to it even when she made the turn at the other corner. She was wearing a long black dress, and at the distance from which we saw her I thought she might easily have been mistaken for a Catholic nun.

But we got the gate open and started through it and into the big vacant lot we had to cross to get to Horst Hauser's car. I held the gate for the other couples, and then for my own date. While I was doing this, I kept one eye on the old woman. But I also peered around the dovecote and saw Nancy O'Connor leave the bright lights of the tennis court and head across the grass under the Japanese lanterns, walking fast in order to catch her grandmother before she reached us. And when I shut the gate after me, I could just imagine the hell the old woman was going to catch.

It wasn't very polite, leaving Nancy's party that way and making trouble in the family—for Nancy was sure to blame the old woman for our going, somehow—but the whole point is that the girl who happened to be my date that night and for whom I had stood there holding the gate was none other than Letitia Ramsey.

Now, there is no use in my not saying right here that all through that spring Letitia's uncle, whom the high-school students generally spoke of as "the Ram," had been having the usual things said about him. And there is no use in my denying that by this time I knew those things were so. For we hadn't had our *other* wonderful times all winter long without running into the Ram at a number of our points of interest—him, along with a couple of his star athletes and his and their girl friends. In fact, I knew by this time that the rumors all of us had heard about him every year since we entered high school were true, and I knew, too, that it was the very athletes he coached and trained and disciplined from the day they first reported for practice, after junior high, that he ended by making his running mates when they were seniors.

But all that sort of thing, in my opinion, is pretty much old hat to most people everywhere. The important thing to me is that when we decided to leave Nancy's wonderful party that night and take our dates with us out to a dine-and-dance joint called Aunt Martha's Tavern, something crossed my mind. And I am not sure that it wasn't something I hoped for instead of something I dreaded, as it should have been. It was that this Aunt Martha's Tavern was exactly where we were most likely to run into the Ram on a Saturday night, which this happened to be, with, of course, one of his girl friends and a couple of his athletes with their girl friends, too.

Well, it couldn't have been worse. We all climbed into Horst Hauser's car and drove out west of town to Aunt Martha's. It was the kind of place where you had to ring several times before they would come and let you in. And when we had rung the bell the second time and were standing outside under the light, with its private flock of bugs whirling around it, waiting there for Aunt Martha to have a look at us through some crack somewhere and decide if she would let us in, a rather upsetting thing happened to me. We were all standing on the stoop together, facing the big, barnlike batten door to the place. Letitia was standing right next to me, and I just thought to myself I would steal a quick glance at her while she wasn't noticing. I turned my head only the slightest bit, but I saw at once that *she* was already looking at *me*. When our eyes met, I felt for the first second or two that she didn't realize they *had* met, because she kept right on looking without changing her expression. I couldn't at once tell what the expression meant. Then it came over me that there was something this girl was expecting me to say—or, at least, hoping I would say. I said the first thing that popped into my mind: "They always make you wait like this." And Letitia Ramsey looked grateful, even for that.

At last, the door was pulled open, though only just about six inches, and inside we saw the face of Aunt Martha's old husband. The old fellow gaped at the girls for a couple of seconds with a stupid grin on his face—he was a deaf-mute and a retired taxi-

dermist—and then he threw the door wide open. We went inside—
and, of course, there the Ram was, out on the floor dancing.

There weren't any lights on to speak of, except around the sides,
in the booths, and the curtains to some of the booths were drawn.
But even so, dark as it was, and with six or eight other couples
swinging around on the dance floor, right off the bat I spotted the
Ram. Maybe I only recognized him because he was doing the old-
time snake-hips dancing that he liked to do when he was high. I
can't be sure. But I have the feeling that when we walked into that
place that night, I would have seen the Ram just as plainly even if
he had not been there—seen the freckled hand he pumped with
when he danced, seen the white sharkskin suit, seen the head of
sandy hair, a little thin on top but with the sweaty curls still thick
along his temples and on the back of his neck.

Once we were inside, I glanced at Letitia again. And for some
reason I noticed now that either before she left the party or in the
car coming out here she had moved the gardenia corsage that I had
sent her from the shoulder strap of her dress to the center of its low-
cut neckline. When I saw this, I suddenly turned to Bob and Horst
and said, "Let's not stay here."

Letitia and the other two girls smiled at each other. "I think he
thinks we'll disgrace him," Letitia said after a moment.

I don't know when she first saw her uncle. It may have been
when I did, right off the bat. It being Letitia, you couldn't tell. Or *I*
couldn't. The one clue I had was that when the old deaf-mute made
signs for us to follow him across the floor to an empty booth, I saw
her throw her little powder blue evening jacket, which was the same
color as her dress, around her shoulders. It was a hot night, and
before that she had only been carrying it over her arm.

Yet it wasn't necessarily her uncle's presence that caused Letitia to
put the jacket around her bare shoulders. It could have been just the

kind of place we were in. It could have been Martha's crazy-looking old husband, with his tufts of white hair sticking out in all directions. It seemed to me at the time that it might be only the sight of the old man's stuffed animal heads, which were hung all around the place. You didn't notice most of these with it so dark, but above the beer counter were the heads of three collie dogs, and as we went across the floor, the bubbly lights of the jukebox would now and again catch a gleam from the glass eyes of those collie dogs. Any other time in the world, I think the effect would have seemed irresistibly funny to me. I would have pointed it out to Horst and Bob, and afterward there would have been cryptic references made to it before girls like Letitia who normally wouldn't ever have been inside such a place.

We went into our booth, which was a big one in a corner, and almost as soon as we sat down, I saw two of the Ram's athletes come out on the dance floor with their girls. The Ram had disappeared, and I didn't see him dancing again. But every so often the two athletes would come out and dance for the length of about half a record and then go back to their booth, pushing the curtains apart just enough to let themselves slip through. None of us said a word about seeing them out there. And, of course, nobody mentioned the Ram. I guess we were all pretty uncomfortable about it, because we made a lot of uncomfortable and silly conversation. All of us except Letitia. We joked and carried on in a very foolish way, trying to cover up. But everything we said or did seemed to make my toes curl under.

For instance: Bob pretended he was going to close the curtains to our booth, and there was a great scramble between him and his date over keeping them open. And all the while, across the way, the curtains to the Ram's booth were never opened wider than it took for one person to slip in or out.

Also: "Where in the world *are* we?" one of the girls asked. That

we were way out in the country, of course, they knew, but *where?*
And it had to be explained that Aunt Martha's Tavern was across
the line in Clark County, about twelve miles due west of Chatham,
which is in Pitt County, and this meant we were only about three
miles from Thompsonville. Thompsonville, I knew, if some of the
others didn't, was where Letitia's uncle and her father grew up. We
were in an area that Letitia's Uncle Louis must have known pretty
well for a long time.

And finally: There was the business about Aunt Martha. She
came herself to take our orders. None of us was hungry, and the
girls wouldn't even order Cokes. But she took us boys' orders for
mixers, and while she was there, Horst Hauser tried to get her to
sing "Temptation" for us. Martha wasn't so very old—you could tell
it by her clear, smooth skin and her bright green eyes—and nobody
really called her Aunt Martha. But she must have weighed about
three hundred pounds and she hadn't a tooth in her head. She wore
her hair in what was almost a crew cut. And she was apt to be
barefoot about half the time; she was barefoot that night. She
wouldn't sing "Temptation" for us, but she talked to the girls and
told them how pretty their dresses were and asked them their
names—"Just your first names, I'm no good at last names," she
said—so she would be sure to remember them next time they came.
"You know," she said. "In case you come with some other fellows,
and not these jelly beans." And she gave them a big wink.

We three boys pretended to look very hurt, and she said, "They
know I'm a tease. These here boys are my honey babes." Then she
looked at us awfully close to make sure that we did know. She hung
around telling the girls how her old husband had built the tavern
singlehanded, as a wedding present for her, and how, after practicing taxidermy "in many parts of the world and for over forty years,"
he had given it up and settled down in the country with her, and
how generally sweet he was. "It mayn't seem likely to you girls," she

said, her green eyes getting a damp look, "but they can be just as fine and just as noble without a tongue in their head as with one." Then, from fear of being misunderstood, maybe, or not wanting to depress the customers, she added, "And just as much fun, honey babes!" She gave us boys a wink and went off in a fit of laughter.

When she had gone, we all agreed that Martha was a good soul and that the old deaf-mute was a lucky man. But we couldn't help trying to take her off. And I laughed with the others till, suddenly, it occurred to me that her accent and her little turns of speech sounded, on our lips, just like things the Ram was quoted as saying in his civics class. He said "territory" and "A-rab" and "how come" and "I'm done." I knew that Letitia's own father didn't say things like that; it only showed the kind of low company Lou Ramsey had always kept, even as a boy in Clark County.

Well, when Martha went for the mixers, it was time for Bob and Horst and me to flip a coin to see who was going outside and buy us a pint of whiskey at the back door, which was where you always had to buy it. Unfortunately, I was odd man, and so I began collecting the money from the other two. Letitia didn't understand about the whiskey, and we had to explain to her about local option and Clark County's being a dry county, and about bootleg's being cheaper than the legal whiskey in Chatham. But while we explained, she didn't seem to listen. She only kept looking at me questioningly, and finally she squinted her eyes and said, "Are you sure you know how to buy it, and where?"

I went out the front door and around to the kitchen door, and bought the whiskey from Martha's husband, who had gone back there to meet me. I was glad for a breath of fresh air and to be away from the others for a few minutes. And yet I was eager to get back to them, too. I hurried toward the front, along the footpath between the parking lot and the side wall of the tavern—a dark wall of unpainted vertical planking. The night seemed even hotter and muggier now than it had earlier. The sky, all overcast, with no stars shining through anywhere, was like an old, washed-out gray sweater. On the far side of the parking lot, a few faint streaks of light caught my eye. I knew they came from Aunt Martha's tourist cabins, which were ranged along the edge of the woods over there. The night was so dark it was hard to tell much about the cars in the parking lot, but I could tell that they were mostly broken down jalopies and that the lot looked more like a junkyard than any real parking lot. Everything I saw looked ugly and raw and unreal to me, and when I came round to the front, where the one big light bulb above the entrance still flickered brightly in its swarm of bugs, I could see a field of waist-high corn directly across the road, and somehow it looked rawer and more unreal to me than anything else.

When I rang at the front door to be let in again, the old man had already come through the place. He opened up for me, grinning as though it were a big joke between us—his having got there as soon as I did. But I didn't want any of his dumb-show joking just then. He was making all kinds of silly signs with his hands, but I passed by him and went on back to our booth. And I was struck right away by how happy Letitia looked when she saw me. She didn't seem to be concerned about her uncle at all, which, of course, was what I was watching to see. I was glad, and yet it didn't ease my mind a bit. What were you to make of such a girl? Ever since we got there, I had been watching her in a way that I felt guilty about, because I knew it was more curiosity than sympathy. And I was certain now that she had been watching me, for some kind of sign. I couldn't have been more uncomfortable. It was strange. She was such a marvelously pretty girl, really!—with her pale yellow hair and her almond eyes, with her firm little mouth that you couldn't help looking at when she opened it a little and smiled, no matter how much respect you had for her, and no matter what else you had on your mind. I kept looking at her, and I tried not to seem too self-conscious when I drew the pint of whiskey out of the pocket of my linen jacket and put it on the table.

But I did feel self-conscious about it, and even more so because she continued to sit there just as casually as though we were having a milkshake somewhere after the show and were settling down to enjoy ourselves for the rest of the evening. When I first came back, she had looked at me as though I were a hero because I had gone around to the back door to buy a pint of bootleg whiskey and had got back alive, and now she commenced puttering around with the glasses and the mixers with a happy, helpful attitude. Bob and Horst and their two dates were still jabbering away as much as before, but Letitia made me feel now that they weren't there at all. She had set the three tumblers in front of me, and so I worked away at opening the pint bottle and then began pouring drinks for us three boys. I wasn't sure how much we ought to have right at first, and I decided I had got too much in two of the glasses. I tried to pour some back into the bottle, and made such a mess of it that I cursed under my breath. During this time, the jukebox was playing away, of course, but I do think I was half aware of some other noise somewhere, though it didn't really sink in. It didn't even sink in when Letitia put her hand on my sleeve, or when I looked up at her and saw her looking at me very much as she had outside the door a while before. The others still went on talking, and after a second Letitia drew away her hand. She began fidgeting with her gardenias, and she wasn't looking at me any more. For a moment, I wondered if she hadn't really expected us to have the drinks. But it wasn't that, and now I saw that she had tilted her head to one side to get a better view of something across the floor. I cut my eyes around and saw that the curtains to the Ram's booth had been pulled apart and that there he was, in plain view, with his girl and his star pitcher and outfielder and their two girls. I thought to myself, She's just now realized that they're all here together. Then I took another look over there, wondering why in hell they hadn't kept those curtains drawn, and I saw that something very unusual was up.

This all happened in an instant, of course—much quicker than I can tell it. The Ram was getting up very slowly from his seat and seemed to be giving some kind of orders to his pitcher and his outfielder. His own girl was still sitting at the table, and she stayed there, but the two other girls were climbing on top of the table. Pretty soon, they had opened the little high window above their booth—there was one above each of the booths—and you could see that the next thing they were going to do was to try to climb out that window. I guess they did climb out, and it wasn't long before people in some of the other booths were doing the same thing.

After a minute or so, there was nobody left on the dance floor, and all of a sudden someone unplugged the jukebox. Without the music, we could hear the knocking on the doors of the tourist cabins, and I began to notice lights flashing outside the little window above our booth. I knew now there was a raid on the cabins, but I didn't want to be the first to mention the existence of those cabins to the girls. And though I was sure enough of it, I just couldn't make myself admit that the raid would be happening to the tavern, too, in about three minutes.

I saw the Ram leave his booth, and he seemed to be starting in the direction of ours. Letitia looked relieved now, and actually leaned forward across the table as though she were trying to catch his eye. Both Bob Southard and I got up and started out to meet him, but he held out a stiff arm, motioning us back, and he went off toward the beer counter without ever looking at Letitia.

When Bob and I turned back toward our booth, Horst and the girls were standing up, saying nothing. But Letitia gave me a comforting smile and she opened her mouth to say something that she never did say. I can almost believe she had been about to tell me how shy her uncle was, and to ask if I noticed how he wouldn't look at her when she was dressed up this way.

But now the Ram was headed back toward us with Martha, and Martha had slipped on some brown loafers. There was loud banging now on the front and back doors of the tavern, but apparently she and her husband weren't set to open up yet; I guessed the old man hadn't finished hiding the whiskey. By now, anybody who was going to get away had to chance it through the windows. We could hear people dropping on the ground outside those little high windows, and hear some of them grunting when they landed.

As soon as the Ram and Martha got near us, he said, "We're going to put you out of sight somewhere. They won't want to take too many in. They just want their quota."

Martha wasn't ruffled a bit. I suppose she could see we were, though. She looked at the girls and said, "Chickabiddies, I wouldn't have had this happen for nothing in this world."

The Ram glanced back at his own booth, to make sure that his athletes were still there—and maybe his girl friend. They hadn't moved a muscle. They just sat there very tense, watching the Ram. You would have thought they were in the bullpen waiting for a signal from him to come in and pitch. But they never got one. The Ram said to Martha, "Just anywhere you stick her and the rest of them is all right, but upstairs in your parlor would be mighty nice." From the way he said it, you would have thought he was speaking to one of the old lady teachers at Westside.

"You know I ain't about to hide nobody upstairs," she said firmly but politely. "Not even for you, honey baby."

"Then put them in the powder room yonder," he said.

"If they'll fit, that's fine," she said. She led the way and we followed.

It was over at the end of the counter—just a little closet, with "SHE" painted on the door and a toilet inside, and not even one of the little high windows. Martha made sure the key was in the lock, inside, and told us to turn off the light and lock ourselves in. We had to squeeze to get in, and one of us would have stood on the toilet except there wasn't a lid. While we were crowding in, the banging on the doors kept getting louder and began to sound more in earnest, and Martha's husband ambled up and stood watching us with his mouth hanging open. Martha looked around at him and burst out laughing. "He can't hear it thunder, bless his heart," she said. And the old fellow laughed, too.

The Ram said, "Get them inside, please, ma'am. They'll *have* to fit."

But Martha merely laughed at him. "You better git yourself *out*side if you expect to git," she said.

"I don't expect to git," he said.

"What'sa matter?"

He looked back over his shoulder at the room, where there were only eight or ten people left, most of them staggering around in the shadows, looking for a window that wasn't so high. "They'll have to have their quota of customers," he said, "or they might make a search."

"Well, it's your funeral you're planning, not mine," Martha said, and she winked at nobody in particular. Then her little green eyes suddenly darted another look at her husband. "O.K.," she said, "and I better take a quick gander to see he left out their quota of whiskey-take." With that, she slipped her feet out of her shoes again and padded along behind the counter and into the kitchen, with the old man following her. The banging on the doors couldn't get any louder, but they could have knocked the doors down by this time if they had really been as earnest about it as they made it sound. And we would long since have been locked inside the toilet except that while the Ram and Martha were having their final words, Letitia had put one foot over the sill again and was waiting to say something to her uncle.

"Uncle Louis," she began very solemnly. The Ram's face turned as red as a beet. Not just his face but the top of his head, too, where his sandy hair had got so thin. And, from the quick way he jerked his head around and fixed his eyes on the front door, it seemed as if he hadn't heard the banging over there till now. The truth was he *didn't* want to look at Letitia. But of course he had to, and it couldn't wait. So he sticks out that square chin, narrows his eyes under those blond eyebrows of his, and gives Letitia the hardest, impatientest look in the world. But it was nothing. The thing that was something was not the expression on *his* face but the one on hers. I won't ever forget it, though I certainly can't describe it. It made me think she was going to thank him from the bottom of her heart or else say how sorry she was about everything, or even ask him if something couldn't be done about hiding those poor athletes of his. I thought most likely it would be something about the athletes, since their being there with him was bound to make a scandal if it got into the newspapers. But in a way what she said was better than any of that. She said, "I don't have any money with me, Uncle Louis. Do you think I ought to have some money?"

"*Good* girl!" he practically shouted. And the guy actually smiled —the very best, most unselfish kind of smile. He reached down in his pocket and pulled out a couple of crumpled-up bills. I saw that one of them was a five. Letitia took the two bills and stuffed them in the pocket of her jacket. "Good girl," he said again, not quite so loud. He was smiling, and seemed nearly bursting with pride because Letitia had thought of something important that he had overlooked.

"It's going to be all right, isn't it?" she said then.

"Why, sure it is," he said. It was as though the whole raid was something that was happening just to them and concerned nobody else. And now she gave him that look again, and what it showed, and what it had shown before, was nothing on earth but the beautiful confidence she had in him—all because he was an uncle of hers, I suppose.

"Good night, darling," she said. She stepped back into the toilet with the rest of us, and it was every bit as exciting to see as if she had been stepping into a lifeboat and leaving him on a sinking ship. My guess, too, is that when the Ram watched her pulling the door to, he wished he *was* about to go down on a real ship, instead of about to be arrested and taken off with his girl friend and his two athletes to the jail in Thompsonville, the town where he grew up, and then to have it all in the Chatham papers and finally lose his job as civics teacher and baseball coach at Westside High. For that, of course, is the way it turned out.

Somebody locked the door and we stood in there in the dark, and then we heard Martha come back and put on her shoes and go to open the front door. But we couldn't hear everything, because at the first sound of the deputies' voices the two other girls began to shake all over and whimper like little sick animals. Bob and Horst managed to hush them up pretty much, however, and before long I heard a man's voice say, "Well, Lou, haven't *you* played hell?" The man sounded surprised and pleased. "This is too bad, Lou," he said. It was a mean, little-town voice, and you could hear the grudge in it against anybody who had got away even as far as Chatham and amounted to even as little as the Ram did. Or that was how I felt it sounded. "That wouldn't be some of your champs over there, would it, Lou?"

Letitia didn't make a sound. She just shivered once, as though a rabbit had run over her grave, or as though, in the awful stink and heat of that airless toilet, she was really cold. It was black as pitch in there, but I was pressed up against Letitia and I felt that shiver go over her. And then, right afterward, I could tell how easily she breathed, how relaxed she was. I wanted to put my arms around her, but I didn't dare—not in a place like that. I didn't dare even think about it twice.

Once our door was shut, we never heard the Ram's voice again.

In a very few minutes, the sheriff's men seemed to have got everybody out of the tavern except Martha and her husband. The two girls had stopped all their whimpering and teeth-chattering now, and we heard one of the men—the sheriff himself, I took it—talking to Martha while the others were carrying away whatever whiskey had been left out for them to find.

"Kind of sad about Lou Ramsey," he said, with a little snicker.

"I don't know him," Martha said, cutting things short. "I don't know any of them by their last names. That's your business, not mine."

The man didn't answer for a minute, but when he did, he sounded as though she had hurt his feelings. "You ought to be fair, Mrs. Mayberry," he said, "and not go blaming me for taking in them that just stands around waiting for it." I thought I could tell now that they were both sitting on stools at the counter.

"I don't mind, if he don't mind," she said. "It's his funeral, not mine." And now it sounded as though it was the Ram she was mad at, even more than the man she was talking to.

After a minute, he said, "I never been so hot as tonight."

"It's growing weather, honey baby," she said, and slapped her hand down on the counter.

"There's not nobody else around?" he asked her suddenly.

"What are you asking me that for, honey baby?" she said. "You got as many as your little jail will 'most hold."

We heard him laugh, and then neither of them said anything more for a minute. The other men seemed to have made their last trips to the kitchen and back now, and I heard the man with Martha get down off his stool at the counter.

"Well'm," he said, "which one of you cares to make the ride this time?"

"Whichever one you favors," she said.

"You know me," he said. "How's them kids?" For a second I was absolutely sure he meant us. But then he said, "How you manage to keep 'em quiet enough up there? You put cotton in their ears?" Martha didn't answer him, and finally he said, "What'sa matter with you tonight, Mrs. Mayberry?"

"You wouldn't kid me about something like my kids, would you, Sheriff?" she asked, in a hard voice.

"Like what?"

"Like saying nobody's never told you they was born just as deaf as their daddy, yonder."

"You don't say, Mrs. Mayberry," he said, sounding out of breath. "Nobody ever told me that, I swear to God. Why, I've seen them two towheads playing around out there in the lot, but nobody said to me they was deaf."

"Can't hear it thunder," she said, and all at once she laughed. Then she let out a long moan, and next thing she was crying.

"Mrs. Mayberry," the sheriff said, "I am sure sorry."

"No," she said, and she stopped crying just as quick as she had begun. "When somebody says they're sorry about it, I say no, it's a blessing. My kids ain't never going to hear the jukebox play all night, and no banging on doors, neither. It's a blessing, I say, all they won't hear, though it's a responsibility to me. But I won't be sitting up wondering where they are, the way you'll likely be doing with your young'uns, Sheriff. It's a blessing the good Lord sends to some people. It's wrong, but it's *something*. It's *something* I got which most people ain't. Till the day they die, they'll be just as true to me as the old man there."

Just then, one of the sheriff's men called him from outside to say they'd better get going, and I couldn't help being glad for the sheriff's sake. "Hell," he said to Martha, "it's too bad, but one of you has to come with me."

I was glad for us, too, because we were about to smother in there and be sick at our stomachs. The sheriff went on out then, taking one of the Mayberrys along. Everything was quiet after that, except for the motor of the sheriff's truck starting up. At first, we couldn't even tell for certain whether it was Martha or the old man who had gone with the sheriff. We waited a couple of minutes, and then, from the way the floor was creaking overhead, we knew it was Martha who had stayed. In the excitement, and after her outburst, she had forgotten all about us and had gone tiptoeing upstairs to see about her little deaf children.

All at once, Bob Southard said, "Let's get out of here," and he turned the key. We burst out onto the dance floor, and the first thing my eyes hit on was Martha's two brown loafers on the pine floor at the end of the counter. They were the first thing I saw, and about the only thing for a minute or so, for we stood there nearly blinded by the bright lights, which the sheriff's men had turned on everywhere and which Martha hadn't bothered to turn out.

It was awful seeing everything lit up that way—not just the mess the place was in, which wasn't so bad considering that there had been a raid, but just seeing the place at all in that light. Those stuffed animal heads of the old man's stared at you from everywhere you could turn—dogs, horses, foxes, bulls, even bobcats and some bears, and one lone zebra—leaning out from the walls, so that their glass eyes were shining right down at you. We got out of there just as quick as we could.

The front door was standing wide open. We didn't stop to pull it to after us. We went outside and around the corner toward the parking lot, and when we showed ourselves there it was the signal for about twenty or thirty people to begin coming out of the woods, where they had been hiding. Some of them came running out, and others kind of wandered out, and at least one came crawling on his hands and knees. With the sky still that nasty gray, we couldn't have seen them at first except for the broad shafts of light that came from the open doorways of the cabins. It was a creepy sight, and the sounds these people made were creepy, too. As they came out of the woods, some of them were arguing, some of them laughing and kidding in a hateful way, and here and there a woman was crying and complaining, as though maybe she had got hurt jumping down from one of those high little windows.

We knew that as soon as they climbed into their old jalopies, there would be a terrific hassle to get out of that parking lot, and so we made a dash for Horst's sedan and all piled into it without caring who sat where or who was whose date. And we were out of that lot and tearing down the road before we even heard a single other motor get started.

All the way to Chatham, and then driving around to take everybody home, we just kept quiet except to talk every now and then about Martha and her old husband's children, about how unfair and terrible it seemed for them to be born deaf, and how unfair and terrible it was to bring up children in a place like that. Even then, it seemed to me unnatural for us not to be mentioning what had happened earlier. But I suppose we were thankful at least to have the other thing to talk about. I was sitting in the back seat, and Letitia was sitting up in the front. I watched her shaking her head or nodding now and then when someone else was talking. There was certainly nothing special I could say to her from the back seat. But when we finally got to her house and I took her up to her door, I did make myself say, "We certainly owe your uncle a lot, Letitia."

"Yes, poor darling," she said. "But it's a good thing he was there, isn't it?" That's all she said. The marvelous thing, I thought, was that she didn't seem to hold anything against me.

I was away from Chatham most of that summer. The first of July, I went down to New Orleans with a friend of mine named Bickford Harris, and he and I got jobs on a freight boat and worked our way over to England and back. We got back on the fourteenth of September, which was only about a week before I had to leave for college. I had seen Letitia at several other parties before we went off to New Orleans, and had called her on the telephone to say goodbye. I sent her a postcard from New Orleans and I sent her three postcards from England. I didn't write her a letter for the same reason that I only telephoned her, instead of asking her for a date or going by to see her, before we left. I didn't want her to think I was trying to make something out of our happening to be put together that night, and didn't want her to think it meant anything special to me. But when we got back in September, I did ask her for a date, and she gave it to me.

And, of course, Letitia hadn't changed a bit—or only a very little bit. I could tell she hadn't, even when I talked with her on the telephone to make the date. She said she loved my postcards, but that's all she said about them, and it was plain they hadn't made any real impression on her. She told me that she was going to be leaving within a couple of weeks, to go to a finishing school in Washington, D.C., and the next summer she was going to Europe herself, before making her debut in the fall. She talked to me about all these plans on the telephone, and I knew that when a girl in Chatham begins talking about her plans to make her debut, she already has her mind on meeting older guys. That's the "very little bit" I mean she had changed. But she did give me the date—on a Monday night, it was. I was awfully glad about it, yet the minute I walked into her house, I began wishing I had left well enough alone.

For right off the bat I heard her uncle's voice. He was back in the dining room, where they were all still sitting around the table. And I had to go in there and tell them how I'd liked working on a freight boat and how I'd liked England. I also had to shake hands all around, even with the Ram, who was already standing up when I came in, speaking rather crossly to Letitia's three little brothers and hurrying them to get through with their dinner. When I shook his hand, I could tell from the indifferent way he looked at me that he didn't know he had ever seen me before. And suddenly I said to myself, "Why, all he knows about me is that I'm not a Ramsey and I'm not a baseball player."

Most of the time I was in the room, he was still hurrying Letitia's little brothers, under his breath, to finish their dinner. Everyone else had finished, and he was waiting to take her brothers somewhere afterward. I knew what he had been doing since June, when he found out he wouldn't be teaching at the high school in the fall. He had landed a soft daytime job with one of the lumber companies in Chatham, which had hired him so it would have him to manage the company's baseball team. As we were going out through the living room, I heard his voice getting louder and very cross again with the boys, the way it had sounded when I came in. Letitia heard it, too, and only laughed to herself. Outside, when we were walking across the lawn toward my car, she explained that her uncle was taking her little brothers to a night baseball game, in the commercial league, and that there was nothing in the world they loved better.

Letitia and I had a nice time that night, I suppose. It was just like other dates we'd had. We ran into some people at the movie, and we all went for a snack somewhere afterward. The thing is I don't pretend that I ever did get to know Letitia Ramsey awfully well. As I have said, it was only by chance that she and I were put together for Nancy O'Connor's dance that year. We simply ran with the same crowd, and in our crowd the boys all knew that they would be going to college (or hoped so), and the girls that they would be going off to finishing school, up East or in Virginia, for a year or two and then be making their debuts, and so we tended not to get too serious about each other. It wasn't a good idea, that's all, because it could break up your plans and your family's. The most that usually happened was some terrific crushes and, naturally, some pretty heavy necking that went along with the crushes. But there was never even anything like that between Letitia and me. I never felt that I knew her half as well as I did several of her friends that I had even fewer dates with.

Still, I do know certain things from that evening at Aunt Martha's Tavern. I know how Letitia looked at an uncle who never had—and never has yet—amounted to anything. And I know now that while I watched her looking at him, I was really wishing that I knew how to make a girl like her look at me that trusting way, instead of the way she had been looking at me earlier. It almost made me wish that I was one of the big, common fellows at Westside High who slipped off and got married to one of the public-school girls in their class and then told the teachers and the principal about it, like a big joke, after they'd got their diplomas on graduation night. But the point is I *didn't* know how to make a girl like her look at me that way. And the question is why *didn't* I know how?

Usually, I tell myself that I didn't because I was such a worrier and that I wouldn't have been such a worrier if there hadn't been a Depression, or if I had known a war was going to come along and solve everything. But I'm not sure. Once, during the war, I told this to a guy who didn't come from the kind of people that I do. He only laughed at me and said he wanted to hear more about those other times we were having that year. I pointed out that those other good times weren't the point and that a girl like Letitia Ramsey was something else again. "Yea," he said, looking rather unfriendly. "That's how all you guys like to talk."

But the worst part, really, is what it's like when you see someone like Letitia nowadays. She may be married to a guy whose family money is in downtown real estate and who has never had a doubt in his life, or maybe to some guy working on commission and drinking himself to death. It doesn't matter which. If it is a girl like Letitia who's married to him, he's part of her family now, and all men outside her family are jokes to her. And she and this fellow will have three or four half-grown children, whom nobody can believe she is really the mother of, since she looks so young. Well, the worst part is when you are back home visiting and meet her at a dinner party, and she tells you before the whole table how she was once on the verge of being head over heels in love with you and you wouldn't give her a tumble. It's always said as a big joke, of course, and everyone laughs. But she goes on and on about it, as though it was really something that had been worrying her. And the more everybody laughs, the more she makes of it and strings it out. And what it shows, more than any number of half-grown children could ever do, is how old she is getting to be. She says that you always seemed to have your mind on other things and that she doesn't know yet whether it was higher things or lower things. Everyone keeps on laughing until, finally, she pretends to look very serious and says that it is all right for them to laugh but that it wasn't funny at the time. Her kidding, of course, is a big success, and nobody really minds it. But all I ever want to say—and don't ever say—is that as far as I am concerned, it isn't one bit funnier now than it was then.

At The Drugstore

Matt Donelson was back home on a visit. He rose early, before any of the others were awake, and set out on foot for the drugstore, where he was going to buy a bottle of shaving lotion. He had left a pretty wife sleeping in the family guest room, two little sons snoozing away in the next room down the hall—both the wife and the sons being exhausted from the long train ride of the day before— and a mother and a father snatching early morning, old-folksy naps in their adjoining rooms at the head of the stairs. At this early hour the house seemed more like its old self than it usually did on his visits home. Though he knew it was a house that would be politely referred to nowadays as "an older house," for a moment it seemed to him again "the new house" that the family had moved into when he was aged six. His room had been the one his father now occupied. He was the baby of the family; his mother had wanted him nearby. His two big brothers had shared the room where his own two boys were sleeping this morning. And his sister, for whose coming-out year the house had been bought, had claimed the guest room for hers during the brief two years she remained at home. She and the brothers had long since, of course, had houses and families of their own. When Matt came back to see his parents he seldom caught more than a glimpse of any of them, and to their children he was a stranger.

Downstairs, just before he left the house, Matt had a brief exchange with the colored cook who was a recent comer and whose name he did not even know.

"I suppose it feels good to you to be back home," she had said.

"There's nothing like it," Matt had replied. "Absolutely nothing."

On his way to the drugstore Matt realized that this was an expedition he had not given any real forethought to. For several days before he left New York he had been intending to buy the bottle of shaving lotion, but he had kept forgetting it or putting it off—refusing somehow to let his mind focus on it. And he had risen this morning and left the house—hatless and on foot—without really thinking of *what* drugstore he was going to. It was with a certain wonderment even that he found himself hiking along a familiar thoroughfare in this sprawling inland city where he had grown up. It was a street that led through what he as a boy had thought of as a newish part of town but a part which he knew must now of course be regarded as "an older section." Once, along the way, he stumbled over an uneven piece of pavement which the roots of one of the maple trees had dislodged. Next, he found himself looking up at the trees, trying to determine whether or not they had grown much since the days when he first remembered them. It seemed to him that they had not. The trees had not leafed out yet this year and even the patterns of the smallest branches against the dull March sky seemed tiresomely familiar. Somehow he felt both bored and disquieted by his observations. And when finally he stood opposite the drugstore and realized that this was his destination, the very sight of the commonplace store front was dismaying to him. How had he got here? It all seemed unreal. It was as though he had climbed out of his warm bed, without thought or care for his wife, his sons, or his aged parents, and walked off down here in his sleep—to a drugstore that he had not thought of in a dozen years.

But it was no dream, no, that is, unless all visits back home be dreams of a kind. He was wide awake, no doubt about that. He was fully and quite properly dressed, except that he wore no hat—he never wore a hat when he was back home—and he was bent on a very specific and practical piece of business . . . But what was the business? Ah, of course, the shaving lotion! He pushed open the heavy glass door and entered the drugstore rather breezily, just as though it were any other drugstore in the world. Fluorescent lights, giving everything an indigo tint, gleamed overhead and behind the counters and even inside some of the glass cases, as they would have done in any other modernized, up-to-date drugstore. But it was still so early in the day that there wasn't another customer in the place. In the artificial light and in the silence, there was the timeless quality of a bank vault. Or, more precisely, the atmosphere was that of a small, out-of-the-way museum where the curator doesn't really expect or welcome visitors.

To call attention to his presence Matt began dragging his leather heels on the tile floor. But at once he checked himself. The black and white tile under foot had suddenly caught his eye! How well he remembered the maddening pattern of it! And he was struck by the thought that this tile was the only feature of the once-familiar drugstore that remained unchanged. Even more striking to him, however, was the coincidence that last night in the railroad station he had had very nearly the same experience. The old Union Depot had, sometime very recently, undergone complete alteration, and when Matt had walked into the lobby just after midnight, he had believed for one moment that he was in the wrong city. During that terrible moment he had looked over the heads of the two sleepy boys at his wife and had given such a hollow laugh that Janie took a quick step toward him, saying, "What is it, dear? What is it, Matt?" Then the expanse of two-toned beige tiling, on which he had long ago played hopscotch, had seemed to come right up at him, and he felt such relief that he had sighed audibly.

Now in the drugstore, with his eyes fixed on the hypnotic black and white diamonds and octagons, he gave another such sigh. He felt relieved all over again not to have gotten Janie and the boys off the train in a strange city in the middle of the night. It really was not something he could possibly have done, of course, but that didn't diminish the relief he felt—last night or this morning. And while he continued to wait in the front part of the drugstore for someone to take notice of him, his mind dwelt further on his confusion last night . . . "What is it?" Janie had asked still again, placing a gloved hand on his sleeve. He had tried to turn his sigh into a yawn, but that had not deceived Janie for one second.

"It's nothing," he had said, watching now for the porter to bring in their luggage. "I was only thinking how I used to play a kind of hopscotch on this floor whenever we came here to meet people."

Janie had looked at him with narrowed eyes, not at all convinced; on their visits home—especially just before they arrived—she always developed her own peculiarly mistaken ideas about what thoughts he was having. "Surely," she said now, "surely you can't have expected anyone to meet us at this hour, Matt. Especially after you insisted so that they not." . . . He wasn't even annoyed by her misreading of his thoughts. In fact, he had had to smile. And he even seized the hand that was resting on his sleeve and whispered, "My little worry-wart!" It was so *like* the notions she always took about his homecomings. She was ever fearful that on these occasions there would be some misunderstanding or quarrel between him and his father, or between him and one of his brothers, or even his gray-haired brother-in-law. Moreover, he knew that in her heart she was firmly convinced that there was some old quarrel between him and his family that had sent him to live away from home in the first place—some quarrel that he would not tell her about. In the early years of their marriage she had not let it bother her very much. But ever since the first baby came she had devoted considerable time to "winning him back to his family." She never put it into so many words—they were *his* words—but he knew what her thoughts were. (She had taken to writing regularly to his mother and even began remembering his father's birthdays.) It had originally seemed to him a good joke on her that she thought there were hidden wounds to be healed, but the joke had gone too far and she had at last become too serious about the matter for him to do more than smile and call her a worry-wart. Yet it really was laughable, almost incredible, to think how little she understood him with respect to his relations with his family. His was simply not a quarreling kind of family; they didn't have the passionate natures for it!—and particularly with respect to how he was affected by the prospect of a short visit with just his parents.

His confusion last night, however, had been a rather extraordinary thing. And he had to acknowledge that it was due partly to the fact that none of the family was there to meet him. Always in the past at least one of them had been there. They thought it silly of him to insist upon coming home on the train instead of flying (they didn't understand what he meant by the transition's being too abrupt; and the difference in the fares was *so* trivial), but still one of them had always trekked down to the dingy old railroad station to welcome him—him and his family. Usually it was his father or one of his two brothers who came, because they considered it strictly a man's job to meet a train that arrived so late at night. They usually seemed amused to find themselves in the Depot again. They hadn't been there since the last time Matt came home! (Who else rode the trains nowadays but Matt?) And Matt was merely amused at their amusement. Why should he take offense at their condescension when he would only be home for a few days? . . . With whoever came to meet the train—father or brother—Matt and Janie and the boys would walk the length of the great Depot lobby, between the rows of straight-back benches on one of which a pathetic family would be huddled together and on another a disreputable-looking old bum would be stretched out, asleep with his head on his bundle and with his hat over his eyes. And when the party came directly under the vast dome that rose above the lobby, Matt's father or brother would tell the boys to look up and see the bats whoozing around up there or see the absurd pigeon that had got himself trapped in the dome and was flapping about from one side to the other.

It had been a very different scene last night, however. The dimly lit lobby of old had been transformed. A false ceiling had been installed no more than ten or twelve feet above the floor. And a new, circular wall, with display windows for advertisers and with bright posters declaring how many people still rode the trains, altered the very shape of the room, hiding the rough stone columns around which children had used to play hide-and-seek. As for the wooden benches, they were replaced by plastic, bucket-bottomed chairs on which huddling together would have been difficult and stretching out alone quite impossible. And the lighting, though indirect, was brilliant; there were no dark corners anywhere.

In view of these changes Matt felt his moment of consternation and confusion upon entering the lobby a very natural response. He did not have to lay it, even in part, to his weariness from the long train ride. Yet when the porter had finally appeared with their luggage and he and his little family had passed out of the lobby and into the large vestibule at the main entrance of the Depot, something even more absurd, if no more confusing, happened. In a huge wall mirror which had always occupied its place there in the vestibule, Matt saw his own reflection; he mistook that reflection for some other male member of his own family. "Oh," he said under his breath. But his "oh" was not so soft that Janie didn't hear it. She perceived at once the mistake he had made. This time he might almost have shown annoyance with her. Her smile said, "You see, you *were* expecting to be met," but the smile was also full of love and was so overly sympathetic—be it sympathy ever so uncalled for—that he could only gently push her and the boys through the doorway and follow them silently to the waiting taxi.

In the drugstore none of the clerks had come to work yet. Only the druggist himself was there, and as soon as he appeared, Matt apprised him of the business he had come on. "What kind will it be—what brand?" the old fellow asked. Matt gaped across the counter. He couldn't believe his eyes at first. It was the same old Mr. Conway who had been the druggist there twenty-odd years before. It was the same old Mr. Conway, and yet of course he didn't recognize Matt.

"I don't know, sir," Matt said respectfully. "Any kind."

The old druggist looked up suspiciously and with obvious irritation. "*Any* kind?"

Matt began to smile, but then he realized his mistake. One large vein stood out on the druggist's forehead precisely as it had used to do whenever he was vexed . . . (Incredible, incredible that he should remember Mr. Conway's vein!) The broad, flat nose twitched like a rabbit's . . . (To think that he should remember. How annoying it was.) One more thing. The small, close-set eyes seemed to draw closer together as the druggist bent across the counter peering up at him. Then the total personality of the man came back to him, and somehow it was all too much to be borne at this hour of the morning. He shifted his gaze away from Mr. Conway. But in the mirror behind Mr. Conway he saw another familiar face (oh, *too familiar*) and was struck by the guilty expression in the round eyes that ogled back at him there.

"*Any* kind?" Mr. Conway was saying again. For a moment the voice seemed to be coming from away at the back of the store. But that was absurd. Mr. Conway was right here before him. There was something back there, however, tugging at Matt's attention.

"Yes, *any* kind," he repeated. They were like two birds or two insects answering each other. Finally, Matt broke the rhythm of it. In the most impersonal, hard, out-of-town voice he could muster, he said, "Any kind, my friend. And I'm afraid I'm in a hell of a hurry."

He even managed to sound a little breathless. Unfortunately, though, it wasn't a very manly breathlessness. It was a boy's breathlessness. It was as if this very morning he had run all the way from home with his school books under one arm and his yellow slicker under the other and was now afraid that the streetcar—the good old Country Day Special—would pass before he could get waited on. How terrible it had been being a boy, and the world so full of Mr. Conways.

Mr. Conway turned away toward the shelves on the wall behind him, to the left of the mirror and toward the rear of the drugstore. (Still, still there was something back there trying to claim Matt's attention. But he couldn't, or wouldn't, look.) He tried to watch Mr. Conway as he examined the various bottles. He was of course searching out the most expensive brand. The old guy's rudeness was insufferable and at the same time fascinating. As soon as his back was turned, Matt felt himself seriously tempted to snatch up some article off the counter and slip it into the pocket of his topcoat. As a boy he had never for a moment been tempted to do such a thing, though he had seen other boys do it. They had taken the most trivial and useless articles—ladies' lipsticks, manicure scissors, get-well cards, though they would not have stooped to stealing candy or chewing gum. Not Country Day boys! But something distracted Matt from his temptation, and distracted him also from watching Mr. Conway's evil, grasping fingers. (The fingers moved with awful deliberation and seemed bent on strangling every bottle they picked up.) What distracted Matt, of course, was that same familiar face in the mirror, his view of it now unobstructed by the figure of his malefactor.

Yet somehow or other it wasn't the same face in the mirror this time. The eyes weren't the guilty eyes of a schoolboy. The face wasn't really familiar at all—not *here*. The person in the mirror now eyed him curiously, even incredulously, and momentarily he resented the intrusion of this third, unfamiliar person on the scene, a person who, so to speak, ought still to have been asleep beside his wife back there in the family's guest room. But he accepted the intrusion philosophically. In effect said to himself, "Look, look, look! Have your fill and let me get back to my important business with Mr. Conway." But the face had a will of its own. It had an impersonal, hard, out-of-town look, like the faces one gets used to seeing everywhere except in the mirror. It was one thing consciously to put those qualities into your voice; it seemed quite another to find them translated and expressed in your face without your even knowing about it.

But the impression lasted only for a moment. The eyes in the mirror grew warm and sympathetic. They were the same fine old eyes. It was the same fine nose too, just the littlest bit beefier than the boy's nose had been. The blond hair was as thick as ever through the temples. (If it lay flatter on top, you could not say for certain that it was really thinning even up there.) And the ruddy complexion was the same as of old, or was except for the "slight purplish cast" that his mother was always imagining when he came home, and had got his wife to imagining, and now had him half believing in.

By the time Mr. Conway had set the bottle on the counter before him, Matt Donelson had recovered himself—had been recovered, that is, by the grown-up self. The thought of his mother and wife had reminded him of the real circumstances of this day in his life. At 7:45 A.M. on a Saturday morning he was in the drugstore where he used to hang out as a boy. It was the man to whom the strange cook had spoken so politely and respectfully that looked at Mr. Conway now—the mature Matt Donelson, aged thirty-five, a man with a family of his own but still a faithful and attentive son, a man whose career was such a going thing that he could easily spare an occasional four or five days for visits back home.

Poor old Mr. Conway. His hand trembled as he set the bottle down. Matt seemed to feel something inside himself tremble. Pitiable little old fellow, he thought. What kind of a career had he had? Probably the most that could be said for him was that he had held his own and kept up with the times. Instead of the white linen jacket that had once upon a time made him look like a butler, he now wore a sleazy, wash-and-wear tunic (with short sleeves and a tight collar) that suggested he was an elderly surgeon fresh from the operating room. Besides the addition of fluorescent lights, his drugstore had been refurbished throughout. The soda fountain was no more, and of course the tables and the booths were gone. There was now a large toy department, a hardware counter, shelves containing men's socks and jockey shorts, a serve-yourself freezer with half-gallon packages of ice cream, cartons of milk, even loaves of bread. Instead of the old lending library, innumerable paperbacks were offered for sale on two revolving stands. Mr. Conway—bless him, dear old fellow—had always had an eye for what brought in the money. No doubt he had a goodly sum stashed away. No doubt he was highly respected by the other storekeepers along this street. Within his lights, he was probably a considerable success. Perhaps his kind was, as everybody always said, the backbone of the community, even the backbone of the country. Matt was on the verge of making himself known to the old man and of reminding him of the days when Country Day boys waited for the streetcar in his store. He was on the verge; then he pulled back.

What was it now? Out of the corner of his eye he had caught a glimpse of the giant mortar and pestle that squatted on a shelf above the entrance to the pharmacist's prescription room. It had squatted up there in the old days; it seemed to be the only piece of the old decor that had been allowed to remain. The bowl was about the size and shape of a large watebasket, and the boys, who had somehow always hated the sight of it, used to toss candy-bar wrappers and other trash up into it . . . Was that what had made him pull back? Was it only this that had been calling for his attention back there all along? Or was it the electric light burning with such fierce brightness in the prescription room beyond the doorway? (How keenly he had felt the fascination of that intense light when he was fourteen.) But presently he answered his own question very positively. It could not be any of that. Surely not. No, it was the bottle of shaving lotion itself that had made him recoil and refuse to introduce himself to Mr. Conway. For, almost without realizing it, he had observed that Mr. Conway had actually set before him—albeit with trembling hand—the most expensive brand that such a drugstore as this would be likely to stock. Matt recognized the label, and despite the bottle's being tightly sealed and neatly cartoned he imagined he could detect the elegant scent.

"Didn't you have something cheaper?" he said.

Mr. Conway grinned, showing—yes—the same old dentures, row upon regular row. And when he spoke there was the familiar clamp and clatter. "I thought you didn't mind what brand," he said. His hand rested solidly on the carton now.

Without seeing himself in the mirror, Matt knew his face was coloring. His lips parted to speak, but at that instant he heard the sound of footsteps in the front part of the store. Someone else had come in.

"You want something cheaper, then," Mr. Conway said, in a loud voice.

"This will do," said Matt.

He quickly drew out a bill and handed it to the druggist. Just as quickly the old man drew change from the cash register and counted it into Matt's open palm. Before Matt's fingers had closed on the change, he glanced over his shoulder to see who it was that had come in. From the first sound of the footsteps he had felt an unnatural curiosity to know who this other person was. He had imagined that it might be someone he knew. But his shock upon glancing back now was greater than any he had received from the face in the mirror.

A rosy-cheeked young man had come up directly behind him—a man ten years or so younger than himself. And the face of this young man, who was at the moment removing from his head a checked cap which matched the checked raglan coat he wore, was indisputably the face of old Mr. Conway as it had been forty years ago—long before even Matt had ever set eyes on him. A black fright seized Matt Donelson. Either this *was* a dream from which he could not wake himself or he was in worse trouble than any of those friends of his and Janie's back in New York—the ones they laughed at so for feeding the revenues of the analysts.

He looked back at Mr. Conway to make out if he saw the apparition too. But Mr. Conway's eyes were on the big clock above the entrance to the store. Matt looked up at the clock; and now he had to concede that there was, after all, another fixture that had been here in the old days. But *had* the clock been there when he came in five minutes ago? Perhaps before his eyes this modern drugstore was going to turn back into the place it had once been. Worst of all, the clock hands said that it was ten minutes to eight!—the time when the Country Day Special was scheduled to pass this corner. *Would* have been the time, that is, on a weekday. *Had* been the time, that is, in the era of streetcars. Nowadays, he reminded himself, the boys rode to school on buses . . . He put his two hands to his head and massaged it gently. He felt a swimming sensation.

"It's ten minutes to eight," Mr. Conway said flatly. Matt sensed at once that the old man wasn't addressing him. He felt better, and removed his hands from his head.

From behind him came the equally flat reponse: "I know."

And now Matt had no choice but to turn around and determine finally whether or not the young man were real. When he confronted him it was really as if he himself were the ghost, because the young man with the rosy cheeks and the shock of dark brown hair did not seem to see *him*. The young fellow was real enough all right but he seemed lost in a dream of his own.

Despite his being the youthful image of old Mr. Conway, with the same squashed nose and small, close-set eyes, he was a pleasant-looking young man. And judging from the dreamy expression on his face, from his snappy clothes, and from the easy way he was now slipping out of his coat, he was a person fairly pleased with the world and not totally displeased with himself. Matt was a trifle offended by the way he seemed to be blind to *his* presence, regarding him as a mere customer and therefore not worthy of his direct gaze. (A family trait, no doubt, since this was certainly Mr. Conway's own flesh and blood.) But still, even before he heard him speak again, Matt was more attracted to the young man than put off by him.

Matt had already turned away and was moving toward the front of the store when he heard the young Conway addressing the old man: "We've morning sickness at our house again this morning." The voice was very masculine, very gentle, expressing keen pleasure in the tidings he brought. "It's a pretty sure thing now," he said.

Matt could not resist taking another glance over his shoulder. He saw that old Mr. Conway was already off to his prescription room, padding down the aisle behind the counter. He responded to his son's good news without bothering even to look at him. But he was clacking away as he went along, his plate making more noise than his footsteps, and speaking so loud that Matt heard him quite distinctly: "Well, that doesn't alter its being ten to eight when you turned up. And there have already been four prescriptions called in which I haven't got started on good."

The old Scrooge, the old bastard! . . . Tyrannizing over this easygoing young fellow! . . . Making no concession even at such an important moment! . . . Matt felt it behooved him almost to go back and shake the young man's hand. But he didn't, of course. He had almost reached the front door now. He halted by the long magazine rack just to the left of the door. (Yes, there had always been such a rack there. Yet the rack was something else he hadn't noticed at first.) From the rear of the store he could hear the young Conway whistling. He let his eye rove over the display of magazines. Somehow he could not bring himself to leave. He tried to identify the jazzy tune young Conway was whistling, but it was something too recent for him. He continued to study the magazines. There was the same old selection. Only *Collier's* was missing. He remembered how the Country Day boys had been forbidden to touch a magazine they were not going to buy.

Presently the whistling was interrupted by the old druggist's voice.

"Is the music necessary?"

The reply was cheerful enough: "Not if you say so."

There was a moment's silence. Then, lowering his voice so slightly that it was only the more insulting to Matt, Mr. Conway asked, "Is that the same customer up there, still hanging around?"

"Yep. The same."

"Better keep an eye on him. He let on to be in 'one hell of a hurry' when he came in."

"All right," said the young man, and Matt thought he heard an indulgent snicker. Boldly, Matt turned around and looked the length of the store at the two men. The older man stepped back into the prescription room. Matt could not be certain but he believed the younger man, who was now in shirtsleeves, winked at him.

He turned back toward the magazines and gazed unseeing through the broad window above the rack. He was reflecting on the young man's undisturbed good spirits, on his indulgence toward his crotchety father. Mr. Conway was lucky indeed to have a son with such an understanding and forgiving nature. And suddenly it was as though the young Conway had communicated to Matt an understanding of the old man's ill humor and impatience this morning: it was due to Matt's interruption while he was trying to get those prescriptions filled. Matt could not restrain a malicious little smile. It was *so* like old times. They had always delighted in interrupting Mr. Conway when he was at work back there in the prescription room. Poor guy seemed to have had a lifetime of having his most important work interfered with. Whenever there was a piece of roughhouse up in the front part of the drugstore and Mr. Conway had to be called from his "laboratory" to deal with it, the boys became almost hysterical in their glee. They were apt to be good as gold if he stood idly here by the front window with his hands behind his back. But somehow they could not bear his being at work in the prescription room crushing a mysterious powder with his pestle or turning up the blue flame of his Bunsen burner under a vial. It was wonderful the things they used to do in order to distract the druggist.

At the soda fountain, in those days, there was a youngish black-haired woman who was believed by some of the boys to be Mr. Conway's wife. Sometimes four or five of the boys would line up on the stools at the soda fountain and place orders for Cokes. Then when the glasses were set before them they would pretend to have no money. At first the dark-haired woman would merely threaten to call "Dr. Conway." The boys, winking at each other, begged her not to, and even pretended to try to borrow the money from some of the other boys who were looking on. Finally, the woman would throw back her head and call out at the top of her voice: "Oh, Dr. Conway! Dr. Conway!"

But the boys continued to search their pockets until the very moment the druggist appeared. (Apparently he worked with his plates out, because he always came through the door of the prescription room with his hand to his mouth as though he were just shoving them in.) Only at that moment did each of the boys make the miraculous discovery that he had the needed money after all. With one accord they all bent forward and plunked their money down on the marble counter. And when they had done this they would be overcome by such a fit of giggling that they couldn't drink their Cokes. Sometimes they would have to go off to school without tasting the drinks they had ordered and paid for.

At another counter in the drugstore, where cigarettes and toilet articles and candy bars were sold in those days, there was usually a somewhat older woman, a woman who was generally believed to be Mr. Conway's mother. Sometimes Mr. Conway himself presided at that counter; that was when the boys actually swiped the useless articles they found on display. But when his "mother" was in charge they always made a point of fumbling . . . As a matter of fact, there was a school of thought which maintained that this older woman was the druggist's wife and the younger woman was his daughter. Since in the boys' eyes Mr. Conway was of an indeterminate age, all of them conceded that the truth might lie either way; and the women themselves would not tolerate questions about their identity. It remained always a mystery . . . At any rate, in an emergency, "mother" Conway would place her two hands on the glass case before her, fix the suspect with her feline eyes, and call out in a coarse, plangent voice: "Do—oc—to-or!"

And the thief stood looking at her blankly until at last the druggist came in sight. The trick at this point, for the boy, was to stoop down and pretend to find the missing article on the floor where he had unknowingly knocked it. Then, handing it to the druggist himself, his next move was to begin making profuse apologies which could not be heard above the gleeful convulsions of the other boys and which continued until some boy at the front door shouted, "Special! Special!" After that, came the chaos of a general exodus. Amid the grabbing up of books and football gear and sheepskin coats, and against the clamor that accompanied the rush for the door, Mr. Conway was helpless. He stood watching them go, his nose twitching, the vein standing out on his forehead, his false teeth no doubt clacking, and holding in his hand a dented lipstick case or a pocket comb with possibly half its fine teeth broken.

Matt felt that he had seen each of these pranks played at least a dozen times. But Mr. Conway seldom took any action against the pranksters; these Country Day boys were the children of his best customers; their parents had the biggest charge accounts on his books; and Mr. Conway had always had a good head for business. Matt had seen even worse tricks than these played on the old man, though he himself had always been a little too timid, a little too well brought up, to have any part in them. He had generally looked on with amusement, but also with a certain disapproval. He had never so much as snatched up a magazine and stuck it under his jacket, or even broken the rule against glancing through a magazine one was not intending to buy. Suddenly now he realized he was at this very moment holding a copy of a news magazine in his hand. He pushed it back into the rack. Then he eased it out again. He held it in his two hands a moment, gazing blankly at the newsworthy face on the front cover. And before he could stop himself he stole a glance over his shoulder . . . From beside the cash register the young Conway was watching him . . . Slowly Matt turned around and, with the magazine he didn't want in one hand and with his other hand delving into his pocket for change, he walked back toward the young man. He had got sufficiently ahold of himself to make it a thoroughly casual performance.

The young Conway accepted the payment for the magazine with a positively friendly kind of smile. In fact, when Matt turned away he was again not sure that the young man had not winked at him. Despite his unfortunate resemblance to his father, the young man was obviously a sensitive, reasonable, affable sort. Matt felt drawn to him, wished they could have some conversation, longed to congratulate him on his wife's morning sickness. Matt felt also that there was some other purchase he had been intending to make which had escaped his mind this morning; surely there was *some* reason why he should not leave the drugstore yet.

This time he stopped before one of the revolving stands that held the paperback books. He began turning the thing slowly. What else was it he had recently been intending to buy in a drugstore? He imagined that it had almost come to him the first moment he had looked back and seen the young Conway removing his checked cap from his head. Perhaps if he went back and made conversation with him now, the thing would come to the surface of his mind. Maybe the young Conway would enjoy hearing about the pranks that the schoolboys used to play on his father. No, that would not do. Especially not if one of those women who used to clerk in the store had been his mother; because, somehow, the worse the prank had been, the more it had always involved one or both of those women. It did seem to Matt in retrospect, however, that probably neither of the women was the real Mrs. Conway. Very likely they were both merely hired clerks, and the real Mrs. Conway—and her mother-in-law too, and the daughter if there was one—kept at home and looked after the young Conway, who would have been a mere infant at that time. Yes, there was a gentleness about the rosy-cheeked young Conway, as seen today, that suggested a careful upbringing by women who didn't go out to work . . . Yet one could not be sure, because those two women clerks, even if they were not in the mother-wife-daughter category, could not possibly have been more respectful of Mr. Conway than they were, or seemed more dependent upon him for protection. They believed absolutely in the old man's authority, and their confidence in him was resented by the boys. What strange power had he over those two women? This question, in the boy's minds, was lumped in with all the other questions they had about Mr. Conway. And all their pranks, if not intended to satisfy their curiosity, were at least intended to show that they knew there was something to be curious about . . . There was the time, for instance, when Ted Harrison threw the stink bomb. The stench of the sulfur made Matt shake his head even now. The memory of it was that vivid. The two women didn't understand what had happened. The odor hadn't yet reached their nostrils when some of the boys began exclaiming in girlish voices: "O, that *awful* Mr. Conway! That *dreadful* Mr. Conway!" The two women stared at each other across the store for a time, then each of them began to spread her nostrils and sniff the malodorous air. The boys all set their faces toward the back of the store, focusing their eyes on the lighted doorway beneath the huge mortar and pestle. Presently, in a dramatic stage whisper, Ted Harrison asked: "*What* can Mr. Conway have *done?*"

Matt himself, standing near the soda fountain that day, had fixed his attention on the face of the younger woman. He was watching her when she inhaled the first whiff of the stink bomb. Suddenly her nostrils quivered, her swarthy skin took on a curious glow, her dark eyebrows contracted. He could tell that her eyes had met those of the older woman, who was behind him at the other counter. Then simultaneously the two women fled their posts, running behind the counters toward the rear of the store. What indeed *had* their Dr. Conway done? They met at the entrance to the prescription room and disappeared through the doorway. There came the sounds of the three excited voices back there, and then presently Mr. Conway emerged, pushing in his dentures. The two women followed close behind him, but he soon sent them scurrying back to their places.

As Mr. Conway approached from the rear, the boys drew away from him toward the front of the store. They really were afraid of him. With downcast eyes they pretended to be looking and smelling all about to find where the stench came from. But suddenly Ted Harrison made a dash for it; he rushed right past Mr. Conway. "It's somewhere back here, I think," he shouted. He rounded the big glass case where hot water bottles and syringes and enema bags were displayed. And then, to the consternation of all, Ted Harrison passed beneath the mortar and pestle and through the bright doorway. He was out of sight for only one second, certainly not long enough to have done any damage or to have had more than a glimpse of the sacrosanct prescription room, but when he reappeared a cheer went up from the other boys. In fact, Ted was already outside again by the time Mr. Conway roared back at him to "get the hell out of there." And when the old druggist slipped in between the counters to try to head him off, Ted was already among his companions again in the front part of the store. Somebody shouted, "Special!" The front door was flung open. The crowd surged out onto the sidewalk, and without slowing their pace moved on into the street, and then, heedless of angry horns and shrieking tires, clambered aboard the waiting streetcar, some of them still chanting, "Special, Special!" until the streetcar doors were safely closed behind them.

There was probably never a worse incident than that one—except one, except one. There was that morning when some boy wrote with soap on the mirror behind the soda fountain. Another boy, probably an accomplice, had fallen or been pushed out of his chair at the little round table where he had gone to drink his morning Coke. As he fell, his knee struck the tile floor—or so he pretended—and presently he lay on the floor moaning and groaning, and writhing in his pain. Of course the two clerks, those same two helpless, artless females, came hurrying to his succor. But he would not let them come near enough to examine the injured knee. "It's killing me!" he wailed, and he began thrashing about as though he were going into a fit. What else were the two honest women to do but cry out for their lord and master? And what else could Mr. Conway do but come forward?

He came warily, though, this time, shoving at his dentures and keeping an eye out for anyone who might make a rush for the prescription room. But his wariness and his precaution were needless and to no point on this occasion. Even before he appeared, a hush had come over the dozen or so boys who were present. Further, silently they had begun to gather up their possessions and to creep toward the front entrance. There was no cry of "Special" this time, and nothing false or pretended about the urgency they felt to be out of the place. Literally they had seen the handwriting on the wall. Clearly the consensus was that this time someone had gone too far. Matt, like a good number of the others, probably had not really seen which of them had done the writing. His whole attention had been directed toward the boy who squirmed on the black and white tile in the center of the store, and as Matt moved with the group toward the entrance, his eyes avoided another contact with the soapy writing on the mirror. But he had no need to see it again. It was written before his mind's eye forever. Twenty years later he could still see it just as distinctly as he could smell the sulfur of the stink bomb: the crude, hurriedly written letters spelling out the simple sentence, "Mr. Conway sleeps with his mother."

And at the door, as he passed out with the others, Matt had

looked back to see that the boy on the floor had got to his feet and, with only the slightest pretense at a limp, was running on tiptoes to join his schoolmates.

Nobody waited to see how the writing on the mirror would affect Mr. Conway or the two women. But during the following two weeks Mr. Conway stationed himself at the entrance each morning and would not let the Country Day boys come inside the drugstore. It was in the dead of winter, and the boys had to wait outside in the cold, stamping their feet and beating their hands together until the Special arrived. When at last Mr. Conway did relent, there was a period of a month or more when the boys came into the drugstore every morning and behaved like the real little gentlemen that Country Day boys were sempiternally and without exception supposed to be. And during that period it was only with the greatest difficulty that Matt had been able to look directly into the eyes of either of the two women clerks. Whenever he wished to make a purchase he couldn't find his voice. If he did finally find his voice it would be either too soft or too loud. Or in the midst of whatever he tried to say his voice would break and change its pitch from high to low, or the other way round. The most painful part, though, was that before he could speak he would stand before the one or the other of the two women for several seconds, scratching his head and looking down at his feet.

That memory of the head-scratching! It was to mean Matt's release and salvation after standing there so long hypnotized by the revolving book stand. He came out of his trance, and he realized that he was actually at this moment scratching his head. And that was it. It was something to soothe his troublesome scalp that he had been meaning to buy in a drugstore. With great self-assurance he strode back to the counter where the young Conway was still on watch.

But when he stood face to face with the amiable sentinel there—so smiling, so fresh complexioned, so luxuriantly thatched (and with the luxuriant thatch so lovingly groomed)—he understood that it was not really he that he wanted to see again. It was the older man. And once again, some twenty feet from where he now stood, it was the giant mortar and pestle with the bright doorway underneath that caught his eye. It was a red flag waved before him—maddening. Ted Harrison had actually got inside the prescription room. But Matt Donelson had never even taken part in any of the pranks. He heard himself saying to the young Conway, "There's a matter I'd like to speak with the pharmacist about. I'd like to get some advice. I'd like him to recommend something."

The young man stopped smiling, and tried to look very serious and professional. "Maybe I can help you," he said. "As a matter of fact, I am a pharmacist myself. And my father is tied up with some prescriptions just now."

Matt continued to look at him for a moment or so without saying more.

The gentleness and sensitivity that showed perpetually in the young man's eyes was momentarily translated into a look of professional consideration for the feelings of a customer. But Matt would have none of that. The young Conway was obviously a mere slave— no man at all really. Else how could he consent to live under the domination of that brute of an old man? Moreover, Matt could tell that the young man thought he had guessed the nature of his ailment. He thought it was hemorrhoids that Matt was so hesitant to mention. "It's my scalp," Matt said abruptly. "I have a more or less chronic scalp complaint. No dandruff, but itching and an occasional breaking out."

"Ah, yes, I see," the young pharmacist began. And lifting his eyebrows he actually looked directly at Matt's head.

Matt looked back at *his* head. "If you don't mind," he said, "I'd like to speak with the senior pharmacist." He relished that last phrase, and he was pleased to observe that finally he had managed to offend the junior pharmacist.

Now the young Conway looked at Matt for a moment without speaking. Presently the inane smile returned to his lips. "Just one moment, please," he said to Matt. He turned and walked away, back to the prescription room. Matt could barely restrain himself from following. The young man stood in the doorway, leaning one shoulder against the jamb while he spoke with his father. Then he came back with a message.

"My father," he said quietly, "suggests that you probably ought to see a doctor."

Matt understood at once that there was more than one interpretation that could be made of that message. "I believe I'd like to speak to the pharmacist myself," he said, and was already striding alongside the counter and toward the doorway to the prescription room. But the young Conway was moving at the same speed behind the counter. They converged at the entrance to Mr. Conway's prescription room. And simultaneously the figure of the old druggist was framed in the doorway. Matt went up on his toes and peered over Mr. Conway's shoulder! He saw it all, the white cabinets and the bottles and the long work shelf, all so like a hundred other pharmacists' shops he had had passing glimpses of. Everything about it looked so innocent and familiar and really quite meaningless. There was no satisfaction in it for him at all—not even in the glass of water which he identified as the receptacle for Mr. Conway's teeth. But what kind of satisfaction should he have got? he asked himself. What had he expected? Something inside him which a moment before had seemed to be swelling to the bursting point suddenly collapsed.

"You told my father you were in a hurry," he heard the young pharmacist say. "I think you'd better get going now." Looking at the young man, Matt observed that he definitely had a nervous tic in one eye. And all the blood had gone out of his cheeks now. He was in a white rage. Why, he even had his right fist tightened and was ready to fight Matt if necessary to protect the old druggist. The incredible thing was that only a moment before, Matt himself would have been willing to fight. Why? What had possessed him? Already the whole incident seemed unreal. Surely he had been momentarily insane; there was no other way to explain it. He backed away from the two men, turned his back to them, and quickly left the drugstore.

On his way back to his parents' house he kept shaking his head as if to rid himself of all thought of his absurd behavior in the drugstore. But at the same time he kept reminding himself of how near he had come to getting into a scrap with the young druggist, and perhaps the old druggist too. How unlike him it would have been, what an anomaly, how incongruous with everything else in a life that was going so well. He would never have been able to explain it to anyone. But even without the incident's ending in a real brawl, his behavior was nonetheless appalling. The only difference was that nobody ever need know about it. Finally he would be able to put it out of his own mind.

Back at the house, he found everyone up and stirring. The odors of the coffee and bacon greeted him in the front hall. From the living room he heard the voices of his two little boys commingled with those of his parents. "There he is now," he heard his mother say. He stepped to the cloak closet and hung up his topcoat, and while still at the closet he slipped the bottle of shaving lotion into the pocket of his jacket. He hesitated a moment, undecided about what to do with the magazine he had bought. It was a magazine he never read himself and one his father "thoroughly detested." Suddenly he stuffed it into the pocket of his father's heaviest winter coat. He knew it wouldn't be discovered there until his mother packed away the winter clothes the first week in May, and it pleased him to think of the mystery it would make and how they would talk about it for days . . . As he left the closet, his father hailed him from the living room doorway with: "Where have you been?"

"Just out," Matt said, and then out of long practice was able to soften such smart-aleckness toward his father with: "Just out for a walk."

"I might have gone with you if you had given me a knock," said his father. The two boys appeared now on either side of their grandfather.

"So would I," said the older boy. He was ten and was beginning to want to dress like a man. He had put on a tie this morning and kept running a finger around the inside of his collar.

"Me too," said the little brother, who was eight and affected nothing.

Matt eyed the three of them. He observed that the old man was wearing the silk smoking jacket he and Janie had sent him at Christmas. "You were both slugabeds," he said to the boys. He went past them and into the living room to kiss his mother on the forehead. "That's a good-looking smoking jacket *he's* wearing," he said to her. His father shrugged, feigning indifference.

"He saves it for special occasions," his mother said. "It's very becoming to him."

"I'm going to run up and shave," Matt said.

On the stairs he met Janie. She had done her long, dull-gold hair in the way his mother liked it, *not* with the dramatic part in the center the way she and he liked it best but parted on the side and brushed softly across her brow and low over her ears to an upswept ratted effect on the back of her head. She looked old-fashioned, like some girl in a 1917 poster.

"Early bird," she said, as he came up toward her.

As they passed, he gave her hand a quick squeeze. "I must shave," he said, rubbing a hand upward over his cheek. "They wouldn't like it this way."

"Oh, must you?"

"I don't look civilized," he said. "I'll hurry."

"No, don't hurry. You're sure to cut yourself if you hurry."

"Worry-wart, I never cut myself," he said.

From the top of the stairs he heard her addressing his parents a good morning . . . It was wonderful being home. It was wonderful having his wife be so attentive to his parents, and his parents so admiring of Janie. It was fine having his parents enjoy the boys, and the boys and Janie enjoy his parents, and fine enjoying them himself the way a grown man ought to do.

He felt that everything was under control and that it was going to be a good visit. Once while he was shaving, in the bathroom, he saw his hand tremble slightly just before he was going to bring the razor up to his bristly throat. But he steadied the hand, and a little smile came upon his lips as he did so. He had already shaved around his mouth, and in the mirror above the lavatory he observed there was a certain cynicism in the smile. It was strange.

When he came down to breakfast, the others had already taken their places around the big dining table. They were all sipping at some kind of juice, but at his plate there was an orange and a fruit knife—as of old. His mother was watching his face, and he smiled at her appreciatively. There was also a box of cigars at his place. He picked up the box, examining it and reading the brand name, holding it gingerly in one hand as though trying to guess its weight. "I haven't had any of these in a long time," he said to his father, who pretended not to be listening. "I can't afford them." He took the box over to the sideboard, aware that his father was watching him, and put it down there. "You'll have to join me in one after breakfast," he said to his father.

"Not for me," the old man said. "Not any more."

Matt stood with his back to the room, looking down at the cigar box on the dark sideboard. Somehow his father's words held him there; he could not turn away. And suddenly a great wave of despair swept over him. It caught him completely off guard. He felt his heartbeat quicken beneath his shirt, and he realized that his shirt was soaked with what must be his own sweat. He placed his two hands on the sideboard as if bracing himself against another wave, which came on now with more fury than the first and which was not of despair but of some other emotion less easily or less willingly identified. It was like regret for lost opportunities, or nearly like that—but already it had passed and already still another wave was imminent. And then it came, the inevitable feeling that Janie had been right last night, and always, about what was happening inside him at these homecomings. His first impulse was to hurl the whole weight of his great good sense and reason against the flood of feeling, but the deeper wisdom of a long-time swimmer in these waters prevailed. He yielded a little to the feeling and let himself be carried out a certain distance, striving only to keep his head clear; and meanwhile he kept telling himself, warning himself, in big, easy strokes . . .

"What are you doing over there?" his father was saying now. Matt rummaged in his pocket for the small silver knife he always carried (mainly for the purpose of paring his nails). He opened the knife and began slitting the paper that sealed the cigar box. He did a very precise job of it, careful not to dig into the surface of the soft wood because he knew one of the boys would want the box. Presently he turned to the table with the lid of the box open and exhibited its fragrant, orderly contents. Everyone strained to see. The smaller boy stood up beside his chair and peered across the table. Apparently everyone took satisfaction from the symmetry of the cigars and the orderly way they were lined up inside the box.

Matt stepped toward his father and said, "Take one for after breakfast."

"I told you I've given up all that," his father said calmly, looking Matt in the eye. His father always sat very erect in his chair, especially at breakfast. And at that hour the old man's bald pate had a smoother, rosier look than it would have later in the day. His face stayed always the same, but by noon the top of his head would have a tired look.

"We'll see," Matt said, winking at his mother, and flipping the box lid closed. He had never felt more self-possessed.

But when he turned again and replaced the cigar box on the sideboard, he again found that something barred his rejoining the family group. This time there was no nonsense about waves sweeping over him or about keeping his eye on the shore. There was a different kind of nonsense: it seemed to him now that he had gone to that drugstore on purpose this morning, that he had planned the whole adventure before he ever left New York. It had been intended to satisfy some passing and unnamed need of his, but the adventure had cut too deep into his memory and into what was far more than mere memory. Inadvertently, he had penetrated beyond all the good sense and reasonableness that made life seem worthwhile—or even tolerable. And through the breach, beyond, behind, or beneath all this, he was now confronted by a thing that had a face and a will of its own. It was there threatening not only him and his father but the others too. Its threat was always present really, in him and in every man. It was in women too, no doubt, but they were so constituted that they never lost sight of it, were always on their guard, were dealing with it every moment of their lives.

Above the sideboard hung a dark still life done in oils. It was protected, in the fashion of an earlier day, by a rather thick pane of glass. Behind this glass a dead fish lay upon a maroon platter, and beside the platter were stretched two dead pheasants in full plumage, their necks drooping over the edge of what seemed to be the same sideboard that the picture hung above. They were not very colorful pheasants, all dull browns and reds; and the leaden-eyed fish, with its lusterless scales and its long, tapering tail, bore more resemblance to a dead rodent than to any game fish. He had been at once fascinated and repelled by the picture as a child, then when he was older he had come to despise its triteness, and later he had learned to find it amusing. It had been painted by one of his great-grandmothers, and like the mahogany sideboard was counted among the family treasures. Suddenly now the limp tail of the dead fish stiffened and moved! Or perhaps it was the neck of one of the lifeless pheasants! . . . It was neither of course. The movement had been the reflection of his own face as he lifted it. He was not amused by the illusion. Momentarily the dim reflection of his face in the glass, superimposed upon the dark, unreal fish and pheasants, appeared to him as the very face of that Thing he had uncovered. The dark face loomed large in the glass and it was a monstrous obtrusion on the relatively bright scene that was reflected all around it—the innocent scene at the breakfast table behind Matt. In the glass he could see his mother nodding her head as she spoke. She was saying that one of his brothers was going to stop by the house to see them on his way to work this morning. And he heard Janie asking whether that brother's oldest child was going to graduate from high school this year . . . How dearly he loved them all! And how bitterly the Thing showing its face in the glass hated them!

"Only out for a walk, eh?" his father was saying, just as though Matt's back were not turned to the room. The tone was playfully sententious. It was their old accustomed tone with each other. Matt massaged his face, as if to transform his features before presenting his face to the family. He reached into the cigar box and took out one cigar for himself, then headed toward the empty chair beside his mother.

"Yes, only out for a walk," he replied cheerfully. "And why not?"

"I don't know. You had a guilty look when you came in."

Matt was standing behind his chair at the table. Already he was able to laugh inwardly about the business of the boogyman in the glass. What nonsense! Perhaps it was a sign of age, letting a visit home upset him so. The truth was, it wasn't just waking up in his father's house and the visit to that drugstore. He had come to the age where waking up anywhere but in his own apartment or in any city but New York could throw him out of kilter. And he reflected that ever since he could remember, his father had disliked sleeping anywhere but in his own bed. It was very wise of the old man, very wise.

As he was getting into his chair he heard the older boy say to his grandfather, "Yes, he looked guilty all right. I noticed it."

"Yes, he sure did," added the younger boy.

"You two little parrots," Matt said fondly. And to his father he said, *"They're* just *like* you."

Janie burst out laughing. He could feel her relief. And his mother said, "You men."

Matt smiled at his father, waiting a moment before taking up his napkin from the table. He was aware that his smile was the same smile he had given his trembling hand upstairs.

"Just out for a walk, eh?" his father said again, childlike in the pleasure he took from the attention his remark had drawn the first time, and even more childlike in his effort to repeat or extend the pleasure. But Matt knew he wouldn't pursue the subject further. He felt that in a sense his father understood him better even than Janie did. And the old man had his own way of communicating it. Yes, it seemed to Matt that he and the man sitting at the head of the table had long, long since reached an understanding and come to terms with one another. Surely no one could say that either he or his father had not made those adjustments and concessions that a happy and successful life requires. They played at being father and son still, played at quarreling still, but they had long ago absolved each other of any guilt. They were free of all that. As two men, they respected each other and enjoyed each other's company. All the rest was nonsense!

Presently the conversation around the table became general. Everyone chattered while they waited for the cook to come and remove the fruit juice glasses. The two boys were behaving extremely well with their grandparents, and Janie had never seemed easier or more at home in the house of her in-laws. Everything was going splendidly. Matt unfolded his napkin and stretched it across his lap. He experienced an exhilarating sense of well-being. He took up his fruit knife and began to peel his orange. He worked with a steady hand, displaying consummate skill, and was conscious that everyone else was looking on admiringly while he performed the rite. As he peeled away at the orange, making the coarse rind come out in long curls like apple peels, it was as though he could already taste the fruit in his mouth. Yet when finally he had put down his knife, he observed with satisfaction that there was nowhere a break on the thin, inner pellicle of the orange. His satisfaction was so complete, in fact, that he could not resist lifting up the piece of fruit—unscathed and whole—between the fingertips of his own hands for a general inspection. Then for a moment he sat looking over the orange and into the faces of his loved ones, and he did not wonder at their grateful smiles.

A Spinster's Tale

My brother would often get drunk when I was a little girl, but that put a different sort of fear into me from what Mr. Speed did. With Brother it was a spiritual thing. And though it was frightening to know that he would have to burn for all that giggling and bouncing around on the stair at night, the truth was that he only seemed jollier to me when I would stick my head out of the hall door. It made him seem almost my age for him to act so silly, putting his white forefinger all over his flushed face and finally over his lips to say, "Sh-sh-sh-sh!" But the really frightening thing about seeing Brother drunk was what I always heard when I had slid back into bed. I could always recall my mother's words to him when he was sixteen, the year before she died, spoken in her greatest sincerity, in her most religious tone: "Son, I'd rather see you in your grave."

Yet those nights put a scaredness into me that was clearly distinguishable from the terror that Mr. Speed instilled by stumbling past our house two or three afternoons a week. The most that I knew about Mr. Speed was his name. And this I considered that I had somewhat fabricated—by allowing him the "Mr."—in my effort to humanize and soften the monster that was forever passing our house on Church Street. My father would point him out through the wide parlor window in soberness and severity to my brother with: "There goes Old Speed, again." Or on Saturdays when Brother was with the Benton boys and my two uncles were over having toddies with Father in the parlor, Father would refer to Mr. Speed's passing with a similar speech, but in a blustering tone of merry tolerance: "There goes Old Speed, again. The rascal!" These designations were equally awful, both spoken in tones that were foreign to my father's manner of addressing me; and not unconsciously I prepared the euphemism, Mister Speed, against the inevitable day when I should have to speak of him to someone.

I was named Elizabeth, for my mother. My mother had died in the spring before Mr. Speed first came to my notice on that late afternoon in October. I had bathed at four with the aid of Lucy, who had been my nurse and who was now the upstairs maid; and Lucy was upstairs turning back the covers of the beds in the rooms with their color schemes of blue and green and rose. I wandered into the shadowy parlor and sat first on one chair, then on another. I tried lying down on the settee that went with the parlor set, but my legs had got too long this summer to stretch out straight on the settee. And my feet looked long in their pumps against the wicker arm. I looked at the pictures around the room blankly and at the stained-glass windows on either side of the fireplace; and the winter light coming through them was hardly bright enough to show the colors. I struck a match on the mosaic hearth and lit the gas logs.

Kneeling on the hearth I watched the flames till my face felt hot. I stood up then and turned directly to one of the full-length mirror panels that were on each side of the front window. This one was just to the right of the broad window and my reflection in it stood out strangely from the rest of the room in the dull light that did not penetrate beyond my figure. I leaned closer to the mirror trying to discover a resemblance between myself and the wondrous Alice who walked through a looking glass. But that resemblance I was seeking I could not find in my sharp features, or in my heavy, dark curls hanging like fragments of hosepipe to my shoulders.

I propped my hands on the borders of the narrow mirror and put my face close to watch my lips say, "Away." I would hardly open them for the "a"; and then I would contort my face by the great opening I made for the "way." I whispered, "Away, away." I whispered it over and over, faster and faster, watching myself in the mirror: "A-way—a-way—away-away-awayaway." Suddenly I burst into tears and turned from the gloomy mirror to the daylight at the wide parlor window. Gazing tearfully through the expanse of plate glass there, I beheld Mr. Speed walking like a cripple with one foot on the curb and one in the street. And faintly I could hear him cursing the trees as he passed them, giving each a lick with his heavy walking cane.

Presently I was dry-eyed in my fright. My breath came short, and I clasped the black bow at the neck of my middy blouse.

When he had passed from view, I stumbled back from the window. I hadn't heard the houseboy enter the parlor, and he must not have noticed me there, I made no move of recognition as he drew the draperies across the wide front window for the night. I stood cold and silent before the gas logs with a sudden inexplicable memory of my mother's cheek and a vision of her in her bedroom on a spring day.

That April day when spring had seemed to crowd itself through the windows into the bright upstairs rooms, the old-fashioned mahogany sick-chair had been brought down from the attic to my mother's room. Three days before, a quiet service had been held there for the stillborn baby, and I had accompanied my father and brother to our lot in the gray cemetery to see the box (large for so tiny a parcel) lowered and covered with mud. But in the parlor now by the gas logs I remembered the day that my mother had sent for the sick-chair and for me.

The practical nurse, sitting in a straight chair busy at her needle-work, looked over her glasses to give me some little instruction in the arrangement of my mother's pillows in the chair. A few minutes before, this practical nurse had lifted my sick mother bodily from the bed, and I had the privilege of rolling my mother to the big bay window that looked out ideally over the new foliage of small trees in our side yard.

I stood self-consciously straight, close by my mother, a maturing little girl awkward in my curls and long-waisted dress. My pale mother, in her silk bed jacket, with a smile leaned her cheek against the cheek of her daughter. Outside it was spring. The furnishings of the great blue room seemed to partake for that one moment of nature's life. And my mother's cheek was warm on mine. This I remembered when I sat before the gas logs trying to put Mr. Speed out of my mind; but that a few moments later my mother beckoned to the practical nurse and sent me suddenly from the room, my memory did not dwell upon. I remembered only the warmth of the cheek and the comfort of that other moment.

I sat near the blue burning logs and waited for my father and my brother to come in. When they came saying the same things about office and school that they said every day, turning on lights beside chairs that they liked to flop into, I realized not that I was ready or unready for them but that there had been, within me, an attempt at a preparation for such readiness.

They sat so customarily in their chairs at first and the talk ran so easily that I thought that Mr. Speed could be forgotten as quickly and painlessly as a doubting of Jesus or a fear of death from the measles. But the conversation took insinuating and malicious twists this afternoon. My father talked about the possibilities of a general war and recalled opinions that people had had just before the

Spanish-American. He talked about the hundreds of men in the Union Depot. Thinking of all those men there, that close together, was something like meeting Mr. Speed in the front hall. I asked my father not to talk about war, which seemed to him a natural enough request for a young lady to make.

"How is your school, my dear?" he asked me. "How are Miss Hood and Miss Herron? Have they found who's stealing the boarders' things, my dear?"

All of those little girls safely in Belmont School being called for by gentle ladies or warm-breasted Negro women were a pitiable sight beside the beastly vision of Mr. Speed which even they somehow conjured.

At dinner, with Lucy serving and sometimes helping my plate (because she had done so for so many years), Brother teased me first one way and then another. My father joined in on each point until I began to take the teasing very seriously, and then he told Brother that he was forever carrying things too far.

Once at dinner I was convinced that my preposterous fears that Brother knew what had happened to me by the window in the afternoon were not at all preposterous. He had been talking quietly. It was something about the meeting that he and the Benton boys were going to attend after dinner. But quickly, without reason, he turned his eyes on me across the table and fairly shouted in his new deep voice: "I saw three horses running away out on Harding Road today! They were just like the mules we saw at the mines in the mountains! They were running to beat hell and with little girls riding them!"

The first week after I had the glimpse of Mr. Speed through the parlor window, I spent the afternoons dusting the bureau and mantel and bedside table in my room, arranging on the chaise longue the dolls which at this age I never played with and rarely even talked to; or I would absent-mindedly assist Lucy in turning down the beds and maybe watch the houseboy set the dinner table. I went to the parlor only when Father came or when Brother came earlier and called me in to show me a shin bruise or a box of cigarettes which a girl had given him.

Finally, I put my hand on the parlor doorknob just at four one afternoon and entered the parlor, walking stiffly as I might have done with my hands in a muff going into church. The big room with its heavy furniture and pictures showed no change since the last afternoon that I had spent there, unless possibly there were fresh antimacassars on the chairs. I confidently pushed an odd chair over to the window and took my seat and sat erect and waited.

My heart would beat hard when, from the corner of my eye, I caught sight of some figure moving up Church Street. And as it drew nearer, showing the form of some Negro or neighbor or drummer, I would sigh from relief and from regret. I was ready for Mr. Speed. And I knew that he would come again and again, that he had been passing our house for inconceivable numbers of years. I knew that if he did not appear today, he would pass tomorrow. Not because I had had accidental, unavoidable glimpses of him from upstairs windows during the past week, nor because there were indistinct memories of such a figure, hardly noticed, seen on afternoons that preceded that day when I had seen him stumbling like a cripple along the curb and beating and cursing the trees did I know that Mr. Speed was a permanent and formidable figure in my life which I would be called upon to deal with; my knowledge, I was certain, was purely intuitive.

I was ready now not to face him with his drunken rage directed at me, but to look at him far off in the street and to appraise him. He didn't come that afternoon, but he came the next. I sat prim and straight before the window. I turned my head neither to the right to anticipate the sight of him nor to the left to follow his figure when it had passed. But when he was passing before my window, I put my eyes full on him and looked though my teeth chattered in my head. And now I saw his face heavy, red, fierce like his body. He walked with an awkward, stomping sort of stagger, carrying his gray topcoat over one arm; and with his other hand he kept poking his walnut cane into the soft sod along the sidewalk. When he was gone, I recalled my mother's cheek again, but the recollection this time, though more deliberate, was dwelt less upon; and I could only think of watching Mr. Speed again and again.

There was snow on the ground the third time that I watched Mr. Speed pass our house. Mr. Speed spat on the snow, and with his cane he aimed at the brown spot that his tobacco made there. And I could see that he missed his aim. The fourth time that I sat watching for him from the window, snow was actually falling outside; and I felt a sort of anixety to know what would ever drive him into my own house. For a moment I doubted that he would really come to my door; but I prodded myself with the thought of his coming and finding me unprepared. And I continued to keep my secret watch for him two or three times a week during the rest of the winter.

Meanwhile my life with my father and brother and the servants in the shadowy house went on from day to day. On week nights the evening meal usually ended with petulant arguing between the two men, the atlas or the encyclopedia usually drawing them from the table to read out the statistics. Often Brother was accused of having looked-them-up-previously and of maneuvering the conversation toward the particular subject, for topics were very easily introduced and dismissed by the two. Once I, sent to the library to fetch a cigar, returned to find the discourse shifted in two minutes' time from the Kentucky Derby winners to the languages in which the Bible was first written. Once I actually heard the conversation slip, in the course of a small dessert, from the comparative advantages of urban and agrarian life for boys between the ages of fifteen and twenty to the probable origin and age of the Icelandic parliament and then to the doctrines of the Campbellite Church.

That night I followed them to the library and beheld them fingering the pages of the flimsy old atlas in the light from the beaded lampshade. They paid no attention to me and little to one another, each trying to turn the pages of the book and mumbling references to newspaper articles and to statements of persons of responsibility. I slipped from the library to the front parlor across the hall where I could hear the contentious hum. And I lit the gas logs, trying to warm my long legs before them as I examined my own response to the unguided and remorseless bickering of the masculine voices.

It was, I thought, their indifferent shifting from topic to topic that most disturbed me. Then I decided that it was the tremendous gaps that there seemed to be between the subjects that was bewildering to me. Still again, I thought that it was the equal interest which they displayed for each subject that was dismaying. All things in the world were equally at home in their arguments. They exhibited equal indifference to the horrors that each topic might suggest; and I wondered whether or not their imperturbability was a thing that they had achieved.

I knew that I had got myself so accustomed to the sight of Mr. Speed's peregrinations, persistent yet, withal, seemingly without destination, that I could view his passing with perfect equanimity. And from this I knew that I must extend my preparation for the day when I should have to view him at closer range. When the day would come, I knew that it must involve my father and my brother and that his existence therefore must not remain an unmentionable thing, the secrecy of which to explode at the moment of crisis, only adding to its confusion.

Now, the door to my room was the first at the top of the long red-carpeted stairway. A wall light beside it was left burning on nights when Brother was out, and, when he came in, he turned it off. The light shining through my transom was a comforting sight when I had gone to bed in the big room; and in the summertime I could see the reflection of light bugs on it, and often one would plop against it. Sometimes I would wake up in the night with a start and would be frightened in the dark, not knowing what had awakened me until I realized that Brother had just turned out the light. On other nights, however, I would hear him close the front door and hear him bouncing up the steps. When I then stuck my head out the door, usually he would toss me a piece of candy and he always signaled to me to be quiet.

I had never intentionally stayed awake till he came in until one night toward the end of February of that year, and I hadn't been certain then that I should be able to do it. Indeed, when finally the front door closed, I had dozed several times sitting up in the dark bed. But I was standing with my door half open before he had come a third of the way up the stair. When he saw me, he stopped still on the stairway resting his hand on the banister. I realized that purposefulness must be showing on my face, and so I smiled at him and beckoned. His red face broke into a fine grin, and he took the next few steps two at a time. But he stumbled on the carpeted steps. He was on his knees, yet with his hand still on the banister. He was motionless there for a moment with his head cocked to one side, listening. The house was quiet and still. He smiled again, sheepishly this time, and kept putting his white forefinger to his red face as he ascended on tiptoe the last third of the flight of steps.

At the head of the stair he paused, breathing hard. He reached his hand into his coat pocket and smiled confidently as he shook his head at me. I stepped backward into my room.

"Oh," he whispered. "Your candy."

I stood straight in my white nightgown with my black hair

hanging over my shoulders, knowing that he could see me only indistinctly. I beckoned to him again. He looked suspiciously about the hall, then stepped into the room and closed the door behind him.

"What's the matter, Betsy?" he said.

I turned and ran and climbed between the covers of my bed.

"What's the matter, Betsy?" he said. He crossed to my bed and sat down beside me on it.

I told him that I didn't know what was the matter.

"Have you been reading something you shouldn't, Betsy?" he asked.

I was silent.

"Are you lonely, Betsy?" he said. "Are you a lonely little girl?"

I sat up on the bed and threw my arms about his neck. And as I sobbed on his shoulder I smelled for the first time the fierce odor of his cheap whiskey.

"Yes, I'm always lonely," I said with directness, and I was then silent with my eyes open and my cheek on the shoulder of his overcoat which was yet cold from the February night air.

He kept his face turned away from me and finally spoke, out of the other corner of his mouth, I thought, "I'll come home earlier some afternoons and we'll talk and play."

"Tomorrow."

When I had said this distinctly, I fell away from him back on the bed. He stood up and looked at me curiously, as though in some way repelled by my settling so comfortably in the covers. And I could see his eighteen-year-old head cocked to one side as though trying to see my face in the dark. He leaned over me, and I smelled his whiskey breath. It was not repugnant to me. It was blended with the odor that he always had. I thought that he was going to strike me. He didn't, however, and in a moment was opening the door to the lighted hall. Before he went out, again I said: "Tomorrow."

The hall light dark and the sound of Brother's footsteps gone, I naturally repeated the whole scene in my mind and upon examination found strange elements present. One was something like a longing for my brother to strike me when he was leaning over me. Another was his bewilderment at my procedure. On the whole I was amazed at the way I had carried the thing off. It was the first incident that I had ever actively carried off. Now I only wished that in the darkness when he was leaning over me I had said languidly, "Oh, Brother," had said it in a tone indicating that we had in common some unmentionable trouble. Then I should have been certain of his presence next day. As it was, though, I had little doubt of his coming home early.

I would not let myself reflect further on my feelings for my brother—my desire for him to strike me and my delight in his natural odor. I had got myself in the habit of postponing such elucidations until after I had completely settled with Mr. Speed. But, as after all such meetings with my brother, I reflected upon the posthumous punishments in store for him for his carousing and drinking, and remembered my mother's saying that she had rather see him in his grave.

The next afternoon at four I had the chessboard on the tea table before the front parlor window. I waited for my brother, knowing pretty well that he would come and feeling certain that Mr. Speed would pass. (For this was a Thursday afternoon; and during the winter months I had found that there were two days of the week on which Mr. Speed never failed to pass our house. These were Thursday and Saturday.) I led my brother into that dismal parlor chattering about the places where I had found the chessmen long in disuse. When I paused a minute, slipping into my seat by the chessboard, he picked up with talk of the senior class play and his chances for being chosen valedictorian. Apparently I no longer seemed an enigma to him. I thought that he must have concluded that I was just a lonely little girl named Betsy. But I doubted that his nature was so different from my own that he could sustain objective sympathy for another child, particularly a younger sister, from one day to another. And since I saw no favors that he could ask from me at this time, my conclusion was that he believed that he had never exhibited his drunkenness to me with all his bouncing about on the stair at night; but that he was not certain that talking from the other corner of his mouth had been precaution enough against his whiskey breath.

We faced each other over the chessboard and set the men in order. There were only a few days before it would be March, and the light through the window was first bright and then dull. During my brother's moves, I stared out the window at the clouds that passed before the sun and watched pieces of newspaper that blew about the yard. I was calm beyond my own credulity. I found myself responding to my brother's little jokes and showing real interest in the game. I tried to terrorize myself by imagining Mr. Speed's coming up to the very window this day. I even had him shaking his cane and his derby hat at us. But the frenzy which I expected at this step of my preparation did not come. And some part of Mr. Speed's formidability seemed to have vanished. I realized that by not hiding my face in my mother's bosom and by looking at him so regularly for so many months, I had come to accept his existence as a natural part of my life on Church Street, though something to be guarded against, or, as I had put it before, to be thoroughly prepared for when it came to my door.

The problem then, in relation to my brother, had suddenly resolved itself in something much simpler than the conquest of my fear of looking upon Mr. Speed alone had been. This would be only a matter of how I should act and of what words I should use. And from the incident of the night before, I had some notion that I'd find a suitable way of procedure in our household.

Mr. Speed appeared in the street without his overcoat but with one hand holding the turned-up lapels and collar of his gray suit coat. He followed his cane, stomping like an enraged blind man with his head bowed against the March wind. I squeezed from between my chair and the table and stood right at the great plate glass window, looking out. From the corner of my eye I saw that Brother was intent upon his play. Presently, in the wind, Mr. Speed's derby went back on his head, and his hand grabbed at it, pulled it back in place, then returned to hold his lapels. I took a sharp breath, and Brother looked up. And just as he looked out the window, Mr. Speed's derby did blow off and across the sidewalk, over the lawn. Mr. Speed turned, holding his lapels with his tremendous hand, shouting oaths that I could hear ever so faintly, and tried to stumble after his hat.

Then I realized that my brother was gone from the room; and he was outside the window with Mr. Speed chasing Mr. Speed's hat in the wind.

I sat back in my chair, breathless; one elbow went down on the chessboard disordering the black and white pawns and kings and castles. And through the window I watched Brother handing Mr. Speed his derby. I saw his apparent indifference to the drunk man's oaths and curses. I saw him coming back to the house while the old man yet stood railing at him. I pushed the table aside and ran to the front door lest Brother be locked outside. He met me in the hall smiling blandly.

I said, "That's Mr. Speed."

He sat down on the bottom step of the stairway, leaning backward and looking at me inquisitively.

"He's drunk, Brother," I said. "Always."

My brother looked frankly into the eyes of this half-grown sister of his but said nothing for a while.

I pushed myself up on the console table and sat swinging my legs and looking seriously about the walls of the cavernous hallway at the expanse of oak paneling, at the inset canvas of the sixteenth-century Frenchman making love to his lady, at the hat rack, and at the grandfather's clock in the darkest corner. I waited for Brother to speak.

"You don't like people who get drunk?" he said.

I saw that he was taking the whole thing as a thrust at his own behavior.

"I just think Mr. Speed is very ugly, Brother."

From the detached expression of his eyes I knew that he was not convinced.

"I wouldn't mind him less if he were sober," I said. "Mr. Speed's like—a loose horse."

This analogy convinced him. He knew then what I meant.

"You mustn't waste your time being afraid of such things," he said in great earnestness. "In two or three years there'll be things that you'll have to be afraid of. Things you really can't avoid."

"What did he say to you?" I asked.

"He cussed and threatened to hit me with that stick."

"For no reason?"

"Old Mr. Speed's burned out his reason with whiskey."

"Tell me about him." I was almost imploring him.

"Everybody knows about him. He just wanders around town, drunk. Sometimes downtown they take him off in the Black Maria."

I pictured him on the main streets that I knew downtown and in the big department stores. I could see him in that formal neighborhood where my grandmother used to live. In the neighborhood of Miss Hood and Miss Herron's school. Around the little houses out where my father's secretary lived. Even in nigger town.

"You'll get used to him, for all his ugliness," Brother said. Then we sat there till my father came in, talking almost gaily about things that were particularly ugly in Mr. Speed's clothes and face and in his way of walking.

Since the day that I watched myself say "away" in the mirror, I had spent painful hours trying to know once more that experience which I now regarded as something like mystical. But the stringent course that I, motherless and lonely in our big house, had brought myself to follow while only thirteen had given me certain mature habits of thought. Idle and unrestrained daydreaming I eliminated almost entirely from my experience, though I delighted myself with fantasies that I quite consciously worked out and which, when concluded, I usually considered carefully, trying to fix them with some sort of childish symbolism.

Even idleness in my nightly dreams disturbed me. And sometimes as I tossed half awake in my big bed I would try to piece together my dreams into at least a form of logic. Sometimes I would complete an unfinished dream and wouldn't know in the morning what part I had dreamed and what part pieced out. I would often smile over the ends that I had plotted in half-wakeful moments but found pride in dreams that were complete in themselves and easy to fix with allegory, which I called "meaning." I found that a dream could start for no discoverable reason, with the sight of a printed page on which the first line was, "Once upon a time"; and soon could have me a character in a strange story. Once upon a time there was a little girl whose hands began to get very large. Grown men came for miles around to look at the giant hands and to shake them, but the little girl was ashamed of them and hid them under her skirt. It seemed that the little girl lived in the stable behind my grandmother's old house, and I watched her from the top of the loft ladder. Whenever there was the sound of footsteps, she trembled and wept; so I would beat on the floor above her and laugh uproariously at her fear. But presently I was the little girl listening to the noise. At first I trembled and called out for my father, but then I recollected that it was I who had made the noises and I felt that I had made a very considerable discovery for myself.

I awoke one Saturday morning in early March at the sound of my father's voice in the downstairs hall. He was talking to the servants, ordering the carriage I think. I believe that I awoke at the sound of the carriage horses' names. I went to my door and called "Goodbye" to him. He was twisting his mustache before the hall mirror, and he looked up the stairway at me and smiled. He was always abashed to be caught before a looking glass, and he called out self-consciously and affectionately that he would be home at noon.

I closed my door and went to the little dressing table that he had had put in my room on my birthday. The card with his handwriting on it was still stuck in the corner of the mirror: "For my young lady daughter." I was so thoroughly aware of the gentleness in his nature this morning that any childish timidity before him would, I thought, seem an injustice, and I determined that I should sit with him and my uncles in the parlor that afternoon and perhaps tell them all of my fear of the habitually drunken Mr. Speed and with them watch him pass before the parlor window. That morning I sat before the mirror of my dressing table and put up my hair in a knot on the back of my head for the first time.

Before Father came home at noon, however, I had taken my hair down, and I was not now certain that he would be unoffended by my mention of the neighborhood drunkard. But I was resolute in my purpose, and when my two uncles came after lunch, and the three men shut themselves up in the parlor for the afternoon, I took my seat across the hall in the little library, or den, as my mother had called it, and spent the first of the afternoon skimming over the familiar pages of *Tales of Ol' Virginny*, by Thomas Nelson Page.

My father had seemed tired at lunch. He talked very little and drank only half his cup of coffee. He asked Brother matter-of-fact questions about his plans for college in the fall and told me once to try cutting my meat instead of pulling it to pieces. And as I sat in the library afterward, I wondered if he had been thinking of my mother. Indeed, I wondered whether or not he ever thought of her. He never mentioned her to us; and in a year I had forgotten exactly how he treated her when she had been alive.

It was not only the fate of my brother's soul that I had given thought to since my mother's death. Father had always had his toddy on Saturday afternoon with his two bachelor brothers. But there was more than one round of toddies served in the parlor on Saturday now. Throughout the early part of this afternoon I could hear the tinkle of the bell in the kitchen, and presently the houseboy would appear at the door of the parlor with a tray of ice-filled glasses.

As he entered the parlor each time, I would catch a glimpse over my book of the three men. One was usually standing, whichever one was leading the conversation. Once they were laughing heartily; and as the Negro boy came out with the tray of empty glasses, there was a smile on his face.

As their voices grew louder and merrier, my courage slackened. It was then I first put into words the thought that in my brother and father I saw something of Mr. Speed. And I knew that it was more than a taste for whiskey they had in common.

At four o'clock I heard Brother's voice mixed with those of the Benton boys outside the front door. They came into the hall, and their voices were high and excited. First one, then another would demand to be heard with: "No, listen now; let me tell you what." In a moment I heard Brother on the stairs. Then two of the Benton brothers appeared in the doorway of the library. Even the youngest, who was not a year older than I and whose name was Henry, wore long pants, and each carried a cap in hand and a linen duster over his arm. I stood up and smiled at them, and with my right forefinger I pushed the black locks which hung loosely about my shoulders behind my ears.

"We're going motoring in the Carltons' machine," Henry said.

I stammered my surprise and asked if Brother were going to ride in it. One of them said that he was upstairs getting his hunting cap, since he had no motoring cap. The older brother, Gary Benton, went back into the hall. I walked toward Henry, who was standing in the doorway.

"But does Father know you're going?" I asked.

As I tried to go through the doorway, Henry stretched his arm across it and looked at me with a critical frown on his face.

"Why don't you put up your hair?" he said.

I looked at him seriously, and I felt the heat of the blush that came over my face. I felt it on the back of my neck. I stooped with what I thought considerable grace and slid under his arm and passed into the hall. There were the other two Benton boys listening to the voices of my uncles and my father through the parlor door. I stepped between them and threw open the door. Just as I did so, Henry Benton commanded, "Elizabeth, don't do that!" And I, swinging the door open, turned and smiled at him.

I stood for a moment looking blandly at my father and my uncles. I was considering what had made me burst in upon them in this manner. It was not merely that I had perceived the opportunity of creating this little disturbance and slipping in under its noise, though I was not unaware of the advantage. I was frightened by the boys' impending adventure in the horseless carriage but surely not so much as I normally should have been at breaking into the parlor at this forbidden hour. The immediate cause could only be the attention which Henry Benton had shown me. His insinuation had been that I remained too much a little girl, and I had shown him that at any rate I was a bold, or at least a naughty, little girl.

My father was on his feet. He put his glass on the mantelpiece. And it seemed to me that from the three men came in rapid succession all possible arrangements of the words, Boys-come-in. Come-in-boys. Well-boys-come-in. Come-on-in. Boys-come-in-the-parlor. The boys went in, rather showing off their breeding and poise, I thought. The three men moved and talked clumsily before them, as the three Benton brothers went each to each of the men carefully distinguishing between my uncles' titles: doctor and colonel. I thought how awkward all of the members of my own family appeared on occasions that called for grace. Brother strode into the room with his hunting cap sideways on his head, and he announced their plans, which the tactful Bentons, uncertain of our family's prejudices regarding machines, had not mentioned. Father and my uncles had a great deal to say about who was going-to-do-the-driving, and Henry Benton without giving an answer gave a polite invitation to the men to join them. To my chagrin, both my uncles accepted with-the-greatest-of-pleasure what really had not been an invitation at all. And they persisted in accepting it even after Brother in his rudeness raised the question of room in the five-passenger vehicle.

Father said, "Sure. The more, the merrier." But he declined to go himself and declined for me Henry's invitation.

The plan was, then, as finally outlined by the oldest of the Benton brothers, that the boys should proceed to the Carltons' and that Brother should return with the driver to take our uncles out to the Carltons' house which was one of the new residences across from Centennial Park, where the excursions in the machine were to be made.

The four slender youths took their leave from the heavy men with the gold watch chains across their stomachs, and I had to shake hands with each of the Benton brothers. To each I expressed my regret that Father would not let me ride with them, emulating their poise with all my art. Henry Benton was the last, and he smiled as though he knew what I was up to. In answer to his smile I said, "Games are *so* much fun."

I stood by the window watching the four boys in the street until they were out of sight. My father and his brothers had taken their seats in silence, and I was aware of just how unwelcome I was in the room. Finally, my uncle, who had been a colonel in the Spanish War and who wore bushy blond sideburns, whistled under his breath and said, "Well, there's no doubt about it, no doubt about it."

He winked at my father, and my father looked at me and then at my uncle. Then quickly in a ridiculously overserious tone he asked, "What, sir? No doubt about what, sir?"

"Why, there's no doubt that this daughter of yours was flirting with the youngest of the Messrs. Benton."

My father looked at me and twisted his mustache and said with the same pomp that he didn't know what he'd do with me if I started that sort of thing. My two uncles threw back their heads, each giving a short laugh. My uncle the doctor took off his pince-nez and shook them at me and spoke in the same mock-serious tone of his brothers: "Young lady, if you spend your time in such pursuits you'll only bring upon yourself and upon the young men about Nashville the greatest unhappiness. I, as a bachelor, must plead the cause of the young Bentons!"

I turned to my father in indignation that approached rage.

"Father," I shouted, "there's Mr. Speed out there!"

Father sprang from his chair and quickly stepped up beside me at the window. Then, seeing the old man staggering harmlessly along the sidewalk, he said in, I thought, affected easiness: "Yes. Yes, dear."

"He's drunk," I said. My lips quivered, and I think I must have blushed at this first mention of the unmentionable to my father.

"Poor Old Speed," he said. I looked at my uncles, and they were shaking their heads, echoing my father's tone.

"What ever did happen to Speed's old-maid sister?" my uncle the doctor said.

"She's still with him," Father said.

Mr. Speed appeared soberer today than I had ever seen him. He carried no overcoat to drag on the ground, and his stagger was barely noticeable. The movement of his lips and an occasional gesture were the only evidence of intoxication. I was enraged by the irony that his good behavior on this of all days presented. Had I been a little younger I might have suspected conspiracy on the part of all men against me, but I was old enough to suspect no person's being even interested enough in me to plot against my understanding, unless it be some vague personification of life itself.

The course which I took, I thought afterward, was the proper one. I do not think that it was because I was then really conscious that when one is determined to follow some course rigidly and is blockaded one must fire furiously, if blindly, into the blockade, but rather because I was frightened and in my fear forgot all logic of attack. At any rate, I fired furiously at the three immutable creatures.

"I'm afraid of him," I broke out tearfully. I shouted at them, "He's always drunk! He's always going by our house drunk!"

My father put his arms about me, but I continued talking as I wept on his shirt front. I heard the barking sound of the machine horn out in front, and I felt my father move one hand from my back to motion my uncles to go. And as they shut the parlor door after them, I felt that I had let them escape me.

I heard the sound of the motor fading out up Church Street, and Father led me to the settee. We sat there together for a long while, and neither of us spoke until my tears had dried.

I was eager to tell him just exactly how fearful I was of Mr. Speed's coming into our house. But he only allowed me to tell him that I *was* afraid; for when I had barely suggested that much, he said that I had no business watching Mr. Speed, that I must shut my eyes to some things. "After all," he said, nonsensically I thought, "you're a young lady now." And in several curiously twisted sentences he told me that I mustn't seek things to fear in this world. He said that it was most unlikely, besides, that Speed would ever have business at our house. He punched at his left side several times, gave a prolonged belch, settled a pillow behind his head, and soon was sprawled beside me on the settee, snoring.

But Mr. Speed did come to our house, and it was in less than two months after this dreary twilight. And he came as I had feared he might come, in his most extreme state of drunkenness and at a time when I was alone in the house with the maid Lucy. But I had done everything that a little girl, now fourteen, could do in preparation for such an eventuality. And the sort of preparation that I had been able to make, the clearance of all restraints and inhibitions regarding Mr. Speed in my own mind and in my relationship with my world, had necessarily, I think, given me a maturer view of my own limited experiences; though, too, my very age must be held to account for a natural step toward maturity.

In the two months following the day that I first faced Mr. Speed's existence with my father, I came to look at every phase of our household life with a more direct and more discerning eye. As I wandered about that shadowy and somehow brutally elegant house, sometimes now with a knot of hair on the back of my head, events and customs there that had repelled or frightened me I gave the closest scrutiny. In the daytime I ventured into such forbidden spots as the servants' and the men's bathrooms. The filth of the former became a matter of interest in the study of the servants' natures, instead of the object of ineffable disgust. The other became a fascinating place of wet shaving brushes and leather straps and red rubber bags.

There was an anonymous little Negro boy that I had seen many mornings hurrying away from our back door with a pail. I discovered that he was toting buttermilk from our icebox with the permission of our cook. And I sprang at him from behind a corner of the house one morning and scared him so that he spilled the buttermilk and never returned for more.

Another morning I heard the cook threatening to slash the house-boy with her butcher knife, and I made myself burst in upon them; and before Lucy and the houseboy I told her that if she didn't leave our house that day, I'd call my father and, hardly knowing what I was saying, I added, "And the police." She was gone, and Lucy had got a new cook before dinnertime. In this way, from day to day, I began to take my place as mistress in our motherless household.

I could no longer be frightened by my brother with a mention of runaway horses. And instead of terrorized I felt only depressed by his long and curious arguments with my father. I was depressed by the number of the subjects to and from which they oscillated. The world as a whole still seemed unconscionably larger than anything I could comprehend. But I had learned not to concern myself with so general and so unreal a problem until I had cleared up more par-ticular and real ones.

It was during these two months that I noticed the difference between the manner in which my father spoke before my uncles of Mr. Speed when he passed and that in which he spoke of him before my brother. To my brother it was the condemning, "There goes Old Speed, again." But to my uncles it was, "There goes Old Speed," with the sympathetic addition, "the rascal." Though my father and his brothers obviously found me more agreeable because a pleasant spirit had replaced my old timidity, they yet considered me a child; and my father little dreamed that I discerned such traits in his character, or that I understood, if I even listened to, their anecdotes and their long funny stories, and it was an interest in the peculiar choice of subject and in the way that the men told their stories.

When Mr. Speed came, I was accustomed to thinking that there was something in my brother's and in my father's natures that was fully in sympathy with the very brutality of his drunkenness. And I knew that they would not consider my hatred for him and for that part of him which I saw in them. For that alone I was glad that it was on a Thursday afternoon, when I was in the house alone with Lucy, that one of the heavy sort of rains that come toward the end of May drove Mr. Speed onto our porch for shelter.

Otherwise I wished for nothing more than the sound of my father's strong voice when I stood trembling before the parlor window and watched Mr. Speed stumbling across our lawn in the flaying rain. I only knew to keep at the window and make sure that he was actually coming into our house. I believe that he was drunker than I had ever before seen him, and his usual ire seemed to be doubled by the raging weather.

Despite the aid of his cane, Mr. Speed fell to his knees once in the muddy sod. He remained kneeling there for a time with his face cast in resignation. Then once more he struggled to his feet in the rain. Though I was ever conscious that I was entering into young womanhood at that age, I can only think of myself as a child at that moment; for it was the helpless fear of a child that I felt as I watched Mr. Speed approaching our door. Perhaps it was the last time I ever experienced the inconsolable desperation of childhood.

Next, I could hear his cane beating on the boarding of the little porch before our door. I knew that he must be walking up and down in that little shelter. Then I heard Lucy's exasperated voice as she came down the steps. I knew immediately, what she confirmed afterward, that she thought it Brother, eager to get into the house, beating on the door.

I, aghast, opened the parlor door just as she pulled open the great front door. Her black skin ashened as she beheld Mr. Speed—his face crimson, his eyes bleary, and his gray clothes dripping water. He shuffled through the doorway and threw his stick on the hall floor. Between his oaths and profanities he shouted over and over in his broken, old man's voice, "Nigger, nigger." I could understand little of his rapid and slurred speech, but I knew his rage went round and round a man in the rain and the shelter of a neighbor's house.

Lucy fled up the long flight of steps and was on her knees at the head of the stair, in the dark upstairs hall, begging me to come up to her. I only stared, as though paralyzed and dumb, at him and then up the steps at her. The front door was still open; the hall was half in light; and I could hear the rain on the roof of the porch and the wind blowing the trees which were in full green foliage.

At last I moved. I acted. I slid along the wall past the hat rack and the console table, my eyes on the drunken old man who was swearing up the steps at Lucy. I reached for the telephone; and when I had rung for central, I called for the police station. I knew what they did with Mr. Speed downtown, and I knew with what I had threatened the cook. There was a part of me that was crouching on the top step with Lucy, vaguely longing to hide my face from this in my own mother's bosom. But there was another part which was making me deal with Mr. Speed, however wrongly, myself. Innocently I asked the voice to send "the Black Maria" to our house number on Church Street.

Mr. Speed had heard me make the call. He was still and silent for just one moment. Then he broke into tears, and he seemed to be chanting his words. He repeated the word "child" so many times that I felt I had acted wrongly, with courage but without wisdom. I saw myself as a little beast adding to the injury that what was bestial in man had already done him. He picked up his cane and didn't seem to be talking either to Lucy or to me, but to the cane. He started out the doorway, and I heard Lucy come running down the stairs. She fairly glided around the newel post and past me to the telephone. She wasn't certain that I had made the call. She asked if I had called my father. I simply told her that I had not.

As she rang the telephone, I watched Mr. Speed cross the porch.

He turned to us at the edge of the porch and shouted one more oath. But his foot touched the wet porch step, and he slid and fell unconscious on the steps.

He lay there with the rain beating upon him and with Lucy and myself watching him, motionless from our place by the telephone. I was frightened by the thought of the cruelty which I found I was capable of, a cruelty which seemed inextricably mixed with what I had called courage. I looked at him lying out there in the rain and despised and pitied him at the same time, and I was afraid to go minister to the helpless old Mr. Speed.

Lucy had her arms about me and kept them there until two gray horses pulling their black coach had galloped up in front of the house and two policemen had carried the limp body through the rain to the dreadful vehicle.

Just as the policemen closed the doors in the back of the coach, my father rode up in a closed cab. He jumped out and stood in the rain for several minutes arguing with the policemen. Lucy and I went to the door and waited for him to come in. When he came, he looked at neither of us. He walked past us saying only, "I regret that the bluecoats were called." And he went into the parlor and closed the door.

I never discussed the events of that day with my father, and I never saw Mr. Speed again. But, despite the surge of pity I felt for the old man on our porch that afternoon, my hatred and fear of what he had stood for in my eyes has never left me. And since the day that I watched myself say "away" in the mirror, not a week has passed but that he has been brought to my mind by one thing or another. It was only the other night that I dreamed I was a little girl on Church Street again and that there was a drunk horse in our yard.

The Fancy Woman

He wanted no more of her drunken palaver. Well, sure enough. Sure enough. And he had sent her from the table like she were one of his half-grown brats. *He,* who couldn't have walked straight around to her place if she *hadn't* been lady enough to leave, sent *her* from the table like either of the half-grown kids he was so mortally fond of. At least she hadn't turned over three glasses of perfectly good stuff during one meal. Talk about vulgar. She fell across the counterpane and slept.

She awoke in the dark room with his big hands busying with her clothes, and she flung her arms about his neck. And she said, "You marvelous, fattish thing."

His hoarse voice was in her ear. He chuckled deep in his throat. And she whispered: "You're an old thingamajig, George."

Her eyes opened in the midday sunlight, and she felt the back of her neck soaking in her own sweat on the counterpane. She saw the unfamiliar cracks in the ceiling and said, "Whose room's this?" She looked at the walnut dresser and the wardrobe and said, "Oh, the kids' room"; and as she laughed, saliva bubbled up and fell back on her upper lip. She shoved herself up with her elbows and was sitting in the middle of the bed. Damn him! Her blue silk dress was twisted about her body; a thin army blanket covered her lower half. "He didn't put that over me, I know damn well. One of those tight-mouth niggers sneaking around!" She sprang from the bed, slipped her bare feet into her white pumps, and stepped toward the door. Oh, God! She beheld herself in the dresser mirror.

She marched to the dresser with her eyes closed and felt about for a brush. There was nothing but a tray of collar buttons there. She seized a handful of them and screamed as she threw them to bounce off the mirror, "This ain't my room!" She ran her fingers through her hair and went out into the hall and into her room next door. She rushed to her little dressing table. There was the bottle half full. She poured out a jigger and drank it. Clearing her throat as she sat down, she said, "Oh, what's the matter with me?" She combed her hair back quite carefully, then pulled the yellow strands out of the amber comb; and when she had greased and wiped her face and had rouged her lips and the upper portions of her cheeks, she smiled at herself in the mirror. She looked flirtatiously at the bottle but shook her head and stood up and looked about her. It was a long, narrow room with two windows at the end. A cubbyhole beside the kids' room! But it *was* a canopied bed with yellow ruffles that matched the ruffles on the dressing table and on the window curtains, as he had promised. She went over and turned back the covers and mussed the pillow. It might not have been the niggers! She poured another drink and went down to get some nice, hot lunch.

The breakfast room was one step lower than the rest of the house; and though it was mostly windows the venetian blinds were lowered all round. She sat at a big circular table. "I can't make out about this room," she said to the Negress who was refilling her coffee cup. She lit a cigarette and questioned the servant, "What's the crazy table made out of, Amelia?"

"It makes a good table, 'spite all."

"It sure enough does make a strong table, Amelia." She kicked the toe of her shoe against the brick column which supported the table top. "But what *was* it, old dearie?" She smiled invitingly at the servant and pushed her plate away and pulled her coffee in front of her. She stared at the straight scar on Amelia's wrist as Amelia reached for the plate. What big black buck had put it there? A lot these niggers had to complain of in her when every one of them was all dosed up.

Amelia said that the base of the table was the old cistern. "He brung that top out f'om Memphis when he done the po'ch up this way for breakfas' and lunch."

The woman looked about the room, thinking, "I'll get some confab out of this one yet." And she exclaimed, "Oh, and that's the old bucket to it over there, then, with the vines on it, Amelia!"

"No'm," Amelia said. Then after a few seconds she added, "They brung that out f'om Memphis and put it there like it was it."

"Yeah . . . yeah . . . go on, Amelia. I'm odd about old-fashioned things. I've got a lot of interest in any antiques."

"That's all."

The little Negro woman started away with the coffee pot and the plate, dragging the soft soles of her carpet slippers over the brick floor. At the door she lingered, and, too cunning to leave room for a charge of impudence, she added to the hateful "That's all" a mutter, "Miss Josephine."

And when the door closed, Miss Josephine said under her breath, "If that black bitch hadn't stuck that on, there wouldn't be another chance for her to sneak around with any army blankets."

George, mounted on a big sorrel and leading a small dapple-gray horse, rode onto the lawn outside the breakfast room. Josephine saw him through the chinks of the blinds looking up toward her bed-room window. "Not for me," she said to herself. "He'll not get *me* on one of those animals." She swallowed the last of her coffee on her feet and then turned and stomped across the bricks to the step-up into the hallway. There she heard him calling:

"Josie! Josie! Get out-a that bed!"

Josephine ran through the long hall cursing the rugs that slipped under her feet. She ran the length of the hall looking back now and again as though the voice were a beast at her heels. In the front parlor she pulled up the glass and took a book from the bookcase nearest the door. It was a red book, and she hurled herself into George's chair and opened to page sixty-five:

> *nity, with anxiety, and with pity. Hamilcar was rubbing him-self against my legs, wild with delight.*

She closed the book on her thumb and listened to George's bellow-ing: "I'm coming after you!"

She could hear the sound of the hoofs as George led the horses around the side of the house. George's figure moved outside the front windows. Through the heavy lace curtains she could see him tying the horses to the branch of a tree. She heard him on the veranda and then in the hall. Damn him! God damn him, he couldn't make her ride! She opened to page sixty-five again as George passed the doorway. But he saw her, and he stopped. He stared at her for a moment, and she looked at him over the book. She rested her head on the back of the chair and put a pouty look on her face. Her eyes were fixed on his hairy arms, on the little bulk in his rolled sleeves, then on the white shirt over his chest, on the brown jodhpurs, and finally on the blackened leather of his shoes set well apart on the polished hall floor. Her eyelids were heavy, and she longed for a drink of the three-dollar whiskey that was on her dressing table.

He crossed the carpet with a smile, showing, she guessed, his delight at finding her. She smiled. He snatched the book from her hands and read the title on the red cover. His head went back, and as he laughed she watched through the open collar the tendons of his throat tighten and take on a purplish hue.

At Josephine's feet was a needlepoint footstool on which was worked a rust-colored American eagle against a background of green. George tossed the red book onto the stool and pulled Josephine from her chair. He was still laughing, and she wishing for a drink.

"Come along, come along," he said. "We've only four days left, and you'll want to tell your friend-girls you learned to ride."

She jerked one hand loose from his hold and slapped his hard cheek. She screamed, "Friend-girl? You never heard me say friend-girl. What black nigger do you think you're talking down to?" She was looking at him now through a mist of tears and presently she broke out into furious weeping.

His laughter went on as he pushed her across the room and into the hall, but he was saying: "Boochie, Boochie. Wotsa matter? Now, old girl, old girl. Listen: You'll want to tell your girl friends, your *girl friends,* that you learned to ride."

That was how George was! He would never try to persuade her. He would never pay any attention to what she said. He wouldn't argue with her. He wouldn't mince words! The few times she had seen him before this week there had been no chance to talk much. When they were driving down from Memphis, Saturday, she had gone through the story about how she was tricked by Jackie Briton and married Lon and how he had left her right away and the pathetic part about the baby she never even saw in the hospital. And at the end of it, she realized that George had been smiling at her as he probably would at one of his half-grown kids. When she stopped the story quickly, he had reached over and patted her hand (but still smiling) and right away had started talking about the sickly-looking tomato crops along the highway. After lunch on Saturday when she'd tried to talk to him again and he had deliberately commenced to play the victrola, she said, "Why won't you take me seriously?" But he had, of course, just laughed at her and kissed her; and they had already begun drinking then. She couldn't resist him (more than other men, he could just drive her wild), and he would hardly look at her, never had. He either laughed at her or cursed her or, of course, at night would pet her. He hadn't hit her.

He was shoving her along the hall, and she had to make herself stop crying.

"Please, George."

"Come on, now! That-a girl!"

"Honest to God, George. I tell you to let up, stop it."

"Come on. *Up* the steps. *Up! Up!*"

She let herself become limp in his arms but held with one hand to the banister. Then he grabbed her. He swung her up into his arms and carried her up the stairs which curved around the back end of the hall, over the doorway to the breakfast room. Once in his arms, she didn't move a muscle, for she thought, "I'm no featherweight, and we'll both go tumbling down these steps and break our skulls." At the top he fairly slammed her to her feet and, panting for breath, he said without a trace of softness: "Now, put on those pants, Josie, and I'll wait for you in the yard." He turned to the stair, and she heard what he said to himself: "I'll sober her. I'll sober her up."

As he pushed Josephine onto the white, jumpy beast he must have caught a whiff of her breath. She knew that he must have! He was holding the reins close to the bit while she tried to arrange herself in the flat saddle. Then he grasped her ankle and asked her, "Did you take a drink upstairs?" She laughed, leaned forward in her saddle, and whispered: "Two. Two jiggers."

She wasn't afraid of the horse now, but she was dizzy. "George, let me down," she said faintly. She felt the horse's flesh quiver under her leg and looked over her shoulder when it stomped one rear hoof.

George said, "Confound it, I'll sober you." He handed her the reins, stepped back, and slapped the horse on the flank. "Hold on!" he called, and her horse cantered across the lawn.

Josie was clutching the leather straps tightly, and her face was almost in the horse's mane. "I could kill him for this," she said, slicing out the words with a sharp breath. God damn it! The horse was galloping along a dirt road. She saw nothing but the yellow dirt. The hoofs rumbled over a three-plank wooden bridge, and she heard George's horse on the other side of her. She turned her face that way and saw George through the hair that hung over her eyes. He was smiling. "You dirty bastard," she said.

He said, "You're doin' all right. Sit up, and I'll give you some pointers." She turned her face to the other side. Now she wished to God she hadn't taken those two jiggers. George's horse quickened his speed and hers followed. George's slowed and hers did likewise. She could feel George's grin in the back of her neck. She had no control over her horse.

They were galloping in the hot sunlight, and Josie stole glances at the flat fields of strawberries. "If you weren't drunk, you'd fall off," George shouted. Now they were passing a cotton field. ("The back of my neck'll be blistered," she thought. "Where was it I picked strawberries once? At Dyersburg when I was ten, visiting some God-forsaken relations.") The horses turned off the road into wooded bottom land. The way now was shaded by giant trees, but here and there the sun shone between foliage. Once after riding thirty feet in shadow, watching dumbly the cool blue-green underbrush, Josie felt the sun suddenly on her neck. Her stomach churned, and the eggs and coffee from breakfast burned her throat as it all gushed forth, splattering her pants leg and the brown saddle and the horse's side. She looked over the horse at George.

But there was no remorse, no compassion, and no humor in George's face. He gazed straight ahead and urged on his horse.

All at once the horses turned to the right. Josie howled. She saw her right foot flying through the air, and after the thud of the fall and the flashes of light and darkness she lay on her back in the dirt and watched George as he approached on foot, leading the two horses.

"Old girl . . ." he said.

"You get the hell away from me!"

"Are you hurt?" He kneeled beside her, so close to her that she could smell his sweaty shirt.

Josie jumped to her feet and walked in the direction from which they had ridden. In a moment George galloped past her, leading the gray horse and laughing like the son-of-a-bitch he was.

"Last night he sent me upstairs! But this is more! I'm not gonna have it." She walked through the woods, her lips moving as she talked to herself. "He wants no more of my drunken palaver!" Well, he was going to get no more of her drunken anything now. She had had her fill of him and everybody else and was going to look out for her own little sweet self from now on.

That was her trouble, she knew. She'd never made a good thing of people. "That's why things are like they are now," she said. "I've never made a good thing out of anybody." But it was real lucky that she realized it now, just exactly when she had, for it was certain that there had never been one whom more could be made out of than George. "God damn him," she said, thinking still of his riding by her like that. "Whatever it was I liked about him is gone now."

She gazed up into the foliage and branches of the trees, and the great size of the trees made her feel real small, and real young. If Jackie or Lon had been different she might have learned things when she was young. "But they were both of 'em easygoin' and just slipped out on me." They *were* sweet. She'd never forget how sweet Jackie always was. "Just plain sweet." She made a quick gesture with her right hand: "If only they didn't all get such a hold on me!"

But she was through with George. This time *she* got through first. He was no different from a floorwalker. He had more sense. "He's educated, and the money he must have!" George had more sense than a floorwalker, but he didn't have any manners. He treated her just like the floorwalker at Jobe's had that last week she was there. But George was worth getting around. She would find out what it was. She wouldn't take another drink. She'd find out what was wrong inside him, for there's something wrong inside everybody, and somehow she'd get a hold of him. Little Josephine would make a place for herself at last. She just wouldn't think about him as a man.

At the edge of the wood she turned onto the road, and across the fields she could see his house. That house was just simply as old and big as they come, and wasn't a cheap house. "I wonder if he looked after getting it fixed over and remodeled." Not likely. She kept looking at the whitewashed brick and shaking her head. "No, by Jesus," she exclaimed. "*She* did it!" George's wife. All of her questions seemed to have been answered. The wife had left him for his meanness, and he was lonesome. There was, then, a place to be filled. She began to run along the road. "God, I feel like somebody might step in before I get there." She laughed, but then the heat seemed to strike her all at once. Her stomach drew in. She vomited in the ditch, and, by God, it was as dry as cornflakes!

She sat still in the grass under a little maple tree beside the road, resting her forehead on her drawn-up knees. All between Josie and her new life seemed to be the walk through the sun in these smelly, dirty clothes. Across the fields and in the house was a canopied bed and a glorious new life, but she daren't go into the sun. She would pass out cold. "People kick off in weather like this!"

Presently Josie heard the voices of niggers up the road. She wouldn't look up, she decided. She'd let them pass, without looking up. They drew near to her and she made out the voices of a man and a child. The man said, "Hursh!" and the voices ceased. There was only the sound of their feet padding along the dusty road.

The noise of the padding grew fainter. Josie looked up and saw that the two had cut across the fields toward George's house. Already she could hear the niggers mouthing it about the kitchen. That little yellow Henry would look at her over his shoulder as he went through the swinging door at dinner tonight. If she heard them grumbling once more, as she did Monday, calling her "she," Josie decided that she was going to come right out and ask Amelia about the scar. Right before George. But the niggers were the least of her worries now.

All afternoon she lay on the bed, waking now and then to look at the bottle of whiskey on the dressing table and to wonder where George had gone. She didn't know whether it had been George or the field nigger who sent Henry after her in the truck. Once she dreamed that she saw George at the head of the stairs telling Amelia how he had sobered Miss Josephine up. When she awoke that time she said, "I ought to get up and get myself good and plastered before George comes back from wherever he is." But she slept again and dreamed this time that she was working at the hat sale at Jobe's and that she had to wait on Amelia who picked up a white turban and asked Josie to model it for her. And the dream ended with Amelia telling Josie how pretty she was and how much she liked her.

Josie had taken another hot bath (to ward off soreness from the horseback ride) and was in the sitting room, which everybody called the back parlor, playing the electric victrola and feeling just prime when George came in. She let him go through the hall and upstairs to dress up for dinner without calling to him. She chuckled to herself and rocked to the time of the music.

George came with a real mint julep in each hand. His hair was wet and slicked down over his head; the part, low on the left side, was straight and white. His cheeks were shaven and were pink with new sunburn. He said, "I had myself the time of my life this afternoon."

Josie smiled and said that she was glad he had enjoyed himself. George raised his eyebrows and cocked his head to one side. She kept on smiling at him, and made no movement toward taking the drink that he held out to her.

George set the glass on the little candle stand near her chair and switched off the victrola.

"George, I was listening . . ."

"Ah, now," he said, "I want to tell you about the cockfight."

"Let me finish listening to that piece, George."

George dropped down into an armchair and put his feet on a stool. His pants and shirt were white, and he wore a blue polka dot tie.

"You're nice and clean," she said, as though she had forgotten the victrola.

"Immaculate!" There was a mischievous grin on his face, and he leaned over one arm of the chair and pulled the victrola plug from the floor socket. Josie reached out and took the glass from the candle stand, stirred it slightly with a shoot of mint, and began to sip it. She thought, "I *have* to take it when he acts this way."

At the dinner table George said, "You're in better shape tonight. You look better. Why don't you go easy on the bottle tonight?"

She looked at him between the two candles burning in the center of the round table. "I didn't ask you for that mint julep, I don't think."

"And you ain't gettin' any more," he said, winking at her as he lifted his fork to his lips with his left hand. This, she felt, was a gesture to show his contempt for her. Perhaps he thought she didn't know the difference, which, of course, was even more contemptuous.

"Nice manners," she said. He made no answer, but at least he could be sure that she had recognized the insult. She took a drink of water, her little finger extended slightly from the glass, and over the glass she said, "You didn't finish about the niggers having a fight after the chickens did."

"Oh, yes." He arranged his knife and fork neatly on his plate. "The two nigs commenced to watch each other before their chickens had done scrapping. And when the big rooster gave his last hop and keeled over, Ira Blakemoor jumped over the two birds onto Jimmy's shoulders. Jimmy just whirled round and round till he threw Ira the way the little mare did you this morning." George looked directly into Josie's eyes between the candles, defiantly unashamed to mention that event, and he smiled with defiance and yet with weariness. "Ira got up and the two walked around looking at each other like two black games before a fight." Josie kept her eyes on George while the story, she felt, went on and on and on.

That yellow nigger Henry was paused at the swinging door, looking over his shoulder toward her. She turned her head and glared at him. He was not even hiding this action from George, who was going on and on about the niggers' fighting. This Henry was the worst hypocrite of all. He who had slashed Amelia's wrist (it was surely Henry who had done it), and probably had raped his own children, the way niggers do, was denouncing her right out like this. Her heart pounded when he kept looking, and then George's story stopped.

A bright light flashed across Henry's face and about the room which was lit by only the two candles. Josie swung her head around, and through the front window she saw the lights of automobiles that were moving through the yard. She looked at George, and his face said absolutely nothing for itself. He moistened his lips with his tongue.

"Guests," he said, raising his eyebrows. And Josie felt that in that moment she had seen the strongest floorwalker weaken. George had scorned and laughed at everybody and every situation. But now he was ashamed. He was ashamed of her. On her behavior would depend his comfort. She was cold sober and would be *up* to whatever showed itself. It was her real opportunity.

From the back of the house a horn sounded, and above other voices a woman's voice rose, calling "Whoohoo!" George stood up and bowed to her beautifully, like something she had never seen, and said, "You'll excuse me?" Then he went out through the kitchen without saying "scat" about what she should do.

She drummed on the table with her fingers and listened to George's greetings to his friends. She heard him say, "Welcome, Billy, and welcome, Mrs. Billy!" They were the only names she recognized. It was likely the Billy Colton she'd met with George one night.

Then these *were* Memphis society people. Here for the night, at least! She looked down at her yellow linen dress and straightened the lapels at the neck. She thought of the women with their lovely profiles and soft skin and natural-colored hair. What if she had waited on one of them once at Jobe's or, worse still, in the old days at Burnstein's? But they had probably never been to one of those cheap stores. What if they stayed but refused to talk to her, or even to meet her? They could be mean bitches, all of them, for all their soft hands and shaved legs. Her hand trembled as she rang the little glass bell for coffee.

She rang it, and no one answered. She rang it again, hard, but now she could hear Henry coming through the breakfast room to the hall, bumping the guests' baggage against the doorway. Neither Amelia nor Mammy, who cooked the evening meal, would leave the kitchen during dinner, Josie knew. "I'd honestly like to go out in the kitchen and ask 'em for a cup of coffee and tell 'em just how scared I am." But too well she could imagine their contemptuous, accusing gaze. "If only I could get something on them! Even catch 'em toting food just once! That Mammy's likely killed enough niggers in her time to fill Jobe's basement."

Josie was even afraid to light a cigarette. She went over to the side window and looked out into the yard; she could see the lights from the automobiles shining on the green leaves and on the white fence around the house lot.

And she was standing thus when she heard the voices and the footsteps in the long hall. She had only just turned around when George stood in the wide doorway with the men and women from Memphis. He was pronouncing her name first: "Miss Carlson, this is Mr. Roberts, Mrs. Roberts, Mr. Jackson, Mrs. Jackson, and Mr. and Mrs. Colton."

Josie stared at the group, not trying to catch the names. She could think only, "They're old. The women are old and plump. George's wife is old!" She stared at them, and when the name Colton struck her ear, she said automatically and without placing his face, "I know Billy."

George said in the same tone in which he had said, "You'll excuse me?" "Josie, will you take the ladies upstairs to freshen up while the men and I get some drinks started? We'll settle the rooming question later." George was the great floorwalker whose wife was old and who had now shown his pride to Josie Carlson. He had shown his shame. Finally he had decided on a course and was following it, but he had given 'way his sore spots. Only God knew what he had told his friends. Josie said to herself, "It's plain he don't want 'em to know who I am."

As Josie ascended the stair, followed by those she had already privately termed the "three matrons," she watched George and the three other men go down the hall to the breakfast room. The sight of their white linen suits and brown and white shoes in the bright hall seemed to make the climb a soaring. At the top of the stairs she stopped and let the three women pass ahead of her. She eyed the costume of each as they passed. One wore a tailored seersucker dress. Another wore a navy-blue linen dress with white collar and cuffs, and the third wore a striped linen skirt and silk blouse. On the wrist of this last was a bracelet from which hung a tiny silver dog, a lock, a gold heart.

Josie observed their grooming: their fingernails, their lipstick, their hair in tight curls. There was gray in the hair of one, but not one, Josie decided now, was much past forty. Their figures were neatly corseted, and Josie felt that the little saggings under their chins and under the eyes of the one in the navy blue made them more charming; were, indeed, almost a part of their smartness. She wanted to think of herself as like them. They were, she realized, at least ten years older than she, but in ten years, beginning tonight, she might become one of them.

"Just go in my room there," she said. She pointed to the open door and started down the steps, thinking that this was the beginning of the new life and thinking of the men downstairs fixing the drinks. And then she thought of the bottle of whiskey on her dressing table in the room where the matrons had gone!

"Oh, hell," she cursed under her breath. She had turned to go up the two steps again when she heard the men's voices below. She heard her own name being pronounced carefully: "Josie Carlson." She went down five or six steps on tiptoe and stood still to listen to the voices that came from the breakfast room.

"You said to come any time, George, and never mentioned having this thing down here."

George laughed. "Afraid of what the girls will say when you get home? I can hear them. 'In Beatrice's own lovely house,'" he mocked.

"Well, fellow, you've a shock coming, too," one of them said. "Beatrice has sent your boys down to Memphis for a month with you. They say she has a beau."

"And in the morning," one said, "your sister Kate's sending them down here. She asked us to bring them, and then decided to keep them one night herself."

"You'd better get *her* out, George."

George laughed. Josie could hear them dropping ice into glasses.

"We'll take her back at dawn if you say."

"What would the girls say to that?" He laughed at them as he laughed at Josie.

"The girls are gonna be decent to her. They agreed in the yard."

"Female curiosity?" George said.

"Your boys'll have curiosity, too. Jock's seventeen."

Even the clank of the ice stopped. "You'll every one of you please to remember," George said slowly, "that Josie's a friend of yours and that she met the girls here by appointment."

Josie tiptoed down the stairs, descending, she felt, once more into her old world. "He'll slick me some way if he has to for his kids, I think." She turned into the dining room at the foot of the stairs. The candles were burning low, and she went and stood by the open window and listened to the counterpoint of the crickets and the frogs while Henry, who had looked over his shoulder at the car lights, rattled the silver and china and went about clearing the table.

Presently, George had come and put his hand on her shoulder. When she turned around she saw him smiling and holding two drinks in his left hand. He leaned his face close to hers and said, "I'm looking for the tears."

Josie said, "There aren't any to find, fellow"; and she thought it odd, really odd, that he had expected her to cry. But he was probably poking fun at her again.

She took one of the drinks and clinked glasses with George. To herself she said, "I bet they don't act any better than I do after they've got a few under their belts." At least she showed her true colors! "I'll keep my eyes open for their true ones."

If only they'd play the victrola instead of the radio. She liked the victrola so much better. She could play "Louisville Lady" over and over. But, *no*. They all wanted to switch the radio about. To get Cincinnati and Los Angeles and Bennie this and Johnny that. If they liked a piece, why did they care who played it? For God's sake! They wouldn't dance at first, either, and when she first got George to dance with her, they sat smiling at each other, grinning. They had played cards, too, but poker didn't go so well after George slugged them all with that third round of his three-dollar-whiskey drinks. Right then she had begun to watch out to see who slapped whose knee.

She asked George to dance because she so liked to dance with him, and she wasn't going to care about what the others did any more, she decided. But finally when two of them had started dancing off in the corner of the room, she looked about the sitting room for the other four and saw that Billy Colton had disappeared not with his own wife but with that guy Jackson's. And Josie threw herself down into the armchair and laughed aloud, so hard and loud that everybody begged her to tell what was funny. But she stopped suddenly and gave them as mean a look as she could manage and said, "Nothin'. Let's dance some more, George."

But George said that he must tell Henry to fix more drinks, and he went out and left her by the radio with Roberts and Mrs. Colton. She looked at Mrs. Colton and thought, "Honey, you don't seem to be grieving about Billy."

Then Roberts said to Josie, "George says you're from Vicksburg."

"I was raised there," she said, wondering why George hadn't told her whatever he'd told them.

"He says you live there now."

Mrs. Colton, who wore the navy blue and was the fattest of the three matrons, stood up and said to Roberts, "Let's dance in the hall where there are fewer rugs." And she gave a kindly smile to Josie, and Josie spit out a "Thanks." The couple skipped into the hall, laughing, and Josie sat alone by the radio wishing she could play the victrola and wishing that George would come and kiss her on the back of her neck. "And I'd slap him if he did," she said. Now and again she would cut her eye around to watch Jackson and Mrs. Roberts dancing. They were at the far end of the room and were dancing slowly. They kept rubbing against the heavy blue drapery at the window and they were talking into each other's ears.

But the next piece that came over the radio was a hot one, and Jackson led Mrs. Roberts to the center of the room and whirled her round and round, and the trinkets at her wrist tinkled like little bells. Josie lit a cigarette and watched them dance. She realized then that Jackson was showing off for her sake.

When George came with a tray of drinks he said, "Josie, move the victrola," but Josie sat still and glared at him as if to say, "What on earth are you talking about? Are you nuts?" He set the tray across her lap and turned and picked up the little victrola and set it on the floor.

"Oh, good God!" cried Josie in surprise and delight. "It's a portable."

George, taking the tray from her, said, "It's not for you to port off, old girl."

The couple in the center of the room had stopped their whirling and had followed George. "We like to dance, but there are better things," Jackson was saying.

Mrs. Roberts flopped down on the broad arm of Josie's chair and took a drink from George. Josie could only watch the trinkets on the bracelet, one of which she saw was a little gold book. George was telling Jackson about the cockfight again, and Mrs. Roberts leaned over and talked to Josie. She tried to tell her how the room seemed to be whirling around. They both giggled, and Josie thought, "Maybe we'll get to be good friends, and she'll stop pretending to be so swell." But she couldn't think of anything to say to her, partly because she just never did have anything to say to women and partly because Jackson, who was not at all a bad-looking little man, was sending glances her way.

It didn't seem like more than twenty minutes or half an hour more before George had got to that point where he ordered her around and couldn't keep on his own feet. He finally lay down on the couch in the front parlor, and as she and Mrs. Roberts went up the stairs with their arms about each other's waists, he called out something that made Mrs. Roberts giggle. But Josie knew that little Josephine was at the point where she could say nothing straight, so she didn't even ask to get the portable victrola. She just cursed under her breath.

The daylight was beginning to appear at the windows of Josie's narrow little room when waking suddenly she sat up in bed and then flopped down again and jerked the sheet about her. "That little sucker come up here," she grumbled, "and cleared out, but where was the little sucker's wife?" Who was with George, by damn, all night? After a while she said, "They're none of 'em any better than the niggers. I knew they couldn't be. Nobody is. By God, nobody's better than I am. Nobody can say anything to me." Every-

one would like to live as free as she did! There was no such thing
as . . . There was no such thing as what the niggers and the whites
liked to pretend they were. She was going to let up, and do things in
secret. Try to look like an angel. It wouldn't be as hard since there
was no such thing.

It was all like a scene from a color movie, like one of the musicals.
It was the prettiest scene ever. And they were like two of those
lovely wax models in the boys' department at Jobe's. Like two of
those models, with the tan skin and blond hair, come to life! And to
see them in their white shorts spring about the green grass under the
blue, blue sky, hitting the little feather thing over the high net, made
Josie go weak all over. She went down on her knees and rested her
elbows on the window sill and watched them springing about before the people from Memphis; these were grouped under a tree,
sitting in deck chairs and on the grass. George stood at the net like a
floorwalker charmed by his wax manikins which had come to life.

It had been George's cries of "Outside, outside!" and the jeers and
applause of the six spectators that awakened Josie. She ran to the
window in her pajamas, and when she saw the white markings on
the grass and the net that had sprung up there overnight, she
thought that this might be a dream. But the voices of George and
Mrs. Roberts and Phil Jackson were completely real, and the movements of the boys' bodies were too marvelous to be doubted.

She sank to her knees, conscious of the soreness which her horseback ride had left. She thought of her clumsy self in the dusty road
as she gazed down at the graceful boys on the lawn and said, "Why,
they're actually pretty. Too pretty." She was certain of one thing:
she didn't want any of their snobbishness. She wouldn't have it from
his two kids.

One boy's racket missed the feather thing. George shouted,
"Game!" The group under the tree applauded, and the men pushed

themselves up from their seats to come out into the sunlight and pat the naked backs of the boys.

When the boys came close together, Josie saw that one was six inches taller than the other. "Why, that one's grown!" she thought. The two of them walked toward the house, the taller one walking with the shorter's neck in the crook of his elbow. George called to them, "You boys get dressed for lunch." He ordered them about just as he did her, but they went off smiling.

Josie walked in her bare feet into the little closet-like bathroom which adjoined her room. She looked at herself in the mirror there and said, "I've never dreaded anything so much in all my life before. You can't depend on what kids'll say." But were they kids? For all their prettiness, they were too big to be called kids. And nobody's as damn smutty as a smart-alecky shaver.

Josephine bathed in the little, square, maroon bathtub. There were maroon and white checkered tile steps built up around the tub, so that it gave the effect of being sunken. After her bath, she stood on the steps and powdered her whole soft body. Every garment which she put on was absolutely fresh. She went to her closet and took out her new white silk dress and slipped it over her head. She put on white shoes first, but, deciding she looked too much like a trained nurse, she changed to her tan pumps. Josie knew what young shavers thought about nurses.

She combed her yellow hair till it lay close to her head, and put on rouge and lipstick. Someone knocked at the bedroom door. "Yeah," she called. No answer came, so she went to the door and opened it. In the hall stood one of the boys. It was the little one.

He didn't look at her; he looked past her. And his eyes *were* as shiny and cold as those on a wax dummy!

"Miss Carlson, my dad says to tell you that lunch is ready. And I'm Buddy."

"Thanks." She didn't know what the hell else she should say.

"Tell him, all right," she said. She stepped back into her room and shut the door.

Josie paced the room for several minutes. "He didn't so much as look at me." She was getting hot, and she went and put her face to the window. The people from Memphis had come indoors, and the sun shone on the brownish green grass and on the still trees. "It's a scorcher," she said. She walked the length of the room again and opened the door. Buddy was still there. Standing there in white, his shirt open at the collar, and his white pants, long pants. He was leaning against the banister.

"Ready?" he said, smiling.

As they went down the steps together, he said, "It's nice that you're here. We didn't know it till just a few minutes ago." He was a Yankee kid, lived with his mother somewhere, and rolled his *r*'s, and spoke as though there was a lot of meaning behind what he said. She gave him a quick glance to see what he meant by that last remark. He smiled, and this time looked right into her eyes.

After lunch, which Josie felt had been awful embarrassing, they traipsed into the back parlor, and George showed off the kids again. She had had a good look at the older one during lunch and could tell by the way the corners of his mouth drooped down that he was a surly one, unless maybe he was only trying to keep from looking so pretty. And all he said to the questions which George asked him about girls and his high school was "Yeah" or "Aw, naw." When Henry brought in the first round of drinks, and he took one, his daddy looked at him hard and said, "Jock?" And the boy looked his daddy square in the eye.

Buddy only shook his head and smiled when Henry offered him a drink, but he was the one that had started all the embarrassment for her at lunch. When they came into the dining room he pulled her chair out, and she looked back at him—knowing how kids like to jerk chairs. Everybody laughed, but she kept on looking at him. And then she knew that she blushed, for she thought how big her behind must look to him with her bent over like she was.

The other thing that was awful was the question that Mrs. Jackson, the smallest matron and the one with the gray streak in her hair, asked her, "And how do *you* feel this morning, Miss Carlson?" It was the fact that it was Jackson's wife which got her most. But then the fool woman said, "Like the rest of us?" And Josie supposed that she meant no meanness by her remark, but she had already blushed; and Jackson, across the table, looked into his plate. Had this old woman and George been messing around? she wondered. Probably Mrs. Jackson hadn't meant anything.

As they all lounged about the sitting room after lunch, she even felt that she was beginning to catch on to these people and that she was going to start a little pretense of her own and make a good thing out of old Georgie. It was funny the way her interest in him, any real painful interest, was sort of fading. "I've never had so much happen to me at one time," she said to herself. She sat on the floor beside George's chair and put her hand on the toe of his brown and white shoe.

Then George said, "Buddy, you've got to give us just one recitation." And Buddy's face turned as red as a traffic light. He was sitting on a footstool and looking down at his hands.

Jock reached over and touched him on the shoulder and said, "Come on, Buddy, the one about 'If love were like a rose.'" Buddy shook his head and kept his eyes on his hands.

Josie said to herself, "The kid's honestly kind-a shy." It gave her the shivers to see anybody so shy and ignorant of things. But then he began to say the poetry without looking up. It was something about a rose and a rose leaf, but nobody could hear him very good.

George said, "Louder! Louder!" The boy looked at him and said a verse about "sweet rain at noon." Next he stood up and moved his hands about as he spoke, and the blushing was all gone. He said the next one to Mrs. Roberts, and it began:

If you were life, my darling,
And I, your love, were death . . .

That verse ended with something silly about "fruitful breath." He went then to Billy Colton's wife, and the verse he said to her was sad. The boy *did* have a way with him! His eyes were big and he could look sad and happy at the same time. "And I were page to joy," he said. He actually looked like one of the pages they have in stores at Christmas.

But now the kid was perfectly sure of himself, and he had acted timid at first. It was probably all a show. She could just hear him saying dirty limericks. She realized that he was bound to say a verse to her if he knew that many, and she listened carefully to the one he said to Mrs. Jackson:

If you were April's lady,
And I were lord in May,
We'd throw with leaves for hours
And draw for days with flowers,
Till day like night were shady
And night were bright like day;
If you were April's lady,
And I were lord in May.

He turned on Josie in his grandest manner:

If you were queen of pleasure,
And I were king of pain,
We'd hunt down love together,
Pluck out his flying-feather

And teach his feet a measure,
And find his mouth a rein;
If you were queen of pleasure,
And I were king of pain.

And Josie sat up straight and gave the brat the hardest look she knew how. It was too plain. "Queen of pleasure" sounded just as bad as whore! Especially coming right after the verse about "April's lady." The boy blushed again when she glared at him. No one made a noise for a minute. Josie looked at George, and he smiled and began clapping his hands, and everybody clapped. Buddy bowed and ran from the room.

"He's good, George. He's good," Jackson said, squinting his beady little eyes. Jackson was really a puny-looking little guy in the light of day! And he hadn't thought the boy was any better than anybody else did. It was just that he wanted to be the first to say something.

"He's really very good," Mrs. Jackson said.

George laughed. "He's a regular little actor," he said. "Get's it from Beatrice, I guess." Everybody laughed.

George's wife was an actress, then! She'd probably been the worst of the whole lot. There was no telling what this child was really like.

"How old is he, Jock?" Jackson asked. How that man liked to hear his own voice!

"Fourteen and a half," Jock said. "Have you seen him draw?" He talked about his kid brother like he was his own child. Josie watched him. He was talking about Buddy's drawings, about the likenesses. She watched him, and then he saw her watching. He dropped his eyes to his hands as Buddy had done. But in a minute he looked up; and as the talking and drinking went on he kept his eyes on Josephine.

It wasn't any of George's business. It wasn't any of his or anybody's how much she drank, and she knew very well that *he* didn't

really give a damn! But it *was* smarter'n hell of him to take her
upstairs, because the boys had stared at her all afternoon and all
through supper. That was really why she had kept on taking the
drinks when she had made up her mind to let up. She had said,
"You're jealous. You're jealous, George." And he had put his hand
over her mouth, saying, "Careful, Josie." But she was sort of cele-
brating so much's happening to her, and she felt good, and she was
plain infuriated when George kissed her and went back downstairs.
"He was like his real self comin' up the steps," she said. He had told
her that she didn't have the gumption God gave a crab apple.

Josie went off to sleep with her lips moving and awoke in the
middle of the night with them moving again. She was feeling just
prime and yet rotten at the same time. She had a headache and yet
she had a happy feeling. She woke up saying, "Thank your stars
you're white!" It was something they used to say around home
when she was a kid. She had been dreaming about Jock. He was all
right. She had dreamed that together she and Jock had watched a
giant bear devouring a bull, and Jock had laughed and for some
reason she had said, "Thank your stars you're white!" He was all
right. She was practically sure. His eyes were like George's, and he
was as stubborn.

It would have been perfectly plain to everybody if supper hadn't
been such an all-round mess. What with Jackson's smutty jokes and
his showing off (trying to get her to look at him), and Mrs. Colton's
flirting with her husband (holding his hand on the table), nobody
but George paid any attention to Jock. And she was glad that she
had smacked Jackson when he tried to carry her up the stairs, for it
made Jock smile his crooked smile.

"They all must be in bed," she thought. The house was so quiet
that she could hear a screech owl, or something, down in the woods.

She thought she heard a noise in her bathroom. She lay still, and
she was pretty sure she had heard it again. She supposed it was a

mouse, but it might be something else; she had never before thought about where that door beside the bathtub might lead. There was only one place it could go. She got up and went in her stocking feet to the bathroom. She switched on the light and watched the knob. She glanced at herself in the mirror. Her new white silk dress was twisted and wrinkled. "Damn him," she whispered to herself. "He *could* have made me take off this dress." Then she thought she had seen the knob move, move as though someone had released it. She stood still, but there wasn't another sound that night.

In the morning when she turned off the bathroom light, she was still wondering. She looked out of the window; the high net was down. No one was in sight.

What they all did was to slip out on her before she woke up! And in the breakfast room that morning Amelia wanted to talk, but Josephine wasn't going to give the nigger the chance. There was no telling what they had let the niggers hear at breakfast. Amelia kept coming to the breakfast room door and asking if everything was all right, if Miss Josephine wanted this or wanted that, but Miss Josephine would only shake her head and say not a word after Amelia had once answered, "They've went back to Memphis." For all she knew, George and the kids had gone too. It would have been like him to leave her and send after her, just because he had promised her she could stay a week. (He talked like it was such a great treat for her. She hadn't given a copper about the place at first. It had been *him*.) But he'd damned well better not have left her. She'd got a taste of this sort of thing for its own sake now, and she'd stay for good!

Buddy opened the outside door of the breakfast room.

"Good morning, Miss Carlson," he said.

"Hello," Josie said. She did wonder what Jock had told Buddy, what he had guessed to tell him. Buddy wasn't at dinner last night, or she couldn't remember him there.

He was wearing khaki riding pants and a short-sleeved shirt. He sat down across the table from her. "I guess we're all that's left," he said. He picked up the sugar bowl and smiled as he examined it. The corners of his mouth turned up like in a picture kids draw on a blackboard.

"Did Jock and George go to Memphis? Did they?"

"Jock did."

"He did?"

"Yes, he did. And Henry told me he didn't much want to go. I was off riding when they all got up this morning. Daddy wanted me to go too, but I wasn't here." He smiled again, and Josie supposed he meant that he'd been hiding from them.

"Where's your dad?"

"He? Oh, he went to the village to see about some hams. What are you going to do now?"

Josie shrugged her shoulders and began to drink her coffee. Jock was gone. He might have just been scorning her with those looks all the time. She should have got that door open somehow and found out what was what. "Why didn't Jock want to go?" she asked Buddy.

"Our pleasant company, I suppose," he said. "Or yours."

She looked at him, and he laughed. She wondered could this brat be poking fun at her? "Queen of pleasure!" she said out loud, not meaning to at all.

"Did you like that poem?" he asked. It was certain that he wasn't timid when he was alone with somebody, not at least when alone with her.

"I don't know," she said. Then she looked at him. "I don't like the one you picked for me."

"That's not one of the best, is it?"

Neither of them spoke while Josie finished her coffee. She put in another spoonful of sugar before taking the last few swallows, and

Buddy reddened when she motioned for him to give up the sugar bowl. Amelia came and removed the breakfast plate and the butter plate. She returned for Josie's coffee cup, and, finding it not quite ready, she stood behind Buddy's chair and put her hands on his shoulders. The scar was right beside his cheek. Buddy smiled and beat the back of his head against her ribs playfully. Finally Josie put her cup down and said, "That's all."

She went upstairs to her room. Jock had tried to get in through her bathroom last night, or he had been so on her mind that her ears and eyes had made up the signs of it. Maybe Buddy had caught Jock trying to open the door and had told George. At any rate George had sent Jock away. If he sent him away, then Jock had definitely had notions. Josie smiled over that one. She was sitting on the side of her little canopied bed, smoking a red-tipped cigarette. There was the noise of an automobile motor in the yard. George was back! Josie went to her dressing table and drank the last of her whiskey.

She sat on the stool before her dressing table, with her eyes on the hall door. She listened to George's footsteps on the stairs, and sat with her legs crossed, twitching the left foot, which dangled. George came in and closed the door behind him.

"I've bought you a ticket on the night train, Josie. You're goin' back tonight."

So he wasn't such a stickler for his word, after all! Not in this case. He was sending her home. Well, what did he expect her to say? Did he think she would beg to stay on? She would clear out, and she wasn't the one beaten. George was beaten. One of his kids that he was so mortally fond of, one for sure had had notions. "Almost for sure." George opened the door and left Josie staring after him. In a few minutes she heard his horse gallop past the house and out onto the dirt road.

She folded her white dress carefully and laid it on the bottom of her traveling bag. She heard Buddy somewhere in the house, singing. She wrapped her white shoes in toilet paper and stuck them at the ends of the bag. Buddy seemed to be wandering through the house, singing. His voice was high like a woman's, never breaking as she sometimes thought it did in conversation. It came from one part of the house and then another. Josie stopped her packing. "There's no such thing," she said.

She went down the steps like a child, stopping both feet on each step, then stepping to the next. One hand was on her hip, the other she ran along the banister. She walked through the front parlor with its bookcases and fancy chairs with the eagles worked in the needlepoint, and through the back parlor with the rocking chairs and the silly candle stand and the victrola. She stepped down into the breakfast room where the sunlight came through the blinds and put stripes on the brick wall. She went into the kitchen for the first time. Mammy, with a white dust cap on the back of her head, had already started supper. She stood by the big range, and Amelia sat in the corner chopping onions. Josie wasn't interested in the face of either. She went through the dark pantry and into the dining room. She looked through the windows there, but no one was in the yard. She went into the hall.

Buddy was near the top of the stairway which curved around the far end of the long hall, looking down at her. "Why don't you come up here?" He pronounced every word sharply and rolled his *r*'s. But his voice was flat, and his words seemed to remain in the hall for several minutes. His question seemed to float down from the ceiling, down through the air like a feather.

"How did he get up there without me hearing him?" Josie mumbled. She took the first two steps slowly, and Buddy hopped up to the top of the stair.

The door to the kids' room was open and Josie went in. Buddy shut the white paneled door and said, "Don't you think it's time you did something nice for me?"

Josie laughed, and she watched Buddy laugh. Queen of pleasure indeed!

"I want to draw you," he said.

"Clothes and all, Bud . . . ?"

"No. That's not what I mean!"

Josie forced a smile. She suddenly felt afraid and thought she was going to be sick again but she couldn't take her eyes off him.

"That's not what I mean," she heard the kid say again, without blinking an eye, without blushing. "I didn't know you were that sort of nasty thing here. I didn't believe you were a fancy woman. Go on out of here. Go away!" he ordered her.

As Josie went down the steps she kept puckering her lips and nodding her head. She was trying to talk to herself about how many times she had been up and down the steps, but she could still see the smooth brown color of his face and his yellow hair, and she could also see her hand trembling on the banister. It seemed like five years since she had come up the steps with the matrons from Memphis.

In the breakfast room she tore open the frail door to George's little liquor cabinet and took a quart of Bourbon from the shelf. Then she stepped up into the hall and went into the sitting room and took the portable victrola and that record. As she stomped back into the hall, Buddy came running down the steps. He opened the front door and ran out across the veranda and across the lawn. His yellow hair was like a ball of gold in the sunlight as he went through the white gate. But Josie went upstairs.

She locked her door and threw the big key across the room. She knocked the bottle of toilet water and the amber brush off her dressing table as she made room for the victrola. When she had started "Louisville Lady" playing, she sat on the stool and began to wonder. "The kid's head was like a ball of gold, but I'm not gonna think about him ever once I get back to Memphis," she told herself. "No, by damn, but I wonder just what George'll do to me." She broke the blue seal of the whiskey with her fingernail, and it didn't seem like more than twenty minutes or half an hour before George was beating and kicking on the door, and she was sitting on the stool and listening and just waiting for him to break the door, and wondering what he'd do to her.

Their Losses

At Grand Junction, the train slowed down for its last stop before getting into the outskirts of Memphis. Just when it had jerked to a standstill, Miss Patty Bean came out of the drawing room. She had not slept there but had hurried into the drawing room the minute she'd waked up to see how her aunt, who was gravely ill and who occupied the room with a trained nurse, had borne the last hours of the trip. Miss Patty had been in there with her aunt for nearly an hour. As she came out the nurse was whispering to her, but Miss Patty pulled the door closed with apparent indifference to what the nurse might be saying. The train had jerked to a standstill. For a moment Miss Patty, clad in a dark dressing gown and with her graying auburn hair contained in a sort of mesh cap, faced the other passengers in the Pullman car with an expression of alarm.

The other passengers, several of whom, already dressed, were standing in the aisle while the porter made up their berths, glanced at Miss Patty, then returned their attention immediately to their luggage or to their morning papers, which had been brought aboard at Corinth. They were mostly businessmen, and the scattering of women appeared to be businesswomen. In the silence and stillness of the train stop, not even those who were traveling together spoke to each other. At least half the berths had already been converted into seats, but the passengers did not look out the windows. They were fifty miles from Memphis, and they knew that nothing outside the windows would interest them until the train slowed down again, for the suburban stop of Buntyn.

After a moment Miss Patty's expression faded from one of absolute alarm to one of suspicion. Then, as though finally gathering her wits, she leaned over abruptly and peered out a window of the first section on her left. What she saw was only a deserted-looking cotton shed and, far beyond it, past winter fields of cotton stalks and dead grass, a two-story clapboard house with a sagging double gallery. The depot and the town were on the other side of the train, but Miss Patty knew this scene and she gave a sigh of relief. "Oh, uh-huh," she muttered to herself. "Grand Junction."

"Yes, sweet old Grand Junction," came a soft whisper.

For an instant Miss Patty could not locate the speaker. Then she became aware of a very tiny lady, dressed in black, seated right beside where she stood; indeed, she was leaning almost directly across the lady's lap. Miss Patty brought herself up straight, throwing her shoulders back and her heavy, square chin into the air, and said, "I was not aware that this section was occupied."

"Why, now, of course you weren't—of course you weren't, my dear," said the tiny lady. She was such an inconspicuous little soul that her presence could not alter the impression that there were only Memphis business people in the car.

"I didn't know you were there," Miss Patty explained again.

"Why, of course you didn't."

"It was very rude of me," Miss Patty said solemnly, blinking her eyes.

"Oh, no," the tiny lady protested gently.

"Oh, but indeed it was," Miss Patty assured her.

"Why, it was all right."

"I didn't see you there. I beg your pardon."

The tiny lady was smiling up at Miss Patty with eyes that seemed as green as the Pullman upholstery. "I came aboard at Sweetwater during the night," she said. She nodded toward the curtains of Miss Patty's berth, across the aisle. "I guess you were as snug as a bug in a rug when I got on."

Miss Patty lowered her chin and scowled.

"You're traveling with your sick aunt, aren't you?" the lady went on. "I saw you go in there awhile ago, and I inquired of the porter." The smile faded from her eyes but remained on her lips. "You see, I haven't been to bed. I'm bringing my mother to Brownsville for burial." She nodded in the direction of the baggage car ahead.

"I see," Miss Patty replied. She had now fixed this diminutive person with a stare of appraisal. She was someone from her own world. If she heard the name, she would undoubtedly know the family. Without the name, she already *knew* the life history of the lady, and she could almost have guessed the name, or made up one that would have done as well. Her impulse was to turn away, but the green eyes of Miss Ellen Watkins prevented her. They were too full of unmistakable sweetness and charity. Miss Patty remained a moment, observing the telltale paraphernalia: the black gloves and purse on the seat beside Miss Ellen; the unobtrusive hat, with its wisp of a veil turned back; the fresh powder on the wrinkled neck.

"I'm Ellen Louise Watkins," the tiny lady said. "I believe you're Miss Bean, from Thornton."

Miss Patty gave a formal little bow—a Watkins from Brownsville, a daughter of the late Judge Davy Watkins. They were kin to the Crocketts. Davy Crockett's blood had come to this end: a whispering old maid in a Pullman car.

"How *is* your aunt this morning?" Miss Ellen whispered, leaning forward.

But Miss Patty had turned her back. She put her head and shoulders inside the curtains of her berth, and as Miss Ellen waited for an answer, all to be seen of Miss Patty was the dark watered silk of her dressing gown, drawn tightly about her narrow hips and falling straight to a hemline just above her very white and very thin and bony ankles.

When Miss Patty pushed herself into the aisle again and faced Miss Ellen, she held, thrown over her arms, a navy-blue dress, various white and pink particulars of underwear, and a pair of extremely long and rumpled silk stockings, and in her hands she had bunched together her black pumps, an ivory comb and brush, and other articles she would need in the dressing room. The train began to move as she spoke. "I believe," she said, as though she were taking an oath, "that there has been no change in my aunt's condition during the night."

Miss Ellen nodded. The display of clothing over Miss Patty's arms brought a smile to her lips, and she was plainly making an effort to keep her eyes off the clothing and on Miss Patty's face. This uninhibited and even unladylike display reminded her of what she had always heard about the Bean family at Thornton. They were eccentric people, and bigoted. But quickly she reproached herself for retaining such gossip in her mind. Some of the Beans used to be in politics, and unfair things are always said about people in public life. Further, Miss Ellen reminded herself, the first instant she had set eyes on Miss Patty, she had *known* the sort of person she was. Even if the porter had not been able to tell her the name, she could almost have guessed it. She knew how Miss Patty would look when she had got into those garments—as though she had dressed in the dark and were proud of it. And there would be a hat—a sort of brown fedora—that she would pull on at the last minute before she got off the train. She had known many a Miss Patty Bean in her time, and their gruffness and their mannish ways didn't frighten her. Indeed, she felt sorry for such women. "Are you going to have breakfast in the diner?" she asked.

"I am," Miss Patty replied.

"Then I'll save you a seat. I'll go ahead and get a table. There's not too much time, Miss Bean."

"As you will, Miss Watkins." Miss Patty turned toward the narrow passage that led to the ladies' dressing room. Suddenly she stopped and backed into Miss Ellen's section. She was making way for the conductor and a passenger who had evidently come aboard at Grand Junction. A porter followed, carrying a large piece of airplane luggage. The Pullman conductor came first, and the passenger, a lady, was addressing him over his shoulder. "But why could not they stop the *Pullman* at the platform, instead of the *coaches?*" It was a remarkably loud voice, and it paused after every word, obviously trying for a humorous effect.

The conductor was smiling grimly. "Here you are, ma'am," he said. "You can sit here till I find space for you—if this lady don't mind. She has the whole section." He indicated Miss Ellen's section and continued down the aisle, followed by the porter, without once looking back.

"But suppose she *does* mind?" the new passenger called after him, and she laughed heartily. Some of the other passengers looked up briefly and smiled. The lady turned to Miss Patty, who was still there holding her possessions. "*Do* you mind?" And then, "Why, Patty Bean! How very nice!"

"It is not my section." Miss Patty thrust herself into the aisle. "It is not my section, Cornelia."

"Then it must be— Why, will wonders never cease? Ellen Louise Watkins!"

Miss Ellen and Miss Patty exchanged surprised glances. "Why, of course you shall sit here with me," Miss Ellen said. "How good to see you, Cornelia!"

Cornelia Weatherby Werner had already seated herself, facing Miss Ellen. She was a large woman in all her dimensions, but a good-looking woman still. She wore a smart three-cornered hat, which drew attention to her handsome profile, and a cloth coat trimmed with Persian lamb. "I declare it's like old times," she said breathlessly. "Riding the Southern from Grand Junction to Memphis and seeing everybody you know! Nowadays it's mostly *that* sort you see on the Southern." She gestured openly toward the other passengers. "I'll bet you two have been gadding off to Washington. Are you traveling together?"

Miss Ellen and Miss Patty shook their heads.

"Ellen and I are old schoolmates, too, Patty," Cornelia continued. "We were at Ward's together after I was dismissed from Belmont. By the way," she said, smiling roguishly and digging into her purse for cigarettes, "I still have that infernal habit. It's old-fashioned now, but I still call them my coffin nails. Which reminds me—" She hesitated, a package of cigarettes in one hand, a silver lighter in the other. "Oh, do either of you smoke? Well, not before breakfast anyhow. And not on a Pullman, even when the conductor isn't looking, I'll bet. I was saying it reminds me I have just been to Grand Junction to put my old mother to her last rest." As she lit her cigarette, she watched their faces, eager for the signs of shock.

Miss Ellen gave a sympathetic "Oh." Miss Patty stared.

"You mustn't look so lugubrious," Cornelia went on. "The old dear hadn't spoken to me in thirty-one years—not since I got married and went to Memphis. I married a Jew, you know. You've both met Jake? He's a bank examiner and a good husband. Let's see, Patty, when was it I came down to Thornton with Jake? During the Depression sometime—but we saw Ellen only last May."

Miss Ellen leaned forward and stopped her, resting a tiny hand on her knee. "Cornelia, dear," she whispered, "we're all making sad trips these days. I'm taking Mother to Brownsville for burial. She died while we were visiting her invalid cousin at Sweetwater."

Cornelia said nothing. Presently she raised her eyes questioningly to Miss Patty.

"My aged aunt," Miss Patty said. "She is not dead. She is in the drawing room with an Irish nurse. I'm bringing her from Washington to spend her last days at Thornton, where she is greatly loved."

Miss Ellen looked up at Miss Patty and said, "I'm sure she is."

"She is," Miss Patty affirmed. There was a civility in her tone that had not been there when she had last addressed Miss Ellen, and the two exchanged a rather long glance.

Cornelia gazed out the window at the passing fields. Her features in repose looked tired. It was with obvious effort that she faced her two friends again. Miss Patty was still standing there, with her lips slightly parted, and Miss Ellen still rested a hand on Cornelia's knee. Cornelia shuddered visibly. She blushed and said, "A rabbit ran over my grave, I guess." Then she blushed again, but now she had regained her spirit. "Oh, just listen to me." She smiled. "I've never said the right thing once in my life. Is there a diner? Can we get any breakfast? You used to get the *best* breakfast on the Southern."

At the word "breakfast," Miss Patty did an about-face and disappeared down the passage to the ladies' room. Miss Ellen seized her purse and gloves. "Of course, my dear," she said. "Come along. We'll all have breakfast together."

There were no other passengers in the diner when Cornelia and Miss Ellen went in. The steward was eating at a small table at the rear of the car. Two Negro waiters were standing by the table talking to him, but he jumped to his feet and came toward the ladies. He stopped at the third table on the right, as though all the others might be reserved, and after wiping his mouth with a large white napkin, he asked if there would be anyone else in their party.

"Why, yes, as a matter of fact," Miss Ellen answered politely, "there will be one other."

"Do you think you can squeeze one more in?" Cornelia asked,

narrowing her eyes and laughing. The steward did not reply. He helped them into chairs opposite each other and by the broad window, and darted away to get menus from his desk at the front of the car. A smiling Negro waiter set three goblets upright, filled them with water, and removed a fourth goblet and a setting of silver. "Sometime during the past thirty years," Cornelia remarked when the waiter had gone, "conductors and stewards lost their sense of humor. It makes you thank God for porters and waiters, doesn't it? Next thing you know— Why, merciful heavens, here's Patty already!"

Miss Ellen glanced over her shoulder. There was Miss Patty, looking as though she had dressed in the dark and were proud of it. She was hatless, her hair pulled into a loose knot on the back of her neck but apparently without benefit of the ivory comb and brush. The steward was leading her toward their table. Without smiling, Cornelia said, "He didn't have to ask her if she were the other member of this party." Miss Ellen raised her eyebrows slightly. "Most passengers don't eat in the diner any more," Cornelia clarified. "They feel they're too near to Memphis to bother." When Miss Patty sat down beside Miss Ellen, Cornelia said, "Gosh a'might, Patty, we left you only two seconds ago and here you are dressed and in your right mind. How do you do it?"

They received their menus, and when they had ordered, Miss Patty smiled airily. "I'm always in my right mind, Cornelia, and I don't reckon I've ever been 'dressed' in my life." As she said "dressed," her eyes traveled from the three-cornered hat to the brocaded bosom of Cornelia's rust-colored dress.

Cornelia looked out the window, silently vowing not to speak again during the meal, or, since speaking was for her the most irresistible of all life's temptations, at least not to let herself speak sharply to either of these crotchety old maids. She sat looking out the window, thanking her stars for the great good luck of being

Mrs. Jake Werner, of Memphis, instead of an embittered old maid from Grand Junction.

Miss Ellen was also looking out the window. "Doesn't it look bleak?" she said, referring to the brown and gray fields under an overcast sky.

"Oh, doesn't it!" Cornelia agreed at once, revealing that Miss Ellen had guessed her very thoughts.

"It *is* bleak," Miss Patty said. "See how it's washed. This land along here didn't use to look like that." The two others nodded agreement, each remembering how it had used to look. "This used to be fine land," she continued, "but it seems to me that all West Tennessee is washing away. Look at those gullies! And not a piece of brush piled in them." Miss Ellen and Cornelia shook their heads vaguely; they were not really certain why there should be brush in the gullies. Cornelia discovered that a glass of tomato juice had been set before her and she began pouring salt into it. Miss Ellen was eating her oatmeal. Miss Patty took a sip from her first cup of coffee. She had specified that it be brought in a cup instead of a pot. It was black and a little cool, the way she liked it. She peered out the window again and pursued her discourse warmly. "And the towns! Look! We're going through Moscow. It's a shambles. Why, half the square's been torn away, and the rest ought to be. Mind you, we went through La Grange without even noticing it. They used to be good towns, fine towns."

"Lovely towns!" responded Miss Ellen. The thought of the vanishing towns touched her.

"There was something about them," Cornelia said, groping. "An atmosphere, I think."

Miss Patty cleared her throat and defined it: "The atmosphere of a prosperous and civilized existence."

Miss Ellen looked bewildered, and Cornelia frowned thoughtfully and pursed her lips. Presently Cornelia said profoundly, "All the business has gone to Memphis."

"Yes," Miss Patty said. "Indeed it has!"

They were being served their main course now. Cornelia looked at her trout and said to the waiter, "It looks delicious. Did you cook this, boy?"

"No, ma'am," the waiter said cheerfully.

"Well, it looks delicious. The same old Southern Railway cooking."

Miss Patty and Miss Ellen had scrambled eggs and ham. Miss Patty eyed hers critically. "The Southern Railway didn't use to cook eggs this way," she said. "And it's no improvement."

Miss Ellen leaned forward and bent her neck in order to look directly up into Miss Patty's face. "Why, now, you probably like them country style, with some white showing," she said. "*These* are what my niece calls Toddle House style. They cook them with milk, of course. They're a little like an omelet." The subject held great interest for her, and she was happy to be able to inform Miss Patty. "And you don't break them into such a hot pan. You don't really break them in the pan, that is." Miss Patty was reaching across Miss Ellen's plate for the pepper. Miss Ellen said no more about the eggs. She busied herself with a small silver box of saccharin, prying the lid open with her fingernail. She saw Cornelia looking at the box and said, "It was my grandmother's snuffbox. For years it was just a keepsake, but now I carry my tablets in it."

The old box, which Miss Patty was now examining admiringly, somehow made Cornelia return to the subject they had left off. "In my grandmother's day, there was a lot of life in this section—entertainment and social life. My own mother used to say, 'In Mama's day, there were people in the country; in my day, there were people in town; now there's nobody.'"

Miss Patty gazed at Cornelia with astonishment. "Your mother was a very wise woman, Cornelia," she said.

"That's a moot question," Cornelia answered. Now they were on a subject that she was sure she knew something about, and she threw caution to the wind. She spoke excitedly and seemed to begin every sentence without knowing how it would end. "My mother is dead now, and I don't mean to ever say another word against her, but just because she is dead, I don't intend to start deceiving myself. The fact remains that she was opinionated and narrow and mentally cruel to her children and her husband and was tied to things that were over and done with before she was born. She's dead now, but I shall make no pretense of mourning someone I did not love. We don't mourn people we don't love. It's not honest."

"No, we don't, do we?" Miss Ellen said sympathetically.

"I beg to differ with you," Miss Patty said with the merest suggestion of a smile. She, too, felt on firm ground. She had already mourned the deaths of all her immediate family and of most of her near kin. She addressed her remarks to Miss Ellen. "Mourning is an obligation. We only mourn those with whom we have some real connection, people who have represented something important and fundamental in our lives."

Miss Ellen was determined to find agreement. "Of course, of course—you are speaking of wearing black."

"I am not speaking of the symbol. I am speaking of the mourning itself. I shall mourn the loss of my aunt when she goes, because she is my aunt, because she is the last of my aunts, and particularly because she is an aunt who has maintained a worthwhile position in the world."

Miss Ellen gasped. "Oh, no, Miss Bean! Not because of her position in the world!"

"Don't mistake me, Miss Watkins."

"I beg you to reconsider. Why, why—" She fumbled, and Miss

Patty waited. "Now that Mother's gone, I've lost nearly everybody, and it has always been my part and my privilege to look after the sick in our family. My two older brothers never married; they were quiet, simple, home-loving men, who made little stir in the world, content to live there in the house with Mother and Nora and me after Father was gone. And Nora, my only sister, developed melancholia. One morning, she could just not finish lacing her high shoes, and after that she seldom left the house or saw anybody. What I want to say is that we also had a younger brother, who was a distinguished professor at Knoxville, with four beautiful children. You see, I've lost them all, one by one, and it's been no different whether they were distinguished or not. I can't conceive—" She stopped suddenly, in real confusion.

"Don't mistake me," Miss Patty said calmly. "I am speaking of my aunt's moral position in the world."

"Why, of course you are," said Miss Ellen, still out of breath.

"My aunt has been an indomitable character," Miss Patty continued. "Her husband died during his first term in Congress, forty years ago, and she has felt it her duty to remain in Washington ever since. With very slight means, she has maintained herself there in the right manner through all the years, returning to Thornton every summer, enduring the heat and the inconvenience, with no definite place of abode, visiting the kin, subjecting herself to the role of the indigent relation, so that she could afford to return to Washington in the fall. Her passing will be a loss to us all, for through her wit and charm she was an influence on Capitol Hill. In a sense, she represented our district in Washington as none of our elected officials has done since the days of"—bowing her head deferentially toward Miss Ellen—"of David Crockett."

"What a marvelous woman!" exclaimed Miss Ellen.

Cornelia looked at Miss Ellen to see whether she meant Miss Patty's aunt or Miss Patty. She had been marveling privately at Miss

Patty's flow of speech, and reflected that she could already see it in print in the county paper's obituary column. "If my mother had been a person of such wit and charm," she said, "I would mourn her, too."

"I never knew your mother," Miss Patty replied, "but from what you say I can easily guess the sort of woman she was. I would mourn her passing if I were in your shoes, Cornelia. She wanted to retain the standards of a past era, a better era for all of *us*. A person can't do that and be a pleasant, charming personality and the darling of a family."

"All I know," said Cornelia, taking the last bite of her trout, "is that my young ladyhood was a misery under that woman's roof and in that town." She glanced dreamily out the window. The train was speeding through the same sort of country as before, perhaps a little more hilly, a little more eroded. It sped through small towns and past solitary stations where only the tiresome afternoon local stopped—Rossville, Collierville, Bailey, Forest Hill. Cornelia saw a two-story farmhouse that was painted up only to the level of the second story. "That house has been that way as long as I can remember," she said, and smiled. "Why do you suppose they don't make them a ladder, or lean out the upstairs windows?" Then, still looking out at the dismal landscape—the uncultivated land growing up in sweet gum and old field pine, with a gutted mud road crossing and recrossing the railroad track every half mile or so—Cornelia said, "I only got away by the skin of my teeth! I came back from Ward's with a scrapbook full of names, but they were nothing but 'cute Vanderbilt boys.' I would have been stuck in Grand Junction for life, nursing Mama and all the hypochondriac kin, if I hadn't met Jake. I met him in Memphis doing Christmas shopping. He was a bank teller at Union Planters." She laughed heartily for the first time since she had come into the diner. "It was an out-and-out pickup. Jake still tells everybody it was an out-and-out pickup."

"I don't like Memphis," said Miss Patty. "I never have."

"I've never felt that Memphis liked me," said Miss Ellen.

"It's a wretched place!" Cornelia said suddenly. And now she saw that she had unwittingly shocked her two friends. The train had passed through Germantown; big suburban estates and scattered subdivisions began to appear in the countryside. There was even a bulldozer at work on the horizon, grading the land for new suburban sites. "It's the most completely snobbish place in the world," she went on. "They can't forgive you for being from the country— they hate the country so, and they can't forgive your being a Jew. They dare not. If you're either one of those, it's rough going. If you're both, you're just out! I mean *socially,* of course. Oh, Jake's done *well,* and we have our friends. But as Mama would have said—and, God knows, probably did say about us many a time—*we're* nobody." Then, for no reason at all, she added, "And we don't have any children."

"What a shame," Miss Ellen said, hastening to explain, "that you have no children, I mean. I've always thought that if—"

"Oh, no, Ellen. They might have liked me about the way I liked Mama. I'm glad that when I die, there'll be no question of to mourn or not to mourn."

"In truly happy families, Cornelia, there is no question," Miss Ellen said softly. She stole a glance at Miss Patty. "I'm just certain that Miss Bean had a very congenial and happy family, and that she loved them all dearly, in addition to being naturally proud of the things they stood for."

Miss Patty had produced a wallet from somewhere on her person and was examining her check. She slammed the wallet on the table, turned her head, and glared at the diminutive Miss Ellen. "How I regarded the members of my family as individuals is neither here nor there, Miss Watkins."

But Miss Ellen raised her rather receding chin and gazed directly up at Miss Patty. "To me, it seems of the greatest consequence." Her voice trembled, yet there was a firmness in it. "I am mourning my mother today. I spent last night remembering every endearing trait she had. Some of them were faults and some were virtues, but they were nonetheless endearing. And so I feel strongly about what you say, Miss Bean. We must love people as people, not for what they are, or were, in the world."

"My people happened to be very much *of* the world, Miss Watkins," said Miss Patty. "Not of *this* world but of *a* world that we have seen disappear. In mourning my family, I mourn that world's disappearance. How could I know whether or not I really loved them, or whether or not we were really happy? There wasn't ever time for asking that. We were all like Aunt Lottie, in yonder, and there was surely never any love or happiness in the end of it. When I went to Washington last week to fetch Aunt Lottie home, I found her living in a hateful little hole at the Stoneleigh Court. All the furniture from larger apartments she had once had was jammed together in two rooms. The tables were covered with framed photographs of the wives of Presidents, Vice-Presidents, senators, inscribed to Lottie Hathcock. But there was not a friend in sight. During the five days I was there, not one person called." Miss Patty stood up and waved her check and two one-dollar bills at the waiter.

Miss Ellen sat watching the check and the two bills with a stunned expression. But Cornelia twisted about in her chair excitedly. "Your aunt was Mrs. Hathcock!" she fairly screamed. "Oh, Patty, of course! She was *famous* in her day. And don't you remember? I met her once with you at the Maxwell House, when we were at Belmont. You took me along, and after supper my true love from Vandy turned up in the lobby. You were so furious, and Mrs. Hathcock was so cute about it. She was the cleverest talker I've ever listened to, Patty. She was interested in spiritualism and offered to take us to a séance at Mr. Ben Allen's house."

Miss Patty looked at Cornelia absent-mindedly. Her antagonism toward the two women seemed suddenly to have left her, and she spoke without any restraint at all. "Aunt Lottie has long since become a Roman Catholic. Her will leaves her little pittance of money and her furniture to the Catholic Church, and her religious oil paintings to me. The nurse we brought along has turned out to be an Irish Catholic." She glanced in the direction of their Pullman car and said, "The nurse has conceived the notion that Aunt Lottie is worse this morning, and she wanted to wire ahead for a Memphis priest to meet us at the Union Station. She knows there won't be any priests at Thornton."

Cornelia, carried away by incorrigible gregariousness, began, "Ah, Patty, might I see her? It would be such fun to see her again, just for old times' sake. It might even cheer her a little."

Miss Patty stared at Cornelia in silence. Finally she said, "My aunt is a mental patient. She doesn't even remember me, Cornelia." She snatched a piece of change from the waiter's tray and hurried past the steward and out of the car.

Miss Ellen was almost staggering as she rose from the table. She fumbled in her purse, trying to find the correct change for the waiter. She was shaking her head from side to side, and opening and closing her eyes with the same rhythm.

Cornelia made no move toward rising. "Depend upon *me,*" she said. "Did you *know?*"

Miss Ellen only increased the speed of her head-shaking. When she saw Cornelia still sitting there, casually lighting a cigarette, she said, "We're approaching Buntyn. I imagine you're getting off there."

"No, that's the country-club stop. I don't get off at the country-club stop."

"There's not much time," Miss Ellen said.

Presently Cornelia pulled a bill from her purse and summoned the waiter. "Well, Ellen," she said, still not getting up, "I guess there's no way I could be of help to you at the station, is there?"

"No, there's nothing, dear."

In her lethargy Cornelia seemed unable to rise and even unable to tell Miss Ellen to go ahead without her. "I suppose you'll be met by a hearse," she said, "and Patty will be met by an ambulance, and—and I'll be met by Jake." For a moment, she sat behind a cloud of cigarette smoke. There was a puzzled expression in her eyes, and she was laughing quietly at what she had said. It was one of those sentences that Cornelia began without knowing how it would end.

Two Pilgrims

We were on our way from Memphis to a small town in northern Alabama, where my uncle, who was a cotton broker, had a lawsuit that he hoped could be settled out of court. Mr. Lowder, my uncle's old friend and lawyer, was traveling with him. I had just turned seventeen, and I had been engaged to come along in the capacity of chauffeur. I sat alone in the front seat of the car. The two men didn't discuss the lawsuit along the way, as I would have expected them to do. I don't know to this day exactly what was involved, or even whether or not Mr. Lowder managed to settle the matter on that trip. From the time we left the outskirts of Memphis, the two men talked instead about how good the bird hunting used to be there in our section of the country. During the two hours while we were riding through the big cotton counties of West Tennessee, they talked of almost nothing but bird dogs and field trials, interrupting themselves only when we passed through some little town or settlement to speak of the fine people they knew who had once lived there. We went through Collierville, La Grange, Grand Junction, Saulsbury. At La Grange, my uncle pointed out a house with a neo-

[216]

classic portico and said he had once had a breakfast there that lasted three hours. At Saulsbury, Mr. Lowder commented that it somehow did his soul good to see the name spelled that way. Though it was November, not all the trees had lost their leaves yet. There was even some color still—dull pinks and yellows mixed with reddish browns —and under a bright, limitless sky the trees and the broad fields of grayish cotton stalks, looking almost lavender in places, gave a kind of faded-tapestry effect.

After we crossed the Tennessee River at Savannah, the country changed. And it was as if the new kind of country we had got into depressed the two men. But it may have been only the weather, because the weather changed, too, after we crossed the river. The sky became overcast, and everything seemed rather closed in. Soon there was intermittent rain of a light, misty sort. I kept switching my windshield wiper on and off, until presently my uncle asked me in a querulous tone why I didn't just let the thing run. For thirty or forty miles, the two men had little to say to each other. Finally, as we were passing through a place called Waynesboro—a hard-looking hill town with a cement-block jailhouse dominating the public square—my uncle said that this town was where General Winfield Scott had made one of his halts on the notorious Trail of Tears, when he was rounding up the Cherokees to move them west, in 1838. The two men spoke of what a cruel thing that had been, but they agreed that one must not judge the persons responsible too harshly, that one must judge them by the light of their times and remember what the early settlers had suffered at the hands of the Indians.

Not very long after we had left Waynesboro, Mr. Lowder remarked that we were approaching the old Natchez Trace section and that the original settlers there had been a mighty rough lot of people. My uncle added that from the very earliest days the whole area had been infested with outlaws and robbers and that even now it was said to be a pretty tough section. They sounded as though they were off to a good start; I thought the subject might last them at least until lunchtime. But just as this thought occurred to me, they were interrupted.

We came over the brow of one of the low-lying hills in that country of scrub oaks and pinewoods, and there before us—in a clearing down in the hollow ahead—was a house with smoke issuing from one window toward the rear and with little gray geysers rising at a half-dozen points on the black-shingled roof. It was an unpainted, one-story house set close to the ground and with two big stone end chimneys. All across the front was a kind of lean-to porch. There was an old log barn beyond the house. Despite my uncle's criticism, I had switched off the windshield wiper a mile or so up the road, and then I had had to switch it on again just as we came over the hill. Even with the wiper going, visibility was not very good, and my first thought was that only the misty rain in the air was keeping the roof of that house from blazing up. Mr. Lowder and my uncle were so engrossed in their talk that I think it was my switching the wiper on again that first attracted their attention. But instantly upon seeing the smoke, my uncle said, "Turn in down there!"

"But be careful how you slow down," Mr. Lowder warned. "This blacktop's slick." Already he and my uncle were perched on the edge of the back seat, and one of them had put a hand on my shoulder as if to steady me.

The little house was in such a clearing as must have been familiar to travelers in pioneer days. There were stumps everywhere, even in the barn lot and among the cabbages in the garden. I suppose I particularly noticed the stumps because a good number were themselves smoldering and sending up occasional wisps of smoke. Apparently, the farmer had been trying to rid himself of the stumps in the old-fashioned way. There was no connection between these fires and the one at the house, but the infernal effect of the whole scene was inescapable. One felt that the entire area within the dark ring of pinewoods might at any moment burst into flame.

I turned the car off the macadam pavement, and we bumped along some two hundred feet, following wagon ruts that led more toward the barn than toward the house. The wide barn door stood open, and I could see the figure of a man inside herding a couple of animals through a door at the other end, where the barn lot was. Then I heard Mr. Lowder and my uncle open the back doors of the car. While the car was still moving, they leaped out onto the ground. They both were big men, more than six feet tall and with sizable stomachs that began just below the breastbone, but they sprinted off in the direction of the house like two boys. As they ran, I saw them hurriedly putting on their black gloves. Next, they began stripping off their topcoats. By the time I had stopped the car and got out, they had pulled their coats over their heads, and I realized then that each had tossed his hat onto the back seat before leaping from the car. Looking like a couple of hooded night riders, they were now mounting the shallow porch steps. It was just as they gained the porch that I saw the woman appear from around the far side of the house. At the sight of the hooded and begloved men on her porch—the porch of her burning house—the woman threw one hand to her forehead and gave such an alarmed and alarming cry that I felt something turn over inside me. Even the two intruders halted for an instant on the porch and looked at her.

I thought at first glance that she was an old woman, she was so stooped. Then something told me—I think it was the plaintive sounds she was making—that she was more young than old. After her first outcry, she continued a kind of girlish wailing, which, it seemed to me, expressed a good deal more than mere emotional shock. The noises she made seemed to say that all this *couldn't* be happening to *her*. Not hooded bandits added to a house-burning! It wasn't right; life *couldn't* be so hard, *couldn't* be as evil as this; it was more than she should be asked to bear!

"Anybody inside, Miss?" my uncle called out to the girl.

She began shaking her head frantically.

"Well, we'll fetch out whatever we can!" he called. Glancing back at me—I was trying to make a hood of my own topcoat and preparing to join them—my uncle shouted, "Don't you come inside! Stay with that girl! And calm her down!" With that, he followed Mr. Lowder through the doorway and into the house.

Presently, they were hurling bedclothes and homemade-looking stools and chairs through the side windows. Then one or the other of them would come dashing out across the porch and into the yard, deposit on the ground a big pitcher and washbasin or a blurry old mirror with a carved wooden frame, and then dash back inside again. Now and then when one of them brought something out, he would pause for just the briefest moment, not to rest but to examine the rescued object before he put it down. It was comical to see the interest they took in the old things they brought out of that burning house.

When I came up to where the woman was standing, she seemed to have recovered completely from her first fright. She looked at me a little shamefacedly, I thought. Her deep-socketed eyes were almost freakishly large. And I noticed at once that they were of two different colors. One was a mottled brown, the other a gray-green. When finally she spoke, she turned her eyes away and toward the house. "Who are you-all?" she asked.

"We were just passing by," I said.

She looked at me and then turned away again. I felt she was skeptical, that she suspected we had been sent by someone. Each time she directed her eyes at me, I read deceit or guilt or suspicion in them.

"Where you coming from?" she asked in an idle tone, craning her neck to see what some object was that had come flying out the window. She seemed abundantly calm now. Without answering her question, I yanked my coat over my head and ran off toward the house. My uncle met me on the porch steps. He handed me a dresser drawer he was carrying, not failing to give the contents a quick inventory. Then he gave me a rather heavy punch on the chest. "*You* stay out there and keep that girl calm," he said. "You hear what I say! She's apt to go to pieces any minute."

The woman was taking a livelier interest in matters now. I set the drawer on a stump, and when I looked up, she peered over me to see which drawer it was I had brought and what extra odds and ends my uncle might have swept into it. On top lay a rusty fire poker and a couple of small picture frames with the glass so smashed up you couldn't make out the pictures. Underneath, there was a jumble of old cloth scraps and paper dress patterns and packages of garden seeds. Seeing all this, the woman opened her mouth and smiled vacantly, perhaps a little contemptuously. She was so close to me that I became aware of the sweetness of her breath! I could not have imagined that her breath would be sweet. Though the skin on her forehead and on her high cheekbones was clear and very fair, there were ugly pimples on her chin and at the corners of her mouth. Her dark hair was wet from the drizzle of rain and was pushed behind her ears and hung in clumps over the collar of her soiled denim jacket. She was breathing heavily through her parted lips. Presently, when our eyes met, I thought I detected a certain momentary glee-fulness in her expression. But her glance darted back toward the house at once.

The two men had pressed on beyond the front rooms and into the ell of the house. Now the woman took a couple of steps in order to look through one of the front windows and perhaps catch a glimpse of them back there.

"We were coming from Memphis," I said. "We're *from* Memphis." But she seemed no longer interested in that subject.

"It's no use what they're doing," she said. "Unless they like it."

"It's all right," I said, still hoping to distract her. "We're on our way to a place in Alabama."

"They your bosses?" she asked. She couldn't take her eyes off the window.

"No, it's my uncle and his lawyer."

"Well, they're right active," she commented. "But there ain't nothing in there worth their bustle and bother. Yet some folks like to take chances. It's just the worst lot of junk in there. We heired this place from my grandma when she passed on last spring; the junk was all hern."

Just then, Mr. Lowder and my uncle came running from the house. Each of them was carrying a coal-oil lamp, his right hand supporting the base of the lamp and his left clamped protectively on the fragile chimney. I almost burst out laughing.

"It's gotten too hot in there," Mr. Lowder said. "We'll have to stop."

When they had set down their lamps, they began examining each other's coats, making sure they weren't on fire. Next, they tossed their coats on the bare ground and set about pulling some of the rescued articles farther from the house. I went forward to help, and the woman followed. She didn't follow to help, however. Apparently, she was only curious to see which of her possessions these men had deemed worth saving. She looked at everything she came to with almost a disappointed expression. Then Mr. Lowder picked up an enameled object, and I noticed that as he inspected it a deep frown appeared on his brow. He held the thing up for my uncle to see, and I imagined for a moment that he was trying to draw laughter from all of us. It was a child's chamber pot, not much larger than a beer mug. "Did you bring this out?" Mr. Lowder asked my uncle.

My uncle nodded, and, still bending over, he studied the pot for a second, showing that he had not really identified it before. Then he looked at the woman. "Where's your child, ma'am?" he asked in a quiet voice.

The woman gaped at him as though she didn't understand what he was talking about. She shifted her eyes to the tiny pot that Mr. Lowder was still holding aloft. Now her mouth dropped wide open, and at the same time her lips drew back in such a way that her bad teeth were exposed for the first time. It was impossible not to think of a death's-head. At that instant, the whole surface of the shingled roof on the side of the house where we were standing burst into flames.

A few minutes before this, the rain had ceased altogether, and now it was as though someone had suddenly doused the roof with kerosene. My back was to the house, but I heard a loud "swoosh" and I spun around in that direction. Then I heard the woman cry out and I spun back again. Mr. Lowder set the chamber pot on the ground and began moving rather cautiously toward her. My uncle stood motionless, watching her as though she were an animal that might bolt. As Mr. Lowder came toward her, she took a step backward, and then she wailed, "My baby! Oh, Lord, my baby! He's in thar!" Mr. Lowder seized her by the wrist and simultaneously gave us a quick glance over his shoulder.

My uncle snatched up a ragged homespun blanket from the ground and threw it over his head. I seized a patchwork quilt that had been underneath the blanket, and this time I followed him inside the house. Even in the two front rooms it was like a blast furnace, and I felt I might faint. The smoke was so dense that you couldn't see anything an arm's length away. But my uncle had been in those two front rooms and he knew there was no baby there. With me at his heels, he ran right on through and into the first room in the ell, where there wasn't so much smoke—only raw flames eating away at the wall toward the rear. The window lights had burst from the heat in there, and there was a hole in the ceiling, so that you could look right up through the flames to the sky. But my eyes were smarting so that I couldn't really see anything in the room, and I was coughing so hard that I couldn't stand up straight. My uncle was coughing, too, but he could still manage to look about. He made two complete turns around the room and then he headed us on into the kitchen. There wasn't anything recognizable to me in the kitchen except the black range. One of the two window frames fell in as we ran through. The next instant, after we had leaped across the burning floorboards and had jumped off the back stoop of the house, the rafters and the whole roof above the kitchen came down.

There must have been a tremendous crash, though I hardly heard it. Even before my uncle and I could shed our smoldering blankets, we saw the man coming toward us from the barn. "You're afire!" he called out to us. But we had already dropped the blankets before I understood what he was saying. He was jogging along toward us. One of his legs was shorter than the other, and he couldn't move very fast. Under one arm he was carrying a little towheaded child of not more than two years. He held it exactly as though it might be a sack of corn meal he was bringing up from the barn.

"Do you have another baby?" my uncle shouted at him.

"No, narry other," the man replied.

My uncle looked at me. He was coughing still, but at the same time he was smiling and shaking his head. "You all right?" he asked me. He gave my clothes a quick once-over, and I did the same for him. We had somehow got through the house without any damage, even to our shoes or our trouser legs.

By the time the man came up to the house, my uncle had dashed off to tell the woman her baby was safe. I tried to explain to the man about the mistake his wife had made. "Your wife thought your baby was in the house," I said.

He was a stocky, black-haired man, wearing overalls and a long-sleeved undershirt. "She *whut?*" he said, looking at me darkly. He glanced up briefly at the flames, which were now leaping twenty or thirty feet above the framework of the kitchen. Then he set out again, in the same jogging pace, toward the front of the house. I caught a glimpse of the baby's intense blue eyes gazing up at the smoke and flames.

"She thought the baby was inside the house," I said, following the man at a trot.

"Like hell she did!" he said under his breath but loud enough for me to hear.

As we rounded the corner of the house, I heard my uncle call out to the woman that her baby was safe. She was seated on a stump with her face hidden in her hands. My uncle and Mr. Lowder once again began pulling rescued objects farther away from the house. As the man passed him, Mr. Lowder looked up and said, "Did you get all the stock out?"

"Yup," said the man.

"I guess you're lucky there's no wind," Mr. Lowder said.

And my uncle said, "It must have started in the kitchen and spread through the attic. You didn't have any water drawn?"

The man stopped for a second and looked at my uncle. He shifted the baby from one hip to the other. "The pump's broke," he said. "It was about wore out, and *she* broke it for good this morning."

"Isn't that the way it goes," my uncle said sympathetically, shaking his head.

Then, still carrying the baby, the man shuffled on toward his wife. The woman kept her face hidden in her hands, but I think she heard him coming. Neither of them seemed to have any awareness that their house and most of their possessions were at that moment going up in flames. I was watching the man when he got to her. He still had the baby under his arm. I saw him draw back his free hand, and saw the hand come down in a resounding slap on the back of her head. It knocked her right off the stump. She hit the ground in a sitting position and still she didn't look up at her husband. "J'you aim to git them fellows burned alive?" he thundered.

Mr. Lowder and my uncle must have been watching, too, because we all three ran forward at the same moment. "Lay off that!" Mr. Lowder bellowed. "Just lay off, now!"

"She knowed this here young'un warn't in no house!" the man said, twisting the baby to his shoulder. "I reckoned she'd like as not lose her head. That's how come I carried him with me, and I told her plain as daylight I was a-goin' to."

"Now, you look here, mister," my uncle said, "the girl was just scared. She didn't know what she was saying."

"Probably she couldn't remember, in her fright," Mr. Lowder said.

The man stood staring down at his wife. "She's feared of her own shadow, and that's how come I carried him to the barn."

"Well, you're not going to beat her with us here," Mr. Lowder said firmly. "She was scared out of her wits, that's all."

"Who sent y' all out here?" the man asked my uncle, turning his back on Mr. Lowder. "Ain't they goan send no fire engine?"

It was as he spoke the word that we heard the fire truck coming. The whine of the siren must have first reached us from a point three or four miles distant, because at least five minutes elapsed before the fire truck and the two carloads of volunteers arrived. It turned out that somebody else had stopped by before we did and had hurried on to the next town to give the alarm. I thought it strange that the woman hadn't told us earlier that they were expecting help from town. But, of course, there was little about the woman's behavior that didn't seem passing strange to me.

As soon as we heard the siren, she began pushing herself up from the ground. Without a glance at any of the rest of us, she went directly to her husband and snatched the baby from him. The baby's little face was dirty, and there were wide streaks on it, where some while earlier there must have been a flow of tears. But his eyes were dry now and wore a glazed look. He seemed to stare up at the flaming house with total indifference. Almost as soon as he was in his mother's arms, he placed his chin on the shoulder of her denim jacket and quietly closed his eyes. He seemed to have fallen asleep at once. With her baby in her arms, the woman strode away into the adjoining field, among the smoking stumps and toward the edge of the pinewoods. There she stopped, at the edge of the woods, and there she remained standing, with her back turned toward the house and toward us and toward all the activity that ensued after the fire truck and the other cars arrived. She was still standing there, with the baby on her shoulder, when we left the scene.

We stayed on for only a few minutes after the local fire brigade arrived. Mr. Lowder and my uncle could see that their work here was done and they were mindful of the pressing business that they hoped to transact in Alabama that afternoon. We lingered just long enough to see most of the articles they had rescued from the flames thoroughly soaked with water. The sight must have been dis-heartening to them, but they didn't speak of it. The inexpert firemen couldn't control the pressure from their tank, and whenever there came a great spurt of water they lost their grip on the hose. They seemed bound to spray everything but the burning house. We withdrew a little way in the direction of our car and joined a small group of spectators who had now come on the scene.

I didn't tell my uncle or Mr. Lowder what I was thinking during the time that we stood there with the local people who had gathered. I could still see the woman down in the field, and I wondered if my uncle or Mr. Lowder were not going to tell some local person how suspicious her behavior had been—and her husband's, too, for that matter. Surely there was some mystery, I said to myself, some questions that ought to be answered or asked. But no question of any kind seemed to arise in the minds of my two companions. It was as if such a fire were an everyday occurrence in their lives and as if they lived always among such queer people as that afflicted poor-white farmer and his simple wife.

Once we had got back into the car and were on our way again, I was baffled by the quiet good humor—and even serenity—of those two men I was traveling with. The moment they had resettled themselves on the back seat of the car, after giving their overcoats a few final brushings and after placing their wide-brimmed fedoras firmly on their heads again, they began chatting together with the greatest ease and nonchalance. I could not see their faces; I had to keep my eyes on the road. But I listened and presently I heard my uncle launch upon a reminiscence. "I did the damndest thing once," he said. "It was when I was a boy of just eight or nine. The family have kidded me about it all my life. One morning after I had been up to mischief of some kind, Father took me into the kitchen and gave me a switching on my legs with a little shoot he had broken off the privet hedge. When I came outside again, I was still yowling, and the other children who were playing there in the house lot commenced guying me about it. All at once, I burst out at them: 'You'd cry, too, if he beat *you* with the shovel handle!' I hadn't aimed to say it; I just said it. My brothers kid me about it to this day."

"Yes," said Mr. Lowder. "It's like that—the things a person will say." He liked my uncle's story immensely. He said it sounded so true. As he spoke, I could hear one of them striking a match. It wasn't long before I caught the first whiff of cigar smoke. Then another match was struck. They were both smoking now. Pretty soon their conversation moved on to other random topics.

Within the next half hour, we got out of that hill country along the Tennessee River and entered the rich and beautiful section to the east of it, near the fine old towns of Pulaski and Fayetteville. I could not help remarking on the change to my uncle. "Seems good to have finally got out of that godforsaken-looking stretch back there," I said over my shoulder.

"How do you mean 'godforsaken'?" my uncle replied. I recognized a testiness in his tone, and his reply had come so quickly that I felt he had been waiting for me to say exactly what I had said.

"It's just ugly, that's all," I mumbled, hoping that would be the end of it.

But Mr. Lowder joined in the attack, using my uncle's tone. "I wouldn't say one kind of country's any better-looking than another—not really."

And then my uncle again: "To someone *your* age, it just depends on what kind of country—if any—you happen to be used to."

"Maybe so," said I, not wanting to say more but unable to stop myself. "Maybe so, but I could live for a hundred years in that scrubby-looking country without ever getting used to it."

No doubt the rolling pasture land on both sides of the highway now—still green in November, and looking especially green after recent rain—caused me to put more feeling into my statement than I might otherwise have done. And it may also have had its effect on the two men in the back seat.

There was a brief pause, and then my uncle fired away again. "Every countryside has its own kind of beauty. It's up to you to learn to see it, that's all."

Then Mr. Lowder: "And if you don't see it, it's just your loss. Because it's *there*."

"Besides, a lot you know about that country," my uncle went on, in what seemed to me an even more captious spirit than before. "And how could you? How could you judge, flying along the highway at fifty miles an hour, flapping that damned wiper off and on?"

"More than that," said Mr. Lowder with renewed energy, "you would have to have seen that country thirty years ago to understand why it looks the way it does now. That was when they cut out the last of the old timber. I've heard it said that when the first white men came through that section it had the prettiest stand of timber on the continent!"

Suddenly I blurted out, "But what's that got to do with it?" I was so irritated that I could feel the blood rising in my cheeks and I knew that the back of my neck was already crimson. "It's how the country looks now I'm talking about. Anyway, I'm only here as your driver. I don't *have* to like the scenery, do I?"

Both men broke into laughter. It was a kind of laughter that expressed both apology and relief. My uncle bent forward, thumped me on the shoulder with his knuckle, and said, "Don't be so touchy, boy." Almost at once, they resumed their earlier dialogue. One of them lowered a window a little way to let out some of the smoke, but the aroma of their cigars continued to fill the car, and they spoke in the same slow cadences as before and in the same tranquil tone.

We reached the town in Alabama toward the middle of the afternoon and we spent the night in an old clapboard hotel on the courthouse square. After dinner that night, the two men sat in the lobby and talked to other men who were staying there in the hotel. I found myself a place near the stove and sat there with my feet on the fender, sometimes dozing off. But even when I was half asleep I was still listening to see whether, in their talk, either Mr. Lowder or my uncle would make any reference to our adventure that morning.

Neither did. Instead, as the evening wore on and they got separated and were sitting with two different groups of men, I heard them both repeating the very stories they had told in the car before we crossed the Tennessee River—stories about bird hunting and field trials and about my uncle's three-hour breakfast in the old house with the neo-classic portico.

What You Hear from 'Em?

⊚⊚⊚⊚⊚⊚⊚⊚⊚⊚⊚⊚⊚⊚⊚⊚⊚⊚⊚⊚⊚⊚⊚⊚⊚⊚⊚⊚⊚

Sometimes people misunderstood Aunt Munsie's question, but she wouldn't bother to clarify it. She might repeat it two or three times, in order to drown out some fool answer she was getting from some fool white woman, or man, either. "What you hear from 'em?" she would ask. And, then, louder and louder: "What you hear from 'em? *What you hear from 'em?*" She was so deaf that anyone whom she thoroughly drowned out only laughed and said Aunt Munsie had got so deaf she couldn't hear it thunder.

It was, of course, only the most utterly fool answers that ever received Aunt Munsie's drowning-out treatment. She was, for a number of years at least, willing to listen to those who mistook her "'em" to mean any and all of the Dr. Tolliver children. And for more years than that she was willing to listen to those who thought she wanted just *any* news of her two favorites among the Tolliver children—Thad and Will. But later on she stopped putting the question to all insensitive and frivolous souls who didn't understand that what she was interested in hearing—and *all* she was interested in hearing—was when Mr. Thad Tolliver and Mr. Will Tolliver were going to pack up their families and come back to Thornton for good.

They had always promised her to come back—to come back sure enough, once and for all. On separate occasions, both Thad and Will had actually given her their word. She had not seen them together for ten years, but each of them had made visits to Thornton now and then with his own family. She would see a big car stopping in front of her house on a Sunday afternoon and see either Will or Thad with his wife and children piling out into the dusty street—it was nearly always summer when they came—and then see them filing across the street, jumping the ditch, and unlatching the gate to her yard. She always met them in that pen of a yard, but long before they had jumped the ditch she was clapping her hands and calling out, "Hai-ee! Hai-ee, now! Look-a-here! Whee! Whee! Look-a-here!" She had got so blind that she was never sure whether it was Mr. Thad or Mr. Will until she had her arms around his waist. They had always looked a good deal alike, and their city clothes made them look even more alike nowadays. Aunt Munsie's eyes were so bad, besides being so full of moisture on those occasions, that she really recognized them by their girth. Will had grown a regular wash pot of a stomach and Thad was still thin as a rail. They would sit on her porch for twenty or thirty minutes— whichever one it was and his family—and then they would be gone again.

Aunt Munsie would never try to detain them—not seriously. Those short little old visits didn't mean a thing to her. He—Thad or Will—would lean against the banister rail and tell her how well his children were doing in school or college, and she would make each child in turn come and sit beside her on the swing for a minute and receive a hug around the waist or shoulders. They were timid with her, not seeing her any more than they did, but she could tell from their big Tolliver smiles that they liked her to hug them and make over them. Usually, she would lead them all out to her back yard and show them her pigs and dogs and chickens. (She always had at least one frizzly chicken to show the children.) They would traipse through her house to the back yard and then traipse through again to the front porch. It would be time for them to go when they came back, and Aunt Munsie would look up at *him*—Mr. Thad or Mr. Will (she had begun calling them "Mr." the day they married)— and say, "Now, look-a-here. When you comin' back?"

Both Thad and Will knew what she meant, of course, and whichever it was would tell her he was making definite plans to wind up his business and that he was going to buy a certain piece of property, "a mile north of town" or "on the old River Road," and build a jim-dandy house there. He would say, too, how good Aunt Munsie's own house was looking, and his wife would say how grand the zinnias and cannas looked in the yard. (The yard was all flowers—not a blade of grass, and the ground packed hard in little paths between the flower beds.) The visit was almost over then. There remained only the exchange of presents. One of the children would hand Aunt Munsie a paper bag containing a pint of whiskey or a carton of cigarettes. Aunt Munsie would go to her back porch or to the pit in the yard and get a fern or a wandering Jew, potted in a rusty lard bucket, and make Mrs. Thad or Mrs. Will take it along. Then the visit was over, and they would leave. From the porch Aunt Munsie would wave goodbye with one hand and lay the other hand, trembling slightly, on the banister rail. And sometimes her departing guests, looking back from the yard, would observe that the banisters themselves were trembling under her hand—so insecurely were those knobby banisters attached to the knobby porch pillars. Often as not Thad or Will, observing this, would remind his wife that Aunt Munsie's porch banisters and pillars had come off a porch of the house where he had grown up. (Their father, Dr. Tolliver, had been one of the first to widen his porches and remove the gingerbread from his house.) The children and their mother would wave to Aunt Munsie from the street. Their father would close the gate, resting his hand a moment on its familiar wrought-iron frame, and wave to her before he jumped the ditch. If the children had not gone too far ahead, he might even draw their attention to the iron fence which, with its iron gate, had been around the yard at the Tolliver place till Dr. Tolliver took it down and set out a hedge, just a few weeks before he died.

But such paltry little visits meant nothing to Aunt Munsie. No more did the letters that came with "her things" at Christmas. She was supposed to get her daughter, Lucrecie, who lived next door, to read the letters, but in late years she had taken to putting them away unopened, and some of the presents, too. All she wanted to hear from *them* was when they were coming back for good, and she had learned that the Christmas letters never told her that. On her daily route with her slop wagon through the square, up Jackson Street, and down Jefferson, there were only four or five houses left where she asked her question. These were houses where the amount of pig slop was not worth stopping for, houses where one old maid, or maybe two, lived, or a widow with one old bachelor son who had never amounted to anything and ate no more than a woman. And so—in the summertime, anyway—she took to calling out at the top of her lungs, when she approached the house of one of the elect, "What you hear from 'em?" Sometimes a Miss Patty or a Miss Lucille or a Mr. Ralph would get up out of a porch chair and come down the brick walk to converse with Aunt Munsie. Or sometimes one of them would just lean out over the shrubbery planted around the porch and call, "Not a thing, Munsie. Not a thing lately."

She would shake her head and call back, "Naw. Naw. Not a thing. Nobody don't hear from 'em. Too busy, they be."

Aunt Munsie's skin was the color of a faded tow sack. She was hardly four feet tall. She was generally believed to be totally bald, and on her head she always wore a white dust cap with an elastic band. She wore an apron, too, while making her rounds with her slop wagon. Even when the weather got bad and she tied a wool scarf about her head and wore an overcoat, she put on an apron over the coat. Her hands and feet were delicately small, which made the old-timers sure she was of Guinea stock that had come to Tennessee out of South Carolina. What most touched the hearts of old ladies on Jackson and Jefferson Streets were her little feet. The sight of her feet "took them back to the old days," they said, because Aunt Munsie still wore flat-heeled, high button shoes. Where ever did Munsie find such shoes any more?

She walked down the street, down the very center of the street, with a spry step, and she was continually turning her head from side to side, as though looking at the old houses and trees for the first time. If her sight was as bad as she sometimes let on it was, she probably recognized the houses only by their roof lines against the Thornton sky. Since this was nearly thirty years ago, most of the big Victorian and ante-bellum houses were still standing, though with their lovely gingerbread work beginning to go. (It went first from houses where there was someone, like Dr. Tolliver, with a special eye for style and for keeping up with the times.) The streets hadn't yet been broadened—or only Nashville Street had—and the maples and elms met above the streets. In the autumn, their leaves covered the high banks and filled the deep ditches on either side. The dark macadam surfacing itself was barely wide enough for two automobiles to pass. Aunt Munsie, pulling her slop wagon, which was a long, low, four-wheeled vehicle about the size and shape of a coffin, paraded down the center of the street without any regard for, if with any awareness of, the traffic problems she sometimes made. Seizing the wagon's heavy, sawed-off-looking tongue, she hauled it after her with a series of impatient jerks, just as though that tongue were the arm of some very stubborn, overgrown white child she had to nurse in her old age. Strangers in town or trifling high-school boys would blow their horns at her, but she was never known to so much as glance over her shoulder at the sound of a horn. Now and then a pedestrian on the sidewalk would call out to the driver of an automobile, "She's so deaf she can't hear it thunder."

It wouldn't have occurred to anyone in Thornton—not in those days—that something ought to be done about Aunt Munsie and her wagon for the sake of the public good. In those days, everyone had equal rights on the streets of Thornton. A vehicle was a vehicle, and a person was a person, each with the right to move as slowly as he pleased and to stop where and as often as he pleased. In the Thornton mind, there was no imaginary line down the middle of the street, and, indeed, no one there at that time had heard of drawing a real line on *any* street. It was merely out of politeness that you made room for others to pass. Nobody would have blown a horn at an old colored woman with her slop wagon—nobody but some Yankee stranger or a trifling high-school boy or maybe old Mr. Ralph Hadley in a special fit of temper. When citizens of Thornton were in a particular hurry and got caught behind Aunt Munsie, they leaned out their car windows and shouted: "Aunt Munsie, can you make a little room?" And Aunt Munsie didn't fail to hear *them*. She would holler, "Hai-ee, now! Whee! Look-a-here!" and jerk her wagon to one side. As they passed her, she would wave her little hand and grin a toothless, pink-gummed grin.

Yet, without any concern for the public good, Aunt Munsie's friends and connections among the white women began to worry more and more about the danger of her being run down by an automobile. They talked among themselves and they talked to her about it. They wanted her to give up collecting slop, now she had got so blind and deaf. "Pshaw," said Aunt Munsie, closing her eyes contemptuously. "Not me." She meant by that that no one would dare run into her or her wagon. Sometimes when she crossed the square on a busy Saturday morning or on a first Monday, she would hold up one hand with the palm turned outward and stop all traffic until she was safely across and in the alley beside the hotel.

Thornton wasn't even then what it had been before the Great World War. In every other house there was a stranger or a mill hand who had moved up from factory town. Some of the biggest old places stood empty, the way Dr. Tolliver's had until it burned. They stood empty not because nobody wanted to rent them or buy them but because the heirs who had gone off somewhere making money could never be got to part with "the home place." The story was that Thad Tolliver nearly went crazy when he heard their old house had burned, and wanted to sue the town, and even said he was going to help get the Republicans into office. Yet Thad had hardly put foot in the house since the day his daddy died. It was said the Tolliver house had caught fire from the Major Pettigru house, which had burned two nights before. And no doubt it had. Sparks could have smoldered in that roof of rotten shingles for a long time before bursting into flame. Some even said the Pettigru house might have caught from the Johnston house, which had burned earlier that same fall. But Thad knew and Will knew and everybody knew the town wasn't to blame, and knew there was no firebug. Why, those old houses stood there empty year after year, and in the fall the leaves fell from the trees and settled around the porches and stoops, and who was there to rake the leaves? Maybe it was a good thing those houses burned, and maybe it would have been as well if some of the houses that still had people in them burned, too. There were houses in Thornton the heirs had never left that looked far worse than the Tolliver or the Pettigru or the Johnston house ever had. The people who lived in them were the ones who gave Aunt Munsie the biggest fool answers to her question, the people whom she soon quit asking her question of or even passing the time of day with, except when she couldn't help it, out of politeness. For, truly, to Aunt Munsie there were things under the sun worse than going off and getting rich in Nashville or in Memphis or even in Washington, D.C. It was a subject she and her daughter Lucrecie sometimes mouthed at each other about across their back fence. Lucrecie was shiftless, and she liked shiftless white people like the ones who didn't have the ambition to leave Thornton. She thought their shiftlessness showed they were *quality.* "Quality?" Aunt Munsie would echo, her voice full of sarcasm. "Whee! Hai-ee! You talk like *you* was *my* mammy, Crecie. Well, if there be quality, there be quality *and* quality. There's quality and there's *has-been* quality, Crecie." There was no end to that argument Aunt Munsie had with Crecie, and it wasn't at all important to Aunt Munsie. The people who still lived in those houses—the ones she called has-been quality—meant little more to her than the mill hands, or the strangers from up North who ran the Piggly Wiggly, the five-and-ten-cent store, and the roller-skating rink.

There was this to be said, though, for the has-been quality: they knew *who* Aunt Munsie was, and in a limited, literal way they understood what she said. But those *others*—why, they thought Aunt Munsie a beggar, and she knew they did. They spoke of her as Old What You Have for Mom, because that's what they thought she was saying when she called out, "What you hear from 'em?" Their ears were not attuned to that soft "r" she put in "from" or the elision that made "from 'em" sound to them like "for Mom." Many's the time Aunt Munsie had seen or sensed the presence of one of those *other* people, watching from next door, when Miss Leonora Lovell, say, came down her front walk and handed her a little parcel of scraps across the ditch. Aunt Munsie knew what they thought of her—how they laughed at her and felt sorry for her and despised her all at once. But, like the has-been quality, they didn't matter, never had, never would. Not ever.

Oh, they mattered in a way to Lucrecie. Lucrecie thought about them and talked about them a lot. She called them "white trash" and even "radical Republicans." It made Aunt Munsie grin to hear Crecie go on, because she knew Crecie got all her notions from her own has-been-quality people. And so it didn't matter, except that Aunt Munsie knew that Crecie truly had all sorts of good sense and had only been carried away and spoiled by such folks as she had worked for, such folks as had really raised Crecie from the time she was big enough to run errands for them, fifty years back. In her heart, Aunt Munsie knew that even Lucrecie didn't matter to her the way a daughter might. It was because while Aunt Munsie had been raising a family of white children, a different sort of white people from hers had been raising her own child, Crecie. Sometimes, if Aunt Munsie was in her chicken yard or out in her little patch of cotton when Mr. Thad or Mr. Will arrived, Crecie would come out to the fence and say, "Mama, some of your chillun's out front."

Miss Leonora Lovell and Miss Patty Bean, and especially Miss Lucille Satterfield, were all the time after Aunt Munsie to give up collecting slop. "You're going to get run over by one of those crazy drivers, Munsie," they said. Miss Lucille was the widow of old Judge Satterfield. "If the Judge were alive, Munsie," she said, "I'd make him find a way to stop you. But the men down at the courthouse don't listen to the women in this town any more. Not since we got the vote. And I think they'd be most too scared of you to do what I want them to do." Aunt Munsie wouldn't listen to any of that. She knew that if Miss Lucille had come out there to her gate, she must have *something* she was going to say about Mr. Thad or Mr. Will. Miss Lucille had two brothers and a son of her own who were lawyers in Memphis, and who lived in style down there and kept Miss Lucille in style here in Thornton. Memphis was where Thad Tolliver had his Ford and Lincoln agency, and so Miss

Lucille always had news about Thad, and indirectly about Will, too.

"Is they doin' any good? What you hear from 'em?" Aunt Munsie asked Miss Lucille one afternoon in early spring. She had come along just when Miss Lucille was out picking some of the jonquils that grew in profusion on the steep bank between the sidewalk and the ditch in front of her house.

"Mr. Thad and his folks will be up one day in April, Munsie," Miss Lucille said in her pleasantly hoarse voice. "I understand Mr. Will and his crowd may come for Easter Sunday."

"One day, and gone again!" said Aunt Munsie.

"We always try to get them to stay at least one night, but they're busy folks, Munsie."

"When they comin' back sure enough, Miss Lucille?"

"Goodness knows, Munsie. Goodness knows. Goodness knows when any of them are coming back to stay." Miss Lucille took three quick little steps down the bank and hopped lightly across the ditch. "They're prospering so, Munsie," she said, throwing her chin up and smiling proudly. This fragile lady, this daughter, wife, sister, mother of lawyers (and, of course, the darling of all their hearts), stood there in the street with her pretty little feet and shapely ankles close together, and holding a handful of jonquils before her as if it were her bridal bouquet. "They're *all* prospering so, Munsie. Mine *and* yours. You ought to go down to Memphis to see them now and then, the way I do. Or go up to Nashville to see Mr. Will. I understand he's got an even finer establishment than Thad. They've done well, Munsie—yours *and* mine—and we can be proud of them. You owe it to yourself to go and see how well they're fixed. They're rich men by our standards in Thornton, and they're going farther—*all* of them."

Aunt Munsie dropped the tongue of her wagon noisily on the

pavement. "What I want to go see 'em for?" she said angrily and with a lowering brow. Then she stooped and, picking up the wagon tongue again, she wheeled her vehicle toward the middle of the street, to get by Miss Lucille, and started off toward the square. As she turned out into the street, the brakes of a car, as so often, screeched behind her. Presently everyone in the neighborhood could hear Mr. Ralph Hadley tooting the insignificant little horn on his mama's coupé and shouting at Aunt Munsie in his own tooty voice, above the sound of the horn. Aunt Munsie pulled over, making just enough room to let poor old Mr. Ralph get by but without once looking back at him. Then, before Mr. Ralph could get his car started again, Miss Lucille was running along beside Aunt Munsie, saying, "Munsie, you be careful! You're going to meet your death on the streets of Thornton, Tennessee!"

"Let 'em," said Aunt Munsie.

Miss Lucille didn't know whether Munsie meant "Let 'em run over me; I don't care" or meant "Let 'em just dare!" Miss Lucille soon turned back, without Aunt Munsie's ever looking at her. And when Mr. Ralph Hadley did get his motor started, and sailed past in his mama's coupé, Aunt Munsie didn't give him a look, either. Nor did Mr. Ralph bother to turn his face to look at Aunt Munsie. He was on his way to the drugstore, to pick up his mama's prescriptions, and he was too entirely put out, peeved, and upset to endure even the briefest exchange with that ugly, uppity old Munsie of the Tollivers.

Aunt Munsie continued to tug her slop wagon on toward the square. There was a more animated expression on her face than usual, and every so often her lips would move rapidly and emphatically over a phrase or sentence. Why should she go to Memphis and Nashville and see how rich they were? No matter how rich they were, what difference did it make; they didn't own any land, did they? Or at least none in Cameron County. She had heard the old

Doctor tell them—tell his boys and tell his girls, and tell the old lady, too, in her day—that nobody was rich who didn't own land, and nobody stayed rich who didn't see after his land firsthand. But of course Aunt Munsie had herself mocked the old Doctor to his face for going on about land so much. She knew it was only something he had heard his own daddy go on about. She would say right to his face that she hadn't ever seen *him* behind a plow. And was there ever anybody more scared of a mule than Dr. Tolliver was? Mules or horses, either? Aunt Munsie had heard him say that the happiest day of his life was the day he first learned that the horseless carriage was a reality.

No, it was not really to own land that Thad and Will ought to come back to Thornton. It was more that if they were going to be rich, they ought to come home, where their granddaddy had owned land and where their money counted for something. How could they ever be rich anywhere else? They could have a lot of money in the bank and a fine house, that was all—like that mill manager from Chi. The mill manager could have a yard full of big cars and a stucco house as big as you like, but who would ever take him for rich? Aunt Munsie would sometimes say all these things to Crecie, or something as nearly like them as she could find words for. Crecie might nod her head in agreement or she might be in a mood to say being rich wasn't any good for anybody and didn't matter, and that you could live on just being quality better than on being rich in Thornton. "Quality's better than land or better than money in the bank here," Crecie would say.

Aunt Munsie would sneer at her and say, "It never were."

Lucrecie could talk all she wanted about the old times! Aunt Munsie knew too much about what they were like, for both the richest white folks and the blackest field hands. Nothing about the old times was as good as these days, and there were going to be better times yet when Mr. Thad and Mr. Will Tolliver came back. Everybody lived easier now than they used to, and were better off. She could never be got to reminisce about her childhood in slavery, or her life with her husband, or even about those halcyon days after the old Mizziz had died and Aunt Munsie's word had become law in the Tolliver household. Without being able to book read or even to make numbers, she had finished raising the whole pack of towheaded Tollivers just as the Mizziz would have wanted it done. The Doctor told her she *had* to—he didn't ever once think about getting another wife, or taking in some cousin, not after his "Molly darling"—and Aunt Munsie *did*. But, as Crecie said, when a time was past in her mama's life, it seemed to be gone and done with in her head, too.

Lucrecie would say frankly she thought her mama was "hard about people and things in the world." She talked about her mama not only to the Blalocks, for whom she had worked all her life, but to anybody else who gave her an opening. It wasn't just about her mama, though, that she would talk to anybody. She liked to talk, and she talked about Aunt Munsie not in any ugly, resentful way but as she would about when the sheep-rains would begin or where the fire was last night. (Crecie was twice the size of her mama, and black the way her old daddy had been, and loud and good-natured the way he was—or at least the way Aunt Munsie wasn't. You wouldn't have known they were mother and daughter, and not many of the young people in town did realize it. Only by accident did they live next door to each other; Mr. Thad and Mr. Will had bought Munsie her house, and Crecie had heired hers from her second husband.) *That* was how she talked about her mama—as she would have about any lonely, eccentric, harmless neighbor. "I may be dead wrong, but I think Mama's kind of hardhearted," she would say. "Mama's a good old soul, I reckon, but when something's past, it's gone and done with for Mama. She don't think about day before yestiddy—yestiddy, either. I don't know, maybe that's the way to be. Maybe that's why the old soul's gonna outlive us all." Then, obviously thinking about what a picture of health she herself was at sixty, Crecie would toss her head about and laugh so loud you might hear her all the way out to the fair grounds.

Crecie, however, knew her mama was not honest-to-God mean and hadn't ever been mean to the Tolliver children, the way the Blalocks liked to make out she had. All the Tolliver children but Mr. Thad and Mr. Will had quarreled with her for good by the time they were grown, but they had quarreled with the old Doctor, too (and as if they were the only ones who shook off their old folks this day and time). When Crecie talked about her mama, she didn't spare her anything, but she was fair to her, too. And it was in no hateful or disloyal spirit that she took part in the conspiracy that finally got Aunt Munsie and her slop wagon off the streets of Thornton. Crecie would have done the same for any neighbor. She had small part enough, actually, in that conspiracy. Her part was merely to break the news to Aunt Munsie that there was now a law against keeping pigs within the city limits. It was a small part but one that no one else quite dared to take.

"They ain't no such law!" Aunt Munsie roared back at Crecie. She was slopping her pigs when Crecie came to the fence and told her about the law. It had seemed the most appropriate time to Lucrecie. "They ain't never been such a law, Crecie," Aunt Munsie said. "Every house on Jackson and Jefferson used to keep pigs."

"It's a brand-new law, Mama."

Aunt Munsie finished bailing out the last of the slop from her wagon. It was just before twilight. The last, weak rays of the sun colored the clouds behind the mock orange tree in Crecie's yard. When Aunt Munsie turned around from the sty, she pretended that that little bit of light in the clouds hurt her eyes, and turned away her head. And when Lucrecie said that everybody had until the first of the year to get rid of their pigs, Aunt Munsie was in a spell of deafness. She headed out toward the crib to get some corn for the chickens. She was trying to think whether anybody else inside the town still kept pigs. Herb Mallory did—two doors beyond Crecie. Then Aunt Munsie remembered Herb didn't pay town taxes. The town line ran between him and Shad Willis.

That was sometime in June, and before July came, Aunt Munsie knew all there was worth knowing about the conspiracy. Mr. Thad and Mr. Will had each been in town for a day during the spring. They and their families had been to her house and sat on the porch; the children had gone back to look at her half-grown collie dog and the two hounds, at the old sow and her farrow of new pigs, and at the frizzliest frizzly chicken Aunt Munsie had ever had. And on those visits to Thornton, Mr. Thad and Mr. Will had also made their usual round among their distant kin and close friends. Everywhere they went, they had heard of the near-accidents Aunt Munsie was causing with her slop wagon and the real danger there was of her being run over. Miss Lucille Satterfield and Miss Patty Bean had both been to the mayor's office and also to see Judge Lawrence to try to get Aunt Munsie "ruled" off the streets, but the men in the courthouse and in the mayor's office didn't listen to the women in Thornton any more. And so either Mr. Thad or Mr. Will—how would which one of them it was matter to Munsie?—had been prevailed upon to stop by Mayor Lunt's office, and in a few seconds' time had set the wheels of conspiracy in motion. Soon a general inquiry had been made in the town as to how many citizens still kept pigs. Only two property owners besides Aunt Munsie had been found to have pigs on their premises, and they, being men, had been docile and reasonable enough to sell what they had on hand to Mr. Will or Mr. Thad Tolliver. Immediately afterward—within a matter of weeks, that is—a town ordinance had been passed forbidding the possession of swine within the corporate limits of Thornton. Aunt Munsie had got the story bit by bit from Miss Leonora and Miss Patty and Miss Lucille and others, including the constable himself, whom she did not hesitate to stop right in the middle of the square on a Saturday noon. Whether it was Mr. Thad or Mr. Will who had been prevailed upon by the ladies she never ferreted out, but that was only because she did not wish to do so.

The constable's word was the last word for her. The constable said yes, it was the law, and he admitted yes, he had sold his own pigs—for the constable was one of those two reasonable souls—to Mr. Thad or Mr. Will. He didn't say which of them it was, or if he did, Aunt Munsie didn't bother to remember it. And after her interview with the constable, Aunt Munsie never again exchanged words with any human being about the ordinance against pigs. That afternoon, she took a fishing pole from under her house and drove the old sow and the nine shoats down to Herb Mallory's, on the outside of town. They were his, she said, if he wanted them, and he could pay her at killing time.

It was literally true that Aunt Munsie never again exchanged words with anyone about the ordinance against pigs or about the conspiracy she had discovered against herself. But her daughter Lucrecie had a tale to tell about what Aunt Munsie did that afternoon after she had seen the constable and before she drove the pigs over to Herb Mallory's. It was mostly a tale of what Aunt Munsie said to her pigs and to her dogs and her chickens.

Crecie was in her own back yard washing her hair when her mama came down the rickety porch steps and into the yard next door. Crecie had her head in the pot of suds, and so she couldn't look up, but she knew by the way Mama flew down the steps that there was trouble. "She come down them steps like she was wasp-nest bit, or like some young'on who's got hisself wasp-nest bit—and

her all of eighty, I reckon!" Then, as Crecie told it, her mama
scurried around in the yard for a minute or so like she thought
Judgment was about to catch up with her, and pretty soon she
commenced slamming at something. Crecie wrapped a towel about
her soapy head, squatted low, and edged over toward the plank
fence. She peered between the planks and saw what her mama was
up to. Since there never had been a gate to the fence around the
pigsty, Mama had taken the wood ax and was knocking a hole in it.
But directly, just after Crecie had taken her place by the plank fence,
her mama had left off her slamming at the sty and turned about so
quickly and so exactly toward Crecie that Crecie thought the poor,
blind old soul had managed to spy her squatting there. Right away,
though, Crecie realized it was not *her* that Mama was staring at.
She saw that all Aunt Munsie's chickens and those three dogs of
hers had come up behind her, and were all clucking and whining to
know why she didn't stop that infernal racket and put out some
feed for them.

Crecie's mama set one hand on her hip and rested the ax on the
ground. "Just look at yuh!" she said, and then she let the chickens
and the dogs—and the pigs, too—have it. She told them what a
miserable bunch of creatures they were, and asked them what right
they had to always be looking for handouts from her. She sounded
like the boss-man who's caught all his pickers laying off before
sundown, and she sounded, too, like the preacher giving his sinners
Hail Columbia at camp meeting. Finally, shouting at the top of her
voice and swinging the ax wide and broad above their heads, she
sent the dogs howling under the house and the chickens scattering
in every direction. "Now, g'wine! G'wine widja!" she shouted after
them. Only the collie pup, of the three dogs, didn't scamper to the
farthest corner underneath the house. He stopped under the porch
steps, and not two seconds later he was poking his long head out
again and showing the whites of his doleful brown eyes. Crecie's

mama took a step toward him and then she halted. "You want to know what's the commotion about? I reckoned you would," she said with profound contempt, as though the collie were a more reasonable soul than the other animals, and as though there were nothing she held in such thorough disrespect as reason. "I tell you what the commotion's about," she said. "They *ain't* comin' back. They ain't never comin' back. They ain't never had no notion of comin' back." She turned her head to one side, and the only explanation Crecie could find for her mama's next words was that that collie pup did look so much like Miss Lucille Satterfield.

"Why don't I go down to Memphis or up to Nashville and see 'em sometime, like *you* does?" Aunt Munsie asked the collie. "I tell you why. Becaze I ain't nothin' to 'em in Memphis, and they ain't nothin' to me in Nashville. *You* can go!" she said, advancing and shaking the big ax at the dog. "A collie dog's a collie dog anywhar. But Aunt Munsie, she's just their Aunt Munsie here in Thornton. I got mind enough to see *that*." The collie slowly pulled his head back under the steps, and Aunt Munsie watched for a minute to see if he would show himself again. When he didn't, she went and jerked the fishing pole out from under the house and headed toward the pigsty. Crecie remained squatting beside the fence until her mama and the pigs were out in the street and on their way to Herb Mallory's.

That was the end of Aunt Munsie's keeping pigs and the end of her daily rounds with her slop wagon, but it was not the end of Aunt Munsie. She lived on for nearly twenty years after that, till long after Lucrecie had been put away, in fine style, by the Blalocks. Ever afterward, though, Aunt Munsie seemed different to people. They said she softened, and everybody said it was a change for the better. She would take paper money from under her carpet, or out of the chinks in her walls, and buy things for up at the church, or buy her own whiskey when she got sick, instead of making somebody bring her a nip. On the square she would laugh and holler with the white folks the way they liked her to and the way Crecie and all the other old-timers did, and she even took to tying a bandanna about her head—took to talking old-nigger foolishness, too, about the Bell Witch, and claiming she remembered the day General N. B. Forrest rode into town and saved all the cotton from the Yankees at the depot. When Mr. Will and Mr. Thad came to see her with their families, she got so she would reminisce with them about their daddy and tease them about all the silly little things they had done when they were growing up: "Mr. Thad—him still in kilts, too—he says, 'Aunt Munsie, reach down in yo' stockin' and git me a copper cent. I want some store candy.'" She told them about how Miss Yola Ewing, the sewing woman, heard her threatening to bust Will's back wide open when he broke the lamp chimney, and how Miss Yola went to the Doctor and told him he ought to run Aunt Munsie off. Then Aunt Munsie and the Doctor had had a big laugh about it out in the kitchen, and Miss Yola must have eavesdropped on them, because she left without finishing the girls' Easter dresses.

Indeed, these visits from Mr. Thad and Mr. Will continued as long as Aunt Munsie lived, but she never asked them any more about when they were sure enough coming back. And the children, though she hugged them more than ever—and, toward the last, there were the children's children to be hugged—never again set foot in her back yard. Aunt Munsie lived on for nearly twenty years, and when they finally buried her, they put on her tombstone that she was aged one hundred years, though nobody knew how old she was. There was no record of when she was born. All anyone knew was that in her last years she had said she was a girl helping about the big house when freedom came. That would have made her probably about twelve years old in 1865, according to her statements and depictions. But all agreed that in her extreme old age Aunt Munsie, like other old darkies, was not very reliable about dates and such things. Her spirit softened, even her voice lost some of the rasping quality that it had always had, and in general she became not very reliable about facts.

A Wife of Nashville

The Lovells' old cook Sarah had quit to get married in the spring, and they didn't have anybody else for a long time—not for several months. It was during the Depression, and when a servant quit, people in Nashville (and even people out at Thornton, where the Lovells came from) tried to see how long they could go before they got another. All through the summer, there would be knocks on the Lovells' front door or on the wooden porch floor, by the steps. And when one of the children or their mother went to the door, some Negro man or woman would be standing there, smiling and holding out a piece of paper. A recommendation it was supposed to be, but the illegible note scribbled with a blunt lead pencil was something no white person could have written if he had tried. If Helen Ruth, the children's mother, went to the door, she always talked a while to whoever it was, but she hardly ever even looked at the note held out to her. She would give a piece of advice or say to meet her around at the back door for a handout. If one of the boys—there were three Lovell boys, and no girls—went to the door, he always brought the note in to Helen Ruth, unless John R., their father, was at home, sick with his back ailment. Helen Ruth would shake her head and say to tell whoever it was to go away! "Tell him to go back home," she said once to the oldest boy, who was standing in the sun-parlor doorway with a smudged scrap of paper in his hand. "Tell him if he had any sense, he never would have left the country."

"He's probably not from the country, Mother."

"They're all from the country," Helen Ruth said. "When they knock on the porch floor like that, they're bound to be from the country, and they're better off at home, where somebody cares something about them. I don't care anything about them any more than you do."

But one morning Helen Ruth hired a cheerful-looking and rather plump, light-complexioned young Negro girl named Jess McGehee, who had come knocking on the front-porch floor just as the others had. Helen Ruth talked to her at the front door for a while; then she told her to come around to the kitchen, and they talked there for nearly an hour. Jess stayed to fix lunch and supper, and after she had been there a few days, the family didn't know how they had ever got along without her.

In fact, Jess got on so well with the Lovells that Helen Ruth even decided to let her come and live on the place, a privilege she had never before allowed a servant of hers. Together, she and Jess moved all of John R.'s junk—a grass duck-hunting outfit, two mounted stags' heads, an outboard motor, and so on—from the little room above the garage into the attic of the house. John R. lent Jess the money for the down payment on a "suit" of furniture, and Jess moved in. "You would never know she was out there," Helen Ruth told her friends. "There is never any rumpus. And her room! It's as clean as yours or mine."

Jess worked for them for eight years. John R. got so one of his favorite remarks was, "The honeymoon is over, but this is the real thing this time." Then he would go on about what he called Helen Ruth's "earlier affairs." The last one before Jess was Sarah, who quit to get married and go to Chicago at the age of sixty-eight. She had been with them for six years and was famous for her pies and her banana dishes.

Before Sarah, there was Carrie. Carrie had been with them when the two younger boys were born, and it was she who had once tried to persuade Helen Ruth not to go to the hospital but to let her act as midwife. She had quit them after five years, to become an undertaker. And before Carrie there was Jane Blakemore, the very first of them all, whom John R. and Helen Ruth had brought with them from Thornton to Nashville when they married. She lasted less than three years; she quit soon after John R., Jr., was born, because, she said, the baby made her nervous.

"It's an honorable record," John R. would say. "Each of them was better than the one before, and each one stayed with us longer. It proves that experience is the best teacher."

Jess's eight years were the years when the boys were growing up; the boys were children when she came, and when she left them, the youngest, little Robbie, had learned to drive the car. In a sense, it was Jess who taught all three boys to drive. She didn't give them their first lessons, of course, because, like Helen Ruth, she had never sat at the wheel of an automobile in her life. She had not ridden in a car more than half a dozen times when she came to the Lovells, but just by chance, one day, she was in the car when John R. let John R., Jr., take the wheel. The car would jerk and lunge forward every time the boy shifted gears, and his father said, "Keep your mind on what you're doing."

"I am," John R., Jr., said, "but it just does that. What makes it do it?"

"Think!" John R. said. "Think! . . . *Think!*"

"I *am* thinking, but what makes it do it?"

Suddenly, Jess leaned forward from the back seat and said, "You letting the clutch out too fast, honey."

Both father and son were so surprised they could not help laughing. They laughed harder, of course, because what Jess said was true. And Jess laughed with them. When they had driven another block, they reached a boulevard stop, and in the process of putting on the brake John R., Jr., killed the engine and then flooded the motor. His father shouted, "Well, let it rest! We're just stuck here for about twenty minutes!"

Jess, who was seated with one arm around a big bag of groceries, began to laugh again. "Turn off the key," she said. "Press down on the starter a spell. Then torectly you turn on the key and she'll start."

John R. looked over his shoulder at her, not smiling, but not frowning, either. Presently, he gave the order, "Try it."

"Try what *Jess said?*" John R., Jr., asked.

"Try what Jess said."

The boy tried it, and in a moment he was racing the motor and grinning at his father. When they had got safely across the boulevard, John R. turned around to Jess again. He asked in a quiet, almost humble manner—the same manner he used when describing the pains in his back to Helen Ruth—where she had learned these things about an automobile. "Law," she said, "I learnt them listening to my brother-in-law that drives a truck talk. I don't reckon I really know'm, but I can say them."

John R. was so impressed by the incident that he did not make it one of his stories. He told Helen Ruth about it, of course, and he mentioned it sometimes to his close friends when they were discussing "the good things" about Negroes. With his sons, he used it as an example of how much you can learn by listening to other people talk, and after that day he would permit John R., Jr., to go for drives in the car without him provided Jess went along in his place. Later on, when the other boys got old enough to drive, there were periods when he turned their instruction over to Jess. Helen Ruth even talked of learning to drive, herself, with the aid of Jess.

But it never came to more than talk with Helen Ruth, though John R. encouraged her, saying he thought driving was perhaps a serious strain on his back. She talked about it for several months, but in the end she said that the time had passed when she could learn new skills. When John R. tried to encourage her in the idea, she would sometimes look out one of the sun-parlor windows toward the street and think of how much she had once wanted to learn to drive. But that had been long ago, right after they were married, in the days when John R. had owned a little Ford coupé. John R. was on the road for the Standard Candy Company then, and during most of the week she was alone in their apartment at the old Vaux Hall. While he was away John R. kept the coupé stored in a garage only two blocks east, on Broad Street; in those days traveling men still used the railroads, because Governor Peay hadn't yet paved Tennessee's highways. At that time, John R. had not believed in women driving automobiles, and Helen Ruth had felt that he must be right about it; she had even made fun of women who went *whizzing* about town, blowing horns at every intersection. Yet in her heart she had longed to drive that coupé! Jane Blakemore was working for them then, and one day Jane had put Helen Ruth's longings into words. "Wouldn't it be dandy," she said, "if me and you clomb in that car one of these weekdays and toured out to Thornton to see all the folks—white and black?"

Without a moment's hesitation, however, Helen Ruth gave the answer that she knew John R. would have given. "Now, think what you're saying, Jane!" she said. "Wouldn't we be a fool-looking pair pulling into the square at Thornton? *Think* about it. What if we should have a flat tire when we got out about as far as Nine Mile

Hill? Who would change it? *You* certainly couldn't! Jane Blakemore, I don't think you use your head about anything!"

That was the way Helen Ruth had talked to Jane on more occasions than one. She was a plain-spoken woman, and she never spoke plainer to anyone than she did to Jane Blakemore during the days when they were shut up together in that apartment at the Vaux Hall. Since Jane was from Thornton and knew how plain-spoken all Helen Ruth's family were, she paid little attention to the way Helen Ruth talked to her. She would smile, or else sneer, and go on with her work of cooking and cleaning. Sometimes she would rebel and speak just as plainly as Helen Ruth did. When Helen Ruth decided to introduce butter plates to their table, Jane said, "I ain't never heard tell of no butter dishes."

Helen Ruth raised her eyebrow. "That's because you are an ignoramus from Thornton, Tennessee," she said.

"I'm ignoramus enough to know ain't no need in nastying up all them dishes for me to wash."

Helen Ruth had, however, made Jane Blakemore learn to use butter plates and had made her keep the kitchen scrubbed and the other rooms of the apartment dusted and polished and in such perfect order that even John R. had noticed it when he came on weekends. Sometimes he had said, "You drive yourself too hard, Helen Ruth."

Jess McGehee was as eager and quick to learn new things as Jane Blakemore had been unwilling and slow. She would even put finger bowls on the breakfast table when there was grapefruit. And how she did spoil the three boys about their food! There were mornings when she cooked the breakfast eggs differently for each one of them while John R. sat and shook his head in disgust at the way she was pampering his sons. John R.'s "condition" in his back kept him at home a lot of the time during the eight years Jess was with them. He had long since left off traveling for the candy company; soon after the first baby came, he had opened an insurance agency of his own.

When Jane Blakemore left them and Helen Ruth hired Carrie (after fifteen or twenty interviews with other applicants), she had had to warn Carrie that John R.'s hours might be very irregular, because he was in business for himself and wasn't able merely to punch a time clock and quit when the day ended. "He's an onsurance man, ain't he?" Carrie had asked and had showed by the light in her eyes how favorably impressed she was. "I know about him," she had said. "He's a life-onsurance man, and that's the best kind to have."

At that moment, Helen Ruth thought perhaps she had made a mistake in Carrie. "I don't like my servant to discuss my husband's business," she said.

"No'm!" Carrie said with enthusiasm. "No, *ma'am!*" Helen Ruth was satisfied, but afterward she had often to tell herself that her first suspicion had been right. Carrie was nosy and prying and morbid—and she gossiped with other people's servants. Her curiosity and her gossiping were especially trying for Helen Ruth during her and John R.'s brief separation. They actually had separated for nearly two months right after Kenneth, the middle boy, was born. Helen Ruth had gone to her father's house at Thornton, taking the two babies and Carrie with her. The boys never knew about the trouble between their parents, of course, until Kenneth pried it out of his mother after they were all grown, and, at the time, people in Nashville and Thornton were not perfectly sure that it was a real separation. Helen Ruth had tried to tell herself that possibly Carrie didn't know it was a real separation. But she was never able to deny completely the significance of Carrie's behavior while they were at Thornton. Carrie's whole disposition had seemed to change the afternoon they left Nashville. Up until then, she had been a moody, shifty, rather loud-mouthed brown woman, full of darky compliments for white folks and of gratuitous promises of extra services she seldom rendered. But at Thornton she had put the old family servants to shame with her industriousness and her respectful, unassuming manner. "You don't find them like Carrie in Thornton any more," Helen Ruth's mother said. "The good ones all go to Nashville or Memphis." But Helen Ruth, sitting by an upstairs window one afternoon, saw her mother's cook and Carrie saunter-ing toward the back gate to meet a caller. She saw Carrie being introduced and then she recognized the caller as Jane Blakemore. Presently the cook returned to the kitchen and Helen Ruth saw Carrie and Jane enter the servants' house in the corner of the yard. During the hour that they visited there, Helen Ruth sat quietly by the window in the room with her two babies. It seemed to her the most terrible hour of her separation from John R. When Carrie and Jane reappeared on the stoop of the servants' house and Carrie was walking with Jane to the gate, there was no longer any doubt in Helen Ruth's mind but that she would return to her husband, and return without any complaints or stipulations. During that hour she had tried to imagine exactly what things the black Jane and the brown Carrie were talking about, or, rather, *how* and in what terms they were talking about the things they must be talking about. In her mind, she reviewed the sort of difficulties she had had with Jane and the sort she had with Carrie and tried to imagine what defense they would make for themselves—Jane for her laziness and contrari-ness, Carrie for her usual shiftiness and negligence. Would they blame her for these failings of theirs? Or would they blandly pass over their own failings and find fault with her for things that she was not even aware of, or that she could not help and could not begin to set right? Had she really misused these women, either the black one or the brown one? It seemed to her then that she had so little in life that she was entitled to the satisfaction of keeping an orderly house and to the luxury of efficient help. There was too much else she had not had—an "else" nameless to her, yet sorely missed—for her to be denied these small satisfactions. As she sat alone with her two babies in the old nursery and thought of the two servants gossiping about her, she became an object of pity to herself. And presently John R., wherever he might be at that moment—in his office or at the club or, more likely, on a hunting or fishing trip somewhere—became an object of pity, too. And her two babies, one in his crib and the other playing on the carpet with a string of spools, were objects of pity. Even Carrie, standing alone by the gate after Jane had gone, seemed a lone and pitiful figure.

A few days later, Helen Ruth and Carrie and the two baby boys returned to Nashville.

In Nashville, Carrie was herself again; everything was done in her old slipshod fashion. Except during that interval at Thornton, Carrie was never known to perform any task to Helen Ruth's complete satisfaction. Hardly a meal came to the table without the soup or the dessert or some important sauce having been forgotten; almost every week something important was left out of the laundry; during a general cleaning the upper sashes of two or three windows were invariably left unwashed. Yet never in her entire five years did Carrie answer back or admit an unwillingness to do the most menial or the most nonessential piece of work. In fact, one of her most exasperating pronouncements was, "You are exactly right," which was often followed by a lengthy description of how she would do the thing from then on, or an explanation of how it happened that she had forgotten to do it. Not only that, she would often undertake to explain to Helen Ruth Helen Ruth's reason for wanting it done. "You are exactly right and I know how you mean. You want them drapes shut at night so it can seem like we're living in a house out in the Belle Meade instead of this here Vox Hall flat, and some fool might be able to look in from the yard."

"Never mind the reasons, Carrie" was Helen Ruth's usual reply. But her answers were not always so gentle—not when Carrie suggested that she have the second baby at home with Carrie acting as midwife, not when Carrie spoke to her about having the third baby circumcised. And the day that Helen Ruth began packing her things to go to Thornton, she was certain that Carrie would speak out of turn with some personal advice. That would have been more than she could bear, and she was prepared to dismiss Carrie from her service and make the trip alone. But neither then nor afterward did Carrie give any real evidence of understanding the reasons for the trip to Thornton.

In fact, it was not until long afterward, when Carrie had quit them to become an undertaker, that Helen Ruth felt that Carrie's gossip with other Nashville servants had, by accident, played a part in her separation from John R. She and John R. had talked of separation and divorce more than once during the first two years they were married, in the era of Jane Blakemore. It was not that any quarreling led to this talk but that each accused the other of being dissatisfied with their marriage. When John R. came in from traveling, on a weekend or in the middle of the week—he was sometimes gone only two or three days at a time—he would find Helen Ruth sitting alone in the living room, without a book or even a deck of cards to amuse herself with, dressed perhaps in something new her mother had sent her, waiting for him. She would rise from her chair to greet him, and he would smile in frank admiration of the tall, graceful figure and of the countenance whose features seemed always composed, and softened by her hair, which was beginning to be gray even at the time of their marriage. But he had not come home many times before Helen Ruth was greeting him with tears instead of smiles. At first, he had been touched, but soon he began to complain that she was unhappy. He asked her why she did not see something of other people while he was away—the wives of his

business and hunting friends, or some of the other Thornton girls
who were married and living in Nashville. She replied that she did
see them occasionally but that she was not the sort of woman who
enjoyed having a lot of women friends. Besides, she was perfectly
happy with her present life; it was only that she believed that he
must be unhappy and that he no longer enjoyed her company. She
understood that he had to be away most of the week, but even when
he was in town, she saw very little of him. When he was not at his
office, he was fishing out on Duck River or was off to a hunt up at
Gallatin. And at night he either took her to parties with those
hunting people, with whom she had little or nothing in common, or
piled up on the bed after supper and slept. All of this indicated that
he was not happy being married to her, she said, and so they talked
a good deal about separating.

After the first baby came, there was no such talk for a long
time—not until after the second baby. After the first baby came,
Helen Ruth felt that their marriage must be made to last, regardless
of hers or John R.'s happiness. Besides, it was at that time that one
of John R.'s hunting friends—a rich man named Rufus Brantley—
had secured the insurance agency for him; and almost before John
R. opened his office, he had sold policies to other rich hunting
friends that he had. For a while, he was at home more than he had
ever been before. But soon, when his business was established, he
began to attend more and more meets and trials, all over Tennessee
and Alabama and Kentucky. He even acquired a few dogs and a
horse of his own. With his friends he began to go on trips to distant
parts of the country. It seemed that when he was not deer hunting
in the State of Maine, he was deep-sea fishing in the Gulf. Helen
Ruth did sometimes go with him to the local horse shows, but one
night, at the Spring Horse Show, she had told Mrs. Brantley that she
had a new machine, and Mrs. Brantley had thought she meant an
automobile instead of a sewing machine. That, somehow, had been

the last straw. She would never go out with "people like the Brantleys" after that. She was pregnant again before the first baby was a year old, and this soon became her excuse for going nowhere in the evening. The women she did visit with very occasionally in the daytime were those she had known as girls in Thornton, women whose husbands were bank tellers and office managers and were barely acquainted with John R. Lovell.

After the second baby came, Helen Ruth saw these women more frequently. She began to feel a restlessness that she could not explain in herself. There were days when she could not stay at home. With Carrie and the two babies, she would traipse about town, on foot or by streetcar, to points she had not visited since she was a little girl and was in Nashville with her parents to attend the State Fair or the Centennial. She went to the Capitol, to Centennial Park and the Parthenon, even out to the Glendale Zoo. Once, with Nancy Tolliver and Lucy Parkes, two of her old Thornton friends, she made an excursion to Cousin Mamie Lovell's farm, which was several miles beyond the town of Franklin. They went by the electric interurban to Franklin, and from there they took a taxi to the farm. Cousin Mamie's husband had been a second cousin of John R.'s father, and it was a connection the Thornton Lovells had once been very proud to claim. But for a generation this branch of the family had been in decline. Major Lovell had been a prominent lawyer in Franklin and had been in politics, but when he died, he left his family "almost penniless." His boys had not gone to college; since the farm was supposed to have been exhausted, they did not try to farm it but clerked in stores in Franklin. There was said to be a prosperous son-in-law in St. Louis, but the daughter was dead and Cousin Mamie was reported to have once called her son-in-law a parvenu to his face. Helen Ruth and her friends made the excursion because they wanted to see the house, which was one of the finest old places in the county and full of antiques.

But Cousin Mamie didn't even let them inside the house. It was a hot summer day, and she had all the blinds closed and the whole L-shaped house shut up tight, so that it would be bearable at night. She received them on the long ell porch. Later, they moved their chairs out under a tree in the yard, where Cousin Mamie's cook brought them a pitcher of iced tea. While they were chatting under the tree that afternoon, they covered all the usual topics that are dealt with when talking to an old lady one doesn't know very well—the old times and the new times, mutual friends and family connections, country living and city living, and always, of course, the lot of woman as it relates to each topic.

"Where are you and John R. living?" Cousin Mamie asked Helen Ruth.

"We're still at the Vaux Hall, Cousin Mamie."

"I'd suppose the trains would be pretty bad for noise there, that close to the depot."

"They're pretty bad in the summer."

"I'd suppose you had a place out from town, seeing how often John R.'s name's in the paper with the hound and hunt set."

"That's John R.'s life," Helen Ruth said, "not mine."

"He runs with a fine pack, I must say," said Cousin Mamie.

Nancy Tolliver and Lucy Parkes nodded and smiled. Lucy said, "The swells of Nashville, Miss Mamie."

But Cousin Mamie said, "There was a day when they weren't the swells. Forty years ago, people like Major Lovell didn't know people like the Brantleys. I think the Brantleys quarried limestone, to begin with. I guess it don't matter, though, for when I was a girl in upper East Tennessee, people said the Lovells started as land speculators hereabouts and at Memphis. But I don't blame you for not wanting to fool with Brantleys, Helen Ruth."

"John R. and I each live our own life, Cousin Mamie."

"Helen Ruth is a woman with a mind of her own, Miss Mamie," Nancy Tolliver said. "It's too bad more marriages can't be like theirs, each living their own life. Everyone admires it as a real achievement."

And Lucy Parkes said, "Because a woman's husband hunts is no reason for her to hunt, any more than because a man's wife sews is any reason for him to sew."

"Indeed not," Cousin Mamie said, actually paying little attention to what Lucy and Nancy were saying. Presently, she continued her own train of thought. "Names like Brantley and Partee and Hines didn't mean a thing in this state even thirty years ago."

What Lucy and Nancy said about her marriage that day left Helen Ruth in a sort of daze and at the same time made her see her situation more clearly. She had never discussed her marriage with anybody, and hearing it described so matter-of-factly by these two women made her understand for the first time what a special sort of marriage it was and how unhappy she was in it. At the time, John R. was away on a fishing trip to Tellico Plains. She did not see him again before she took the babies and Carrie to Thornton. She sent a note to his office saying that she would return when he decided to devote his time to his wife and children instead of to his hounds and horses. While she was at Thornton her letters from John R. made no mention of her note. He wrote about his business, about his hounds and horses, about the weather, and he always urged her to hurry home as soon as she had seen everybody and had a good visit. Meanwhile, he had a room at the Hermitage Club.

When Helen Ruth returned to Nashville, their life went on as before. A year later, the third boy, Robbie, was born, and John R. bought a large bungalow on Sixteenth Avenue, not too far from the Tarbox School, where they planned to send the boys. Carrie was with them for three years after the separation, and though her work did not improve, Helen Ruth found herself making excuses for her. She began to attribute Carrie's garrulity to "a certain sort of bashfulness, or the Negro equivalent to bashfulness." And with the three small boys, and the yard to keep, too, there was so much more for

Carrie to do than there had been before! Despite the excuses she made for her, Helen Ruth could see that Carrie was plainly getting worse about everything and that she now seemed to take pleasure in lying about the smallest, most unimportant things. But Helen Ruth found it harder to confront Carrie with her lies or to reprimand her in any way.

During the last months before Carrie quit, she would talk sometimes about the night work she did for a Negro undertaker. To make Helen Ruth smile, she would report things she had heard about the mourners. Her job, Carrie always said, was to sweep the parlors after the funeral and to fold up the chairs. It was only when she finally gave notice to Helen Ruth that she told her what she professed was the truth. She explained that during all those months she had been learning to embalm. "Before you can get a certificate," she said, "you has to handle a bad accident, a sickness, a case of old age, a drowning, a burning, and a half-grown child or less. I been waiting on the child till last night, but now I'll be getting my certificate."

Helen Ruth would not even let Carrie go to the basement to get her hat and coat. "You send somebody for them," she said. "But *you*, you get off these premises, Carrie!" She was sincerely outraged by what Carrie had told her, and when she looked at Carrie's hands she was filled with new horror. Yet something kept her from saying all the things that one normally said to a worthless, lying servant who had been guilty of one final outrage. "*Leave*, Carrie!" she said, consciously restraining herself. "*Leave* this place!" Carrie went out the kitchen door and down the driveway to the street, bareheaded, coatless, and wearing her kitchen slippers.

After Carrie, there was old Sarah, who stayed with them for six years and then quit them to get married and go to Chicago. Sarah was too old to do heavy work even when she first came, and before she had been there a week, John R. had been asked to help move the sideboard and to bring the ladder up from the basement. He said it seemed that every minute he was in the house, he was lifting or moving something that was too much for Sarah. Helen Ruth replied that perhaps she should hire a Negro man to help in the house and look after the yard. But John R. said no, he was only joking, he thought Sarah far and away the best cook they had ever had, and besides business conditions didn't look too good and it was no time to be taking on more help. But he would always add he did not understand why Helen Ruth babied Sarah so. "From the first moment old Sarah set foot in this house, Helen Ruth has babied her," he would say to people in Helen Ruth's presence.

Sarah could neither read nor write. Even so, it took her only a short while to learn all Helen Ruth's special recipes and how to cook everything the way the Lovells liked it. For two weeks, Helen Ruth stayed in the kitchen with Sarah, reading to her from *How We Cook in Tennessee* and giving detailed instructions for every meal. It was during that time that her great sympathy for Sarah developed. Sarah was completely unashamed of her illiteracy, and it was this that first impressed Helen Ruth. She admired Sarah for having no false pride and for showing no resentment of her mistress's impatience. She observed Sarah's kindness with the children. And she learned from Sarah about Sarah's religious convictions and about her long, unhappy marriage to a Negro named Morse Wilkins, who had finally left her and gone up North.

While Sarah was working for them, John R. and Helen Ruth lived the life that Helen Ruth had heard her friends describe to John R.'s Cousin Mamie. It was not until after Sarah had come that Helen Ruth, recalling the afternoon at Cousin Mamie's, identified Lucy Parkes's words about a wife's sewing and a husband's hunting as the very answer she had once given to some of Carrie's impertinent prying. That afternoon, the remark had certainly sounded familiar, but she had been too concerned with her own decision to leave her husband to concentrate upon anything so trivial. And after their reconciliation, she tried not to dwell on things that had led her to leave John R. Their reconciliation, whatever it meant to John R., meant to her the acceptance of certain mysteries—the mystery of his love of hunting, of his choice of friends, of his desire to maintain a family and home of which he saw so little, of his attachment to her, and of her own devotion to him. Her babies were now growing into little boys. She felt that there was much to be thankful for, not the least of which was a servant as fond of her and of her children as Sarah was. Sarah's affection for the three little boys often reminded Helen Ruth how lonely Sarah's life must be.

One day, when she had watched Sarah carefully wrapping up little Robbie in his winter play clothes before he went out to play in the snow, she said, "You love children so much, Sarah, didn't you ever have any of your own?"

Sarah, who was a yellow-skinned woman with face and arms covered with brown freckles, turned her gray eyes and fixed them solemnly on Helen Ruth. "Why, I had the cutest little baby you ever did see," she said, "and Morse went and killed it."

"Morse *killed* your baby?"

"He rolled over on it in his drunk sleep and smothered it in the bed."

After that, Helen Ruth would never even listen to Sarah when she talked about Morse, and she began to feel a hatred toward any and all of the men who came to take Sarah home at night. Generally, these men were the one subject Sarah did not discuss with Helen Ruth, and their presence in Sarah's life was the only serious complaint Helen Ruth made against her. They would come sometimes as early as four in the afternoon and wait on the back porch for Sarah to get through. She knew that Sarah was usually feeding one of them out of her kitchen, and she knew that Sarah was living with first one and then another of them, but when she told John R. she was going to put her foot down on it, he forbade her to do so. And so through nearly six years she tolerated this weakness of Sarah's. But one morning in the late spring Sarah told her that Morse Wilkins had returned from up North and that she had taken him back as her husband. Helen Ruth could not find anything to say for a moment, but after studying the large diamond on her engagement ring for awhile she said, "My servant's private life is her own affair, but I give you fair warning now, Sarah, I want to see no more of your men friends—Morse or *any other*—on this place again."

From that time, she saw no more men on the place until Morse himself came, in a drunken rage, in the middle of a summer's day. Helen Ruth had been expecting something of the sort to happen. Sarah had been late to work several times during the preceding three weeks. She had come one morning with a dark bruise on her cheek and said she had fallen getting off the streetcar. Twice, Helen Ruth had found Sarah on her knees, praying, in the kitchen. The day Helen Ruth heard the racket at the back-porch door, she knew at once that it was Morse. She got up from her sewing machine and went directly to the kitchen. Sarah was on the back porch, and Morse was outside the screen door of the porch, which was hooked on the inside. He was a little man, shriveled up, bald-headed, not more than five feet tall, and of a complexion very much like Sarah's. Over his white shirt he wore a dark sleeveless sweater. "You come on home," he was saying as he shook the screen door.

Helen Ruth stepped to the kitchen door. "Is that her?" Morse asked Sarah, motioning his head toward Helen Ruth.

When Sarah turned her face around, her complexion seemed several shades lighter than Morse's. "I got to go," she said to Helen Ruth.

"No, Sarah, *he's* got to go. But *you* don't."

"He's gonna leave me again."

"That's the best thing that could happen to you, Sarah."

Sarah said nothing, and Morse began shaking the door again.

"Is he drunk, Sarah?" Helen Ruth asked.

"He's so drunk I don't know how he find his way here."

Helen Ruth went out onto the porch. "Now, you get off this place, and quick about it," she said to Morse.

He shook the screen door again. "You didn't make me come here, Mrs. Lovellel, and you can't make me leave, Mrs. Lovellel."

"I can't make you leave," Helen Ruth said at once, "but there's a bluecoat down on the corner who can."

Suddenly Sarah dropped to her knees and began praying. Her lips moved silently, and gradually she let her forehead come to rest on the top of the rickety vegetable bin. Morse looked at her through the screen, putting his face right against the wire. "Sarah," he said, "you come on home. You better come on now if you think I be there."

Sarah got up off her knees.

"I'm going to phone the police," Helen Ruth said, pretending to move toward the kitchen.

Morse left the door and staggered backward toward the driveway. "Come on, Sarah," he shouted.

"I got to go," Sarah said.

"I won't let you go, Sarah!"

"She can't make you stay!" Morse shouted. "You better come on if you coming!"

"It will be the worst thing you ever did in your life, Sarah," said Helen Ruth. "And if you go with him, you can't ever come back here. He'll kill you someday, too—the way he did your baby."

Sarah was on her knees again, and Morse was out of sight but still shouting as he went down the driveway. Suddenly, Sarah was on her feet. She ran into the kitchen and on through the house to the front porch.

Helen Ruth followed, calling her back. She found Sarah on the front porch waving to Morse, who was halfway down the block, running in a zigzag down the middle of the street, still shouting at the top of his voice. Sarah cried out to him, "Morse! Morse!"

"Sarah!" Helen Ruth said.

"Morse!" Sarah cried again, and then she began mumbling words that Helen Ruth could not quite understand at the time. Afterward, going over it in her mind, Helen Ruth realized that what Sarah had been mumbling was, "If I don't see you no more on this earth, Morse, I'll see you in Glory."

Sarah was with the Lovells for four more months, and then one night she called up on the telephone and asked John R., Jr., to tell his mother that she was going to get married to a man named Racecar and they were leaving for Chicago in the morning.

Jess McGehee came to them during the Depression. Even before Sarah left the Lovells, John R. had had to give up all of his "activities" and devote his entire time to selling insurance. Rufus Brantley had shot himself through the head while cleaning a gun at his hunting lodge, and most of John R.'s other hunting friends had suffered the same financial reverses that John R. had. The changes in the Lovells' life had come so swiftly that Helen Ruth did not realize for awhile what the changes meant in her relationship with John R. It seemed as though she woke up one day and discovered that she was not married to the same man. She found herself spending all her evenings playing Russian bank with a man who had no interest in anything but his home, his wife, and his three boys. Every night, he would give a brief summary of the things that had happened at his office or on his calls, and then he would ask her and the boys for an account of everything they had done that day. He took an interest in the house and the yard, and he and the boys made a lily pool in the back yard, and singlehanded he screened in the entire front porch. Sometimes he took the whole family to

Thornton for a weekend, and he and Helen Ruth never missed the family reunions there in September.

In a sense, these were the happiest years of their married life. John R.'s business got worse and worse, of course, but since part of their savings was in the bank at Thornton that did not fail, they never had any serious money worries. Regardless of their savings, however, John R.'s loss of income and his having to give up his friends and his hunting wrought very real, if only temporary, changes in him. There were occasions when he would sit quietly and listen to his family's talk without correcting them or pointing out how foolish they were. He gave up saying "Think!" to the boys, and instead would say, "Now, let's see if we can't reason this thing out." He could never bring himself to ask for any sympathy from Helen Ruth for his various losses, but as it was during this time that he suffered so from the ailment in his back (he and Helen Ruth slept with boards under their mattress for ten years), the sympathy he got for his physical pain was more than sufficient. All in all, it was a happy period in their life, and in addition to their general family happiness they had Jess.

Jess not only cooked and cleaned, she planned the meals, did the marketing, and washed everything, from handkerchiefs and socks to heavy woolen blankets. When the boys began to go to dances, she even learned to launder their dress shirts. There was nothing she would not do for the boys or for John R. or for Helen Ruth. The way she idealized the family became the basis for most of the "Negro jokes" told by the Lovells during those years. In her room she had a picture of the family, in a group beside the lily pool, taken with her own box Brownie; she had tacked it and also a picture of each of them on the wall above her washstand. In her scrapbook she had pasted every old snapshot and photograph that Helen Ruth would part with, as well as old newspaper pictures of John R. on horseback or with a record-breaking fish he had caught. She had even begged from Helen Ruth an extra copy of the newspaper notice of their wedding.

Jess talked to the family a good deal at mealtime, but only when they had addressed her first and had shown that they wanted her to talk. Her remarks were mostly about things that related to the Lovells. She told a sad story about a "very loving white couple" from Brownsville, her home town, who had been drowned in each other's arms when their car rolled off the end of a river ferry. The point of the story was that those two people were the same, fine, loving sort of couple that John R. and Helen Ruth were. All three of the boys made good grades in school, and every month Jess would copy their grades in her scrapbook, which she periodically passed around for the family to appreciate. When Kenneth began to write stories and articles for his high-school paper, she would always borrow the paper overnight; soon it came out that she was copying everything he wrote onto the big yellow pages of her scrapbook.

After three or four years, John R. began to say that he thought Jess would be with them always and that they would see the day when the boys' children would call her "Mammy." Helen Ruth said that she would like to agree with him about that, but actually she worried, because Jess seemed to have no life of her own, which wasn't at all natural. John R. agreed that they should make her take a holiday now and then. Every summer, they would pack Jess off to Brownsville for a week's visit with her kinfolks, but she was always back in her room over the garage within two or three days; she said that her people fought and quarreled so much that she didn't care for them. Outside her life with the Lovells, she had only one friend. Her interest was the movies, and her friend was "the Mary who works for Mrs. Dunbar." Jess and Mary went to the movies together as often as three or four times a week, and on Sunday afternoons Mary came to see Jess or Jess went to see Mary, who lived over the Dunbar's garage. Jess always took along her scrapbook and her most recent movie magazines. She and Mary swapped movie magazines, and it was apparent from Jess's talk on Monday mornings that they also swapped eulogies of their white families.

Sometimes Helen Ruth would see Mrs. Dunbar downtown or at a P.T.A. meeting; they would discuss their cooks and smile over the reports that each had received of the other's family. "I understand that your boys are all growing into very handsome men," Mrs. Dunbar said once, and she told Helen Ruth that Jess was currently comparing one of the boys—Mrs. Dunbar didn't know which one— to Neil Hamilton, and that she was comparing Helen Ruth to Irene Rich, and John R. to Edmund Lowe. As the boys got older, they began to resent the amount of authority over them—though it was small—that Jess had been allowed by their parents and were embarrassed if anyone said Jess had taught them to drive the car. When John R., Jr., began at the university, he made his mother promise not to let Jess know what grades he received, and none of the boys would let Jess take snapshots of them any more. Their mother tried to comfort Jess by saying that the boys were only going through a phase and that it would pass in time. One day, she even said this in the presence of Robbie, who promptly reported it to the older boys, and it ended with John R., Jr.'s, complaining to his father that their mother ought not to make fun of them to Jess. His father laughed at him but later told Helen Ruth that he thought she was making a mistake, that the boys were getting big enough to think about their manly dignity, and that she would have to take that into consideration.

She didn't make the same mistake again, but although Jess never gave any real sign of her feelings being hurt, Helen Ruth was always conscious of how the boys were growing away from their good-natured servant. By the time Robbie was sixteen, they had long since ceased to have any personal conversation with Jess, and nothing would have induced Robbie to submit to taking drives with her but the knowledge that his father would not allow him to use the car on dates until he had had months of driving practice. Once, when Robbie and Jess returned from a drive, Jess reported, with a grin, that not a word had passed between them during the entire hour and a half. Helen Ruth only shook her head sadly. The next day she bought Jess a new bedside radio.

The radio was the subject of much banter among the boys and their father. John R. said Helen Ruth had chosen the period of hard times and the Depression to become more generous with her servant than she had ever been before in her life. They recalled other presents she had given Jess recently, and from that time on they teased her regularly about how she spoiled Jess. John R. said that if Jess had had his back trouble, Helen Ruth would have retired her at double pay and nursed her with twice the care that he received. The boys teased her by saying that at Christmas time she reversed the custom of shopping for the servant at the ten-cent stores and for the family at the department stores.

Yet as long as Jess was with them, they all agreed that she was the best help they had ever had. In fact, even afterward, during the war years, when John R.'s business prospered again and his back trouble left him entirely and the boys were lucky enough to be stationed near home and, later, continue their education at government expense, even then John R. and the boys would say that the years when Jess was with them were the happiest time of their life and that Jess was the best servant Helen Ruth had ever had. They said that, and then there would be a silence, during which they were probably thinking about the summer morning just before the war when Jess received a telephone call.

When the telephone rang that morning, Helen Ruth and John R. and the boys had just sat down to breakfast. As was usual in the summertime, they were eating at the big drop-leaf table in the sun parlor. Jess had set the coffee urn by Helen Ruth's place and was starting from the room when the telephone rang. Helen Ruth, supposing the call was for a member of the family, and seeing that Jess lingered in the doorway, said for her to answer it there in the sun parlor instead of running to the telephone in the back hall.

Jess answered it, announcing whose residence it was in a voice so like Helen Ruth's that it made the boys grin. For a moment, everyone at the table kept silent. They waited for Jess's eyes to single out one of them. John R., Jr., and Kenneth even put down their grapefruit spoons. But the moment Jess picked up the instrument, she fixed her eyes on the potted fern on the window seat across the room. At once her nostrils began to twitch, her lower lip fell down, and it seemed only an act of will that she was twice able to say, "Yes, ma'am," in answer to the small, unreal, metallic voice.

When she had replaced the telephone on its cradle, she turned quickly away and started into the dining room. But Helen Ruth stopped her. "Jess," she asked, her voice full of courtesy, "was the call for you?"

Jess stopped, and they all watched her hands go up to her face. Without turning around, she leaned against the door jamb and began sobbing aloud. Helen Ruth sprang up from the table, saying, "Jess, honey, what *is* the matter?" John R. and the boys stood up, too.

"It was a telegram for me—from Brownsville."

Helen Ruth took her in her arms. "Is someone dead?"

Between sobs, Jess answered, "My little brother—our baby brother —the only one of 'em I cared for." Then her sobs became more violent.

Helen Ruth motioned for John R. to move the morning paper from the big wicker chair, and she led Jess in that direction. But Jess would not sit down, and she could not be pulled away from Helen Ruth. She held fast to her, and Helen Ruth continued to pat her gently on the back and to try to console her with gentle words. Finally, she said, "Jess, you must go to Brownsville. Maybe there's been some mistake. Maybe he's not dead. But you must go, anyway."

Presently, Jess did sit in the chair, and dried her eyes on Helen Ruth's napkin. The boys shook their heads sympathetically and John R. said she certainly must go to Brownsville. She agreed, and said she believed there was a bus at ten that she would try to catch. Helen Ruth patted her hand, telling her to go along to her room when she felt like it, and said that *she* would finish getting breakfast.

"I want to go by to see Mary first," Jess said, "so I better make haste." She stood up, forcing a grateful smile. Then she burst into tears again and threw her arms about Helen Ruth, mumbling, "Oh, God! Oh, God!" The three boys and their father saw tears come into Helen Ruth's eyes, and through her tears Helen Ruth saw a change come over their faces. It was not exactly a change of expression. It couldn't be that, she felt, because it was exactly the same on each of the four faces. It hardly seemed possible that so similar a change could reflect four men's individual feelings. She concluded that her own emotion, and probably the actual tears in her eyes, had made her imagine the change, and when Jess now pulled away and hurried off to her room, Helen Ruth's tears had dried and she could see no evidence of the change she had imagined in her husband's and her sons' faces.

While Jess was in her room preparing to leave, they finished breakfast. Then Helen Ruth began clearing the table, putting the dishes on the teacart. She had said little while they were eating, but in her mind she was all the while going over something that she knew she must tell her family. As she absent-mindedly stacked the dishes, her lips moved silently over the simple words she would use in telling them. She knew that they were watching her, and when

Robbie offered to take Jess to the bus station, she knew that the change she had seen in all their faces had been an expression of sympathy for *her* as well as of an eagerness to put this whole episode behind them. "I'll take Jess to her bus," he said.

But Helen Ruth answered, in the casual tone she had been preparing to use, that she thought it probably wouldn't be the thing to do.

"Why, what do you mean, Helen Ruth?" John R. asked her.

"It was very touching, Mother," Kenneth said in his new, manly voice, "the way she clung to you." He, too, wanted to express sympathy, but he also seemed to want to distract his mother from answering his father's question.

At that moment, Jess passed under the sun-parlor windows, walking down the driveway, carrying two large suitcases. Helen Ruth watched her until she reached the sidewalk. Then, very quietly, she told her family that Jess McGehee had no baby brother and had never had one. "Jess and Mary are leaving for California. They think they're going to find themselves jobs out there."

"You knew that right along?" John R. asked.

"I knew it right along."

"Did she know you did, Helen Ruth?" he asked. His voice had in it the sternness he used when questioning the boys about something.

"No, John R., she did not. I didn't learn it from her."

"Well, I don't believe it's so," he said. "Why, I don't believe that for a minute. Her carrying on was too real."

"They're going to California. They've already got their two tickets. Mrs. Dunbar got wind of it somehow, by accident, from Mrs. Lon Thompson's cook, and she called me on Monday. They've saved their money and they're going."

"And you let Jess get away with all that crying stuff just now?" John R. said.

Helen Ruth put her hands on the handlebar of the teacart. She pushed the cart a little way over the tile floor but stopped when he repeated his question. It wasn't to answer his question that she stopped, however. "Oh, my dears!" she said, addressing her whole family. Then it was a long time before she said anything more. John R. and the three boys remained seated at the table, and while Helen Ruth gazed past them and toward the front window of the sun parlor, they sat silent and still, as though they were in a picture. What could she say to them, she kept asking herself. And each time she asked the question, she received for answer some different memory of seemingly unrelated things out of the past twenty years of her life. These things presented themselves as answers to her question, and each of them seemed satisfactory to her. But how little sense it would make to her husband and her grown sons, she reflected, if she should suddenly begin telling them about the long hours she had spent waiting in that apartment at the Vaux Hall while John R. was on the road for the Standard Candy Company, and in the same breath should tell them about how plainly she used to talk to Jane Blakemore and how Jane pretended that the baby made her nervous and went back to Thornton. Or suppose she should abruptly remind John R. of how ill at ease the wives of his hunting friends used to make her feel and how she had later driven Sarah's worthless husband out of the yard, threatening to call a bluecoat. What if she should suddenly say that because a woman's husband hunts, there is no reason for *her* to hunt, any more than because a man's wife sews, there is reason for him to sew. She felt that she would be willing to say anything at all, no matter how cruel or absurd it was, if it would make them understand that everything that happened in life only demonstrated in some way the lonesomeness that people felt. She was ready to tell them about sitting in the old nursery at Thornton and waiting for Carrie and Jane Blakemore to come out of the cabin in the yard. If it would make them see what she had been so long in learning to see, she would even talk at last about the "so much else" that had been missing from her life and that she had not been able to name, and about the foolish mysteries she had so nobly accepted upon her reconciliation with John R. To her, these things were all one now; they were her loneliness, the loneliness from which everybody, knowingly or unknowingly, suffered. But she knew that her husband and her sons did not recognize her loneliness or Jess Mc-Gehee's or their own. She turned her eyes from the window to look at their faces around the table, and it was strange to see that they were still thinking in the most personal and particular terms of how they had been deceived by a servant, the ignorant granddaughter of an ignorant slave, a Negro woman from Brownsville who was crazy about the movies and who would soon be riding a bus, mile after mile, on her way to Hollywood, where she might find the friendly faces of the real Neil Hamilton and the real Irene Rich. It was with effort that Helen Ruth thought again of Jess McGehee's departure and the problem of offering an explanation to her family. At last, she said patiently, "My dears, don't you see how it was for Jess? How else can they tell us anything when there is such a gulf?" After a moment she said, "How can I make you understand this?"

Her husband and her three sons sat staring at her, their big hands, all so alike, resting on the breakfast table, their faces stamped with identical expressions, not of wonder but of incredulity. Helen Ruth was still holding firmly to the handle of the teacart. She pushed it slowly and carefully over the doorsill and into the dining room, dark and cool as an underground cavern, and spotlessly clean, the way Jess McGehee had left it.

Cookie

Two nights a week, he *had* to be home for supper, and some weeks, when his conscience was especially uneasy, he turned up three or four times. Tonight, she had a dish of string beans, cooked with cured side meat, on the table when he came in. The smoky odor of the fat struck him when he opened the front door, but he couldn't believe it until he went back to the dining room and saw the dish on the table. "Good God!" he said to himself. "That's fine. Where did she get fresh beans at this time of year?"

Presently his wife, who was, like himself, past fifty, came through the swinging door from the pantry.

"Ah," she said, "my husband is right on time tonight." She came to him and undid the buttons of his overcoat, as she used to undo the children's. It was his lightweight "fall coat," which she had brought down from the attic only two weeks before. She took it and folded it over the back of a dining-room chair, as she would have a visitor's. She knew that he would be leaving right after coffee.

He leaned over the dish and smelled it, and then sat down at the place that was set for him. It was directly across the round dining-

[281]

room table from her place. She stepped to the pantry door and called: "Cookie, we're ready when you are." She pulled out her chair and sat down.

"Shall we have the blessing tonight?" she said, with some small hope in her smile.

"Oh, let's not." He smiled back. It was a cajoling smile.

"All right, then." She smoothed the tablecloth with her fingers.

He served himself from the dish of beans and selected a piece of the side meat. He bent his head over and got one whiff of the steaming dish. "You're too good to me," he said evenly. He pushed the dish across the table to within her reach.

"Nothing's too good for one's husband."

"You're much too good to me," he said, now lowering his eyes to his plate.

Cookie came through the swinging door with a vegetable dish in each hand. She was a brown, buxom Negro woman, perhaps a few years older than her mistress. She set the dishes on the table near her mistress's plate.

"Good evenin', Cookie," he said to her as she started back to the kitchen.

"Yessuh," she said, and went on through the doorway.

His wife was serving herself from a dish. "Here are some of your baked potatoes," she said.

"Ah!" he said. "You *are* too good . . ." This time he left the sentence unfinished.

She passed him the dish. "And here are simply some cold beets."

"Fine . . . fine . . . fine."

"Do you think we would like a little more light?" she said. She pushed herself back from the table.

"We might. We might."

She went to the row of switches by the doorway that led to the hall. She pushed the second switch, and the light overhead was increased. She pushed the third, and the wall lights by the sideboard came on. With each increase of light in the room her husband said, "Ah . . . fine . . . ah . . . fine." It was a small dining room—at least, it seemed so in the bright light, for the house was old and high-ceilinged. The woodwork was a natural pine, with heavy door facings and a narrow chair rail. The paper above the chair rail was a pale yellow, and no pictures were on the walls. There were two silver candlesticks and a punch bowl on the sideboard. Through the glass doors of the press the cut glassware showed. The large light fixture, a frosted glass bowl, hung from a heavy "antiqued" chain low over the table, and the bright light brought out a spot here and there on the cloth.

She was taking her seat again when Cookie pushed through the door with the meat and the bread.

"What's this? A roast? You're outdoing yourself tonight, Cookie," he said.

"Y'all want all iss light?" Cookie said, blinking, and she set the meat down before him.

"Well, it's—well, it's cold-water cornbread!" He took two pieces of bread from the plate that Cookie held to him.

"Y'all want all iss light?" Cookie said to her mistress, who was selecting a small piece of bread and smiling ingenuously at her husband.

"Yes, Cookie," she said, "I think so. I thought I'd turn 'em up some."

"Wull, I could a done it, Mizz."

"It's all right, Cookie. I didn't want the bread burned."

"Wull, it ain't Judgment Day, Mizz. Y'all could a waited. I'd a done it, stead of you havin' to do it." She put the bread on the table and covered it with the napkin that she had held the plate with.

"It's all right, Cookie."

Cookie opened the door to go back to the kitchen. As she went through, she said, "Lawd a *mercy!*"

His wife pushed her plate across the table, and he put on it a slice of roast that he had carved—an outside piece, because it was more done. He cut several slices, until he came to one that seemed rare enough for himself. "Any news from the chillun?" he said.

"Yes," she said. "Postcards from all three."

"Only postcards?"

She began to taste her food, taking so little on her fork that it was hardly visible.

"Now, that's just rotten!" he said. He brought a frown to his face. "They ought to write you letters. They ought to write you at least once a week! I'm going to write the boys tomorrow and tell 'em."

"Now, please, honey! Please don't! They're well. They said so, and that's all I need to know. They're just busy. Young people don't have time for letters." She eased her knife and fork down on her plate. "They're young!"

"What's that got to do with it?" he said. "They ought always to have time for *you.*" He went on eating and talking at the same time. "These beets are fine," he said. Then, after swallowing, "I won't have that! They ought to write their mother once a week. When I was in med school, you know how much I wrote Mama. Father would have beaten me, I believe, and taken me out, if I hadn't. I ought to take them out just once." He stopped eating for a moment, and shaking his fork at her, he spoke even more earnestly: "And just one month I should forget to send *her* that check."

His wife sat, somewhat paled, making no pretense of eating. "Now, please, honey," she said. "She has two little children and a husband who is far from well. I had a letter from her last week, written while the children were taking a little nap. Remember that she has two little children to look after." Her lips trembled. "There's nothing for the boys to write. They say on every single card they miss being home."

He saw that her lips were quivering, and he began eating again. He frowned. Then he smiled suddenly and said, as if with relief, "I'll tell you. Yes. You ought to go up and see 'em. You haven't been to Nashville since they were *both* in med."

She wiped her mouth with her napkin and smiled. "No, there's no need in my going," she said. And she began to eat her dinner again.

Cookie came in with a small pan of hot bread, holding it with a kitchen towel. She uncovered the plate of bread on the table and stacked the hot bread on top of what was there. With her free hand, she reached in front of her mistress and felt the untouched piece of bread on her plate. " 'S got cole on ya," she said. She picked it up in her brown hand and threw it on the cooking pan. She placed a piece of hot bread on her mistress's plate, saying, "Now, gwine butter't while 't's hot."

Her mistress pushed the bread plate across the table toward her husband. She said to him, "Cookie and I are going to get a box of food off to 'em next week, like we used to send 'em in military school. Aren't we, Cookie?"

"Fine . . . fine . . . fine," he said. He took a piece of the cornbread and began to butter it.

Cookie nodded her head toward him and said to her mistress, *"He* hear from 'em?" Then she took several steps around the table, picked up the bread plate, and returned it to its former place. She was tucking the napkin about its edges again.

"No, I have *not!*" He brought the frown to his face again. "They ought to write their mammy, oughtn't they, Cookie?"

"Sho-God ought. 'S a shame," Cookie said. She looked at her mistress. And her mistress put her knife and fork down again. Her lips began to quiver. She gazed tearfully at her husband.

He looked away and spoke out in a loud voice that seemed almost to echo in the high-ceilinged room: "What are you goin' to send 'em? What are you going to send them young'ons, Cookie?"

Cookie looked at him blankly and then at the butter plate, which was in the center of the table. "Whatever she say."

"Well, what do you say, Mother?"

She cleared her throat and ran her hand in a series of pats over her thick and slightly graying hair that went in soft waves back over her ears. "I had thought that we might get hold of two fat guinea hens," she said.

"Fine . . . fine."

"I thought we might get some smoked sausage, not too new and—"

"Ah . . . fine."

"And we might spare one of the fruitcakes we've got soaking."

"How does that suit you, Cookie?" he said.

Cookie was on her way toward the kitchen again. "Yessuh," she said.

He ate in silence for several minutes, took a second helping of string beans, and another piece of bread. She nibbled at a piece of bread. She put more salt and pepper on her meat and ate a few bites. And then she arranged her knife and fork on her plate. Finally, he put his knife and fork down on his empty plate and, with his mouth still full, said, "There's not more, surely?"

She smiled, nodding her head. "Pie."

"No! What kind!"

"I cooked it myself." She picked up a little glass call bell beside her plate and tinkled it. He sat chewing his last bite, and presently Cookie appeared in the doorway with two plates of yellow lemon pie topped with an inch of white meringue.

"This is where she can beat you, Cookie," he said as the cook set the piece of pie before him.

Cookie made a noise that was somewhat like "Psss." She looked at her mistress and gave her a gold-toothed smile. She started to leave with the dinner plates.

"Wait a minute, Cookie," he said. She stopped and looked at him, with her lower lip hanging open. He was taking big bites of the pie. "Cookie, I've been wantin' to ask you how your 'corporosity' is."

"M'whut, Boss-Man?"

"And, furthermore, I understand from what various people are saying around that you have ancestors." He winked at his wife. She dropped her eyes to her plate.

"Whut's he mean, Mizz?" Cookie asked, standing with the two dinner plates in hand.

"Just some of his foolishness, Cookie," she said, with her eyes still on her plate.

He thought to himself that his wife was too good to tease even Cookie. He said to himself, "She doesn't realize that they really eat it up."

"M' coffee's bilin'," Cookie said, and she went through the swinging door.

His wife looked up from her plate. "You know Cookie never has liked to joke. Now, please, honey, don't tease her. She's getting along in her years now. Her temper's quicker than it used to be."

He had finished his pie when Cookie brought in the coffee. She brought it on a tray—two cups and a kitchen pot. She set a cup at each place, filled them, and set the pot on the tablecloth.

"How's that church of yours comin', Cookie?" he said.

"It's makin' out, Boss-Man."

"Haven't you-all churched nobody lately?"

"No, suh, not us."

"How about Dr. Palmer's cook, Cookie? Is she a member in standing?"

"Sho. Mean 'at gal Hattie?" She looked at her mistress and smiled.

He looked at his wife, who he thought was shaking her head at Cookie. Then he looked at Cookie. "Yes," he said, almost absent-mindedly. "He brought her in from the country. That's it—Hattie! That's her name."

"Yessuh. She's from out on Pea Ridge."

"She's givin' 'im some trouble. Drinkin', ain't she, Cookie?"

" 'Cep' *he* didn't get her from Pea Ridge."

"No, Cookie?"

"She put in a year for some ladies he know out near the sand banks, and—"

"She's a drinker, ain't she, Cookie?"

"Yessuh. I *reckon* she is." She tilted her head back and gave him her gold-toothed laugh, which ended in a sort of sneer this time. "She uz dancin' roun' outside chuch las' night an' say to me she want to teach me how to do dat stuff. I tell huh she's drunk, an' she say, 'Sho I is. I teach you how to hit de bottle, too!' "

He pushed his chair away from the table, still holding his coffee, and laughed aloud. He saw that his wife was looking threateningly at Cookie. "What else did she say, Cookie?" he pressed her.

"Oh, dat gal's a big talker. She's full of lies. De way she lies 'bout huh boss-man's terble. She lie 'bout anybody an' everybody in Thornton. She call names up an' down de street."

"What sort of lies?" He leaned forward, smiling, and winked at his wife.

"Them ladies from the sand banks—she say they's in an' out his place mos' any night. Doc Palmer's a bachlorman, sho, but Hattie say hit ain't jus' Doc Palmer! They comes there to meet the ladies—

all sorts of menfolks, married or not. She say she see 'em *all* 'bout his place sooner later."

His wife had quit sipping her coffee and was staring at Cookie.

"Who, for instance, Cookie? Let us in on it," he said.

The cook turned to him and looked at him blankly. "You, Boss-Man."

His wife stood up at her place, her napkin in her hand. Her eyes filled with tears. "After all these years!" she said. "Cookie, you've forgotten your place for the first time, after all these years."

Cookie put her hands under her apron, looked at her feet a moment, and then looked up at him, her own eyes wet. Her words came almost like screams. "Hattie say she *seen* ya! But she's a liar, ain't she, Boss-Man?"

Her mistress sat down, put one elbow on the table, and brought her napkin up to cover her face. "I'm disappointed in you, Cookie. Go to the kitchen."

Cookie went through the swinging door without looking at her mistress.

In a moment, his wife looked up at him and said, "I'm sorry. I'd not thought she was capable of a thing like that."

"Why, it's all right—for what she said. Doctors will get talked about. Even Cookie knows the girl's a liar."

His wife seemed, he thought, not to have heard him. She was saying, "A servant of mine talking to my husband like that!"

"It's only old-nigger uppitiness," he reassured her.

"I shall speak to her tonight," she said. "I promise you."

"Oh, I suppose you'll think you have to fire her."

She looked at him, her features composed again. She ran her hand over her hair in a series of pats. "No, no," she said. "I can't fire Cookie. I'll speak to her tonight. It'll never happen again."

"Now I think of it, perhaps she ought to be sent on her way after talking like that."

"I'll look after the matter."

He poured himself a second cup of coffee and, as he drank it, he watched his wife closely. He frowned again and said, "Why, she might talk to *you* that way some day. That's all I thought."

She smiled at him. "There's no danger. I'll have a talk with her tonight."

She helped him on with his overcoat. He said, "Got to see some country people tonight. Might even have to drive over to Hunts-boro." She was buttoning his coat. "There's a lot of red throat over there."

"I can't have her talking that way to my husband," she said aloud, yet to herself. "But I won't fire her," she told him. "She's too much one of us—too much one of the family, and I know she'll be full of remorse for speaking out of turn like that."

He looked directly into her eyes, and she smiled confidently. She told him she would leave the back light on, because lately the nights had been cloudy and dark. As he stopped in the hall to pick up his hat and his case, he heard Cookie come through the swinging door.

"Now, Cookie, I want to have a little talk with you," his wife said, and Cookie said, "Yes'm, Mizz."

He went out, closing the door softly behind him, and as he crossed the porch, he could still hear their voices inside—the right-eousness and disillusion of Cookie's, the pride and discipline of his wife's. He passed down the flight of wooden steps and stepped from the brick walk onto the lawn. He hesitated a moment; he could still hear their voices indistinctly—their senseless voices. He began walking with light, sure steps over the grass—their ugly, old voices. In the driveway, his car, bright and new and luxurious, was waiting for him.

Venus, Cupid, Folly and Time

Their house alone would not have made you think there was anything so awfully wrong with Mr. Dorset or his old-maid sister. But certain things about the way both of them dressed had, for a long time, annoyed and disturbed everyone. We used to see them together at the grocery store, for instance, or even in one of the big department stores downtown, wearing their bedroom slippers. Looking more closely, we would sometimes see the cuff of a pajama top or the hem of a hitched-up nightgown showing from underneath their ordinary daytime clothes. Such slovenliness in one's neighbors is so unpleasant that even husbands and wives in West Vesey Place, which was the street where the Dorsets lived, had got so they didn't like to joke about it with each other. Were the Dorsets, poor old things, losing their minds? If so, what was to be done about it? Some neighbors got so they would not even admit to themselves what they saw. And a child coming home with an ugly report on the Dorsets was apt to be told that it was time he learned to curb his imagination.

Mr. Dorset wore tweed caps and sleeveless sweaters. Usually he

had his sweater stuffed down inside his trousers with his shirt tails.
To the women and young girls in West Vesey Place this was extremely distasteful. It made them feel as though Mr. Dorset had just
come from the bathroom and had got his sweater inside his trousers
by mistake. There was, in fact, nothing about Mr. Dorset that was
not offensive to the women. Even the old touring car he drove was
regarded by most of them as a disgrace to the neighborhood. Parked
out in front of his house, as it usually was, it seemed a worse
violation of West Vesey's zoning than the house itself. And worst of
all was seeing Mr. Dorset wash the car.

Mr. Dorset washed his own car! He washed it not back in the
alley or in his driveway but out there in the street of West Vesey
Place. This would usually be on the day of one of the parties which
he and his sister liked to give for young people or on a day when
they were going to make deliveries of the paper flowers or the home-
grown figs which they sold to their friends. Mr. Dorset would
appear in the street carrying two buckets of warm water and wearing a pair of skin-tight coveralls The skin-tight coveralls, of khaki
material but faded almost to flesh color, were still more offensive to
the women and young girls than his way of wearing his sweaters.
With sponges and chamois cloths and a large scrub brush (for use
on the canvas top) the old fellow would fall to and scrub away,
gently at first on the canvas top and more vigorously as he pro-
gressed to the hood and body, just as though the car were something
alive. Neighbor children felt that he went after the headlights
exactly as if he were scrubbing the poor car's ears. There was an
element of brutality in the way he did it and yet an element of
tenderness too. An old lady visiting in the neighborhood once said
that it was like the cleansing of a sacrificial animal. I suppose it was
some such feeling as this that made all women want to turn away
their eyes whenever the spectacle of Mr. Dorset washing his car
presented itself.

As for Mr. Dorset's sister, her behavior was in its way just as offensive as his. To the men and boys in the neighborhood it was she who seemed quite beyond the pale. She would come out on her front terrace at midday clad in a faded flannel bathrobe and with her dyed black hair all undone and hanging down her back like the hair of an Indian squaw. To us whose wives and mothers did not even come downstairs in their negligees, this was very unsettling. It was hard to excuse it even on the grounds that the Dorsets were too old and lonely and hard-pressed to care about appearances any more.

Moreover, there was a boy who had gone to Miss Dorset's house one morning in the early fall to collect for his paper route and saw this very Miss Louisa Dorset pushing a carpet sweeper about one of the downstairs rooms without a stitch of clothes on. He saw her through one of the little lancet windows that opened on the front loggia of the house, and he watched her for quite a long while. She was cleaning the house in preparation for a party they were giving for young people that night, and the boy said that when she finally got hot and tired she dropped down in an easy chair and crossed her spindly, blue-veined, old legs and sat there completely naked, with her legs crossed and shaking one scrawny little foot, just as unconcerned as if she didn't care that somebody was likely to walk in on her at any moment. After a little bit the boy saw her get up again and go and lean across a table to arrange some paper flowers in a vase. Fortunately he was a nice boy, though he lived only on the edge of the West Vesey Place neighborhood, and he went away without ringing the doorbell or collecting for his paper that week. But he could not resist telling his friends about what he had seen. He said it was a sight he would never forget! And she an old lady more than sixty years old who, had she not been so foolish and self-willed, might have had a house full of servants to push that carpet sweeper for her!

This foolish pair of old people had given up almost everything in life for each other's sake. And it was not at all necessary. When they were young they could have come into a decent inheritance, or now that they were old they might have been provided for by a host of rich relatives. It was only a matter of their being a little tolerant—or even civil—toward their kinspeople. But this was something that old Mr. Dorset and his sister could never consent to do. Almost all their lives they had spoken of their father's kin as "Mama's in-laws" and of their mother's kin as "Papa's in-laws." Their family name was Dorset, not on one side but on both sides. Their parents had been distant cousins. As a matter of fact, the Dorset family in the city of Chatham had once been so large and was so long established there that it would have been hard to estimate how distant the kinship might be. But still it was something that the old couple never liked to have mentioned. Most of their mother's close kin had, by the time I am speaking of, moved off to California, and most of their father's people lived somewhere up East. But Miss Dorset and her old bachelor brother found any contact, correspondence, even an exchange of Christmas cards with these in-laws intolerable. It was a case, so they said, of the in-laws respecting the value of the dollar above all else, whereas they, Miss Louisa and Mr. Alfred Dorset, placed importance on other things.

They lived in a dilapidated and curiously mutilated house on a street which, except for their own house, was the most splendid street in the entire city. Their house was one that you or I would have been ashamed to live in—even in the lean years of the early thirties. In order to reduce taxes the Dorsets had had the third story of the house torn away, leaving an ugly, flat-topped effect without any trim or ornamentation. Also, they had had the south wing pulled down and had sealed the scars not with matching brick but with a speckled stucco that looked raw and naked. All this the old couple did in violation of the strict zoning laws of West Vesey Place, and for doing so they would most certainly have been prosecuted except that they were the Dorsets and except that this was during the Depression when zoning laws weren't easy to enforce in a city like Chatham.

To the young people whom she and her brother entertained at their house once each year Miss Louisa Dorset liked to say: "We have given up everything for each other. Our only income is from our paper flowers and our figs." The old lady, though without showing any great skill or talent for it, made paper flowers. During the winter months, her brother took her in that fifteen-year-old touring car of theirs, with its steering wheel on the wrong side and with isinglass side curtains that were never taken down, to deliver these flowers to her customers. The flowers looked more like sprays of tinted potato chips than like any real flowers. Nobody could possibly have wanted to buy them except that she charged next to nothing for them and except that to people with children it seemed important to be on the Dorsets' list of worthwhile people. Nobody could really have wanted Mr. Dorset's figs either. He cultivated a dozen little bushes along the back wall of their house, covering them in the wintertime with some odd-looking boxes which he had had constructed for the purpose. The bushes were very productive, but the figs they produced were dried up little things without much taste. During the summer months he and his sister went about in their car, with the side curtains still up, delivering the figs to the same customers who bought the paper flowers. The money they made could hardly have paid for the gas it took to run the car. It was a great waste and it was very foolish of them.

And yet, despite everything, this foolish pair of old people, this same Miss Louisa and Mr. Alfred Dorset, had become social arbiters of a kind in our city. They had attained this position entirely through their fondness for giving an annual dancing party for young people. To *young* people—to *very* young people—the Dorsets' hearts went out. I don't mean to suggest that their hearts went out to orphans or to the children of the poor, for they were not foolish in that way. The guests at their little dancing parties were the thirteen- and fourteen-year-olds from families like the one they had long ago set themselves against, young people from the very houses to which, in season, they delivered their figs and their paper flowers. And when the night of one of their parties came round, it was in fact the custom for Mr. Alfred to go in the same old car and fetch all the invited guests to his house. His sister might explain to reluctant parents that this saved the children the embarrassment of being taken to their first dance by Mommy or Daddy. But the parents knew well enough that for twenty years the Dorsets had permitted no adult person, besides themselves, to put foot inside their house.

At those little dancing parties which the Dorsets gave, peculiar things went on—unsettling things to the boys and girls who had been fetched round in the old car. Sensible parents wished to keep their children away. Yet what could they do? For a Chatham girl to have to explain, a few years later, why she never went to a party at the Dorsets' was like having to explain why she had never been a debutante. For a boy it was like having to explain why he had not gone up East to school or even why his father hadn't belonged to the Chatham Racquet Club. If when you were thirteen or fourteen you got invited to the Dorsets' house, you went; it was the way of letting people know from the outset who you were. In a busy, modern city like Chatham you cannot afford to let people forget who you are—not for a moment, not at any age. Even the Dorsets knew that.

Many a little girl, after one of those evenings at the Dorsets', was heard to cry out in her sleep. When waked, or half waked, her only explanation might be: "It was just the fragrance from the paper flowers." Or: "I dreamed I could really smell the paper flowers." Many a boy was observed by his parents to seem "different" after-

ward. He became "secretive." The parents of the generation that had
to attend those parties never pretended to understand what went on
at the Dorsets' house. And even to those of us who were in that
unlucky generation, it seemed we were half a lifetime learning what
really took place during our one evening under the Dorsets' roof.
Before our turn to go ever came round, we had for years been
hearing about what it was like from older boys and girls. Afterward,
we continued to hear about it from those who followed us. And,
looking back on it, nothing about the one evening when you were
actually there ever seemed quite so real as the glimpses and snatches
which you got from those people before and after you—the second-
hand impressions of the Dorsets' behavior, of things they said, of
looks that passed between them.

Since Miss Dorset kept no servants, she always opened her own
door. I suspect that for the guests at her parties the sight of her
opening her door, in her astonishing attire, came as the most violent
shock of the whole evening. On these occasions, she and her brother
got themselves up as we had never seen them before and never
would again. The old lady invariably wore a modish white evening
gown, a garment perfectly fitted to her spare and scrawny figure and
cut in such high fashion that it must necessarily have been new that
year. And never to be worn but that one night! Her hair, long and
thick and newly dyed for the occasion, would be swept upward and
forward in a billowy mass which was topped by a corsage of yellow
and coral paper flowers. Her cheeks and lips would be darkly
rouged. On her long bony arms and her bare shoulders she would
have applied some kind of suntan powder. Whatever else you had
been led to expect of the evening, no one had ever warned you
sufficiently about the radical change to be noted in her appearance—
or in that of her brother, either. By the end of the party Miss Louisa
might look as dowdy as ever, and Mr. Alfred a little worse than
usual. But at the outset, when the party was assembling in their

drawing room, even Mr. Alfred appeared resplendent in a nattily
tailored tuxedo, with exactly the shirt, the collar, and the tie which
fashion prescribed that year. His gray hair was nicely trimmed, his
puffy old face freshly shaven. He was powdered with the same dark
powder that his sister used. One felt even that his cheeks had been
lightly touched with rouge.

A strange perfume pervaded the atmosphere of the house. The
moment you set foot inside, this awful fragrance engulfed you. It
was like a mixture of spicy incense and sweet attar of roses. And
always, too, there was the profusion of paper flowers. The flowers
were everywhere—on every cabinet and console, every inlaid table
and carved chest, on every high, marble mantelpiece, on the book-
shelves. In the entrance hall special tiers must have been set up to
hold the flowers, because they were there in overpowering masses.
They were in such abundance that it seemed hardly possible that
Miss Dorset could have made them all. She must have spent weeks
and weeks preparing them, even months, perhaps even the whole
year between parties. When she went about delivering them to her
customers, in the months following, they were apt to be somewhat
faded and dusty; but on the night of the party, the colors of the
flowers seemed even more impressive and more unlikely than their
number. They were fuchsia, they were chartreuse, they were coral,
aquamarine, brown, they were even black.

Everywhere in the Dorsets' house too were certain curious illuminations and lighting effects. The source of the light was usually
hidden and its purpose was never obvious at once. The lighting was
a subtler element than either the perfume or the paper flowers, and
ultimately it was more disconcerting. A shaft of lavender light
would catch a young visitor's eye and lead it, seemingly without
purpose, in among the flowers. Then just beyond the point where
the strength of the light would begin to diminish, the eye would
discover something. In a small aperture in the mass of flowers, or

sometimes in a larger grotto-like opening, there would be a piece of sculpture—in the hall a plaster replica of Rodin's "The Kiss," in the library an antique plaque of Leda and the Swan. Or just above the flowers would be hung a picture, usually a black and white print but sometimes a reproduction in color. On the landing of the stairway leading down to the basement ballroom was the only picture that one was likely to learn the title of at the time. It was a tiny color print of Bronzino's "Venus, Cupid, Folly and Time." This picture was not even framed. It was simply tacked on the wall, and it had obviously been torn—rather carelessly, perhaps hurriedly—from a book or magazine. The title and the name of the painter were printed in the white margin underneath.

About these works of art most of us had been warned by older boys and girls; and we stood in painful dread of that moment when Miss Dorset or her brother might catch us staring at any one of their pictures or sculptures. We had been warned, time and again, that during the course of the evening moments would come when she or he would reach out and touch the other's elbow and indicate, with a nod or just the trace of a smile, some guest whose glance had strayed among the flowers.

To some extent the dread which all of us felt that evening at the Dorsets' cast a shadow over the whole of our childhood. Yet for nearly twenty years the Dorsets continued to give their annual party. And even the most sensible of parents were not willing to keep their children away.

But a thing happened finally which could almost have been predicted. Young people, even in West Vesey Place, will not submit forever to the prudent counsel of their parents. Or some of them won't. There was a boy named Ned Meriwether and his sister Emily Meriwether, who lived with their parents in West Vesey Place just one block away from the Dorsets' house. In November, Ned and

Emily were invited to the Dorsets' party, and because they dreaded it they decided to play a trick on everyone concerned—even on themselves, as it turned out . . . They got up a plan for smuggling an uninvited guest into the Dorsets' party.

The parents of this Emily and Ned sensed that their children were concealing something from them and suspected that the two were up to mischief of some kind. But they managed to deceive themselves with the thought that it was only natural for young people— "mere children"—to be nervous about going to the Dorsets' house. And so instead of questioning them during the last hour before they left for the party, these sensible parents tried to do everything in their power to calm their two children. The boy and the girl, seeing this was the case, took advantage of it.

"You must not go down to the front door with us when we leave," the daughter insisted to her mother. And she persuaded both Mr. and Mrs. Meriwether that after she and her brother were dressed for the party they should all wait together in the upstairs sitting room until Mr. Dorset came to fetch the two young people in his car.

When, at eight o'clock, the lights of the automobile appeared in the street below, the brother and sister were still upstairs—watching from the bay window of the family sitting room. They kissed Mother and Daddy goodbye and then they flew down the stairs and across the wide, carpeted entrance hall to a certain dark recess where a boy named Tom Bascomb was hidden. This boy was the uninvited guest whom Ned and Emily were going to smuggle into the party. They had left the front door unlatched for Tom, and from the upstairs window just a few minutes ago they had watched him come across their front lawn. Now in the little recess of the hall there was a quick exchange of overcoats and hats between Ned Meriwether and Tom Bascomb; for it was a feature of the plan that

Tom should attend the party as Ned and that Ned should go as the uninvited guest.

In the darkness of the recess, Ned fidgeted and dropped Tom Bascomb's coat on the floor. But the boy, Tom Bascomb, did not fidget. He stepped out into the light of the hall and began methodically getting into the overcoat which he would wear tonight. He was not a boy who lived in the West Vesey Place neighborhood (he was in fact the very boy who had once watched Miss Dorset cleaning house without any clothes on), and he did not share Emily's and Ned's nervous excitement about the evening. The sound of Mr. Dorset's footsteps outside did not disturb him. When both Ned and Emily stood frozen by that sound, he continued buttoning the unfamiliar coat and even amused himself by stretching forth one arm to observe how high the sleeve came on his wrist.

The doorbell rang, and from his dark corner Ned Meriwether whispered to his sister and to Tom: "Don't worry. I'll be at the Dorsets' in plenty of time."

Tom Bascomb only shrugged his shoulders at this reassurance. Presently when he looked at Emily's flushed face and saw her batting her eyes like a nervous monkey, a crooked smile played upon his lips. Then, at a sign from Emily, Tom followed her to the entrance door and permitted her to introduce him to old Mr. Dorset as her brother.

From the window of the upstairs sitting room the Meriwether parents watched Mr. Dorset and this boy and this girl walking across the lawn toward Mr. Dorset's peculiar-looking car. A light shone bravely and protectively from above the entrance of the house, and in its rays the parents were able to detect the strange angle at which Brother was carrying his head tonight and how his new fedora already seemed too small for him. They even noticed that he seemed a bit taller tonight.

"I hope it's all right," said the mother.

"What do you mean 'all right'?" the father asked petulantly.

"I mean—" the mother began, and then she hesitated. She did not want to mention that the boy out there did not look like their own Ned. It would have seemed to give away her feelings too much. "I mean that I wonder if I should have put Sister in that long dress at this age and let her wear my cape. I'm afraid the cape is really inappropriate. She's still young for that sort of thing."

"Oh," said the father, "I thought you meant something else."

"Whatever else did you think I meant, Edwin?" the mother said, suddenly breathless.

"I thought you meant the business we've discussed before," he said, although this was of course not what he had thought she meant. He had thought she meant that the boy out there did not look like their Ned. To him it had seemed even that the boy's step was different from Ned's. "The Dorsets' parties," he said, "are not very nice affairs to be sending your children to, Muriel. That's all I thought you meant."

"But we *can't* keep them away," the mother said defensively.

"Oh, it's just that they are growing up faster than we realize," said the father, glancing at his wife out of the corner of his eye.

By this time Mr. Dorset's car had pulled out of sight, and from downstairs Muriel Meriwether thought she heard another door closing. "What was that?" she said, putting one hand on her husband's.

"Don't be so jumpy," her husband said irritably, snatching away his hand. "It's the servants closing up in the kitchen."

Both of them knew that the servants had closed up in the kitchen long before this. Both of them had heard quite distinctly the sound of the side door closing as Ned went out. But they went on talking and deceiving themselves in this fashion during most of the evening.

Even before she opened the door to Mr. Dorset, little Emily

Meriwether had known that there would be no difficulty about passing Tom Bascomb off as her brother. In the first place, she knew that without his spectacles Mr. Dorset could hardly see his hand before his face and knew that due to some silly pride he had he never put on his spectacles except when he was behind the wheel of his automobile. This much was common knowledge. In the second place, Emily knew from experience that neither he nor his sister ever made any real pretense of knowing one child in their general acquaintance from another. And so, standing in the doorway and speaking almost in a whisper, Emily had merely to introduce first herself and then her pretended brother to Mr. Dorset. After that the three of them walked in silence from her father's house to the waiting car.

Emily was wearing her mother's second-best evening wrap, a white lapin cape which, on Emily, swept the ground. As she walked between the boy and the man, the touch of the cape's soft silk lining on her bare arms and on her shoulders spoke to her silently of a strange girl she had seen in her looking glass upstairs tonight. And with her every step toward the car the skirt of her long taffeta gown whispered her own name to her: *Emily . . . Emily.* She heard it distinctly, and yet the name sounded unfamiliar. Once during this unreal walk from house to car she glanced at the mysterious boy, Tom Bascomb, longing to ask him—if only with her eyes—for some reassurance that she was really she. But Tom Bascomb was absorbed in his own irrelevant observations. With his head tilted back he was gazing upward at the nondescript winter sky where, among drifting clouds, a few pale stars were shedding their dull light alike on West Vesey Place and on the rest of the world. Emily drew her wrap tightly about her, and when presently Mr. Dorset held open the door to the back seat of his car she shut her eyes and plunged into the pitch blackness of the car's interior.

Tom Bascomb was a year older than Ned Meriwether and he was

nearly two years older than Emily. He had been Ned's friend first. He and Ned had played baseball together on Saturdays before Emily ever set eyes on him. Yet according to Tom Bascomb himself, with whom several of us older boys talked just a few weeks after the night he went to the Dorsets', Emily always insisted that it was she who had known him first. On what she based this false claim Tom could not say. And on the two or three other occasions when we got Tom to talk about that night, he kept saying that he didn't understand what it was that had made Emily and Ned quarrel over which of them knew him first and knew him better.

We could have told him what it was, I think. But we didn't. It would have been too hard to say to him that at one time or another all of us in West Vesey had had our Tom Bascombs. Tom lived with his parents in an apartment house on a wide thoroughfare known as Division Boulevard, and his only real connection with West Vesey Place was that that street was included in his paper route. During the early morning hours he rode his bicycle along West Vesey and along other quiet streets like it, carefully aiming a neatly rolled paper at the dark loggia, at the colonnaded porch, or at the ornamented doorway of each of the palazzi and châteaux and manor houses that glowered at him in the dawn. He was well thought of as a paper boy. If by mistake one of his papers went astray and lit on an upstairs balcony or on the roof of a porch, Tom would always take more careful aim and throw another. Even if the paper only went into the shrubbery, Tom got off his bicycle and fished it out. He wasn't the kind of boy to whom it would have occurred that the old fogies and the rich kids in West Vesey could very well get out and scramble for their own papers.

Actually, a party at the Dorsets' house was more a grand tour of the house than a real party. There was a half hour spent over very light refreshments (fruit Jello, English tea biscuits, lime punch). There was another half hour ostensibly given to general dancing in the basement ballroom (to the accompaniment of victrola music). But mainly there was the tour. As the party passed through the house, stopping sometimes to sit down in the principal rooms, the host and hostess provided entertainment in the form of an almost continuous dialogue between themselves. This dialogue was famous and was full of interest, being all about how much the Dorsets had given up for each other's sake and about how much higher the tone of Chatham society used to be than it was nowadays. They would invariably speak of their parents, who had died within a year of each other when Miss Louisa and Mr. Alfred were still in their teens; they even spoke of their wicked in-laws. When their parents died, the wicked in-laws had first tried to make them sell the house, then had tried to separate them and send them away to boarding schools, and had ended by trying to marry them off to "just anyone." Their two grandfathers had still been alive in those days and each had had a hand in the machinations, after the failure of which each grandfather had disinherited them. Mr. Alfred and Miss Louisa spoke also of how, a few years later, a procession of "young nobodies" had come of their own accord trying to steal the two of them away from each other. Both he and she would scowl at the very recollection of those "just anybodies" and those "nobodies," those "would-be suitors" who always turned out to be misguided fortune hunters and had to be driven away.

The Dorsets' dialogue usually began in the living room the moment Mr. Dorset returned with his last collection of guests. (He sometimes had to make five or six trips in the car.) There, as in other rooms afterward, they were likely to begin with a reference to the room itself or perhaps to some piece of furniture in the room. For instance, the extraordinary length of the drawing room—or reception room, as the Dorsets called it—would lead them to speak of an even longer room which they had had torn away from the house. "It grieved us, we wept," Miss Dorset would say, "to have Mama's French drawing room torn away from us."

"But we tore it away from ourselves," her brother would add, "as we tore away our in-laws—because we could not afford them." Both of them spoke in a fine declamatory style, but they frequently interrupted themselves with a sad little laugh which expressed something quite different from what they were saying and which seemed to serve them as an aside not meant for our ears.

"That was one of our greatest sacrifices," Miss Dorset would say, referring still to her mother's French drawing room.

And her brother would say: "But we knew the day had passed in Chatham for entertainments worthy of that room."

"It was the room which Mama and Papa loved best, but we gave it up because we knew, from our upbringing, which things to give up."

From this they might go on to anecdotes about their childhood. Sometimes their parents had left them for months or even a whole year at a time with only the housekeeper or with trusted servants to see after them. "You could trust servants then," they explained. And: "In those days parents could do that sort of thing, because in those days there was a responsible body of people within which your young people could always find proper companionship."

In the library, to which the party always moved from the drawing room, Mr. Dorset was fond of exhibiting snapshots of the house taken before the south wing was pulled down. As the pictures were passed around, the dialogue continued. It was often there that they told the story of how the in-laws had tried to force them to sell the house. "For the sake of economy!" Mr. Dorset would exclaim, adding an ironic "Ha ha!"

"As though money—" he would begin.

"As though money ever took the place," his sister would come in, "of living with your own kind."

"Or of being well born," said Mr. Dorset.

After the billiard room, where everyone who wanted it was permitted one turn with the only cue that there seemed to be in the house, and after the dining room, where it was promised refreshments would be served later, the guests would be taken down to the ballroom—purportedly for dancing. Instead of everyone's being urged to dance, however, once they were assembled in the ballroom, Miss Dorset would announce that she and her brother understood the timidity which young people felt about dancing and that all that she and he intended to do was to set the party a good example . . . It was only Miss Louisa and Mr. Alfred who danced. For perhaps thirty minutes, in a room without light excepting that from a few weak bulbs concealed among the flowers, the old couple danced; and they danced with such grace and there was such perfect harmony in all their movements that the guests stood about in stunned silence, as if hypnotized. The Dorsets waltzed, they two-stepped, they even fox-trotted, stopping only long enough between dances for Mr. Dorset, amid general applause, to change the victrola record.

But it was when their dance was ended that all the effects of the Dorsets' careful grooming that night would have vanished. And, alas, they made no effort to restore themselves. During the remainder of the evening Mr. Dorset went about with his bow tie hanging limply on his damp shirtfront, a gold collar button shining above it. A strand of gray hair, which normally covered his bald spot on top, now would have fallen on the wrong side of his part and hung like fringe about his ear. On his face and neck the thick layer of powder was streaked with perspiration. Miss Dorset was usually in an even more disheveled state, depending somewhat upon the fashion of her dress that year. But always her powder was streaked, her lipstick entirely gone, her hair falling down on all sides, and her corsage dangling somewhere about the nape of her neck. In this condition they led the party upstairs again, not stopping until they had reached the second floor of the house.

On the second floor we—the guests—were shown the rooms which the Dorsets' parents had once occupied (the Dorsets' own rooms were never shown). We saw, in glass museum cases along the hallway, the dresses and suits and hats and even the shoes which Miss Louisa and Mr. Alfred had worn to parties when they were very young. And now the dialogue, which had been left off while the Dorsets danced, was resumed. "Ah, the happy time," one of them would say, "was when we were *your* age!" And then, exhorting us to be happy and gay while we were still safe in the bosom of our own kind and before the world came crowding in on us with its ugly demands, the Dorsets would recall the happiness they had known when they were very young. This was their *pièce de résistance*. With many a wink and blush and giggle and shake of the forefinger—and of course standing before the whole party—they each would remind the other of his or her naughty behavior in some old-fashioned parlor game or of certain silly little flirtations which they had long ago caught each other in.

They were on their way downstairs again now, and by the time they had finished with this favorite subject they would be downstairs. They would be in the dark, flower-bedecked downstairs hall and just before entering the dining room for the promised refreshments: the fruit Jello, the English tea biscuits, the lime punch.

And now for a moment Mr. Dorset bars the way to the dining room and prevents his sister from opening the closed door. "Now, my good friends," he says, "let us eat, drink, and be merry!"

"For the night is yet young," says his sister.

"Tonight you must be gay and carefree," Mr. Dorset enjoins.

"Because in this house we are all friends," Miss Dorset says. "We are all young, we all love one another."

"And love can make us all young forever," her brother says.

"Remember!"

"Remember this evening always, sweet young people!"

"Remember!"

"Remember what our life is like here!"

And now Miss Dorset, with one hand on the knob of the great door which she is about to throw open, leans a little toward the guests and whispers hoarsely: "This is what it is like to be young forever!"

Ned Meriwether was waiting behind a big japonica shrub near the sidewalk when, about twenty minutes after he had last seen Emily, the queer old touring car drew up in front of the Dorsets' house. During the interval, the car had gone from the Meriwether house to gather a number of other guests, and so it was not only Emily and Tom who alighted on the sidewalk before the Dorsets' house. The group was just large enough to make it easy for Ned to slip out from his dark hiding place and join them without being noticed by Mr. Dorset. And now the group was escorted rather unceremoniously up to the door of the house, and Mr. Dorset departed to fetch more guests.

They were received at the door by Miss Dorset. Her eyesight was no doubt better than her brother's, but still there was really no danger of her detecting an uninvited guest. Those of us who had gone to that house in the years just before Ned and Emily came along could remember that, during a whole evening, when their house was full of young people, the Dorsets made no introductions and made no effort to distinguish which of their guests was which. They did not even make a count of heads. Perhaps they did vaguely recognize some of the faces, because sometimes when they had come delivering figs or paper flowers to a house they had of necessity encountered a young child there, and always they smiled sweetly at it, asked its age, and calculated on their old fingers how many years must pass before the child would be eligible for an invitation. Yet at those moments something in the way they had held up their fingers and in the way they had gazed *at* the little face instead of into it had revealed their lack of interest in the individual child. And later, when the child was finally old enough to receive their invitation, he found it was still no different with the Dorsets. Even in their own house it was evidently to the young people as a group that the Dorsets' hearts went out; while they had the boys and girls under their roof they herded them about like so many little thoroughbred calves. Even when Miss Dorset opened the front door she did so exactly as though she were opening a gate. She pulled it open very slowly, standing half behind it to keep out of harm's way. And the children, all huddled together, surged in.

How meticulously this Ned and Emily Meriwether must have laid their plans for that evening! And the whole business might have come out all right if only they could have foreseen the effect which one part of their plan—rather a last-minute embellishment of it—would produce upon Ned himself. Barely ten minutes after they entered the house, Ned was watching Tom as he took his seat on the piano bench beside Emily. Ned probably watched Tom closely, because certainly he knew what the next move was going to be. The moment Miss Louisa Dorset's back was turned Tom Bascomb slipped his arm gently about Emily's little waist and commenced kissing her all over her pretty face. It was almost as if he were kissing away tears.

This spectacle on the piano bench, and others like it which followed, had been an inspiration of the last day or so before the party. Or so Ned and Emily maintained afterward when defending themselves to their parents. But no matter when it was conceived, a part of their plan it was, and Ned must have believed himself fully prepared for it. Probably he expected to join in the round of giggling which it produced from the other guests. But now that the time had come—it is easy to imagine—the boy Ned Meriwether found himself not quite able to join in the fun. He watched with the others, but he was not quite infected by their laughter. He stood a little apart, and possibly he was hoping that Emily and Tom would not notice his failure to appreciate the success of their comedy. He was no doubt baffled by his own feelings, by the failure of his own enthusiasm, and by a growing desire to withdraw himself from the plot and from the party itself.

It is easy to imagine Ned's uneasiness and confusion that night. And I believe the account which I have given of Emily's impressions and her delicate little sensations while on the way to the party has a ring of truth about it, though actually the account was supplied by girls who knew her only slightly, who were not at the party, who could not possibly have seen her afterward. It may, after all, represent only what other girls imagined she would have felt. As for the account of how Mr. and Mrs. Meriwether spent the evening, it is their very own. And they did not hesitate to give it to anyone who would listen.

It was a long time, though, before many of us had a clear picture of the main events of the evening. We heard very soon that the parties for young people were to be no more, that there had been a wild scramble and chase through the Dorsets' house, and that it had ended by the Dorsets locking some boy—whether Ned or Tom was not easy to determine at first—in a queer sort of bathroom in which the plumbing had been disconnected, and even the fixtures removed, I believe. (Later I learned that there was nothing literally sinister about the bathroom itself. By having the pipes disconnected to this, and perhaps other bathrooms, the Dorsets had obtained further reductions in their taxes.) But a clear picture of the whole evening wasn't to be had—not without considerable searching. For one thing, the Meriwether parents immediately, within a week after the party, packed their son and daughter off to boarding schools. Accounts from the other children were contradictory and vague—perversely so, it seemed. Parents reported to each other that the little girls had nightmares which were worse even than those which their older sisters had had. And the boys were secretive and elusive, even with us older boys when we questioned them about what had gone on.

One sketchy account of events leading up to the chase, however, did go the rounds almost at once. Ned must have written it back to some older boy in a letter, because it contained information which no one but Ned could have had. The account went like this: When Mr. Dorset returned from his last roundup of guests, he came hurrying into the drawing room where the others were waiting and said in a voice trembling with excitement: "Now, let us all be seated, my young friends, and let us warm ourselves with some good talk."

At that moment everyone who was not already seated made a dash for a place on one of the divans or love seats or even in one of the broad window seats. (There were no individual chairs in the room.) Everyone made a dash, that is, except Ned. Ned did not move. He remained standing beside a little table rubbing his fingers over its polished surface. And from this moment he was clearly an object of suspicion in the eyes of his host and hostess. Soon the party moved from the drawing room to the library, but in whatever room they stopped Ned managed to isolate himself from the rest. He would sit or stand looking down at his hands until once again an explosion of giggles filled the room. Then he would look up just in time to see Tom Bascomb's cheek against Emily's or his arm about her waist.

For nearly two hours Ned didn't speak a word to anyone. He endured the Dorsets' dialogue, the paper flowers, the perfumed air, the works of art. Whenever a burst of giggling forced him to raise his eyes, he would look up at Tom and Emily and then turn his eyes away. Before looking down at his hands again, he would let his eyes travel slowly about the room until they came to rest on the figures of the two Dorsets. That, it seems, was how he happened to discover that the Dorsets understood, or thought they understood, what the giggles meant. In the great mirror mounted over the library mantel he saw them exchanging half-suppressed smiles. Their smiles lasted precisely as long as the giggling continued, and then, in the mirror, Ned saw their faces change and grow solemn when their eyes—their identical, tiny, dull, amber-colored eyes—focused upon himself.

From the library the party continued on the regular tour of the house. At last when they had been to the ballroom and watched the Dorsets dance, had been upstairs to gaze upon the faded party clothes in the museum cases, they descended into the downstairs hall and were just before being turned into the dining room. The guests had already heard the Dorsets teasing each other about the silly little flirtations and about their naughtiness in parlor games when they were young and had listened to their exhortations to be gay and happy and carefree. Then just when Miss Dorset leaned toward them and whispered, "This is what it is like to be young forever," there rose a chorus of laughter, breathless and shrill, yet loud and intensely penetrating.

Ned Meriwether, standing on the bottom step of the stairway, lifted his eyes and looked over the heads of the party to see Tom and Emily half hidden in a bower of paper flowers and caught directly in a ray of mauve light. The two had squeezed themselves into a little niche there and stood squarely in front of the Rodin statuary. Tom had one arm placed about Emily's shoulders and he was kissing her lightly first on the lobe of one ear and then on the tip of her nose. Emily stood as rigid and pale as the plaster sculpture behind her and with just the faintest smile on her lips. Ned looked at the two of them and then turned his glance at once on the Dorsets.

He found Miss Louisa and Mr. Alfred gazing quite openly at

Tom and Emily and frankly grinning at the spectacle. It was more than Ned could endure. "Don't you *know?*" he wailed, as if in great physical pain. "Can't you *tell?* Can't you see who they *are?* They're *brother* and *sister!*"

From the other guests came one concerted gasp. And then an instant later, mistaking Ned's outcry to be something he had planned all along and probably intended—as they imagined—for the very cream of the jest, the whole company burst once again into laughter—not a chorus of laughter this time but a volley of loud guffaws from the boys, and from the girls a cacophony of separately articulated shrieks and trills.

None of the guests present that night could—or would—give a satisfactory account of what happened next. Everyone insisted that he had not even looked at the Dorsets, that he, or she, didn't know how Miss Louisa and Mr. Alfred reacted at first. Yet this was precisely what those of us who had gone there in the past *had* to know. And when finally we did manage to get an account of it, we knew that it was a very truthful and accurate one. Because we got it, of course, from Tom Bascomb.

Since Ned's outburst came after the dancing exhibition, the Dorsets were in their most disheveled state. Miss Louisa's hair was fallen half over her face, and that long, limp strand of Mr. Alfred's was dangling about his left ear. Like that, they stood at the doorway to the dining room grinning at Tom Bascomb's antics. And when Tom Bascomb, hearing Ned's wail, whirled about, the grins were still on the Dorsets' faces even though the guffaws and the shrieks of laughter were now silenced. Tom said that for several moments they continued to wear their grins like masks and that you couldn't really tell how they were taking it all until presently Miss Louisa's face, still wearing the grin, began turning all the queer colors of her paper flowers. Then the grin vanished from her lips and her mouth fell open and every bit of color went out of her face. She took a step backward and leaned against the doorjamb with her mouth still open and her eyes closed. If she hadn't been on her feet, Tom said he would have thought she was dead. Her brother didn't look at her, but his own grin had vanished just as hers did, and his face, all drawn and wrinkled, momentarily turned a dull copperish green.

Presently, though, he too went white, not white in faintness but in anger. His little brown eyes now shone like resin. And he took several steps toward Ned Meriwether. "What we know is that you are not one of us," he croaked. "We have perceived that from the beginning! We don't know how you got here or who you are. But the important question is, What are you doing here among these nice children?"

The question seemed to restore life to Miss Louisa. Her amber eyes popped wide open. She stepped away from the door and began pinning up her hair which had fallen down on her shoulders, and at the same time addressing the guests who were huddled together in the center of the hall. "Who is he, children? He is an intruder, that we know. If you know who he is, you must tell us."

"Who *am* I? Why, I am Tom Bascomb!" shouted Ned, still from the bottom step of the stairway. "I am Tom Bascomb, your paper boy!"

Then he turned and fled up the stairs toward the second floor. In a moment Mr. Dorset was after him.

To the real Tom Bascomb it had seemed that Ned honestly believed what he had been saying; and his own first impulse was to shout a denial. But being a level-headed boy and seeing how bad things were, Tom went instead to Miss Dorset and whispered to her that Tom Bascomb was a pretty tough guy and that she had better let *him* call the police for her. She told him where the telephone was in the side hall, and he started away.

But Miss Dorset changed her mind. She ran after Tom telling

him not to call. Some of the guests mistook this for the beginning of another chase. Before the old lady could overtake Tom, however, Ned himself had appeared in the doorway toward which she and Tom were moving. He had come down the back stairway and he was calling out to Emily, "We're going *home*, Sis!"

A cheer went up from the whole party. Maybe it was this that caused Ned to lose his head, or maybe it was simply the sight of Miss Dorset rushing at him that did it. At any rate, the next moment he was running up the front stairs again, this time with Miss Dorset in pursuit.

When Tom returned from the telephone, all was quiet in the hall. The guests—everybody except Emily—had moved to the foot of the stairs and they were looking up and listening. From upstairs Tom could hear Ned saying, "All right. All right. All right." The old couple had him cornered.

Emily was still standing in the little niche among the flowers. And it is the image of Emily Meriwether standing among the paper flowers that tantalizes me whenever I think or hear someone speak of that evening. That, more than anything else, can make me wish that I had been there. I shall never cease to wonder what kind of thoughts were in her head to make her seem so oblivious to all that was going on while she stood there, and, for that matter, what had been in her mind all evening while she endured Tom Bascomb's caresses. When, in years since, I have had reason to wonder what some girl or woman is thinking—some Emily grown older—my mind nearly always returns to the image of that girl among the paper flowers. Tom said that when he returned from the telephone she looked very solemn and pale still but that her mind didn't seem to be on any of the present excitement. Immediately he went to her and said, "Your dad is on his way over, Emily." For it was the Meriwether parents he had telephoned, of course, and not the police.

It seemed to Tom that so far as he was concerned the party was now over. There was nothing more he could do. Mr. Dorset was upstairs guarding the door to the strange little room in which Ned was locked up. Miss Dorset was serving lime punch to the other guests in the dining room, all the while listening with one ear for the arrival of the police whom Tom pretended he had called. When the doorbell finally rang and Miss Dorset hurried to answer it, Tom slipped quietly out through the pantry and through the kitchen and left the house by the back door as the Meriwether parents entered by the front.

There was no difficulty in getting Edwin and Muriel Meriwether, the children's parents, to talk about what happened after they arrived that night. Both of them were sensible and clear-headed people, and they were not so conservative as some of our other neighbors in West Vesey. Being fond of gossip of any kind and fond of reasonably funny stories on themselves, they told how their children had deceived them earlier in the evening and how they had deceived themselves later. They tended to blame themselves more than the children for what had happened. They tried to protect the children from any harm or embarrassment that might result from it by sending them off to boarding school. In their talk they never referred directly to Tom's reprehensible conduct or to the possible motives that the children might have had for getting up their plan. They tried to spare their children and they tried to spare Tom, but unfortunately it didn't occur to them to try to spare the poor old Dorsets.

When Miss Louisa opened the door, Mr. Meriwether said, "I'm Edwin Meriwether, Miss Dorset. I've come for my son Ned."

"And for your daughter Emily, I hope," his wife whispered to him.

"And for my daughter Emily."

Before Miss Dorset could answer him, Edwin Meriwether spied Mr. Dorset descending the stairs. With his wife, Muriel, sticking

close to his side Edwin now strode over to the foot of the stairs. "Mr.
Dorset," he began, "my son Ned—"

From behind them, Edwin and Muriel now heard Miss Dorset
saying, "All the invited guests are gathered in the dining room."
From where they were standing the two parents could see into the
dining room. Suddenly they turned and hurried in there. Mr. Dorset
and his sister of course followed them.

Muriel Meriwether went directly to Emily who was standing in a
group of girls. "Emily, where is your brother?"

Emily said nothing, but one of the boys answered: "I think
they've got him locked up upstairs somewhere."

"Oh, no!" said Miss Louisa, a hairpin in her mouth—for she was
still rather absent-mindedly working at her hair. "It is an intruder
that my brother has upstairs."

Mr. Dorset began speaking in a confidential tone to Edwin. "My
dear neighbor," he said, "our paper boy saw fit to intrude himself
upon our company tonight. But we recognized him as an outsider
from the start."

Muriel Meriwether asked: "Where *is* the paper boy? Where is the
paper boy, Emily?"

Again one of the boys volunteered: "He went out through the
back door, Mrs. Meriwether."

The eyes of Mr. Alfred and Miss Louisa searched the room for
Tom. Finally their eyes met and they smiled coyly. *"All* the children
are being mischievous tonight," said Miss Louisa, and it was quite
as though she had said, "all *we* children." Then, still smiling, she
said, "Your tie has come undone, Brother. Mr. and Mrs. Meriwether
will hardly know what to think."

Mr. Alfred fumbled for a moment with his tie but soon gave it
up. Now with a bashful glance at the Meriwether parents, and
giving a nod in the direction of the children, he actually said, "I'm

afraid we've all decided to play a trick on Mr. and Mrs. Meriwether."

Miss Louisa said to Emily: "We've hidden our brother somewhere, haven't we?"

Emily's mother said firmly: "Emily, tell me where Ned is."

"He's upstairs, Mother," said Emily in a whisper.

Emily's father said: "I wish you to take me to the boy upstairs, Mr. Dorset."

The coy, bashful expressions vanished from the faces of the two Dorsets. Their eyes were little dark pools of incredulity, growing narrower by the second. And both of them were now trying to put their hair in order. "Why, *we* know nice children when we see them," Miss Louisa said peevishly. There was a pleading quality in her voice, too. "We knew from the beginning that that boy upstairs didn't belong amongst us," she said. "Dear neighbors, it isn't just the money, you know, that makes the difference." All at once she sounded like a little girl about to burst into tears.

"It isn't just the money?" Edwin Meriwether repeated.

"Miss Dorset," said Muriel with new gentleness in her tone, as though she had just recognized that it was a little girl she was talking to, "there has been some kind of mistake—a misunderstanding."

Mr. Alfred Dorset said: "Oh, we wouldn't make a mistake of that kind! People *are* different. It isn't something you can put your finger on, but it isn't the money."

"I don't know what you're talking about," Edwin said, exasperated. "But I'm going upstairs and find that boy." He left the room with Mr. Dorset following him with quick little steps—steps like those of a small boy trying to keep up with a man.

Miss Louisa now sat down in one of the high-backed dining chairs which were lined up along the oak wainscot. She was trembling, and Muriel came and stood beside her. Neither of them spoke, and in almost no time Edwin Meriwether came downstairs again with Ned. Miss Louisa looked at Ned, and tears came into her eyes. "Where is my brother?" she asked accusingly, as though she thought possibly Ned and his father had locked Mr. Dorset in the bathroom.

"I believe he has retired," said Edwin. "He left us and disappeared into one of the rooms upstairs."

"Then I must go up to him," said Miss Louisa. For a moment she seemed unable to rise. At last she pushed herself up from the chair and walked from the room with the slow, steady gait of a somnambulist. Muriel Meriwether followed her into the hall and as she watched the old woman ascending the steps, leaning heavily on the rail, her impulse was to go and offer to assist her. But something made her turn back into the dining room. Perhaps she imagined that her daughter, Emily, might need her now.

The Dorsets did not reappear that night. After Miss Louisa went upstairs, Muriel promptly got on the telephone and called the parents of some of the other boys and girls. Within a quarter of an hour, half a dozen parents had assembled. It was the first time in many years that any adult had set foot inside the Dorset house. It was the first time that any parent had ever inhaled the perfumed air or seen the masses of paper flowers and the illuminations and the statuary. In the guise of holding consultations over whether or not they should put out the lights and lock up the house, the parents lingered much longer than was necessary before taking the young people home. Some of them even tasted the lime punch. But in the presence of their children they made no comment on what had happened and gave no indication of what their own impressions were—not even their impressions of the punch. At last it was decided that two of the men should see to putting out the lights everywhere on the first floor and down in the ballroom. They were a long time in finding the switches for the indirect lighting. In most cases, they simply resorted to unscrewing the bulbs. Meanwhile the children went to the large cloak closet behind the stairway and got their wraps. When Ned and Emily Meriwether rejoined their parents at the front door to leave the house, Ned was wearing his own overcoat and held his own fedora in his hand.

Miss Louisa and Mr. Alfred Dorset lived on for nearly ten years after that night, but they gave up selling their figs and paper flowers and of course they never entertained young people again. I often wonder if growing up in Chatham can ever have seemed quite the same since. Some of the terror must have gone out of it. Half the dread of coming of age must have vanished with the dread of the Dorsets' parties.

After that night, their old car would sometimes be observed creeping about town, but it was never parked in front of their house any more. It stood usually at the side entrance where the Dorsets could climb in and out of it without being seen. They began keeping a servant too—mainly to run their errands for them, I imagine. Sometimes it would be a man, sometimes a woman, never the same one for more than a few months at a time. Both of the Dorsets died during the Second World War while many of us who had gone to their parties were away from Chatham. But the story went round—and I am inclined to believe it—that after they were dead and the house was sold, Tom Bascomb's coat and hat were found still hanging in the cloak closet behind the stairs.

Tom himself was a pilot in the war and was a considerable hero. He was such a success and made such a name for himself that he never came back to Chatham to live. He found bigger opportunities elsewhere I suppose, and I don't suppose he ever felt the ties to Chatham that people with Ned's kind of upbringing do. Ned was in the war too, of course. He was in the navy and after the war he did return to Chatham to live, though actually it was not until then that he had spent much time here since his parents bundled him off to boarding school. Emily came home and made her debut just two or three years before the war, but she was already engaged to some boy in the East; she never comes back any more except to bring her children to see their grandparents for a few days during Christmas or at Easter.

I understand that Emily and Ned are pretty indifferent to each other's existence nowadays. I have been told this by Ned Meriwether's own wife. Ned's wife maintains that the night Ned and Emily went to the Dorsets' party marked the beginning of this indifference, that it marked the end of their childhood intimacy and the beginning of a shyness, a reserve, even an animosity between them that was destined to be a sorrow forever to the two sensible parents who had sat in the upstairs sitting room that night waiting until the telephone call came from Tom Bascomb.

Ned's wife is a girl he met while he was in the navy. She was a Wave, and her background isn't the same as his. Apparently, she isn't too happy with life in what she refers to as "Chatham proper." She and Ned have recently moved out into a suburban development, which she doesn't like either and which she refers to as "greater Chatham." She asked me at a party one night how Chatham got its name (she was just making conversation and appealing to my interest in such things) and when I told her that it was named for the Earl of Chatham and pointed out that the city is located in Pitt County, she burst out laughing. "How very elegant," she said. "Why has nobody ever told me that before?" But what interests me most about Ned's wife is that after a few drinks she likes to talk about Ned and Emily and Tom Bascomb and the Dorsets. Tom Bascomb has become a kind of hero—and I don't mean a wartime hero—in her eyes, though of course not having grown up in Chatham she has never seen him in her life. But she is a clever girl, and there are times when she will say to me, "Tell me about Chatham. Tell me

about the Dorsets." And I try to tell her. I tell her to remember that
Chatham looks upon itself as a rather old city. I tell her to remember that it was one of the first English-speaking settlements west of
the Alleghenies and that by the end of the American Revolution,
when veterans began pouring westward over the Wilderness Road
or down the Ohio River, Chatham was often referred to as a
thriving village. Then she tells me that I am being dull, because it is
hard for her to concentrate on any aspect of the story that doesn't
center around Tom Bascomb and that night at the Dorsets'.

But I make her listen. Or at least one time I did. The Dorset
family, I insisted on saying, was in Chatham even in those earliest
times right after the Revolution, but they had come here under
somewhat different circumstances from those of the other early
settlers. How could that really matter, Ned's wife asked, after a
hundred and fifty years? How could distinctions between the first
settlers matter after the Irish had come to Chatham, after the
Germans, after the Italians? Well, in West Vesey Place it could
matter. It had to. If the distinction was false, it mattered all the
more and it was all the more necessary to make it.

But let me interject here that Chatham is located in a state about
whose history most Chatham citizens—not newcomers like Ned's
wife, but old-timers—have little interest and less knowledge. Most of
us, for instance, are never even quite sure whether during the 1860's
our state did secede or didn't secede. As for the city itself, some of us
hold that it is geographically Northern and culturally Southern.
Others say the reverse is true. We are all apt to want to feel mis-
placed in Chatham, and so we are not content merely to say that it is
a border city. How you stand on this important question is apt to
depend entirely on whether your family is one of those with a good
Southern name or one that had its origin in New England, because
those are the two main categories of old society families in
Chatham.

But truly—I told Ned's wife—the Dorset family was never in either of those categories. The first Dorset had come, with his family and his possessions and even a little capital, direct from a city in the English Midlands to Chatham. The Dorsets came not as pioneers, but paying their way all the way. They had not bothered to stop for a generation or two to put down roots in Pennsylvania or Virginia or Massachusetts. And this was the distinction which some people wished always to make. Apparently those early Dorsets had cared no more for putting down roots in the soil of the New World than they had cared for whatever they had left behind in the Old. They were an obscure mercantile family who came to invest in a new Western city. Within two generations the business—no, the industry!—which they established made them rich beyond any dreams they could have had in the beginning. For half a century they were looked upon, if any family ever was, as our first family.

And then the Dorsets left Chatham—practically all of them except the one old bachelor and the one old maid—left it just as they had come, not caring much about what they were leaving or where they were going. They were city people, and they were Americans. They knew that what they had in Chatham they could buy more of in other places. For them Chatham was an investment that had paid off. They went to live in Santa Barbara and Laguna Beach, in Newport and on Long Island. And the truth which it was so hard for the rest of us to admit was that, despite our families of Massachusetts and Virginia, we were all more like the Dorsets—those Dorsets who left Chatham—than we were unlike them. Their spirit was just a little closer to being the very essence of Chatham than ours was. The obvious difference was that we had to stay on here and pretend that our life had a meaning which it did not. And if it was only by a sort of chance that Miss Louisa and Mr. Alfred played the role of social arbiters among the young people for a number of years, still no one could honestly question their divine right to do so.

"It may have been their right," Ned's wife said at this point, "but just think what might have happened."

"It's not a matter of what might have happened," I said. "It is a matter of what did happen. Otherwise, what have you and I been talking about?"

"Otherwise," she said with an irrepressible shudder, "I would not be forever getting you off in a corner at these parties to talk about my husband and my husband's sister and how it is they care so little for each other's company nowadays."

And I could think of nothing to say to that except that probably we had now pretty well covered our subject.

1939

❖◈❖◈❖◈❖◈❖◈❖◈❖◈❖◈❖◈❖◈❖◈❖◈❖◈❖◈❖◈❖◈❖

Twenty years ago, in 1939, I was in my senior year at Kenyon College. I was restless, and wasn't sure I wanted to stay on and finish college. My roommate at Kenyon was Jim Prewitt. Jim was restless, too. That fall, he and I drove to New York City to spend our Thanksgiving holiday. Probably both of us felt restless and uneasy for the same reasons that everyone else did in 1939, or for just the obvious reasons that college seniors always do, but we imagined our reasons to be highly individual and beyond the understanding of the other students.

It was four o'clock on Wednesday afternoon when we left Gambier, the little Ohio village that gives Kenyon its post office address. We had had to wait till the four o'clock mail was put in the Gambier post office, because each of us was expecting a check from home. My check came. Jim's did not. But mine was enough to get us to New York, and Jim's would be enough to get us back. "Enough to get back, *if* we come back!" That became our motto for the trip. We had both expressed the thought in precisely the same words and at precisely the same moment as we came out of the post

[326]

office. And during the short time it took us to dash back across the village street, with its wide green in the center, and climb the steps up to our room in Douglass House and then dash down again with our suitcases to the car, we found half a dozen excuses for repeating our motto.

The day was freakishly warm, and all of our housemates were gathered on the front stoop when we made our departure. In their presence, we took new pleasure in proclaiming our motto and repeating it over and over while we threw our things into the car. The other boys didn't respond, however, as we hoped they would. They leaned against the iron railing of the stoop, or sat on the stone steps leaning against one another, and refused to admit any interest in our "childish" insinuation: *if* we came back. All seven of them were there and all seven were in agreement on the "utter stupidity" of our long Thanksgiving trip as well as that of our present behavior. But they didn't know our incentive, and they couldn't be expected to understand.

For two years, Jim and I had shared a room on the second floor of old Douglass House. I say "old" because at Kenyon in those days there was still a tendency to prefix that adjective to the name of everything of any worth on the campus or in the village. Oldness had for so many years been the most respected attribute of the college that it was natural for its prestige to linger on a few years after what we considered the new dispensation and the intellectual awakening. Old Douglass House *was* an oldish house, but it had only been given over for use as a dormitory the year that Jim and I—and most of our friends—came to Kenyon. The nine of us moved into it just a few weeks after its former occupants—a retired professor and his wife, I believe—had moved out. And we were to live there during our three years at Kenyon (all of us having transferred from other colleges as sophomores)—to live there without ever caring to inquire into the age or history of the house. We were not the kind of students who cared about such things. We were hardly aware, even, of just how quaint the house was, with its steep white gables laced with gingerbread work, and its Gothic windows and their arched window blinds. Our unawareness—Jim's and mine—was probably never more profound than on that late afternoon in November, when we set out for New York. Our plan was to spend two days in Manhattan and then go on to Boston for a day with Jim's family, and our only awareness was of that plan.

During the previous summer, Jim Prewitt had become engaged to a glorious, talented girl with long flaxen hair, whom he had met at a student writers' conference somewhere out West. And I, more attached to things at home in St. Louis than Jim was to things in Boston—*I* had been "accepted" by an equally glorious dark-eyed girl in whose veins ran the Creole blood of old-time St. Louis. By a happy coincidence both of these glorious girls were now in New York City. Carol Crawford, with her flaxen hair fixed in a bun on the back of her neck and a four-hundred-page manuscript in her suitcase, had headed East from the fateful writers' conference in search of a publisher for her novel. Nancy Gibault had left St. Louis in September to study painting at the National Academy. The two girls were as yet unacquainted, and it was partly to the correcting of this that Jim and I meant to dedicate our Thanksgiving holiday.

The other boys at Douglass House didn't know our incentive, and when we said goodbye to them there on the front steps I really felt a little sorry for them. Altogether, they were a sad, shabby, shaggy-looking lot. All of us who lived at Douglass House were, I suppose. You have probably seen students who look the way we did—especially if you have ever visited Bard College or Black Mountain or Rollins or almost any other college nowadays. Such students seem to affect a kind of hungry, unkempt look. And yet they don't really know what kind of impression they want to make; they only know that there are certain kinds they *don't* want to make.

Generally speaking, we at Douglass House were reviled by the rest of the student body, all of whom lived in the vine-covered dormitories facing the campus, and by a certain proportion of the faculty. I am sure we were thought of as a group as closely knit as any other in the college. We were even considered a sort of fraternity. But we didn't see ourselves that way. We would have none of that. Under that high gabled roof, we were all independents and meant to remain so. Housing us "transfers" together this way had been the inspiration of the dean or the president under the necessity of solving a problem of overflow in the dormitories. Yet we did not object to his solution, and of our own accord we ate together in the Commons, we hiked together about the countryside, we went together to see girls in nearby Mount Vernon, we enrolled in the same classes, flocked more or less after the same professors, and met every Thursday night at the creative writing class, which we all acknowledged as our reason for being at Kenyon. But think of ourselves as a club, or as dependent upon each other for companionship or for anything else, we would not. There were times when each of us talked of leaving Kenyon and going back to the college or university from which he had come—back to Ann Arbor or Olivet, back to Chapel Hill, to Vanderbilt, to Southwestern, or back to Harvard or Yale. It was a moderately polite way each of us had of telling the others that *they* were a bunch of Kenyon boys but that *he* knew something of a less cloistered existence and was not to be confused with their kind. We were so jealous of every aspect of our independence and individuality that one time, I remember, Bruce Gordon nearly fought with Bill Anderson because Bill, for some strange reason, had managed to tune in, with his radio, on a Hindemith sonata that Bruce was playing on the electric phonograph in his own room.

Most of us had separate rooms. Only Jim Prewitt and I shared a room, and ours was three or four times as big as most dormitory cubicles. It opened off the hall on the second floor, but it was on a somewhat lower level than the hall. And so when you entered the door, you found yourself at the head of a little flight of steps, with the top of your head almost against the ceiling. This made the room seem even larger than it was, as did the scarcity and peculiar arrangement of the furniture. Our beds, with our desks beside them, were placed in diagonally opposite corners, and we each had a wobbly five-foot bookshelf set up at the foot of his bed, like a hospital screen. The only thing we shared was a little three-legged oak table in the very center of the room, on which were a hot plate and an electric coffeepot, and from which two long black extension cords reached up to the light fixture overhead.

The car that Jim and I were driving to New York did not belong to either of us. It didn't at that time belong to anybody, really, and I don't know what ever became of it. At the end of our holiday, we left it parked on Marlborough Street in Boston, with the ignition key lost somewhere in the gutter. I suppose Jim's parents finally disposed of the car in some way or other. It had come into our hands the spring before, when its last owner had abandoned it behind the college library and left the keys on Jim's desk up in our room. He, the last owner, had been one of us in Douglass House for a while—though it was, indeed, for a very short while. He was a poor boy who had been at Harvard the year that Jim was there, before Jim transferred to Kenyon, and he was enormously ambitious and possessed enough creative energy to produce in a month the quantity of writing that most of us were hoping to produce in a lifetime. He was a very handsome fellow, with a shock of yellow hair and the physique of a good trackman. On him the cheapest department store clothes looked as though they were tailor-made, and he could never have looked like the rest of us, no matter how hard he might have tried. I am not sure that he ever actually

matriculated at Kenyon, but he was there in Douglass House for
about two months, clicking away on first one typewriter and then
another (since he had none of his own); I shall never forget the
bulk of manuscript that he turned out during his stay, most of
which he left behind in the house or in the trunk of the car. The
sight of it depressed me then, and it depresses me now to think of it.
His neatly typed manuscripts were in every room in the house—
novels, poetic dramas, drawing-room comedies, lyrics, epic poems,
short stories, scenarios. He wasn't at all like the rest of us. And
except for his car he has no place in this account of our trip to New
York. Yet since I have digressed this far, there is something more
that I somehow feel I ought to say about him.

Kenyon was to him only a convenient place to rest awhile (for
writing was not work to him) on his long but certain journey from
Harvard College to Hollywood. He used to say to us that he wished
he could do the way we were doing and really dig in at Kenyon for
a year or so and get his degree. The place appealed to him, he said,
with its luxuriant countryside, and its old stone buildings sending
up turrets and steeples and spires above the treetops. If he stayed, he
would join a fraternity, so he said, and walk the Middle Path with
the other fraternity boys on Tuesday nights, singing fraternity songs
and songs of old Kenyon. He said he envied us—and yet he hadn't
himself time to stay at Kenyon. He was there for two months, and
while he was there he was universally admired by the boys in
Douglass House. But when he had gone, we all hated him. Perhaps
we were jealous. For in no time at all stories and poems of his began
appearing in the quarterlies as well as in the popular magazines.
Pretty soon one of his plays had a good run on Broadway, and I
believe he had a novel out even before that. He didn't actually go to
Hollywood till after the war, but get there at last he did, and now, I
am told, he has a house in the San Fernando Valley and has the two
requisite swimming pools, too.

To us at Kenyon he left his car. It was a car given to him by an elderly benefactor in Cambridge, but a car that had been finally and quite suddenly rendered worthless in his eyes by a publisher's advance, which sent him flying out of our world by the first plane he could get passage on. He left us the car without any regret, left it in the same spirit that American tourists left their cars on the docks at European ports when war broke out that same year. In effect, he tossed us his keys from the first-class deck of the giant ship he had boarded at the end of his plane trip, glad to know that he would never need the old rattletrap again and glad to be out of the mess that all of us were in for life.

I have said that I somehow felt obliged to include everything I have about our car's last real owner. And now I know why I felt so. Without that digression it would have been impossible to explain what the other boys were thinking—or what we thought they were thinking—when we left them hanging about the front stoop that afternoon. They were thinking that there was a chance Jim and I had had an "offer" of some kind, that we had "sold out" and were headed in the same direction that our repudiated brother had taken last spring. Perhaps they did not actually think that, but that was how we interpreted the sullen and brooding expressions on their faces when we were preparing to leave that afternoon.

Of course, what their brooding expressions meant made no difference to Jim or me. And we said so to each other as, with Jim at the wheel, we backed out of the little alleyway beside the house and turned into the village street. We cared not a hoot in hell for what they thought of us or of our trip to New York. Further, we cared no more—Jim and I—for each other's approval or disapproval, and we reminded each other of this then and there.

We were all independents in Douglass House. There was no spirit of camaraderie among us. We were not the kind of students who cared about such things as camaraderie. Besides, we felt that there was more than enough of that spirit abroad at Kenyon, among the students who lived in the regular dormitories and whose fraternity lodges were scattered about the wooded hillside beyond the village. In those days, the student body at Kenyon was almost as picturesque as the old vine-clad buildings and the rolling countryside itself. So it seemed to us, at least. We used to sit on the front stoop or in the upstairs windows of Douglass House and watch the fops and dandies of the campus go strolling and strutting by on their way to the post office or the bank, or to Jean Val Dean's short-order joint. Those three establishments, along with Dicky Doolittle's filling station, Jim Lynch's barber shop, Jim Hayes's grocery store, Tom Wilson's Home Market, and Mrs. Titus's lunchroom and bakery (the Kokosing Restaurant), constituted the business district of Gambier. And it was in their midst that Douglass House was situated. Actually, those places of business were strung along just one block of the village's main thoroughfare. Each was housed in its separate little store building or in a converted dwelling house, and in the spring and in the fall, while the leaves were still on the low hanging branches of the trees, a stranger in town would hardly notice that they were places of business at all.

From the windows of Douglass House, between the bakery and the barber shop, we could look down on the dormitory students who passed along the sidewalk, and could make our comment on what we considered their silly affectations—on their provincial manners and their foppish, collegiate clothing. In midwinter, when all the leaves were off the trees, we could see out into the parkway that divided the street into two lanes—and in the center of the parkway was the Middle Path. For us, the Middle Path was the epitome of everything about Kenyon that we wanted no part of. It was a broad gravel walkway extending not merely the length of the village green; it had its beginning, rather, at the far end of the campus, at the worn doorstep of the dormitory known as Old

Kenyon, and ran the length of the campus, on through the village, then through the wooded area where most of the faculty houses were, and ended at the door of Bexley Hall, Kenyon's Episcopal seminary. In the late afternoon, boys on horseback rode along it as they returned from the polo field. At noon, sometimes, boys who had just come up from Kenyon's private airfield appeared on the Middle Path still wearing their helmets and goggles. And after dinner every Tuesday night the fraternity boys marched up and down the path singing their fraternity songs and singing fine old songs about early days at Kenyon and about its founder, Bishop Philander Chase:

> *The first of Kenyon's goodly race*
> *Was that great man Philander Chase.*
> *He climbed the hill and said a prayer*
> *And founded Kenyon College there.*

> *He dug up stones, he chopped down trees,*
> *He sailed across the stormy seas,*
> *And begged at ev'ry noble's door,*
> *And also that of Hannah Moore.*

> *He built the college, built the dam,*
> *He milked the cow, he smoked the ham;*
> *He taught the classes, rang the bell,*
> *And spanked the naughty freshmen well.*

At Douglass House we wanted none of that. We had all come to Kenyon because we were bent upon becoming writers of some kind or other and the new president of the college had just appointed a famous and distinguished poet to the staff of the English Department. Kenyon was, in our opinion, an obscure little college that had for more than a hundred years slept the sweet, sound sleep that only a small Episcopal college can ever afford to sleep. It was a quaint and pretty spot. We recognized that, but we held that against it. That was not what we were looking for. We even collected stories about other people who had resisted the beauties of the campus and the surrounding countryside. A famous English critic had stopped here on his way home from a long stay in the Orient, and when asked if he did not admire our landscape he replied, "No. It's too rich for my blood." We all felt it was too rich for ours, too. Another English visitor was asked if the college buildings did not remind him of Oxford, and by way of reply he permitted his mouth to fall open while he stared in blank amazement at his questioner.

Despite our feeling that the countryside was too rich for our blood, we came to know it a great deal better—or at least in more detail—than did the polo players or the fliers or the members of the champion tennis team. For we were nearly all of us walkers. We walked the country roads for miles in every direction, talking every step of the way about ourselves or about our writing, or if we exhausted those two dearer subjects, we talked about whatever we were reading at the time. We read W. H. Auden and Yvor Winters and Wyndham Lewis and Joyce and Christopher Dawson. We read *The Wings of the Dove* (aloud!) and *The Cosmological Eye* and *The Last Puritan* and *In Dreams Begin Responsibilities*. (Of course, I am speaking only of books that didn't come within the range of the formal courses we were taking in the college.) On our walks through the country—never more than two or three of us together— we talked and talked, but I think none of us ever listened to anyone's talk but his own. Our talk seemed always to come to nothing. But our walking took us past the sheep farms and orchards and past some of the old stone farmhouses that are scattered throughout that township. It brought us to the old quarry from which most of the stone for the college buildings and for the farmhouses had been taken, and brought us to Quarry Chapel, a long since deserted and "deconsecrated" chapel, standing on a hill two miles from the college and symbolizing there the failure of Episcopalianism to take root among the Ohio country people. Sometimes we walked along the railroad track through the valley at the foot of the college hill, and I remember more than once coming upon two or three tramps warming themselves by a little fire they had built or even cooking a meal over it. We would see them maybe a hundred yards ahead, and we would get close enough to hear them laughing and talking together. But as soon as they noticed us we would turn back and walk in the other direction, for we pitied them and felt that our presence was an intrusion. And yet, looking back on it, I remember how happy those tramps always seemed. And how sad and serious we were.

Jim and I headed due East from Gambier on the road to Coshocton and Pittsburgh. Darkness overtook us long before we ever reached the Pennsylvania state line. We were in Pittsburgh by about 9 p.m., and then there lay ahead of us the whole long night of driving. Nothing could have better suited our mood than the prospect of this ride through the dark, wooded countryside of Pennsylvania on that autumn night. This being before the days of the turnpike—or at least before its completion—the roads wound about the great domelike hills of that region and through the deep valleys in a way that answered some need we both felt. We spoke of it many times during the night, and Jim said he felt he knew for the first time the meaning of "verdurous glooms and winding mossy ways." The two of us were setting out on this trip not in search of the kind of quick success in the world that had so degraded our former friend in our eyes; we sought, rather, a taste—or foretaste— of "life's deeper and more real experience," the kind that dormitory life seemed to deprive us of. We expressed these yearnings in just those words that I have put in quotation marks, not feeling the need for any show of delicate restraint. We, at twenty, had no abhorrence of raw ideas or explicit statement. We didn't hesitate to say what we wanted to be and what we felt we must have in order to become that. We wanted to be writers, and we knew well enough that before we could write we had to have "mature and adult experience." And, by God, we *said* so to each other, there in the car as we sped through towns like Turtle Creek and Greensburg and Acme.

I have observed in recent years that boys the age we were then and with our inclinations tend to value ideas of this sort above all else. They are apt to find their own crude obsession with mere ideas the greatest barrier to producing the works of art they are after. I have observed this from the vantage ground of the college professor's desk, behind which the irony of fate has placed me from time to time. From there, I have also had the chance to observe something about *girls* of an artistic bent or temperament, and for that reason I am able to tell you more about the two girls we were going to see in New York than I could possibly have known then.

At the time—that is, during the dark hours of the drive East— each of us carried in his mind an image of the girl who had inspired him to make this journey. In each case, the image of the girl's face and form was more or less accurate. In my mind was the image of a brunette with dark eyes and a heart-shaped face. In Jim's was that of a blonde, somewhat above average height, with green eyes and perhaps a few freckles on her nose. That, in general, was how we pictured them, but neither of us would have been dogmatic about the accuracy of his picture. Perhaps Carol Crawford didn't have any freckles. Jim wasn't sure. And maybe her eyes were more blue than green. As for me, I wouldn't have contradicted anyone who said Nancy Gibault's face was actually slightly elongated, rather than heart-shaped, or that her hair had a decided reddish cast to it. Our impressions of this kind were only more or less accurate, and we would have been the first to admit it.

But as to the talent and the character and the original mind of the two glorious girls, we would have brooked no questioning of our concepts. Just after we passed through Acme, Pennsylvania, our talk turned from ourselves to these girls—from our inner yearnings for mature and adult experience to the particular objects toward which we were being led by these yearnings. We agreed that the quality we most valued in Nancy and Carol was their "critical" and "objective" view of life, their unwillingness to accept the standards of "the world." I remember telling Jim that Nancy Gibault could always take a genuinely "disinterested" view of any matter—"disinterested in the best sense of the word." And Jim assured me that, whatever else I might perceive about Carol, I would sense at once the originality of her mind and "the absence of anything commonplace or banal in her intellectual make-up."

It seems hard to believe now, but that was how we spoke to each other about our girls. That was what we thought we believed and felt about them then. And despite our change of opinions by the time we headed back to Kenyon, despite our complete and permanent disenchantment, despite their unkind treatment of us—as worldly and as commonplace as could be—I know now that those two girls were as near the concepts we had of them to begin with as any two girls their age might be, or should be. And I believe now that the decisions *they* made about *us* were the right decisions for *them* to make. I have only the vaguest notion of how Nancy Gibault has fared in later life. I know only that she went back to St. Louis the following spring and was married that summer to Lon Havemeyer. But as for Carol Crawford, everybody with any interest in literary matters knows what became of her. Her novels are read everywhere. They have even been translated into Javanese. She is, in her way, even more successful than the boy who made the long pull from Harvard College to Hollywood.

Probably I seem to be saying too much about things that I understood only long after the events of my story. But the need for the above digression seemed no less urgent to me than did that concerning the former owner of our car. In his case, the digression dealt mostly with events of a slightly earlier time. Here it has dealt with a wisdom acquired at a much later time. And now I find that I am still not quite finished with speaking of that later time and wisdom. Before seeing me again in the car that November night in 1939, picture me for just a moment—much changed in appearance and looking at you through gold-rimmed spectacles—behind the lectern in a classroom. I stand before the class as a kind of journeyman writer, a type of whom Trollope might have approved, but one who has known neither the financial success of the facile Harvard boy nor the reputation of Carol Crawford. Yet this man behind the lectern is a man who seems happy in the knowledge that he knows—or thinks he knows—what he is about. And from behind his lectern he is saying that any story that is written in the form of a memoir should give offense to no one, because before a writer can make a person he has known fit into such a story—or any story, for that matter—he must do more than change the real name of that person. He must inevitably do such violence to that person's character that the so-called original is forever lost to the story.

The last lap of Jim's and my all-night drive was the toughest. The night had begun as an unseasonably warm one. I recall that there were even a good many insects splattered on our windshield in the hours just after dark. But by the time we had got through Pittsburgh the sky was overcast and the temperature had begun to drop. Soon after 1 a.m. we noticed the first big, soft flakes of snow. I was driving at the time, and Jim was doing most of the talking. I raised one finger from the steering wheel to point out the snow to Jim, and he shook his head unhappily. But he went on talking. We had maintained our steady stream of talk during the first hours of the night partly to keep whoever was at the wheel from going to sleep, but from this point on it was more for the purpose of making us forget the threatening weather. We knew that a really heavy snowstorm could throw our holiday schedule completely out of gear. All night long we talked. Sometimes the snow fell thick and fast, but there were times, too, when it stopped altogether. There was a short period just before dawn when the snow turned to rain—a cold rain, worse than the snow, since it began to freeze on our windshield. By this time, however, we had passed through Philadelphia and we knew that somehow or other we would make it on to New York.

We had left Kenyon at four o'clock in the afternoon, and at eight the next morning we came to the first traffic rotary outside New York, in New Jersey. Half an hour later we saw the skyline of the city, and at the sight of it we both fell silent. I think we were both conscious at that moment not so much of having arrived at our destination as of having only then put Kenyon College behind us. I remember feeling that if I glanced over my shoulder I might still see on the horizon the tower of Pierce Hall and the spires of Old Kenyon Dormitory. And in my mind's eye I saw the other Douglass House boys—all seven of them—still lingering on the stone steps of the front stoop, leaning against the iron railing and against one another, staring after us. But more than that, after the image had gone I realized suddenly that I had pictured not seven but *nine* figures there before the house, and that among the other faces I had glimpsed my own face and that of Jim Prewitt. It seemed to me that we had been staring after ourselves with the same fixed, brooding expression in our eyes that I saw in the eyes of the other boys.

Nancy Gibault was staying in a sort of girls' hotel, or rooming house, on 114th Street. Before she came down from her room that Thanksgiving morning, she kept me waiting in the lobby for nearly forty-five minutes. No doubt she had planned this as a way of preparing me for worse things to come. As I sat there, I had ample time to reflect upon various dire possibilities. I wondered if she had been out terribly late the night before and, if so, with whom. I thought of the possibility that she was angry with me for not letting her know what day I would get there. (I had had to wait on my check from home, and there had not been time to let her know exactly when we would arrive.) I reflected, even, that there was a remote chance she had not wanted me to come at all. What didn't occur to me was the possibility that *all* of these things were true. I sat in that dreary, overheated waiting room, still wearing my overcoat and holding my hat in my lap. When Nancy finally came down, she burst into laughter at the sight of me. I rose slowly from my chair and said angrily, "What are you laughing at? At how long I've waited?"

"No, my dear," she said, crossing the room to where I stood. "I was laughing at the way you were sitting there in your overcoat with your hat in your lap like a little boy."

"I'm sweating like a horse," I said, and began unbuttoning my coat. By this time Nancy was standing directly in front of me, and I leaned forward to kiss her. She drew back with an expression of revulsion on her face.

"Keep your coat on!" she commanded. Then she began giggling and backing away from me. "If you expect me to be seen with you," she said, "you'll go back to wherever you're staying and shave that fuzz off your lip."

For three weeks I had been growing my first mustache.

I had not yet been to the hotel where Jim and I planned to stay. It was a place that Jim knew about, only three or four blocks from where Nancy was living, and I now set out for it on foot, carrying my suitcase. Our car had broken down just after we came up out of the Holland Tunnel. It had been knocking fiercely for the last hour of the trip, and we learned from the garage man with whom we left it that the crankcase was broken. It seems we had burned out a bearing, because we had forgotten to put any oil in the crankcase. I don't think we realized at the time how lucky we were to find a garage open on Thanksgiving morning and, more than that, one that would have the car ready to run again by the following night.

After I had shaved, I went back to Nancy's place. She had gone upstairs again, but this time she did not keep me waiting so long. She came down wearing a small black hat and carrying a chesterfield coat. Back in St. Louis, she had seldom worn a hat when we went out together, and the sight of her in one now made me feel uncomfortable. We sat down together near the front bay window of that depressing room where I had waited so long, and we talked there for an hour, until it was time to meet Jim and Carol for lunch.

While we talked that morning, Nancy did not tell me that Lon Havemeyer was in town from St. Louis, much less that she had spent all her waking hours with him during the past week. I could not have expected her to tell me at once that she was now engaged to marry him, instead of me, but I did feel afterward that she could have begun at once by telling me that she had been seeing Lon and that he was still in town. It would have kept me from feeling quite so much at sea during the first hours I was with her. Lon was at least seven or eight years older than Nancy, and for five or six years he had been escorting debutantes to parties in St. Louis. His family were of German origin and were as new to society there as members of Nancy's family were old to it. The Havemeyers were also as rich nowadays as the Gibaults were poor. Just after Nancy graduated from Mary Institute, Lon had begun paying her attentions. They went about together a good deal while I was away at college, but between Nancy and me it had always been a great joke. To us, Lon was the essence of all that we were determined to get away from there at home. I don't know what he was really like. I had heard an older cousin of Nancy's say that Lon Havemeyer managed to give the impression of not being dry behind the ears but that the truth was he was "as slick as a newborn babe." But I never exchanged two sentences with him in my life—not even during the miserable day and a half that I was to tag along with him and Nancy in New York.

It may be that Nancy had not known that she was in love with Lon or that she was going to marry him until she saw me there, with the fuzz on my upper lip, that morning. Certainly I must have been an awful sight. Even after I had shaved my mustache, I was still the seedy-looking undergraduate in search of "mature experience." It must have been a frightful embarrassment to her to have to go traipsing about the city with me on Thanksgiving Day. My hair was long, my clothes, though quite genteel, were unpressed, and even rather dirty, and for some reason I was wearing a pair of heavy brogans. Nancy had never seen me out of St. Louis before, and since she had seen me last, she had seen Manhattan. To be fair to her, though, she had seen something more important than that. She had, for better or for worse, seen herself.

We had lunch with Jim and Carol at a little joint over near Columbia, and it was only after we had left them that Nancy told me Lon Havemeyer was in town and waiting that very moment to go with us to the Metropolitan Museum. I burst out laughing when she told me, and she laughed a little, too. I don't remember when I fully realized the significance of Lon's presence in New York. It wasn't that afternoon, or that night, even. It was sometime during the next day, which was Friday. I suppose that I should have realized it earlier and that I just wouldn't. From the time we met Lon on the museum steps, he was with us almost continuously until the last half hour before I took my leave of Nancy the following night. Sometimes I would laugh to myself at the thought of this big German oaf's trailing along with us through the galleries in the

afternoon and then to the ballet that night. But I was also angry at
Nancy from the start for having let him horn in on our holiday
together, and at various moments I pulled her aside and expressed
my anger. She would only look at me helplessly, shrug, and say, "I
couldn't help it. You really have got to try to see that I couldn't help
it."

After the ballet, we joined a group of people who seemed to be
business acquaintances of Lon's and went to a Russian nightclub—
on Fourteenth Street, I think. (I don't know exactly where it was,
for I was lost in New York and kept asking Nancy what part of
town we were in.) The next morning, about ten, Nancy and I took
the subway down to the neighborhood of Fifty-seventh Street,
where we met Lon for breakfast. Later we looked at pictures in
some of the galleries. I don't know what became of the afternoon.
We saw an awful play that night. I know it was awful, but I don't
remember what it was. The events of that second day are almost
entirely blotted from my memory. I only know that the mixture of
anger and humiliation I felt kept me from ducking out long before
the evening was over—a mixture of anger and humiliation and
something else, something that I had begun to feel the day before
when Nancy and I were having lunch with Jim and Carol Crawford.

Friday night, I was somehow or other permitted to take Nancy
home alone from the theater. We went in a taxi, and neither of us
spoke until a few blocks before we reached 114th Street. Finally I
said, "Nancy." And Nancy burst into tears.

"You won't understand, and you will never forgive me," she said
through her tears, "but I am so terribly in love with him."

I didn't say anything till we had gone another block. Then I said,
"How have things gone at the art school?"

Nancy blew her nose and turned her face to me, as she had not done when she spoke before. "Well, I've learned that I'm not an artist. They've made me see that."

"Oh," I said. Then, "Does that make it necessary to—"

"It makes everything in the world look different. If I could only have known in time to write you."

"When did you know?"

"I don't know. I don't know when I knew."

"Well, it's a good thing you came to New York," I said. "You almost made a bad mistake."

"No," she said. "You mustn't think I feel that about you."

"Oh, not about me," I said quickly. "About being an artist. When we were at lunch yesterday, you know, with Jim and his girl, it came over me suddenly that you weren't an artist. Just by looking at you I could tell."

"What a cruel thing to say," she said quietly. All the emotion had gone out of her voice. "Only a child could be so cruel," she said.

When the taxi stopped in front of her place, I opened the door for her but didn't get out, and neither of us said goodbye. I told the driver to wait until she was inside and then gave him the address of my hotel. When, five minutes later, I was getting out and paying the driver, I didn't know how much to tip him. I gave him fifteen cents. He sat with his motor running for a moment, and then, just before he pulled away, he threw the dime and the nickel out on the sidewalk and called out to me at the top of his voice, "You brat!"

The meeting between Nancy and Carol was supposed to be one of the high points of our trip. The four of us ate lunch together that first day sitting in the front booth of a little place that was crowded with Columbia University students. Because this was at noon on Thanksgiving Day, probably not too many restaurants in that neighborhood were open. But I felt that every student in the dark little lunchroom was exulting in his freedom from a certain turkey dinner somewhere, and from some particular family gathering. We four had to sit in the very front booth, which was actually no booth at all but a table and two benches set right in the window. Some people happened to be getting up from that table just as we came in and Carol, who had brought us there, said, "Quick! We must take this one." Nancy had raised up on her tiptoes and craned her neck, looking for a booth not quite so exposed.

"I think there may be some people leaving back there," she said.

"No," said Carol in a whisper. "Quick! In here." And when we had sat down, she said, "There are some dreadful people I know back there. I'd rather die than have to talk to them."

Nancy and I sat with our backs almost against the plate-glass window. There was scarcely room for the two of us on the bench we shared. I am sure the same was true for Jim and Carol, and they faced us across a table so narrow that when our sandwiches were brought, the four plates could only be arranged in one straight row. There wasn't much conversation while we ate, though Jim and I tried to make a few jokes about our drive through the snow and about how the car broke down. Once, in the middle of something Jim was saying, Carol suddenly ducked her head almost under the table. "Oh, God!" she gasped. "Just my luck!" Jim sat up straighter and started peering out into the street. Nancy and I looked over our shoulders. There was a man walking along the sidewalk on the other side of the broad street.

"You mean that man way over there?" Nancy asked.

"Holy God, yes," hissed Carol. "Do please stop gaping at him."

Nancy giggled. "Is he dreadful, too?" she asked.

Carol straightened and took a sip of her coffee. "No, he's not exactly dreadful. He's the critic Melville Bland." And after a moment: "He's a full professor at Columbia. I was supposed to have dinner today with him and his stupid wife—she's the playwright Dorothy Lewis and really *awfully* stupid—at some chichi place in the East Sixties, and I told them an awful lie about my going out to Connecticut for the day. I'd rather be shot than talk to either of them for five minutes."

I was sitting directly across the table from Carol. While we were there, I had ample opportunity to observe her, without her seeming to notice that I was doing so. My opportunity came each time anyone entered the restaurant or left it. For nobody could approach the glass-front door, either from the street or from inside, without Carol's fastening her eyes upon that person and seeming to take in every detail of his or her appearance. Here, I said to myself, is a real novelist observing people—*objectively* and *critically*. And I was favorably impressed by her obvious concern with literary personages; it showed how committed she was to a life of writing. Carol seemed to me just the girl that Jim had described. Her blond hair was not really flaxen. (It was golden, which is prettier but which doesn't sound as interesting as flaxen.) It was long and carelessly arranged. I believe Jim was right about its being fixed in a knot on the back of her neck. Her whole appearance showed that she cared as little about it as either Jim or I did about ours . . . Perhaps *this* was what one's girl really ought to look like.

When we got up to leave, Nancy lingered at the table to put on fresh lipstick. Carol wandered to the newspaper stand beside the front door. Jim and I went together to pay our bills at the counter. As we waited for our change, I said an amiable, pointless "Well?"

"Well what?" Jim said petulantly.

"Well, they've met," I said.

"Yeah," he said. "They've met." He grinned and gave his head a little shake. "But Nancy's just another society girl, old man," he said. "I had expected something more than that." He suddenly looked very unhappy, and rather angry, too. I felt the blood rising in my cheeks and knew in a moment that I had turned quite red. Jim was much heavier than I was, and I would have been no match for him in any real fight, but my impulse was to hit him squarely in the face with my open hand. He must have guessed what I had in mind, for with one movement he jerked off his horn-rimmed glasses and jammed them into the pocket of his jacket.

At that moment, the man behind the counter said, "Do you want this change or not, fellows?"

We took our change and then glared at each other again. I had now had time to wonder what had come over Jim. Out of the corner of my eye I caught a glimpse of Carol at the newsstand and took in for the first time, in that quick glance, that she was wearing huaraches and a peasant skirt and blouse, and that what she now had thrown around her shoulders was not a topcoat but a long green cape. "At least," I said aloud to Jim, "Nancy's not the usual bohemian. She's not the run-of-the-mill arty type."

I fully expected Jim to take a swing at me after that. But, instead, a peculiar expression came over his face and he stood for a moment staring at Carol over there by the newsstand. I recognized the expression as the same one I had seen on his face sometimes in the classroom when his interpretation of a line of poetry had been questioned. He was reconsidering.

When Nancy joined us, Jim spoke to her very politely. But once we were out in the street there was no more conversation between the two couples. We parted at the first street corner, and in parting there was no mention of our joining forces again. That was the last time I ever saw Carol Crawford, and I am sure that Jim and Nancy never met again. At the corner, Nancy and I turned in the direction of her place on 114th Street. We walked for nearly a block without either of us speaking. Then I said, "Since when did you take to wearing a hat everywhere?"

Nancy didn't answer. When we got to her place, she went upstairs for a few minutes, and it was when she came down again that she told me Lon Havemeyer was going to join us at the Metropolitan.

Looking back on it, I feel that it may have been only when I asked that question about her hat that Nancy decided definitely about how much Lon and I were going to be seeing of each other during the next thirty-six hours. It is possible, at least, that she called him on the telephone while she was upstairs.

I didn't know about it then, of course, but the reception that Jim Prewitt found awaiting him that morning had, in a sense, been worse even than mine. I didn't know about it and Jim didn't tell me until the following spring, just a few weeks before our graduation from Kenyon. By that time, it all seemed to us like something in the remote past, and Jim made no effort to give me a complete picture of his two days with Carol. The thing he said most about was his reception upon arriving.

He must have arrived at Carol's apartment, somewhere on Morningside Heights, at almost the same moment that I arrived at Nancy's place. He was not, however, kept waiting for forty-five minutes. He was met at the door by a man whom he described as a flabby middle-aged man wearing a patch over one eye, a T shirt, and denim trousers. The man did not introduce himself or ask for Jim's name. He only jerked his head to one side, to indicate that Jim should come in. Even before the door opened, Jim had heard strains of the Brandenburg Concerto from within. Now, as he stepped into the little entryway, the music seemed almost deafening, and when he was led into the room where the phonograph was playing, he could not resist the impulse to make a wry face and clap his hands over his ears.

But although there were half a dozen people in the room, nobody saw the gesture or the face he made. The man with the patch over his eye had preceded him into the room, and everyone else was sitting with eyes cast down or actually closed. Carol sat on the floor tailor fashion, with an elbow on each knee and her face in her hands. The man with the patch went to her and touched the sole of one of her huaraches with his foot. When she looked up and saw Jim, she gave him no immediate sign of recognition. First she eyed him from head to foot with an air of disapproval. Jim's attire that day, unlike my own, was extremely conventional (though I won't say he ever looked conventional for a moment). At Kenyon, he was usually the most slovenly and ragged-looking of us all. He really went about in tatters, sometimes even with the soles hanging loose from his shoes. But in his closet, off our room, there were always to be found his "good" shoes, his "good" suit, his "good" coat, his "good" hat, all of which had been purchased for him at Brooks Brothers by his mother. Today he had on his "good" things. Probably it was that that made Carol stare at him as she did. At last she gave him a friendly but slightly casual smile, placed a silencing forefinger over her lips, and motioned for him to come sit down beside her and listen to the deafening tones of the concerto.

While the automatic phonograph was changing records, Carol introduced Jim to the other people in the room. She introduced him and everyone else—men and women alike—by their surnames only: "Prewitt, this is Carlson. Meyer, this is Prewitt." Everyone nodded, and the music began again at the same volume. After the Bach there was a Mozart symphony. Finally Jim, without warning, seized Carol by the wrist, forcibly led her from the room, and closed the door after them. He was prepared to tell her precisely what he thought of his reception, but he had no chance to. "Listen to me," Carol began at once—belligerently, threateningly, all but shaking her finger in his face. "I have sold my novel. It was definitely accepted three days ago and is going to be published in the spring. And two sections from it are going to be printed as stories in the *Partisan Review*."

From that moment, Jim and Carol were no more alone than Nancy and I were. Nearly everywhere they went, they went with the group that had been in Carol's apartment that morning. After lunch with us that first noon, they rejoined the same party at someone else's apartment, down in Greenwich Village. When Jim told me about it, he said he could never be sure whose apartment he was in, for they always behaved just as they did at Carol's. He said that once or twice he even found himself answering a knock at the door in some strange apartment and jerking his head at whoever stood outside. The man with the patch over his eye turned out to be a musicologist and composer. The others in the party were writers whose work Jim had read in New Directions anthologies and in various little magazines, but they seemed to have no interest in anything he had to say about what they had written, and he noticed that their favorite way of disparaging any piece of writing was to say "it's *so* naïve, *so* undergraduate." After Jim got our car from the garage late Friday afternoon, they all decided to drive to New Jersey to see some "established writer" over there, but when they arrived at his house the "established writer" would not receive them.

Jim said there were actually a few times when he managed to get Carol away from her friends. But her book—the book that had been accepted by a publisher—was Carol's Lon Havemeyer, and her book was always with them.

Poor Carol Crawford! How unfair it is to describe her as she was that Thanksgiving weekend in 1939. Ever since she was a little girl on a dairy farm in Wisconsin she had dreamed of becoming a writer and going to live in New York City. She had not merely dreamed of it. She had worked toward it every waking hour of her life, taking jobs after school in the wintertime, and full-time jobs in the summer, always saving the money to put herself through the state university. She had made herself the best student—the prize pupil—in every grade of grammar school and high school. At the university she had managed to win every scholarship in sight. Through all those years she had had but one ambition, and yet I could not have met her at a worse moment in her life. Poor girl, she had just learned that she *was* a writer.

Driving to Boston on Saturday, Jim and I took turns at the wheel again. But now there was no talk about ourselves or about much of anything else. One of us drove while the other slept. Before we reached Boston, in mid-afternoon, it was snowing again. By night, there was a terrible blizzard in Boston.

As soon as we arrived, Jim's father announced that he would not hear of our trying to drive back to Kenyon in such weather and in such a car. Mrs. Prewitt got on the telephone and obtained a train schedule that would start us on our way early the next morning and put us in Cleveland sometime the next night. (From Cleveland we would take a bus to Gambier.) After dinner at the Prewitts' house, I went with Jim over to Cambridge to see some of his prep-school friends who were still at Harvard. The dinner with his parents had been painful enough, since he and I were hardly speaking to each other, but the evening with him and his friends was even worse for me. In the room of one of these friends, they spent the time drinking beer and talking about the undergraduate politics at Harvard and about the Shelley Poetry Prize. One of the friends was editor of the *Crimson,* I believe, and another was editor of the *Advocate*—or perhaps he was just on the staff. I sat in the corner pretending to read old copies of the *Advocate.* It was the first time I had been to Boston or to Cambridge, and ordinarily I would have been interested in forming my own impressions of how people like the Prewitts lived and of what Harvard students were like. But, as things were, I only sat cursing the fate that had made it necessary for me to come on to Boston instead of returning directly to Kenyon. That is, my own money having been exhausted, I was dependent upon the money Jim would get from his parents to pay for the return trip.

Shortly before seven o'clock Sunday morning, I followed Jim
down two flights of stairs from his room on the third floor of his
family's house. A taxi was waiting for us in the street outside. We
were just barely going to make the train. In the hall I shook hands
with each of his parents, and he kissed them goodbye. We dashed
out the front door and down the steps to the street. Just as we were
about to climb into the taxi, Mrs. Prewitt came rushing out,
bareheaded and without a wrap, calling to us that we had forgotten
to leave the key to the car, which was parked there in front of the
house. I dug down into my pocket and pulled out the key along
with a pocketful of change. But as I turned back toward Mrs.
Prewitt I stumbled on the curb, and the key and the change went
flying in every direction and were lost from sight in the deep snow
that lay on the ground that morning. Jim and Mrs. Prewitt and I
began to search for the key, but Mr. Prewitt called from the
doorway that we should go ahead, that we would miss our train.
We hopped in the taxi, and it pulled away. When I looked back
through the rear window I saw Mrs. Prewitt still searching in the
snow and Mr. Prewitt moving slowly down the steps from the
house, shaking his head.

On the train that morning Jim and I didn't exchange a word or a
glance. We sat in the same coach but in different seats, and we did
not go into the diner together for lunch. It wasn't until almost
dinnertime that the coach became so crowded that I had either to
share my seat with a stranger or to go and sit beside Jim. The day
had been long, I had done all the thinking I wanted to do about the
way things had turned out in New York. Further, toward the
middle of the afternoon I had begun writing in my notebook, and I
now had several pages of uncommonly fine prose fiction, which I
did not feel averse to reading aloud to someone.

I sat down beside Jim and noticed at once that *his* notebook was open, too. On the white, unlined page that lay open in his lap I saw the twenty or thirty lines of verse he had been working on. It was in pencil, quite smudged from many erasures, and was set down in Jim's own vigorous brand of progressive-school printing.

"What do you have there?" I said indifferently.

"You want to hear it?" he said with equal indifference.

"I guess so," I said. I glanced over at the poem's title, which was "For the Schoolboys of Douglass House," and immediately wished I had not got myself into this. The one thing I didn't want to hear was a preachment from him on his "mature experience" over the holiday. He began reading, and what he read was very nearly this (I have copied this part of the poem down as it later appeared in *Hika*, our undergraduate magazine at Kenyon):

> *Today while we are admissibly ungrown,*
> *Now when we are each half boy, half man,*
> *Let us each contrast himself with himself,*
> *And weighing the halves well, let us each regard*
> *In what manner he has not become a man.*

> *Today let us expose, and count as good,*
> *What is mature. And childish peccadillos*
> *Let us laugh out of our didactic house—*
> *The rident punishment one with reward*
> *For him bringing lack of manliness to light.*

But I could take no more than the first two stanzas. And I knew how to stop him. I touched my hand to his sleeve and whispered, "Shades of W. B. Yeats." And I commenced reciting:

> *Now that we're almost settled in our house*
> *I'll name the friends that cannot sup with us*
> *Beside a fire of turf in th' ancient tower . . .*

Before I knew it, Jim had snatched my notebook from my hands, and began reading aloud from it:

She had told him—Janet Monet had, for some inscrutable reason which she herself could not fathom, and which, had he known—as she so positively and with such likely assurance thought he knew—that if he came on to New York in the weeks ensuing her so unbenign father's funeral, she could not entertain him alone. . . .

Then he closed my notebook and returned it to me. "I can put it into rhyme for you, Mr. Henry James," he said. "It goes like this:

She knew that he knew that her father was dead.
And she knew that he knew what a life he had led—

While he was reciting, with a broad grin on his face and his eyes closed, I left him and went up into the diner to eat dinner. The next time we met was in the smoking compartment, at eight o'clock, an hour before we got into Cleveland.

It was I who wandered into the smoking compartment first. I went there not to smoke, for neither Jim nor I started smoking till after we left college, but in the hope that it might be empty, which, oddly enough, it was at that moment. I sat down by the window, at the end of the long leather seat. But I had scarcely settled myself there and begun staring out into the dark when the green curtain in the doorway was drawn back. I saw the light it let in reflected in the windowpane, and I turned around. Jim was standing in the doorway with the green curtain draped back over his head and shoulders. I don't know why, but it was only then that I realized that Jim, too, had been jilted. Perhaps it was the expression on his face—an expression of disappointment at not finding the smoking compartment empty, at being deprived of his one last chance for solitude before returning to Douglass House. And now—more than I had all day—I hated the sight of him. My lips parted to speak, but he literally took the sarcastic words out of my mouth.

"Ah, you'll get over it, little friend," he said.

Suddenly I was off the leather seat and lunging toward him. And he had snatched off his glasses, with the same swift gesture he had used in the restaurant, and tossed them onto the seat. The train was moving at great speed and must have taken a sharp turn just then. I felt myself thrown forward with more force than I could possibly have mustered in the three or four steps I took. When I hit him, it was not with my fists, or even my open hands, but with my shoulder, as though I was blocking in a game of football. He staggered back through the doorway and into the narrow passage, and for a moment the green curtain separated us. Then he came back. He came at me just as I had come at him, with his arms half folded over his chest. The blow he struck me with his shoulders sent me into the corner of the leather seat again. But I, too, came back.

Apparently neither of us felt any impulse to strike the other with his fist or to take hold and wrestle. On the contrary, I think we felt a mutual abhorrence and revulsion toward any kind of physical contact between us and if our fight had taken any other form than the one it did, I think that murder would almost certainly have been committed in the smoking compartment that night. We shoved each other about the little room for nearly half an hour, with ever-increasing violence, our purpose always seeming to be to get the other through the narrow doorway and into the passage—out of sight behind the green curtain.

From time to time, after our first exchange of shoves, various would-be smokers appeared in the doorway. But they invariably beat a quick retreat. At last one of them found the conductor and sent him in to stop us. By then it was all over, however. The conductor stood in the doorway a moment before he spoke, and we stared at him from opposite corners of the room. He was an old man with an inquiring and rather friendly look on his face. He looked like a man who might have fought gamecocks in his day, and I think he must have waited that moment in the doorway in the hope of seeing something of the spectacle that had been described to him. But by then each of us was drenched in sweat, and I know from a later examination of my arms and chest and back that I was covered with bruises.

When the old conductor was satisfied that there was not going to be another rush from either of us, he glanced about the room to see if we had done any damage. We had not even upset the spittoon. Even Jim's glasses were safe on the leather seat. "If you boys want to stay on this train," the conductor said finally, "you'll hightail it back to your places before I pull that emergency cord."

We were only thirty minutes out of Cleveland then, but when I got back to my seat in the coach I fell asleep at once. It was a blissful kind of sleep, despite the fact that I woke up every five minutes or so and peered out into the night to see if I could see the lights of Cleveland yet. Each time, as I dropped off to sleep again, I would say to myself what a fine sort of sleep it was, and each time it seemed that the wheels of the train were saying: *Not yet, not yet, not yet.*

After Cleveland there was a four-hour ride by bus to Gambier. Sitting side by side in the bus, Jim and I kept up a continuous flow of uninhibited and even confidential talk about ourselves, about our writing, and even about the possibility of going to graduate school next year if the army didn't take us. I don't think we were silent a moment until we were off the bus and, as we paced along the Middle Path, came in sight of Douglass House. It was 1 a.m., but through the bare branches of the trees we saw a light burning in the front dormer of our room. Immediately our talk was hushed, and we stopped dead still. Then, though we were as yet two hundred feet from the house and there was a blanket of snow on the ground, we began running on tiptoe and whispering our conjectures about what was going on in our room. We took the steps of the front stoop two at a time, and when we opened the front door, we were met by the odor of something cooking—bacon, or perhaps ham. We went up the long flight to the second floor on tiptoe, being careful not to bump our suitcases against the wall or the banisters. The door to our room was the first one at the top of the stairs. Jim seized the knob and threw the door open. The seven whom we had left lolling around the stoop on Wednesday were sprawled about our big room in various stages of undress, and all of them were eating. Bruce Gordon and Bill Anderson were in the center of the room, leaning over my hot plate.

Jim and I pushed through the doorway and stood on the doorstep looking down at them. I have never before or since seen seven such sober—no, such frightened-looking—people. Most eyes were directed at me, because it was my hot plate. But when Jim stepped down into the room, the two boys lounging back on his bed quickly stood up.

I remember my first feeling of outrage. The sacred privacy of that room under the eaves of Douglass House had been violated; this on top of what had happened in New York seemed for a moment more than flesh and blood could bear. Then, all of a sudden, Jim Prewitt and I began to laugh. Jim dropped his suitcase and went over to where the cooking was going on and said, "Give me something to eat. I haven't eaten all day."

I stood for a while leaning against the wall just inside the door. I was thinking of the tramps we had seen cooking down along the railroad track in the valley. Finally I said, "What a bunch of hoboes!" Everyone laughed—a little nervously, perhaps, but with a certain heartiness, too.

I continued to stand just inside the door, and presently I leaned my head against the wall and shut my eyes. My head swam for a moment. I had the sensation of being on the train again, swaying from side to side. It was hard to believe that I was really back in Douglass House and that the trip was over. I don't know how long I stood there that way. I was dead for sleep, and as I stood there with my eyes closed I could still hear the train wheels saying *Not yet, not yet, not yet.*

There

"Let me tell you something about the Busbys," the old gentleman said to me. "The Busbys don't wash themselves—not adequately. And especially not as they grow older."

That was how he opened our last conversation. It was our last meeting aboard ship, and the last he and I will be likely to have in this world. He was the kind of shipboard acquaintance you make who never seems real afterward. You remember him more distinctly than you do someone you have met on a plane or a train, but it is only because you were with him for a longer time. Nowadays particularly, there seems something unreal about people you have known on a sea voyage. To me, at least, it is nearly always as though I have met some character out of the past or out of a novel. And I never know whether it seems stranger when they *do* or when they *don't* explain why they are traveling by ship instead of by plane. In any case, the odd thing was that this man was a shipboard acquaintance who had come originally from my own home town, and it was of people back *there* he was speaking, not of our fellow passengers. We two had grown up in the same inland city, and we came more or less from the same stock there; yet the thirty or forty years that separated us made us strangers to one another as no distance across the surface of the earth nowadays, and no difference in nationality, could possibly have . . . At least so it seemed to me at the time. And nothing could have amused me more than his assumption that I would be acquainted with the same families that had once so absorbed his interest.

"Those Busbys! Those Busbys!" said he, thumping on the smoking table between us with his long lean middle finger. "It all comes to one thing: such people have no imagination about themselves!" At first he resorted to this finger-thumping and those exclamations to make sure he got my full attention. But finally, seeing me comfortably fixed in my chair, my academic pipe lighted, and my whole attention directed to his discourse, he spoke without bothering to look at me. "That's what made the Busbys a laughingstock. Lack of imagination about themselves. Of course the Busbys were not alone in this lack of theirs, but, despite all the good company they were in, it was no less damaging to them. There was a Busby boy named David, for instance, about the age of two young-lady cousins of mine. They used to visit us every summer when I was a small boy, and David Busby would try to court the younger girl. But she, being an out-of-town girl and not impressed by the Busby money, mocked him behind his back. Whenever he had been especially attentive to her, she and her sister had a little parody they would recite. It began, 'David, David, dirty but true . . .' Moreover, when there was a series of parties, they used to count the times that David appeared wearing the same shirt with the same soiled spots on it. He would change his collar, so they said, for any little old chafing-dish party (his detachable collar, you know—the kind Americans never wear any more), but it took an affair of the first magnitude to bring him out in a clean shirt . . . Poor fellow, I guess he never knew what a little fresh linen might have done for him with the girls."

As the old gentleman spoke he gazed off across the public room, as though trying to see out of first one porthole and then another. He was a strikingly handsome old man, with a decidedly clean and well-scrubbed look, and he had described himself to me as a retired career man from the diplomatic service, which I see no reason to doubt he was. I'd judge that he was well past seventy, but his figure was very slender still and straight, and by day he was given to wearing a beige or a checked waistcoat under a close-fitted tweed jacket. Or sometimes he wore a double-breasted navy jacket with brass buttons. There was always a handkerchief in the breast pocket of his jacket, and he owned at least one pair of brown suede shoes. Though his hair was white it was quite thick, and always perfectly groomed of course. His face was almost incredibly youthful looking. There were neat little wrinkles about his eyes and at the corners of his mouth, but otherwise his skin was as smooth and pink as a little child's. Somehow this had the effect of making me think a good deal about his age and about how he must have appeared when he was younger. I am confident that he had been a beautiful, tow-headed child, that his hair became black in young manhood, that after forty his temples turned becomingly gray, and that finally his entire panache had gone snow white in his sixty-fifth year or thereabouts.

He impressed me from the beginning as someone with great personal reserve and reticence. And until that last day on shipboard he had never revealed to me anything about himself—not even inadvertently. But as people of genuine reserve very often are, he was voluble enough on other subjects—particularly on the subject of *other* people . . . He had a way of making you feel that he couldn't say what he was saying to anyone but you. From the outset I observed in him what seemed a mixture of masculine frankness and almost feminine gossipiness. It was this mixture which must always have constituted his charm for people. Yet at that time I imagined he could only speak to me as he did because we came originally from the same place and because we had both asserted, right away, that we would never under any circumstances go back *there* to live. "Our home town is a cultural desert, as I'm sure you'll agree," he had said to me when he learned that I was an academic. "Most people there haven't even the imagination to see how urgent it is that they get away from the place if they are going to stay alive."

Though he had not himself really lived at home since he went East to college in 1906, the old man's voice still retained a flavor that I recognized even before we had introduced ourselves. I had sat eavesdropping in the bar one night—the night of our second day out—and heard how his voice contrasted with those of the other passengers with whom he associated, an assortment of Englishmen and Eastern seaboard types. That was really what made me distinguish him from the others in the first place. And soon after we began our nightly talks he and I discovered that he had known— ever so slightly—an uncle of mine who had died before I was born. And it turned out that I knew a girl—ever so slightly—who had married the son of one of his boyhood friends. That's how it went. At no point did we discover a mutual acquaintance. We missed completely when it came to individuals, but there was no mistaking the city that he and I had in mind or the kind of people there about whom Mr. Charles Varnell and I knew most.

During that last session of ours we were alone in the first-class smoking lounge. Though there was little likelihood of anyone's wishing to join us, Mr. Varnell had deliberately selected two chairs that were set well apart from all others. Our ship had docked that afternoon at Cherbourg and was resting in port while the continental passengers were let off and others were received on board for the return voyage to New York. During the night ahead the ship

would cross over to Southampton, and in the morning Mr. Varnell
and I would say our brief goodbyes before going down the gangplank. Actually I did catch another glimpse of him in customs, and
I even spotted him again, at a considerable distance, after we had
detrained at Waterloo Station an hour later. He and his wife were
being greeted there by some old-fashioned, rather toney-looking
English friends. As a matter of fact, I recalled his having told me,
when with mere perfunctory politeness I suggested we might run
into each other in London, that he and his wife were stopping with
friends for only a few hours. They would be in London "almost no
time at all." They had been "out to New York" for six weeks, and
now they had to rush down to Surrey and put their house there in
order before going up to Scotland for a month ("We're going up to
Scotland to shoot"—or some such elegant and wonderfully dated
remark). I never knew whether his wife was English or American
or of some other nationality. As for her appearance, it is sufficient to
say that she looked the way *his* wife *should* look. I was never
introduced to her, not even that morning at the gangplank when he
and I shook hands and parted. Our leavetaking was so brief and
casual that the other passengers, and perhaps even his own wife,
may have supposed that neither of us was sure of when, during the
voyage, he had talked to the other. But our real farewell had already
taken place—in the dead stillness of the port of Cherbourg. It was
he who did the talking on that occasion, and I imagine that what he
said to me then had had to wait until he knew that he and I would
not talk again.

   I laughed outright of course when he said the sort of thing he did
about the Busbys' not washing themselves. I suppose he expected me
to. But he didn't laugh. "It is no small matter," he insisted, "for
people not to wash—regardless of how rich or well-to-do they are. It
kept all the Busbys from ever amounting to anything outside their
own little bailiwick. Let me tell you. I used to sit behind that same

David Busby's grandfather in church—Mr. Lionel Busby. I was just a little fellow at the time, and what I chiefly remember about him are the deep creases and wrinkles in the back of his neck. I have never seen anything to equal it on a man of his position in the world—the visible dirt, that is to say, caked in those creases on the neck of that extremely rich old man. The Busbys were *very* wealthy at that time. I used to hear it debated at home whether Mr. Lionel was our second or third richest citizen. And he was no self-made man. If I am not mistaken, they had owned downtown real estate since before the Civil War. Mr. Lionel himself went East somewhere to college. But even up there they couldn't teach a Busby to wash his neck properly. And after college he came back, the way most of those people do, and married somebody at home—some girl who, I suppose, didn't care about or was willing to overlook the peculiar characteristics of the Busbys.

"Now, a man *can* be careless about his personal cleanliness. I understand that. A man *can* be somewhat slovenly in his dress. Some of my closest friends are so—to a certain degree. But what I found most revolting was its being the trait of a whole family, and a trait that the community regarded with a tolerance beyond all comprehension. Further, whereas it is possible for a gentleman to have such a weakness, it is not possible for a lady. And yet there were two Busby maiden ladies of my mother's generation, aunts to said David Busby, daughters to old Mr. Lionel; and *they* managed it, and *they,* by the community at large, were forgiven. They were a laughingstock, yes; but the point is that their defect *was* regarded as a laughing matter. I remember them as two old creatures with dyed black hair and reeking of perfume. Their fondness for personal finery, their tendency to be always overdressed, was proverbial. But the state and condition of their clothing was generally a scandal. My mother used to speak of a certain black lace mantilla that one of them wore. It slipped from the lady's shoulder one day when

Mother was sitting beside her on our parlor settee, and when Mother helped her retrieve it she found the thing as stiff with old spillage as though it had been freshly starched. Those two ladies were renowned also for the jewels they possessed and for the number they ornamented themselves with on all occasions. They were not averse to telling the history and value of every brooch, bracelet, or pendant earring they had on. They spoke of their jewels always as their 'stones,' and some rustic wit out there once remarked that the Busby ladies ought to put fewer precious stones on their fingers and more pumice stone on their elbows.

"But the prize story about the two Busby ladies is a very old and familiar sort of story. It is that of the burglar and the two old maids . . . The Misses Busby came in from a party one evening and heard the intruder moving about upstairs. He was after some of their 'stones' of course, and of course they were wearing most of what he was after. The two intrepid ladies didn't even call in the servants or the neighbors or send out for help of any kind. With an ice pick and an ax they hunted down their man, who, as it fortunately happened, was unarmed . . . There were several versions to the story, all of them ending with the man stretched out—in a dead faint—on the floor of one of the upstairs bedrooms. One version, probably the correct one, had it that the fellow was such a coward that he passed out cold at the sight of the ice pick and the ax. And then there was a pornographic version, of course, which I shall spare you. And there was also a third version, in its way as indelicate as the second, being the version which found favor amongst people most intimately acquainted with the Busby family. It seems the man had hidden himself in an old-fashioned clothespress, and the condition of the garments stored therein was so strong that when the old maids found their man he was already overcome by the rank and musty emanations. They dragged him out into the room, but he did not recover consciousness until after the police had finally been summoned and had removed him from the scene of the crime. His own version of what happened will never be known. He maintained through his trial and ultimate conviction that he could remember nothing. He may only have been possuming, of course, but it is possible on the other hand that the fellow had suffered an awful shock—of one kind or another."

Mr. Varnell told these anecdotes about the Busbys with never a smile and with but little discernible relish for the details he brought forth. He seemed to know the stories so well that it was not really necessary for him to think of what he was saying or how he would say it. One felt, even, that most of his phrases had been used in the exact context before. What made it interesting, though, was that one got the impression it had been such a long, long time before. There were moments when he seemed to listen to his own voice with a certain detachment and wonder. He was like a man delving into a trunk he had packed away years ago and who did not know, himself, what he would come upon next. His transition from the Busbys to the Jenkinses was quite abrupt and at the same time seemed very natural and easy, too. It was as though he had put down one old photograph or letter and picked up another. "The astonishing thing to me was always that the Busbys, like the Jenkinses and other families with equally marked peculiarities, remained in the very cream of society *there*. Nobody there minded them as they were, and so why need they change themselves? *Anything* was forgivable. If you ever met a Jenkins, for instance—as I am sure you have—you simply expected to meet a fat man, or, worse, a fat woman. It was entirely because the Jenkinses wouldn't stop eating. Jenkins apologists liked to put out that their trouble was glandular, just as the Busbys were all supposed to be nearsighted, or farsighted, or whichever it is that would excuse their not knowing that the backs of their necks were dirty. But once I saw Alice Jenkins eat eight pieces of fried chicken, three servings of potato salad, and a whole half of a watermelon in one sitting. It was on a picnic at Riverview Mills. Alice, you see, was the only Jenkins of my generation, but she was a plenty. That day at Riverview Mills we all went out on the pond in rowboats. The couples paired off, sitting side by side in the boats—in general they did. But there was never any pairing off on Alice's part. Without any companion she occupied the entire poop seat in her boat. There was a great deal of merriment over the fact, and she joined right in with it. But there was something repulsive to me about the way the boat sank down under her weight; and somehow it was worse because the image of all the other Jenkinses, all her fat relations, rose up in my mind.

"A couple of years later Alice was a debutante, and during the summer before her coming out she starved herself until she got to be quite decent looking. In fact, she appeared that fall looking a very handsome woman and with quite elegant manners. She got engaged soon after Christmas, however, and by the time she married in May she was a full-size Jenkins again. In the years just after that I used to see her when I would be back home on a visit. It would be at the Sunday night buffet supper at the country club; and not many years passed before she was surrounded there by a tribe of little Jenkins elephants (I forget now what her married name was). They occupied a long table that the Jenkinses had been occupying every Sunday night for years, and Alice's parents would still be there with them, as well as some of her enormous cousins and uncles and aunts. How they all heaped up the food on their plates! I can see them now trooping back to the buffet for second and third helpings. The food at the country club was the best in town in those days, and the Sunday night buffet supper was surely the best bargain ever offered anywhere. Probably it was only this combination that could bring the Jenkinses out in full force, because they were great home-bodies really, and the men in the family as well as the women were said to be splendid cooks. On his first trip to the buffet Alice's father used to take a tiny serving of every dish, even a pinch of each relish and a few drops of every sauce. Back at his table you would see him tasting away very thoughtfully. He had a high, rounded-out stomach, wonderfully symmetrical (like a giant tureen), and almost no chest. He wore a little gray, two-pronged imperial that stuck down like a meat fork over the white napkin which was tucked under his collar. While eating, he eyed his food intently, though, if some passerby happened to catch his eye, he would throw back his head and laugh aloud at himself and wave one corner of the napkin at the spectator. On his second trip to the buffet he narrowed his choice to four or five of the principal dishes. He became even more selective on his third trip. And the highest compliment he could pay the club chef was to go back for a fourth serving of some single dish.

"After supper, on a hot summer evening, the whole herd of elephantine Jenkinses would repair to the capacious wicker chairs out on the terrace beside the golf course. A special chair was reserved there for old Mrs. Jenkins, who outweighed her husband by at least fifty pounds and whose wide posterior could not be accommodated between the arms of any ordinary chair. Once they were all seated out there, they didn't rise until it was time to leave. Friends passing along the terrace, or seated in other groups nearby, would call out to them, asking how they had enjoyed their supper. They would reply in an enthusiastic chorus: 'Marvelously! Enormously!' Frequently, when it was time to go home, or if a little shower had come up, it would be discovered that Mrs. Jenkins had fallen into a deep sleep in her chair. There would be a great stir and commotion with even the grandchildren joining in the effort to wake the sleeper and prize her out of her chair. All over the club grounds people would hear them and would smile at each other and say, 'It's only the Jenkinses trying to wake Miss Nanny.'

"Not a very edifying picture, is it?" said Mr. Varnell, looking altogether serious, and disregarding my audible signs of amusement.

"And let me tell you," he continued, "the Busbys and the Jenkinses were not very exceptional people in our home town. It used to seem to me that every family there had some awful deficiency—I might almost say affliction—that marked them as a family. It wasn't so, of course. Or it was nearly always only something they might have overcome if they hadn't been so self-satisfied and so mutually indulgent. You and I know what it was they needed to do, of course. But why was it those people with so much money and so much leisure couldn't understand what their next step ought to be? More often than not they were people of genuine capability. The men were actually men of imagination when it came to business and money matters. The women, though you could not say they were cultivated, were not without charm and manners of a kind. But they stuck themselves off there and lived their sort of tribal life. Of course some of them would pick up and leave for a while. Even the Lionel Busbys did, I think. But they couldn't stick it out long enough. They always came back saying that 'people in Europe' or 'people up East' were condescending to them. Naturally! What else can you do but condescend to people until they have learned to wash themselves and eat with moderation. Some of them even enlarged their fortunes by taking their capital with them and investing it in bigger things than we had there. But still they came back at last, singing that false old tune that there's no place like home.

"Even when I was an adolescent I used to wonder how I could ever really fall in love with any girl who came from one of those families. And I never developed a genuine romantic interest in one of them till after I was in college. She was a Morris—Laura Nell Morris. I won't bore you by telling you what a beautiful creature Laura Nell was. Suffice it to say that it was love at first sight for me. And suffice it to say, on another score, that she bore only the very slightest family resemblance to her brothers and sisters and to her parents. She was a silly, harum-scarum kind of girl. I won't pretend otherwise. She had *no* conversation, and yet at a party she would never stop talking. She recited limericks, and riddles, and shaggy-dog stories, and she remembered and would make us listen to every poor joke she had ever heard at vaudeville and minstrel shows. Further, she was the sort of person who prided herself on always taking a dare, no matter how foolish it was. You couldn't afford to speak the word in her presence. It is a wonder she never got into serious trouble, whereas actually the most punishment I think she ever took was one night when somebody dared her to keep silent for fifteen minutes. She succeeded all right. But I was her escort on that occasion and afterward when I was taking her home I saw Laura Nell Morris, for the only time ever, in what I would call low spirits.

"There is even worse to be said about Laura Nell, however, and I might as well get the worst over with. She had a passion for playing elaborate practical jokes, not on her friends and contemporaries but on members of her own family—particularly on the older members. The odium of this was somewhat mitigated, perhaps, by the happy fact that the family did not mind her jokes so much as they might have done. They thought it childish of her, and they were baffled by her willingness to take such pains as she did in the preparation of her jokes. But it was their view that if Laura Nell derived real satisfaction and amusement from the practice, then they must not absolutely forbid her continuing and must not resent being, themselves, her objects. That was what the Morrises were like. If such extreme tolerance and disinterested regard for one another made them seem ridiculous, it was at the same time a most appealing quality for a family to have. And among its consequences, I am perfectly convinced, was the measure of individuality which all its members developed.

"I have already said how little the Morrises looked alike. There was a redheaded grandfather whose coloring did turn up in two of the older children. And Laura Nell, who was the youngest of the five, had just a suggestion of red in her dark hair. Perhaps there was something about the eyes of all the children to remind you of the father, if you noticed carefully. And there was a gentleness of speech general amongst them—even in the case of Laura Nell—that made you know they had been brought up by the same mother. But surely they had nothing more in common. There was a very tall brother, a short brother, and one of medium height. The middle-sized one was athletic, the tall one bookish, and the short one socially inclined. Laura Nell's only sister was the eldest child, and she was known for her quiet and responsive disposition, for her way of drawing out other people in conversation so that they would appear to best advantage.

"Part of Laura Nell's attraction for me—need I say it even?—was the very absence of any strong family marking. At our first meeting I didn't realize that she was at all related to the other Morrises. She was three years younger than I, and she had grown into a young lady since I went away to school. I was convinced that I had never laid eyes on her or on any of her family before. It turned out that I had in fact been acquainted with two of her brothers but had always supposed that they were, at most, distant cousins to each other. I found the very idea of such a family intriguing, and I find it so even to this day. Their mere unlikeness to one another, alone, would not of course have accounted for the impression they gave. It was their dissimilarity plus, in every case, without exception, a very strong and attractive personality. It was inconceivable to me that such a family should be content, generation after generation, to waste themselves on a town like ours. Mr. Morris was a lawyer with a national reputation in his profession. A good proportion of his clients were in New York and Philadelphia, not to mention Chicago and other cities nearer by. It would have been a very natural thing for him to have moved his family to New York. With such connections as he had, with Mrs. Morris's considerable fortune, and with all their natural social graces and intellectual capabilities, what interesting lives they might have had, what *serious* careers they might have made for themselves, if only they had got away from there. For the Morrises there would have been no handicaps, no bars of any kind.

"Once when I was talking to Mr. Morris about Laura Nell I made a point of telling him what an interesting and admirable family I thought they were. I even went into some detail as to why I found them so. 'Well,' he said to me, 'you *are* in love with my daughter if you think she and we are as different from the rest of the world as all that. In fact, you have about the worst case I've ever encountered. Laura Nell is a fortunate young lady. I wish you success with her. Sincerely I do.' But he treated the matter casually and even lightly. He made no objection to my suit. But he did not offer to speak in my favor to Laura Nell. If he had, the matter might have come out differently. I am not sure, though. At any rate, it couldn't have come out worse.

"Laura Nell's mother did not take such a disinterested view of my suit. She was a most amiable and sympathetic woman, and she told me that she could not imagine a more satisfactory son-in-law than I was certain to make. Still, she would not try to influence Laura Nell. In our conversations she spoke of Laura Nell almost as if she were someone else's daughter and spoke as if I were a son whom she was comforting and encouraging. There was always *some* of that in Mr. Morris's tone, too. If my own parents had lived until I was a grown man, I think they might have talked to me as Mr. and Mrs. Morris did. I like to think so. But I had no very near relative of any kind after I was in my teens, and the elderly banker and old bachelor who was my guardian and who had controlled my trust fund till I came of age was not anybody to turn to. My real confidants were Mr. and Mrs. Morris.

"Soon after Laura Nell refused me the first time, I came to call one day when she wasn't at home. It was during the last week of

September, and Mrs. Morris took me down to the end of the garden to show me her chrysanthemums. The late summer and fall flowers were a specialty with her, and she was certain that there was going to be a killing frost that night. There were splendid arrays of asters and dahlias on either side of the garden walk, but we had to go to the very end of the garden and climb to the top of a little terrace there in order to look back toward the house and have a proper view of the chrysanthemums. It was a chilly late afternoon, with the air bright and dry. I stood beside Mrs. Morris on the brick terrace and was able for a moment to admire the beds of russet and gold just below where we were standing. But it was only for a moment. At the other end of the garden I saw the great neo-Georgian house with its Palladian windows upstairs and its wide porch below. The muscular wistaria vines on the trellis of the porch were already leafless at that season. Suddenly I said to Mrs. Morris, 'Laura Nell has refused me . . . I am convinced now that there is no hope for my cause.'

"I was not really convinced of it—sad to relate. The passing of nearly two years and a considerably more drastic gesture on Laura Nell's part would be required for that. But Mrs. Morris herself was, there can be little doubt, convinced even then. She did not tell me to give Laura Nell time, or anything of that kind. When I withdrew my gaze from the house and looked at her, there was the sweetest, gentlest look in her gray eyes that I believe I have ever beheld in human eyes. And when she spoke it was not encouragement but consolation she offered me.

"The consolation came in a strange form. Laura Nell's practical jokes on her family were something that the family kept very much to themselves. I mean to say, they often referred to the fact that she had such a weakness, and on some occasions they were cautious in their behavior for fear of being led into one of her traps. But they would never oblige you with an account of any particular joke. If pressed, they would only laugh and say, 'It's much too grim. For Laura Nell's own sake it can't be told.' And since Laura Nell would not discuss the subject herself, I had never had any clue to what her jokes were like until that afternoon when I was out there at the end of the garden with Mrs. Morris. What she revealed to me is all I know to this day of Laura Nell's jokes.

" 'My dear,' she began, 'I can't blame you for being so in love with Laura Nell. She's an enchanting little person. But I want to tell you about two pranks that a certain young lady played on members of her own family. It may amuse you, and you may want to reflect on what caprices such a girl might some day treat her lawful husband to.' With no more preface than that and with no further explanation of her reason for doing so, she then told me about a joke that the certain young lady had once played on her father and about another she had played on her maternal grandmother only a year before the old lady died . . . It seems that the grandmother had a great fondness for attending funerals, and especially the funerals of indigent relations and friends and even slight acquaintances who were not so well-to-do as herself. The measure of her sympathy for the bereaved and the strength of her determination to be present at the funeral depended in each case on how straitened the family's circumstances were. Well, the old lady's granddaughter did a terrible thing. She arranged that she herself should accompany her grandmother to one of these funerals, and then when the hour came she got them into the wrong funeral. And she did it on purpose, as a joke. The poor acquaintance who was dead was one that the old lady had not seen in many years and that she probably would not have recognized had she met her on the street. Whereas the funeral they attended was that of a wealthy neighbor whom she had been seeing with some regularity in recent years but whose death did not seem to touch her at all.

"Since the grandmother's hearing and sight were not what they had once been, she managed to sit through the funeral service without discovering the trick that was being played on her. It was only at the end when they had gone up to view the remains and she had looked down into the face of her dead neighbor that she understood whose funeral it was. The shock was such that she had to lean on her granddaughter's arm all the way to the carriage, but by the time the driver, whom she reprimanded for having taken them to the Presbyterian instead of to the Methodist Church—by the time the driver had helped them inside the carriage and closed the door she had realized that the 'mistake' was all her granddaughter's doing. The girl didn't deny her guilt for a moment, and she only restrained her merriment until they had got out of the sight and hearing of the mourners. 'It's only what you deserve, Grandma,' she said to the old lady, who sat staring at her incredulously, 'for being so unsympathetic to your own kind.'

"The practical joke that the girl played on her father was not so bad as that, but it had a similar theme. The father prided himself on the tradition that his ancestors back in Virginia, a hundred years before, had been ruined by the 'cult of hospitality.' In fact, he kept in touch with a host of distant kin in Virginia; furthermore, new and seemingly ever more distant members of the connection were continually being made known to him. It was not uncommon for them to come and put up at his house overnight when they were (ostensibly) passing through town on their way to the West Coast or to the Deep South; and they did not scruple to write to him from time to time for small loans or free legal advice. He spoke of them censoriously as 'broken-down aristocrats,' but still he was proud of them as living proof of the old family tradition . . . A telephone call came on a Saturday night, purportedly from a relative that had never been heard from before. The male voice said that the speaker was 'having certain difficulties with the law' and that he, along with his wife and their seven children, were stranded 'temporarily' at a downtown rooming house without the means of buying their Sunday dinner next day. The desired invitation to dinner was obtained, of course, and at one o'clock the next day the host and his family had assembled in the front drawing room to welcome their troubled cousins. Instead of their cousins, however, there arrived at precisely one o'clock another family quite well known to all present. It was a Mr. and Mrs. Herman Miller, their two married sons, their daughters-in-law, and their grandchildren. Mr. Miller's investment and brokerage company had recently collapsed, he had been indicted by the grand jury, and it was generally conceded that in the end he would not avoid a jail sentence. The Millers' home had already been foreclosed on, and they were preparing to move from it the following Monday morning. For a number of years they had been living in very fine style, and by their host that Sunday noon they had always been regarded as parvenues and fourflushers. They were received for dinner that day, however, in a most cordial and hospitable manner by a family who grasped at once whose work the whole business had been.

"I can only account for Laura Nell's practical jokes and for her overbearing, chatterbox ways by attributing it all to an excess of vitality. She had a store of energy that she didn't know what to do with. She ought to have found some sensible use to put it to, but somehow she couldn't. She remained a silly, harum-scarum girl when she ought to have been maturing into the wonderful young woman that she might have been. And yet her very vitality and animation were what attracted me first. I fell in love with her on first sight almost, and when I discovered that, though she would listen to no one else, she *would* listen to me, it seemed to me that I had only then begun to live and I was sure for the first time that I was going to be able to make something of my life.

"I suppose she was in love with me, at first. During the first weeks and months of our acquaintance she gave every sign of being so—every sign that a young lady of that day could give. And during that period I had but one object in life. It was finding moments when I could be alone with her. Laura Nell seemed as eager as I for those moments, and by the time we had known each other a year we had discoursed upon every subject that a young lady and a young gentleman of that day were permitted to discourse upon. I was no longer living there at home even then. I had begun training for my career immediately after college (I was one of the first to have any formal training in the field). But I took every opportunity to go back home and see Laura Nell. I was confident that she would someday be my wife, and I could already imagine her as a brilliant hostess and as the heroine of a thousand drawing rooms from St. Petersburg to Buenos Aires. I was sure of how swiftly she would be transformed into a really serious person once I got her away from *there*.

"From the very earliest days of my courting Laura Nell I found myself talking to her about the other families that moved in our own circle—that is, about the other people whom we both had more or less grown up with. At the beginning she was greatly amused by all I had to say about those people. I can hear her pretty laughter now and hear her urging me to continue and say more. 'What else?' she would say. 'What else? Go on.' The truth is, I wonder now if she understood that all my criticism of others implied a favorable comparison of them to herself, and wonder if she realized that while I was giving my true opinion of those people and the life they lived and while I had a genuine interest in the whole subject, I was also using it to pay her the most direct compliment that good taste and the proprieties of that age permitted—permitted at that stage of our courtship. Perhaps she did understand, but, as time passed, my talk itself—particularly my talk about the peculiar traits those families had—became even more interesting to her and ceased altogether to be a matter of amusement. And finally she came to reject all my complaints and strictures against those people, who were so unlike herself and her own family, and she even became their stanch defender and apologist. It is hard for me to remember accurately how long a time was required for this transition. Sometimes it seems to me that the entire course of our friendship lasted but one brief summer. Other times it seems to me that it must have consumed half my youth. I know in fact, of course, that it was a period of three years—three years when I was making the final break back there and committing myself once and for all to another life.

"It was not until the second summer after I had met Laura Nell that I felt myself in a position to speak of marriage. By then I felt I could give her some concrete image of the life I was offering her. But by then Laura Nell was no longer in love with me. I can say that now, though I could not have said it at the time. I believed there to be certain difficulties in her mind about the life that I proposed for us, certain imaginary obstacles to our happiness, but I thought that with time she—or I—would overcome such doubts as she had. It was not, you see, as though she were any less fond of my company than she had been formerly or any less interested in the career I was bent upon or in my ideas about the place and the people that she and I knew best. No, despite the serious way she had listened to all I had ever said to her, she was very much the same silly girl that I had met a year and a half before. I was not in the least surprised that she burst out laughing when I made my formal proposal or even that she should treat it as a joke and tease me about it before her parents and other members of her family. 'He's too serious for me, much too critical,' she would say when we were all assembled in the drawing room before dinner on a Sunday (I would be visiting back home, taking most of my meals at their house). 'You should hear the way he analyzes other people. Within a month he'd know what I'm really like, and then there would be the devil to pay.'

" 'What she's saying,' her oldest brother said on one occasion, 'is that you're too good for her. I'd take heart from that. There couldn't be a better omen.'

"But the trouble was, Laura Nell said the same things to me in private. And she said, in effect, that she was too simple and artless a person to be taken out into the great world that I wanted to live in. She would be nothing but an embarrassment to a man who was as 'serious' and 'critical' as I was. At last I began to feel that it truly was all those things I said about such people as the Jenkinses and the Busbys that disquieted her so. I came to realize that no one was readier than Laura Nell to overlook those people's limitations and forgive their failure to find a way out of that little pond in which they were such big fish. She was prepared to forgive them *everything*. When I ridiculed those who went away only to come back with their tails between their legs, she said she couldn't blame them for wanting to live amongst friends. When I talked about what wonderful experiences might be in store for her family if they got away from there, she replied that it would be the same with them as with 'everybody like us.' To me it was amazing to hear her equating herself and her remarkable family with those other, unattractive, unimaginative, provincial people. But that was what she did. 'I know how it would be,' she said. 'We'd do very well for a while, like the others. Then the truth would dawn on us suddenly.'

" 'What truth?' I asked. 'What is it that would dawn on you? I don't think you really know, yourself, what you mean.'

"She laughed at me, as if to say I was much too stupid. 'Why, it's easy: dawn on us that we'd gone too far from home and that we'd better get back before it was too late.'

"It is hard to remember, after so many years, precisely the things she said. I do remember certain things, though. Once when I went home for a few days in February I had the happiness, for some moments, of believing that she might be coming round. We had attended a large reception together which turned out to be an announcement party for two of our friends. When we returned from the party to her house we went, for some reason, into a little card room that opened off the drawing room. We sat down in two little gilded chairs, facing each other across the card table's polished surface of inlaid woods. She was still wearing her furs, her gloves, and even her hat and veil. The hat was of brown velvet with a very high crown and little, cream-colored bows pinned all over it. It was the most becoming hat I ever saw her wear; somehow it made you want to reach out your hand and take hold of her tiny pointed chin, or even lift the veil and kiss that tight little mouth. When she first spoke, it even crossed my mind that in another moment I might be holding her in my arms. 'Would it make you miserable,' she began, 'to think you were going to end your days here where you grew up?' Through her veil I could not quite make out the expression in her eyes. I imagined that she was giving me an opening, that in my absence she had missed me, that she was now willing to debate with me how and where we might make a life together. I imagined that this was our critical hour and that I must be firm.

" 'I am only made miserable,' I said, 'by the thought that you may end *your* life here in a kind of misery you can't foresee.'

"But as usual, she laughed at me. 'I was not thinking about *us*,' she said. 'I was thinking about *them*'—the engaged couple, she meant, whom we had seen that afternoon. 'You know very well there is no chance for us. And please don't be so silly as to worry about me. Don't ever, ever worry about me. I was not made for misery of any kind.' . . . It is the sentence she wound up with that I remember most distinctly, of course: 'I was not made for misery of any kind.' As she spoke those words, her voice carried an impossible mixture of utter frivolity and total despair. And her eyes seemed to shine through her face veil with a luminosity that could not be explained and that cannot be described—a light both bright and dim, warm and cold, both shimmering and glassy.

"That was in February, and I went out to see Laura Nell again in April of that year. She never seemed more radiant to me than she did that spring. But the real reason for my visit was that during the month of March she had ceased to answer my letters and—in addition—I had learned from a mutual friend that Laura Nell Morris had made a March trip to New York to buy her spring and summer wardrobe—had done so, you understand, without letting me know she was in that part of the country. Her Easter outfit was a coatsuit of cerulean blue! I went to church with her and her family on Easter morning, and as I sat beside her in the family pew—and knelt beside her and rose with her to sing the old hymns—I think I was conscious in a way I had never been before of the glory of Laura Nell's physical beauty, frankly conscious, that is to say, of the wonderfully womanly figure beneath the snug-fitting coatsuit. When the congregation sang the hymns and spoke the words of the psalm, it was only Laura Nell's voice that I heard, and when I heard her I felt sure there had never been one of God's creatures more thoroughly alive or so full of the joy of being so . . . On her head she wore a hat made entirely of feathers dyed the same shade as that of her suit. What a perfect hat it was for her—designed to complement the smooth texture of her skin as well as the reddish tints in her hair. Her eyes, which often seemed a gray-green, were pure blue that morning. Now and then during the service she turned to me and smiled. Each time she did so, I had the illusion immediately afterward that she had actually spoken to me and said what she could not possibly have said there.

"But I had come home that time with a suspicion, and now that I had seen her I believed that my suspicion was bound to be confirmed. Even on my February visit I had observed that she was more attentive to her dress and to her appearance in general than she had ever been in the past. The brown velvet hat with cream-colored bows was not something she would have worn a year earlier. And since then there had been her trip to New York, and now the evidence of the satisfaction and pleasure she had taken in her shopping presented itself each time she appeared. There was a question in my mind that I could not go away without asking. I wanted to know who my rival was.

"On Easter afternoon we went for a drive in her father's trap. The little vehicle was spanking new, and drawn by a pretty bay mare that stepped along smartly. I drove the mare of course, and as we rode along Laura Nell took to counting the automobiles—the 'machines,' we called them—that were on the streets. She counted seven, and I suspect that represented the total number owned in the city at that time. It was a warm day for mid-April, but the sky was gray and overcast, and when finally we turned and headed for home I commented on what a dreary sky it was. 'I don't think it's dreary at all,' Laura Nell said. 'It is a lovely shade of gray.' When I looked at her with a skeptical smile, she said, 'Is there any real reason why a gray sky cannot be thought as beautiful as a blue one?'

"It seemed to me that she was *trying* to make a quarrel between us. Suddenly I asked: 'Why have you stopped answering my letters?'

"She looked straight ahead and gave a little shrug. 'Letters are no good any more,' she said. 'I'll always be glad to see you when you come, but let's give up letters.'

" 'Is there someone else, Laura Nell?' I asked.

"She didn't answer until we had driven half a block. I watched her face, and what I felt most was pity. I could see it was going to be so hard for her to tell me. It *was* hard for her, and I can't ever forget how she said it. 'No, there is no one,' she said. It was as though she wished with all her heart and soul that that had not been the answer she had to give me. After a moment she laughed, and actually slipped her arm through mine. A futile gesture and a meaningless laugh. There was no concealing the emptiness in her heart. There was nothing more I could say.

"I didn't see her again until she was taken ill in the summer of 1911, more than a year later . . . But I must tell you about something she had said to me long before that Easter. It was after she had already listened to me many a time on the subject of people like the Jenkinses and the Busbys. She had at first, you remember, found it very amusing to hear me describe how their family traits got on my nerves and how it annoyed me that they took refuge in a place that seemed willing to forgive them everything. Then, after a period during which she found it merely interesting or curious, she came to reject my criticism and showed that in her mind she associated herself and her own family with those people! It was while so disposed that she once said to me: 'Since you are so critical of everyone else, and so intolerant, I wonder that you're willing to forgive the terrible trait all we Morrises have in common.'

" 'There is no such trait,' I said. We were alone in the family parlor in the back of the house, and we were seated together in one of those wicker conversation chairs that are considered antiques nowadays but which were then merely hopelessly out of fashion and mid-Victorian and so, quite naturally, relegated to the back parlor. 'There is no such trait in this family,' I said, letting my eyes skip about the parlor walls from one gilt-framed studio portrait to another.

"She tossed her head and laughed, and then looking me squarely in the eye she said, 'Ours is worse than obesity or dirtiness. My redheaded grandfather used to point it out whenever someone said how unlike we all were, or whenever we bragged on ourselves in any way.'

" 'Some of you have his red in your hair . . .'

" 'Oh, it's nothing like that,' she said. 'It is an unpardonable trait.'

She went on at great length, saying she supposed it was what kept them from ever wanting to leave home and that it made her feel very close to the very people that I was so 'unsympathetic' with. 'I tell you what!' she said at last, bringing her hand down on the wicker arm between us. 'I'll make a bargain with you. If ever you can guess what it is without asking anybody—without getting any hints even—then *I'll* forgive *you* everything. Do you understand what I mean?'

"I thought I understood what she meant, but I told her that I wanted no such bargain. If she could not accept me because she loved me, then I wouldn't try to win her in a bargaining. I put it down as more of her silliness—as another of her jokes, and whenever she brought it up again I changed the subject.

"After she was taken sick I used to go out to see her every three or four weeks—as often as I could get away from my work. They took her all about the country to different kinds of specialists, just trying to get a diagnosis, if nothing more. I have come to suppose that it must have been some kind of cancer that she had, but in those days one didn't so much as breathe the word . . . When I would see her between her journeyings about the country to visit doctors, she enjoyed pointing out to me that doctors were quite as ignorant in other places as they were *there*. During the year that we did not see each other, Laura Nell had written to me occasionally, and I had always answered her letters, but in our letters and when I saw her afterward during her illness we wrote and spoke as old friends reminiscing about old, old times that had little relation to our present and future. Her mother, overhearing us once, took me aside and said that it broke her heart to hear Laura Nell talking that way—as though her youth, and even her life itself, were something in the past. I expressed my regret at having led her into that kind of conversation, but Mrs. Morris quickly reassured me, saying that it was not just with me that Laura Nell talked so. She confided in me that the doctors everywhere were as disturbed by her indifference to finding the cause and cure of her suffering as they were by her physical symptoms. Now, I am not going to tell you that Laura Nell Morris died because she lacked a will to live. I have no doubt that had she lived today the nature of her illness might have been better understood and that some means might have been found at least to retard the work of her disease. I am convinced that today we should not have had to watch her strength ebb away month after month without respite or restitution even for the briefest period. And, even as it was, the poor girl took a certain joy from the life that went on around her till the end. Her indifference was not to life but to illness. In fact, as illness drew those she loved closer about her she seemed almost to relish the condition. And, silly girl that she was, she would not think of what the final consequence might be. Or would not think of it in a serious way. If the worst should come, she told her mother, she could not imagine a 'better worst' than hers would be—with everybody she 'cared about' being so 'darling' to her and so 'close at hand.'

"It was after this and other similar remarks had been reported to me that I asked Mrs. Morris to walk out into her garden with me one afternoon. We went to the very spot where she had tried to console me, nearly two years before, with her accounts of Laura Nell's practical jokes. It was in the late spring, this time, that we stood on the low terrace and looked back toward the house. Pink and white peonies were in bloom on the borders of the center path. There were red and white roses in the big square rose bed just below us. Jonquils and narcissuses had already gone, and the summer flowers were not in yet. There was no other color at all except the fresh verdure of the trees all around and the new foliage of the wistaria on the porch trellises. While we eyed the garden (both of us wishing, I believe, that we had the heart to speak of its beauty, or wishing that it were not so beautiful), I began to say mechanically the thing I had brought Mrs. Morris out there to hear. I cannot remember the words I used, but I told her that Laura Nell had once tried to tease me with the idea that there was some terrible family trait they all shared. I wondered if she knew what it was Laura Nell had in mind and, if so, would she be willing to tell me.

"She gazed at me at first without comprehension. And so then I went on to say that it was something her grandfather used to mention when anyone pointed out how different they all were from each other. Mrs. Morris's mouth fell open, and she stared at me as though I had spoken an obscenity. I believe I suffered more during the seconds that that lady's eyes were so fixed on me than I did at any other time. But the pain was of short duration. Mrs. Morris suddenly turned away, and I could see that she had brought her hands up to her face and that she was pressing her fingertips against her eyes as if to force back tears. I stepped toward her and put one arm about her. I half expected her to draw away, but when she didn't I took her in my arms and began trying to comfort her. That she permitted me to comfort her was the deepest consolation I could possibly have known. It was perhaps the most consoling moment of my adult life. It was as though my own parents had not been taken from me when I was only a boy really, as though I had had a sort of second chance that everyone wishes for with his mother. And presently she looked up at me and said, 'I can tell you what Laura Nell meant.' She was smiling now, and I knew from her voice that there would be no more tears. 'It was only a grim little joke that Laura Nell's grandfather used to make,' she said, 'and it is just like Laura Nell to have remembered it. He used to say that the Morrises were all alike in at least one respect: they all had to die some time or other . . . A fairly trite kind of joke, I used to think—and still think. I do apologize for having given way so just now.'

"We stayed in the garden a few minutes longer. Then we walked back between the peonies to the house, and I went away without going up to see Laura Nell again. Next morning I took the train back East.

"But ten days later I was there again. And now I resolved to carry through my original purpose. Seated at her bedside, I told Laura Nell that I had discovered what the Morrises' dreadful failing was, and I gave proof of my knowledge. She lay with her eyes closed, and without making any sign that she understood me. But I continued. 'I must remind you of your promise,' I said. 'Now you must get well so that you can keep your end of the bargain and marry me.'

"She opened her eyes and smiled at me. I was filled with hope, for I actually believed—had believed from the start—that my scheme might work. I had thought that the very fatuousness of what I was attempting might appeal to Laura Nell, and I believed that even while she lay there already so near death she still possessed resources that would enable her to respond to a challenge of that kind. It was impossible for me to believe otherwise. When I was persuading her parents and her doctors to grant me that last quarter hour alone with her I concealed my purpose from them, but I think that they too believed I might work a magic with her.

"I took the frail hand that lay on the coverlet and was about to say more when she asked in a whisper, 'Did I make you such a promise?'

" 'You did,' I said. 'Or that was how I understood you.'

" 'You did not want to make the bargain, though.'

" 'I had no choice.'

" 'But the condition—' she whispered. 'I made a condition.'

"I knew what she meant, and she saw at once that I did. And also at once I saw that she knew I had not met her condition.

" 'You asked someone what it was,' she said.

"I nodded and bent down and kissed her hand in an effort to hide my face.

" 'Well, I forgive you anyway,' she said. 'I think I understand you better than in the old days . . . It *is* a little frightening even at best . . . Probably it is just as well always to run away from it.' Until that moment I had never understood what our differences were or realized how close we were to each other. But when I raised my head, her eyes were already closed, and I never saw them open again . . . The doctors could not predict how long she might linger, and so I was not there at the end. The telegram saying that she had died came on the third of July. I went out to the funeral, of course, and when I returned to Washington my first assignment to a foreign post was awaiting me.

"For a number of years I corresponded with Mrs. Morris, and of course I always called on the family on the rare occasions when some matter of my property took me back there. This was not often, though, and I eventually got rid of all my interests that made the trips necessary. Gradually over the years I have lost touch with everyone there. None of them ever comes over here for any length of time except an occasional stray lamb like yourself. When they come, they come only as tourists or—nowadays—on flying business trips; and invariably the first question they have to ask a person like myself is, don't I ever get 'the least bit' homesick. What rot. What utter rot! It's something more than home *they're* sick for, if only they knew. *She* knew at the last. And knew it was no better to welcome and want the inevitable than to turn your back on it and let it overtake you when and wherever it will. I say they'd do better to stay at home altogether than to come the way they do. Their little tours abroad must be as painful to them as my little excursions back home were to me after Laura Nell was dead. But, anyhow, I seldom see them when they do come. In the profession that I followed, I learned at last not to complicate my life with entertaining the tourists."

The Elect

Though it was past two in the afternoon, Judge Larwell was still sleeping like a baby. The best thing his wife could do was to keep busy. The telephone was off the hook, and the doorbell had been muffled. It was really as though someone were dead and black crape were draped on the front door. Actually, their faithful son-in-law Joseph, along with several other of Judge Larwell's ardent supporters—and two state troopers, as well—was stationed on the wide front porch to receive and ultimately drive away any of the television people or even any of the party's own public-relations people who might come banging on the door. The judge had fought a long, hard battle, and he had won. He was now governor-elect of the state. Surely the governor-elect was entitled to his rest. In his wife's opinion, at any rate, among the spoils belonging to the victor there should be included at least some small measure of privacy.

When the wall clock in the downstairs hallway struck a quarter past two, the state's first lady-elect was at her little desk at the end of the living room, writing checks. She was paying last month's bills from the department stores and the oil company, from the grocer and the dry cleaner and the drugstore. In the last weeks of the campaign, she had let everything go. As a matter of fact, she had actually taken up residence in a suite of rooms at the hotel opposite the capitol building. She had lived as she had never imagined she could possibly live. She had, in those last weeks, joined in the campaign and, much as she hated it all, had taken to the road with the rest of the family, appearing on platforms in twenty counties, waving, smiling, giving the victory sign.

She had even made half a dozen impromptu two-minute speeches when nobody else from the judge's family was there to speak up. Even the opposition newspapers had called her a good trouper and had said she was "well-spoken." Her best and most oft-quoted words were those delivered to a jokester in a crowd, who had called out, asking if she wanted to go keep house in that "musty old governor's mansion." She had replied with: "Whither he goes, there I shall go also. His people shall be my people." And the crowd had roared its crude, infelicitous approval: "Give 'em hell, Nell."

But now it was over. In the hotel ballroom at 3 a.m., posturing before the television cameras, Judge Larwell's opposition had conceded. The race was over. And now the judge's wife could once again enjoy the dignity of being Mrs. Larwell and not Nell Larwell, as the newspapers—opposition and otherwise—had insisted on calling her. During the campaign, you had to endure almost anything—that is, you did if, in the modern way, you joined in the fray alongside your husband.

Halfway through the campaign, when things began to seem uncertain for the judge and she had to begin climbing on platforms and making a spectacle of herself, she realized who were the two most sympathetic figures in American public life. They were Bess Truman and Mamie Eisenhower. Clearly, those two had hated it all as much as she had. They were women of "some background," like herself. And like herself, they had recognized their duty and had carried on. Everyone had said that she, unlike them, must have known what to expect, coming as she did from a political family—having even once, as a child, lived in the "musty old mansion."

But in her papa's day, it had been different. In those days, a candidate's wife stayed at home with her family, went her usual social rounds, got her bills paid on time. The intrusions of television and the pressures from PR men had not existed then. It had been very different. Mrs. Larwell's mother, as first lady of the state, had said that the principal adjustment she had had to make was to the ever-present sense of living beyond her means. Yes, in those days the family of a successful politician had to learn to live like rich people. Nowadays, they had to learn to live like—like show people!

With the sheet still over his face, Judge Larwell stirred in his bed. He became aware of the silence in the house and aware that it was being imposed for his sake. He had not got to bed till after 6 a.m. Suddenly he threw back the sheet, to see what time it was now. The window shades were drawn, and so he had to put on a light to see the face of the clock. Then, when he saw what time it was, it didn't seem to matter. He reflected only that he couldn't have imagined he would really sleep so soundly after last night. When he was leaving the hotel, someone asked if he were not going to get up to catch the morning television reports. They simply weren't able to believe that he would want to sleep through such a morning.

On the bedside table, he read the notes he had scribbled to himself as he was getting into bed. "Oh, Lord!" he exclaimed, reaching for the telephone. But the telephone was dead, of course, being off the hook downstairs. He jiggled the instrument several times. Then suddenly none of it seemed so all-fired urgent. Besides, Jake Ransom, the PR man, and Miss Ledbetter and Billy Henderson and his son-in-law Joseph would go on looking after things, as they had throughout the campaign. The great trick had been turned. They had won! Now he could hold the world at arm's length for a few hours—the very world he had been courting yesterday. Now he could relax for a while.

Yet suddenly it was the silence of the house itself that seemed real to him above anything else and that demanded his full attention. Somehow, he felt he couldn't bear it, could never bear silence of that sort again. Pulling on his robe, he went into the hall and listened for some sound of life. Hearing none, he moved on to the head of the stairs. Still only the silence, the unspeakable, intolerable silence of this private house. All at once he threw back his head and called at the top of his campaign-roughened but still powerful voice: "I—am—hun—gree!"

Mrs. Larwell appeared in the doorway from the living room and stood at the foot of the stairs. She was smiling up at him. It was a good sign if he was hungry. It meant he had not fixed his mind on her yet. The cook could give him his breakfast—or lunch—and she could finish paying last month's bills. "I'll tell Nola you're up," she called. "Would you like to have her bring you something on a tray?"

"I would not," he replied, clearing his throat. Then, striking a Napoleonic pose, slipping his hand inside his plaid robe and dropping his chin onto his bare chest, he intoned, "The governor does not choose to eat alone."

Mrs. Larwell laughed obligingly. She recognized his elated mood and knew, of course, that that was what she could have expected today. "All right," she said. "Is it breakfast or lunch you want?"

"Half and half," he announced solemnly from the head of the stairs, still holding the pose and fixing her with a simulated frown.

"Very well. I'll tell Nola. And while you get yourself dressed, I'll finish a little job I've begun in here."

Mrs. Larwell turned back to the living-room doorway. There were not many governors-elect, she reflected, who could and would sleep till two on this day. It was very healthy and youthful of him to be able to do so. She had known without asking, of course, what he would want to eat—tomato salad, a ham sandwich and scrambled eggs, with perhaps dry cereal for dessert—and she had known, as well, that he would not want to eat alone. Moreover, she knew that he would wish to get fully dressed before going downstairs. It was one of his old-fashioned, formal traits that he would never go down in his nightclothes. She was glad of that, too, because now it would allow her a few more minutes to work on her bills and perhaps even get started on a letter to one of her two old aunts. Her personal correspondence was, as a matter of fact, in worse need of attention than her bills.

But she was hardly through the doorway and in the living room before she heard him call again. He simply called her name: "Nell!" She heard him clearly, but at the far end of the long living room her little spinet desk beckoned to her. No, not the desk itself so much as the stack of bills with their address panes, and her own business envelopes in the half-open drawer, and the checkbooks spread out on the surface of the desk, and even the tiny roll of stamps and her own stick-on return addresses. They held out their arms to her, like so many little children.

But Mrs. Larwell knew where her first duty lay. She knew that some secretary could take care of her personal bills and even her personal correspondence in the future. The small satisfaction of writing those checks and scratching the bills off her list was not important. What difference did those bills make? She heard the voice at the top of the stairs asking, "Do you know where my new tattersall shirt is? I want to wear it with my blue suit." Yes, some secretary would have to take care of her personal bills in the future.

Presently she was walking quickly up the stairs. And she was wondering, Would it come now? Would he speak to her now of his appreciation for her joining in the campaign when she had hated it so? She stopped for a moment and then went to the kitchen to put the telephone on the hook and to tell Nola that Judge Larwell was ready to eat something now. Then she started upstairs again. And again the question filled her mind: Would it come now? How she longed to postpone the moment when he would try to speak to her of it! How she dreaded the moment! And yet she could not say why she did.

When she got upstairs, she found him rifling through the drawers of the big, old-fashioned chiffonier that had once belonged to her father. He was going through it like a burglar looking for money or jewels hidden among the clothes.

When she went into the room, he faced her momentarily in the wide mirror above the chiffonier and asked in a suspicious voice, "Where is it?"

"Where's what, dear?"

"The new tattersall shirt you bought me. I've decided that's what I ought to wear today—and with the blue suit."

"It's on the closet shelf, where I always put your new shirts."

He started toward the closet. He had already removed his robe and the top to his paisley pajamas. He now wore only the pants, which were tied with a drawstring around his narrow hips and over the sizable, low, and rather assertive belly he had developed in recent years. His narrow hips and long legs made him still look decidedly athletic, despite his belly, and in his present garb he looked like anything but his wife's idea of a governor of the state. Seeing him still in that wide mirror made it all too easy for her to remember how her father had appeared at such moments.

Her revered papa would have stood before her in a dark silk dressing gown, or if she had, as a little girl, burst into the room unexpectedly, she might have found him in his billowing white nightshirt, clipping his mustache before the mirror. *That* was how a governor should look in the privacy of his bedchamber. Yet here was this youngish-looking man, who, though already a grandfather, still played tennis and handball and sailed his own sloop on the reservoir lake. And whereas Papa had grown his mustache to make himself look old enough to be governor, *her* husband had often, during the campaign, gone about with his stomach sucked in, so that he would look even more boyish than he naturally did.

And in the chiffonier mirror, Mrs. Larwell saw herself, still a good-looking woman, who had kept her figure (because it was required of her) and whose pancake make-up and frosted hair deceived some people into thinking she was perhaps fifteen years younger than she was and certainly fifteen years younger than she sometimes felt. They were a handsome-looking pair, no doubt about it, and that was what politics *demanded* of you nowadays. It was a far cry from the way it once was, and a far cry from the way she had imagined it would be if ever her husband should occupy the gubernatorial chair.

She followed him to the closet, where he had pulled the new shirt from the shelf and was removing the pins. She took out his navy-blue pinstripe suit and began flicking off particles of lint. This was the sort of thing she liked doing for him. No matter how many servants she might have, she liked looking after his everyday needs, and as long as he was practicing law and later when he was on the bench, she had liked listening to his accounts of his courtroom battles and of the judgments he had to make—liked it especially when he said or implied that she was not really supposed to follow or understand all he told her.

Now she handed him the blue suit and took from him the shirt and the four round-head pins he had already pulled out of it. She placed the pins, points first, between her lips and proceeded to extricate the other pins from the folds of the shirt. Then, with all the pins between her lips and after removing the tissue paper and cardboard liner from the collar, she gave the shirt a good shaking, as if to shake out all its stiff newness. She eyed it critically and mumbled through the pins: "Mibb-ee I sh'ld give thizz crisses a few strocks wi' th' i'on."

Her husband understood her perfectly. Talking with pins in her mouth was something she had always seemed to relish. He glanced over his shoulder at the shirt she was holding up and shrugged. "I wouldn't bother," he said. He had laid his suit on the big double bed and was once again looking over the memoranda he had written himself last night, at the bedside table. "The phone is off the hook downstairs," he commented, in a relatively unconcerned tone.

"No," she corrected him. "I put it back on just before I came up."

"Ah," he said, with somewhat more interest, and he reached for the receiver. But then he shrugged again and didn't take it up.

She methodically and with evident satisfaction—even pleasure—unbuttoned the shirt buttons for him, even those at the cuffs. She was placing the shirt beside the suit on the bed when suddenly she changed her mind. "No," she mumbled, still through the pins. "I b'lev I'll j'st touch it up." She took the shirt and turned to go across the hallway to the little sewing room, where her ironing board was kept set up. There was an ironing board in the basement laundry and another in the kitchen, but she was a woman who would always have to have an ironing board of her very own and have to have it handy. She left him still standing at the bedside table, pulling a white undervest over his head.

The iron had to be plugged in and warmed up before she could begin pressing the creases out of the new shirt. Draping the shirt over the back of a straight oak chair, she moved toward the sewing machine. Her sewing machine was even more important to her than her iron and was always kept open, with only a little square of India print thrown over it as protection against dust. She moved toward the sewing machine now with the intention of sticking the pins, which she still carried between her lips, into the big strawberry pincushion there.

Instead, however, her attention was caught by several skirts and dresses of her own that were lying on the cutting table nearby. They had been lying there for many weeks, and her purpose had been to shorten the hems. One of her daughters had said to her once, "If you became Queen of England, you would still take up your own hems." And the other daughter had added, "Yes, and wash out your own bathtub." On that occasion, as on others, she had quoted her own mother to them: "There are some things that a lady will always do for herself."

She noticed that on the tweed and flannel skirts she had already marked with chalk where the new hem was to be folded. Inadvertently, almost, she took up the brown tweed skirt and, using the pins she held in her mouth, began pinning the new hem in place. Just as she had taken the last pin from her mouth, she heard a familiar creaking sound and realized that the iron was ready for use. She hesitated a moment, holding the warm woolen material between her thumb and forefinger, enjoying the sensation, relishing the feel of its texture on her fingertips. Then she stuck the last pin firmly into the skirt and moved directly to the more urgent business of ironing her husband's new shirt.

She finished with the iron after only two or three minutes. But when she had removed the electric plug and hung the shirt on a hanger, her attention was caught once again by the skirts to be hemmed. Returning to the cutting table, she could not resist taking up a paper of pins and continuing to pin the hem of the brown tweed.

When she had it in place all around, she held the skirt to her waist and observed it in the long mirror on the closet door. It was shorter than the skirt of the dress she wore, but it was the fashionable length this year. She had been conscious all through the campaign that her skirts were a little longer than was fashionable; but since she was on the platform so much, she thought it more becoming to a woman of her age to wear them somewhat longer than fashion prescribed. But now that the campaign was over, of course, she would feel free to conform to feminine fashion once more.

Putting aside the tweed skirt, she took up a gray flannel skirt, and hardly knowing what her fingers were doing, she began pinning the hem in place. Her fingers functioned rapidly and with great precision in such work, and she had got nearly halfway around the hem when suddenly the door from the hall was pushed open and Judge Larwell strode into the room. He had on his blue trousers, was wearing his shoes; he had even shaved.

"Ah," he said, seeing his shirt on the coat hanger beside the ironing board.

She raised her eyes, though continuing to push the pins into the soft flannel, and she said, "I'm sorry. Were you waiting for it? I got involved in this. Does it look all right, the shirt?"

"It looks great, but you shouldn't have bothered." As he was getting into the shirt and moving back toward the door to the hall, he asked casually, "What are you doing there?"

"Oh, I'm just pinning up these hems. I'm going to whip them in today. This has all been lying here for weeks." She glanced up to see him standing in the doorway with his eyes fixed on her.

Suddenly lowering his eyes, instead of letting them meet hers, he began slowly buttoning his shirt. Even before he spoke, she perceived that he was irritated. "Couldn't you get someone else to do that?" he asked.

"Silly, I like doing it. Taking up a few skirts is nothing."

"It's time-consuming, though—that sort of little job is. One has to learn to delegate such work," he said.

Then he was gone from the doorway. And it was as though he had given her an explicit order to put down her sewing and follow him. Also, it was somehow as though she were working in an office somewhere, as though she had been widowed and had had to go to work in a man's world and would have to try to forget that she had brought up two children and try to forget—that is, try not to "dwell upon" the fact—that she had known those many happy years of keeping house and entertaining for and being cherished by an affectionate husband.

As she left the sewing room, she gave one glance backward. The room seemed unreal to her quick glance, like a room she was remembering fondly if somewhat indistinctly from a long-ago childhood. She felt a lump in her throat. And then she laughed at herself. Why, what were a few skirts to her?

When she went back into the bedroom, he accused her frankly of trying to avoid him this morning.

"This afternoon, you mean," she said, laughing at him. And she went over and kissed him, saying, "How silly can a governor-elect be?"

He returned her kiss and smiled a shamefaced smile.

But as they went down the stairs, arm in arm, she wondered if she hadn't, after all, been avoiding him. Because now she was consciously dreading it again, the moment when he would thank her for her part in the campaign. When would it come? Or perhaps he was going to spare her. Oh, what *did* she mean by such silly nonsense? she asked herself. Yet the possibility that he was not going into the matter lifted her spirits almost magically.

She began to chatter about the three newspaper photographers who had been perched all morning, like three big birds, on the fenders of cars across the street, and about how everyone knew the judge had vowed, win or lose, to sleep all day on the day after the election, and about how faithfully Joseph, their son-in-law, had been guarding the front door, greeting people who came but turning them away. Now, she said, they must make Joseph come in and have brunch with them.

In the breakfast room, she found that Nola had places set for three. Somehow overlooking this obvious fact, she called through the kitchen doorway for Nola to set additional places for herself and Joseph.

"Yes'm, I already have," replied Nola cheerfully.

"Oh, yes, I see you have." And Mrs. Larwell detected in her own voice an absurd, resentful note. She ought to have been glad, she told herself, that the cook could guess she and Joseph would wish to have a bite while the judge ate. But she was so keenly, so painfully aware of being out of touch with the operation of her own kitchen and household that she had a *silly, silly* sense of being superseded. Nola had even sent Horace, the yardman and chauffeur, who had been guarding the back door, around to the front porch to invite Joseph to come in.

And presently Joseph appeared, his face flushed from being out in the autumn weather all morning and his manner all smiles and congratulations.

"List, oh, list!" began Joseph, sitting down at the breakfast table. "Really, you would hardly believe how many important folks have tried to force their way past me this morning. Ah, I could tell thee a tale!"

Joseph was considered quite literary and had even helped the judge with the wording in a good many of his speeches, though Mrs. Larwell was not always sure that his additions and corrections were beneficial. Sometimes in the middle of a speech, she had recognized Joseph's words on the judge's lips, and somehow from that point on, the speech would not ring true to her. Her own father had never allowed anyone to tamper with his speeches, and to him the very idea of hiring a ghost writer—an idea the judge had recently been entertaining—would have been abhorrent.

Still, Joseph was a loyal admirer of the judge's, and that had to be appreciated. The other son-in-law, out in California, was an engineer and was openly scornful of politics and politicians. But Joseph had been at the judge's side throughout the campaign, had been there, in fact, at times when his mother-in-law had thought he ought to be at home with his pregnant wife. During these same months, the daughter in California had also been pregnant, and the engineer had given this as their excuse for not coming home for the election. Well, at any rate, Joseph had not slept at all last night and had been on the front porch this morning, protecting the judge's well-earned right to rest.

"You just couldn't believe," Joseph said now, "how little consideration some of these fellows show for a man who has fought the hard campaign you have, or how little respect, in fact, they have for the office of governor of this state. I really don't believe I could have kept them out if those two troopers hadn't been there with me. One newspaperman pretended he had a note to you from Senator Brice, and when I asked to see the note, he just laughed in my face and walked away—wadding up the paper and stuffing it in his pocket."

The judge laughed pleasurably at Joseph's reporting of this last little incident. "Well, I'm afraid that's how it's going to be from here out," he declared. "The campaign was nothing to how it will be now. I'll be needing you all the way, Joseph. I don't know what your title will be, but I'll be needing you to keep such fellows off my back."

"Oh!" exclaimed Mrs. Larwell, interrupting suddenly. "I should think your secretaries and the state troopers together could do that, without taking up your own son-in-law's time."

There was an asperity in her words that she had not intended should be there and that seemed to draw her husband's attention entirely away from Joseph. She saw him drop his eyes from Joseph to the plate that Nola had just set before him and then lift them to her own face. It was a trick of his she had often observed in the past. She had observed that, in any conversation, he seldom moved directly from one important subject to another. That is, there was always an effort to prevent your detecting the mental associations he made or the logic of his transitions. She had always acknowledged to him that he was too subtle and too deep for her; but there *were* moments when she had consciously to conceal from him her knowledge of his depths and subtleties.

"Nola!" she called over her shoulder, turning her face away from him and toward the kitchen. "Give us luncheon forks, please, and not these big dinner forks. Nola!" But there was no answer from the kitchen.

"Nell, darling, I don't—" began the judge.

But she pretended not to hear him. Although she and Joseph, as well as the judge, had already been served, she snatched the forks from beside their plates. And rising from her chair, she set out for the kitchen. Nola was nowhere to be seen. After serving them, she had no doubt stepped to her room for a moment. Or she might, so far as her mistress knew, have put on her hat and coat and left the house forever! *That* was how little Mrs. Larwell felt she knew of what her own cook might do nowadays.

"Nola!" she called again. And the silence she got for answer somehow made her think of the names of other cooks she had had over the years. She was tempted, almost, to stand there calling their names: "Minerva! Gertrude! Maybelle! Clara!" Nola seemed no less someone out of the past than they.

But realizing that her husband and her son-in-law were waiting for their forks, Mrs. Larwell scurried back through the breakfast room and into the dining room. She went there to fetch the luncheon forks. But where were they? She had pulled open the top, shallow drawer of the buffet and found that they were not in their accustomed place. *Where* could Nola have put them? It seemed incredible that she no longer knew where her own flat silver was kept.

She was tempted, almost, to return to the breakfast room and announce that Nola and the flat silver were missing. Instead, when she opened the swinging door and saw her son-in-law and her husband waiting there without forks, she quickly crossed over and put one of the dinner forks in Judge Larwell's hand.

He accepted it but simultaneously seized her free hand in his own. "Thank you," he said gently. "Thank you for the fork, my darling, and thank you for everything else." She saw him glance across the table at Joseph and heard him say, "She's been a wonderful campaigner, hasn't she, Joe?"

She knew his glance at Joseph meant nothing, and yet she had a sense of discovering a conspiracy between them. Only, of course, it wasn't merely between them. The whole world, somehow, was conspiring against her. She could feel the blood draining from her cheeks. It seemed she might actually faint.

"I never saw anything like it," Joseph was saying as he wrested his fork from her. "Boy, what a campaigner she turned out to be! The timid, reserved little Mrs. Larwell! I'll never forget that night at Lawrenceburg when the rest of us sat there tongue-tied, how she stepped up to the lectern and began: 'I plead guilty to the soft impeachment!' Until that night, I hadn't known my pretty little mother-in-law had such powers of rhetoric."

"It was a quotation I used," Mrs. Larwell said in a whisper, her voice trembling. She was remembering that wreched moment at Lawrenceburg, when it had seemed anything would be better than the silence. Someone in the crowd had called out a phrase used in one of the opposition papers that morning: "The genteel judge." She had felt he was being attacked for the decent good manners she had always encouraged in him. And this had happened on the very first night he had been able to persuade her to sit on the platform.

"What I won't soon forget," the judge was saying, "is the sight of her shaking hands with that line of mill workers at Cedar Point. When those old codgers and those young roughnecks, who had been heckling me only fifteen minutes before, saw who they were going to shake hands with, they came flocking from all over the plant." The judge held on to her hand now and gave it a series of squeezes as he spoke.

And it really was as if she were out there in the rain at Cedar

Point again, wearing her rain hat and raincoat and shaking hands with all those young boys and old men. While she had stood there in the rain, it had come over her that there were no middle-aged men among the mill hands. There were only smooth-faced young boys, mixed with young boys who had at some point turned into rough-faced old men. Her heart had gone out unreservedly to those young boys and those old boys.

And afterward, at home that night, the memory that there had been no middle-aged men among them had touched her. But what had troubled her most, when she was alone that night, was the realization that she had shaken their hands with a genuine cordiality and she was not capable of a professional cordiality. She had acted on her real feelings, and the result was that the persons she had deceived that day were not the mill hands but her husband and her son-in-law and Miss Ledbetter and Jake Ransom and Billy Henderson.

"My darling Nell," the judge was saying now, still holding her hand and, though Joseph was present, addressing her in a language and tone that he had always heretofore reserved for their private exchanges, "my darling, you do have powers I never suspected you possessed. I owe you a debt that I can never repay, and the bad part is that I have no doubt that you will go on increasing that debt of mine so long as we live."

Mrs. Larwell burst into tears. With her own dinner fork clutched in one hand and with the judge holding on to her other hand, she began heaving and sobbing, the contorted features of her face completely exposed.

Now the moment had come. She had known how it would be without knowing she knew. What she had dreaded, what she had known to expect (without knowing she knew), was that his expression of gratitude would be but an expression of his desire, his will, that she not now discontinue her public role. Tears quite literally flooded her eyes and flowed down her cheeks. It was as though, quite literally, some dam within her had burst. She knew that there was no turning back and no answering him.

As he came to his feet and looked directly into her eyes, she felt a flash of hatred for him. She remembered his saying to Joseph at some point in the campaign, "Do only small favors for others on the ticket, and ask only large ones." She hated him—but only for the one moment. She loved him; he was her life. But her life would be changed now. The world was changed now, however, and it was only that she must change with it. *Everybody* had to change with the times. And it was her duty to him to change. *Politicians no longer had to learn to live like rich people; they had to learn to live like show people.* Somehow, she would learn.

The judge had his arms about her, and Joseph had come around to her, too. They were calling her a perfect darling. They were touched that she should shed tears over his expression of gratitude.

Beyond Joseph's tear-blurred silhouette, she had an even more blurred glimpse of the kitchen and saw that Nola had returned and was in command there. Drying her eyes and cheeks on a napkin the judge had handed her, Mrs. Larwell said, "I'm being *so* silly. How silly *can* a woman be? The wife of the governor-elect! This should be the happiest day of our life, and I shouldn't spoil it with tears." Looking at her son-in-law, she said, with a baffled smile, "Many are called but few are chosen."

"Wonderful!" replied her literary son-in-law.

Then, to her husband, she said, "I'm through with crying now." And she went up on her toes and kissed him on his clean-shaven cheek.

Then the three of them sat down to their brunch, busying themselves with their large dinner folks. And it seemed to the wife of the governor-elect that she was quite literally through with crying, that she might never shed another tear as long as she lived.

Guests

◈◇◈◇◈◇◈◇◈◇◈◇◈◇◈◇◈◇◈◇◈◇◈◇◈◇◈◇◈◇◈

The house was not itself. Relatives were visiting from the country. It was an old couple this time, an old couple who could not sleep after the sun was up and who began yawning as soon as dinner was over in the evening. They were silent at table, leaving the burden of conversation to their host and hostess, and they declined all outside invitations issued in their honor. Cousin Johnny was on a strict diet. Yet wanting to be no trouble, both he and Cousin Annie refused to reveal any principle of his diet. If he couldn't eat what was being served, he would do without. They made their own beds, washed out their own tubs, avoided using salad forks and butter knives. Upon arriving, they even produced their own old-fashioned ivory napkin rings, and when either of them chanced to spill something on the tablecloth, they begged the nearest Negro servant's pardon. As a result, everybody, including the servants, was very uncomfortable from the moment the old couple entered the house.

Edmund Harper, their host, was most uncomfortable of all. What's more, he had to conceal the fact from his wife, Henrietta, because otherwise he would be accused of "not seeing her through."

[407]

Henrietta was a planner, an arranger, a straighten-outer—especially of other people's lives. Somehow she always managed to involve Edmund in her good works, and never more so than when it was a matter of relatives from the country. Cousin Johnny and Cousin Annie, for instance, had clearly not wanted to make this visit. In fact, they had struggled valiantly against Henrietta's siege. But they couldn't withstand Henrietta's battering for very long. Henrietta knew that neither of them had ever set foot in the capital city of Nashville; and she couldn't bear the thought of the poor old souls' not seeing Nashville before they died. It ended by Edmund's going with Henrietta in her car to bring the unwilling visitors "bodily" into Nashville.

Some weeks before the visit, Henrietta had written a letter suggesting that she might enter the old couple's house and do their packing for them—that is, if Cousin Annie didn't feel up to it. And this was what finally made Cousin Annie run up the white flag and pretend to accept Henrietta's terms. Come what might, the old lady's little clapboard Gothic citadel, with its bay windows and gingerbread porches, was *not* going to be entered. In its upright posture on the rockiest hill of Cousin Johnny's stock farm—a farm where the land was now mostly rented out and the stock disposed of, because of Cousin Johnny's advanced years—the house was like Cousin Annie's very soul, and it would be defended at all costs. The morning that Henrietta's new Chrysler car turned through the stone gateposts at the bottom of the hill, the old lady not only had herself and her husband thoroughly packed up, she had them fully dressed for their journey, their hats on their heads, and, with the door to the house already stoutly locked, they were seated side by side on the porch swing—rigid as two pieces of graveyard statuary. As the car pulled up the hill, turning cautiously between the scrub pines and the cedar trees, Edmund Harper saw Cousin Annie rise slowly, in one continuous, wraithlike movement, from her place in the swing. Once on her feet, she stood there still and erect as a sentinel. In the swing, which until now had remained motionless, Cousin Johnny permitted himself a quick, little solo flight, so short and tentative that he must barely have touched his toe to the porch floor. Edmund interpreted this motion as a favorable sign. But then, almost immediately, he saw the old lady's hand go out to one of the swing's chains. The mere touch of her gloved hand was enough to halt the swing, but for several moments she kept her hand there on the chain. And the figures of the two old people, thus arranged, made a kind of *tableau vivant,* which Edmund was to carry in his mind throughout the visit.

For twenty-five years, Edmund had been seeing Henrietta through such plans as the present one. Three country nieces had been presented to Nashville society from the Harper house. Countless nephews had stayed there while working their way through the university—or as far through it as it seemed practicable for them to try to go. And Henrietta scarcely ever returned from a visit back home without bringing news of some ailing connection who needed to see a Nashville specialist, needed a place to stay while seeing the specialist, needed a place to stay while convalescing from the inevitable operation. The worst of all this, for Edmund, was not what he was called upon to do during these visitations but what he was called upon to feel, and the moral support he was expected to give Henrietta. For something nearly always went wrong. Two of the three nieces had eloped with worthless louts from back home before their seasons in Nashville were half over. Most of the countless nephews had taken to a wild life, for which their parents tended to blame the influence of the Harper household more than that of university and fraternity life. Worse still, the convalescents always outstayed their welcome, and Edmund had to support Henrietta in taking a firm hand when it was time for each poor old creature to return to his or her nearest of kin in the country.

In a sense, though, these larger projects of Henrietta's had been less trying for Edmund than the smaller ones—the ones that she had gone in for in recent years. She had turned more and more to brightening the lives of people like Cousin Johnny and Cousin Annie, people whose lives didn't seem absolutely to require her touch. It was three and four day visits from the likes of Cousin Johnny and Cousin Annie that Edmund found it hardest to adjust to—visits from people not really too far removed from his own generation. He found a part of himself always reaching out and wanting to communicate with them and another part forever holding back, as though afraid of what *would* be communicated. And the same seemed to be true for the guests themselves, particularly for the men.

Cousin Johnny Kincaid was not, of course, a real contemporary of Edmund Harper's. There was a twelve-year difference in their ages. Edmund was fifty-eight, and Cousin Johnny was seventy. It was a delicate difference. A certain respect was due the older man, but it had to be manifested in a way that would not offend him and make him feel that he was an old man and that Edmund was not. On the second day of the visit, when the old couple's silence had already become pretty irksome to her, Henrietta telephoned Edmund at his office and said that she had a simple suggestion to make. At breakfast she had noticed that Cousin Johnny seemed to wince every time Edmund addressed him as "Cousin" Johnny. She thought he might be sensitive about his age. She suggested that that night Edmund should try calling him just plain Johnny.

Now, this was the kind of thing that was always coming up. It seemed that every year Henrietta had to dig deeper into the kin and deeper into the country to find suitable objects for her good works. The couples were invariably rather distant kin of his or hers, people Edmund had known all his life but not known very well. Either Edmund couldn't remember what he had called them as a boy or he had literally never called them anything. But the problem had never come into such focus as it did now. On the telephone he didn't dispute Henrietta's point, though it was inconceivable to him that

Cousin Johnny had ever in his seventy years winced over a small matter of personal vanity—if that's what it was. Since, at the moment of the telephone call, Edmund's law partner was with him in his office and since the firm's most moneyed and currently most troubled client was also there, Edmund said only, "I'll see what I can do about it tonight." And he wrote the word "Johnny" on the pad of paper in front of him.

"I can tell from your voice that you're terribly busy," Henrietta said apologetically.

"No, not particularly," Edmund said.

"I probably shouldn't have called about something so—"

"Oh, nonsense!" Edmund laughed. And he wound up the conversation in hearty tones meant to convince everybody in earshot of his imperturbability.

But it *was* a serious matter, of course. And when he put down the telephone he still sat for a moment staring rather intently at the instrument. As a matter of fact, he was trying to think the problem through right then and there. It was his habit of mind, as a good trial lawyer, to think any question through and find a positive answer to it as soon as it came up. It wasn't the truth of Henrietta's observation he was debating; he had long since accepted her contention that she was "more sensitive to people" than he was, and so he had to assume that she was right about something like this. Nor was it a question of his willingness to do what she asked of him. It was a simple matter of whether or not he could bring himself to call Cousin Johnny Kincaid just plain "Johnny." Then in a flash he saw he could. He could because—but he didn't go into that at the time. The immediate question was answered, and he was free now to return to his client's urgent affairs.

It wasn't till several hours later that he let himself think again about this silly piece of business that Henrietta had cooked up. He was driving home from work in his hardtop convertible, and the moment he opened the subject with himself, his mind took him back to the previous day. They were making the return trip from the country, with Cousin Annie and Cousin Johnny in the car. It was a seventy-five-mile drive back into Nashville; they had to pass through sections of three counties. Since they were in Henrietta's car, she was doing the driving, and she was providing most of the conversation, too. Cousin Annie, wearing a plain black coat and an even plainer black hat, was in the front seat beside Henrietta. In the back seat of the big car the two long-legged men sat in opposite corners, each with one leg crossed stiffly over the other. They had traveled some twelve or fifteen miles when something made Edmund glance down at Cousin Johnny's foot. He found himself observing with great interest the high-topped shoe, the lisle sock held up by an elastic supporter, and, since it was still early April, the long underwear showing above the sock where the old man's trouser leg was pulled up.

Somehow to be thus reminded that there were still men who dressed in the old style was unaccountably pleasant to Edmund. At the same time it saddened him, too. For here was the kind of old man that he had once upon a time supposed he would himself someday become. And now he knew, of course, he never would. It seemed like being denied an experience without which life wouldn't be complete. It seemed almost the same as discovering that no matter how long he lived he would never *be* an old man. For how could you really *be* old and have it mean anything if you lived in a world where you weren't expected to dress and behave in a special way, in a world where you went on dressing and trying to behave like a young man or at least a middle-aged man till the very end? It was bad enough to be childless and therefore grandchildless, as he and Henrietta of course were, without also being denied any prospect of ever *feeling* or being *treated* like a grandfather, something which Cousin Johnny, also childless and grandchildless, must for a long time now have felt and been treated like. Edmund found the subject absorbing.

The foot gave an involuntary little kick, and Edmund realized that this was probably what had drawn his attention to it in the first place. The twitch was presently followed by another and then, at irregular intervals, by another and another. This was bound to interest a mind like Edmund's, especially in its present mood. With his lawyer's eye he soon made out that the kicks occurred always when the car was passing a field where cattle grazed. He wasn't surprised when Cousin Johnny finally came right out with it: "Seems like the livestock gets fatter every mile we pull in towards Nashville." But as soon as he had said this the old man's eyes narrowed and he bit his lower lip with such vehemence that it was plain he wished it was his tongue he was biting. His utterance had been as involuntary as any of those kicks his foot was giving.

It was as if Fate and Cousin Annie had been waiting together for such a slip from him. The car had just left a fine stretch of low ground where he had seen the herd that brought forth his comment. Now the car was climbing a long, wooded hill, and in a little clearing near the summit Cousin Annie spied a herd of bunched-up, scrawny, and altogether sorry-looking milk cows. For the only time during the long trip, she turned around and showed her face to the two men in the back seat. And it was only the profile of her face, at that. She merely turned and stared out the window, on Cousin Johnny's side, at those cows in the clearing.

"Yes, but—" Cousin Johnny began, exactly as though the old lady had spoken. And then, Cousin Annie having already turned her back to him again, he broke off. That was the whole of the interchange between them. When Cousin Johnny spoke again, which was surprisingly soon, Edmund felt his words had no reference to what had passed between him and Cousin Annie. He said directly to Edmund, "I guess a fellow who's been concerned with cattle as long as I have won't ever see much out a car window but cows, no matter where he goes."

It was some kind of an apology. An apology for what? For a certain boorishness he felt he had been guilty of? An apology for his own narrow interest in life. Or was it, rather, an indication of the old man's awareness of the figure he must be cutting with Edmund?

Edmund's reply to the outburst and the apology was a ten-minute discourse on the history of stock farming in Middle Tennessee. Most of what he said came out of some research he had had one of the young men in his office do for a case he had tried a few years back. He wasn't showing off. He was honestly trying to reassure Cousin Johnny and to draw him out, because already Edmund's interest in this man and his desire to win his confidence and to find a common ground on which they could meet was considerable. But the discourse on cattle farming did not produce a single remark from Cousin Johnny.

A long silence followed. Then there was a period of give-and-take between Henrietta and Cousin Annie about the illnesses and deaths of various relatives. After that, there was more silence. Cousin Johnny's lips seemed to have been permanently sealed. But in the last miles before Nashville, his caution must have been lulled by Henrietta's fresh chatter about the Nashville sights they would be seeing in the days just ahead. When a colossal city limits sign suddenly hove into view at the roadside, Cousin Johnny's mouth dropped open. "Why," he said. "It's a funny thing. When I was just married and was still just a young fellow, I almost came here to work." It was as if until then he hadn't known, or hadn't believed, where it was they were taking him. "In a shoe factory, it was. But my wife and I decided against it. I was to start at the bottom and maybe later go on the road for them."

How different the whole visit might have been if Cousin Johnny had not said that. Because, after that, Edmund Harper would have consented to almost any scheme of Henrietta's to promote understanding between him and his house guest. Why, what wonderful things mightn't they say to each other if only they could talk together man to man! In a flight of fancy that was utterly novel to him, Edmund visualized Cousin Johnny as he would have appeared today had he taken that job at the shoe factory. He saw him now as president of the shoe company after years of working up from the bottom, and saw himself as a country lawyer in Nashville on a visit with his rich relatives. Why, it was *Maud Muller* twice reversed! Moreover, that client Edmund was going to see in his office tomorrow morning and who had been in his office nearly every day for the past two weeks, that richest and currently most troubled of the firm's clients, was none other than the president of a shoe company, probably the very shoe company that Cousin Johnny would have gone to work for . . . *That* was precisely how Cousin Johnny might have turned out. And to think it was only a difference of seventy-five miles.

Cousin Johnny's response to being called just plain "Johnny" was, to say the least, disconcerting. He did exactly what Henrietta said he had done when Edmund called him "Cousin Johnny." He winced. He drew in his chin—almost imperceptibly, though not quite— batted his eyes, and gave his head a quick little shake. And then, as Edmund hurried on to finish the long sentence which he had dropped his "Johnny" in the midst of, Cousin Johnny gazed past Edmund into a fire the houseboy had just now lit in the fireplace. Plainly he was trying to decide how he liked the sound of it—the sound of his Christian name on the lips of this man, this strange kind of man who could come in from work at four-thirty in the afternoon, disappear above stairs to change from a dark doublebreasted suit to a plaid jacket and gray trousers, and then reappear and settle down to a long evening, without ever mentioning the work that had kept him all day.

Edmund had carefully waited, before springing that "Johnny" on the old man, till a moment when Henrietta and Cousin Annie were well on the other side of the living room. Afterward, he realized that Henrietta had been conspiring with him without his knowing it. She had lured Cousin Annie over there beyond the piano to see a scrapbook that she kept in the piano bench for just such moments. During the hour since Edmund came in the house, she hadn't mentioned the subject of their telephone conversation. But she knew well enough that he was going to follow her suggestion. And he knew what her attitude would be by now; they were in this together, and she wanted to make his part as easy for him as possible—and as interesting. One quick glance told him that however much he had tried to slur his articulation of the name, Henrietta had heard it. As for Cousin Annie, whose back was toward him, he could not at the moment tell whether or not she heard. Probably he could not have told if he had had a clear view of her face. And, for that matter, the incident was to pass without his knowing what conclusion Cousin Johnny had reached—whether he did or didn't like the sound of it.

They went into dinner at six o'clock. At first the table talk was livelier than it had been the previous night. Cousin Annie, right away, spoke a number of complete sentences which were not dragged out of her by direct questions. She spoke with enthusiasm of the sights they had taken in that day: the Parthenon, the capitol building, old Fort Nashboro. There was, in fact, every indication that matters had taken a real turn for the better. Edmund found himself wondering if Cousin Annie weren't going to turn out to be like all the other country ladies who had come here in recent years— vain, garrulous, and utterly susceptible to the luxuries of Henrietta's commodious, well-staffed, elegantly appointed house. The bright look on Henrietta's face at the opposite end of the table informed him that she was thinking the same thing. And then, as though conscious of just how far into the woods she had led them, Cousin Annie Kincaid began quietly closing in.

"You mustn't think," she said, "that Mr. Kincaid and I can't dine at whatever your accustomed dinner hour is." This was very much in her usual vein—making known her awareness that they were dining earlier than was normal for the Harpers. Since the houseboy was removing the soup bowls at the time, it might have been supposed that what she said was meant for his ears and that she had phrased it with that in mind. But the old lady wasn't long in finding another occasion to refer to Cousin Johnny as "Mr. Kincaid." She did it a third and fourth time, even. Each time it was as if she feared they hadn't understood her before. Finally, though, she made it absolutely clear. During the meat course, while everyone except Cousin Johnny was working away at the roast lamb and baked potatoes, she drove the point home to her own satisfaction. "It isn't that Mr. Kincaid doesn't like roast lamb," she said, addressing herself to Edmund and speaking in the most old-fashioned country-genteel voice that Edmund had heard since he was a boy at home. "It isn't that he doesn't like roast lamb," she repeated. "It's that he dined alone with ladies at noon and so had to eat the greater share of an uncommonly fine cut of sirloin steak. He isn't, you understand, used to eating a great deal of meat." Now she turned to Henrietta. "He seldom eats any meat at all for supper . . ." Edmund, remembering the other country ladies who had sat where Cousin Annie now sat, supposed that she would continue endlessly on this fascinating subject. But once she saw that she had the attention of both host and hostess, she suddenly turned to Cousin Johnny and said genially, "You seldom eat any meat at all for supper, do you, Mr. Kincaid?" It was the voice of a woman from an earlier generation than the Harpers', addressing her husband with the respect due a husband. How could anyone call him just plain Johnny after that?

The meat course was finished in almost total silence, but Edmund had two things to think about. After putting her question to Cousin Johnny, Cousin Annie had turned a triumphant gaze on Henrietta, indicating that she recognized who her real adversary was. That was one thing. The other thing was Cousin Johnny's response to being addressed as Mr. Kincaid. There was but one way to describe it. He winced. And there was but one conclusion that Edmund could draw: the poor fellow had lived so long in isolation that he would always wince when singled out in company and addressed directly by any name whatever.

Cousin Annie and Cousin Johnny retired within less than thirty minutes after dinner. As soon as they were safely upstairs, Edmund expected Henrietta to launch into Cousin Annie's performance. She did nothing of the kind. While he was setting up the card table and fetching the cards for a game of double solitaire, she turned on the television set and stood switching aimlessly from one channel to another—a practice she often criticized him for. She seemed to be avoiding conversation. Once they were seated at the table with the cards laid out and the television playing a favorite Western, Edmund said cozily, "*They* disapprove of cards, and *they* detest TV." These were two points that Cousin Annie had made clear the first night.

"I think they're awfully sweet, all the same," Henrietta said gently, smiling a little, and keeping her eyes on her cards.

"Oh, I like them," Edmund said defensively. "Everything they do or say takes me back forty years."

"They have real character."

"Yes," Edmund agreed. "It was pretty marvelous the way she let me have it at the table. She fairly rubbed my nose in it."

Henrietta looked up at him for the first time. "You mean—?"

"I mean the name business, of course. What else?"

"I don't know about that. I suppose she always calls him Mr. Kincaid."

"Well, what else did you think I meant?"

"Didn't you understand what she was saying? Of course I may be wrong."

"What on earth?"

"I'm afraid she was offended because you left Cousin Johnny to have lunch 'alone'—with the ladies. What else could you make of her emphasis?"

"She meant I should have come home to lunch today?"

"I don't know, darling. Maybe not."

"But you think I might come home tomorrow? Or take you all out somewhere?"

She smiled at him appreciatively. "Or better still," she offered, "take Cousin Johnny to lunch with some men downtown. I wonder if he wouldn't like that?"

"But would Cousin Annie let him?"

Henrietta leaned across the table and spoke in a conspiratorial whisper. "We could see," she said.

Edmund was silent. "Well, we'll see about it," he said finally, not promising anything but knowing in his heart that everything was already promised.

At the breakfast table next morning, Edmund sat admiring the graceful curve of Henrietta's wrist as she poured coffee from the silver urn into his cup. He had asked for this third cup mostly for the sake of admiring again the way she lifted the heavy urn and then let the weight of it pull her wrist over in that pretty arc. And the ruffles on the collar of Henrietta's breakfast gown seemed particularly becoming to her, and Edmund admired the soft arrangement of her hair and the extraordinary freshness of her complexion. She really looked incredibly young. She was a beautiful woman in every sense, and nothing about her this morning was more beautiful than the way she had been so right about Cousin Annie. Cousin Annie and Cousin Johnny had already finished their breakfast, and the old lady had gone back upstairs with her husband to prepare him for his morning at the office with Edmund and his noonday luncheon at the Hermitage Club. Edmund was now waiting for Cousin Johnny to come down in his "other suit" and "good tie."

He wouldn't have thought it possible for it to turn out this way. He was convinced all over again of how much more sensitive to people Henrietta was than he was. And he was so grateful to her. No sooner had he issued the invitation to Cousin Johnny than Cousin Annie became positively affable. And at once Cousin Johnny had begun nodding his head in agreement. Edmund noticed also that the old man began pulling rather strenuously at his lower lip, but all such lip pullings and winces and twitches Edmund was now willing to lump together as meaningless nervous habits. He wasn't at all sure he wouldn't end by having lunch alone with Cousin Johnny in a booth at Jackson's Stable, where they could talk without interruption.

And what a relief it was, anyway, that the thing was settled one way or the other. He had spent his last hour in bed this morning tossing about and wishing that he didn't have to raise the question and yet knowing that he wanted to. Long before the cook came in to fix breakfast, he had heard the old couple stirring in the guest room. It had been this way the day before, too. The monotonous buzz of the two old people's lowered voices seemed to penetrate the walls of the house in a way that no ordinary speech would have done. At that hour they seemed to feel that they must speak in the voice that one normally uses only when there is someone dead in the house or when something has gone awfully wrong. They were hard of hearing, of course, and believed they were whispering! Edmund had to smile at the thought of how carefully they concealed the fact of their deafness in company. At any rate, he woke to the drone of these old country people's voices. And with Cousin Johnny so much on his mind, he couldn't go back to sleep again. He knew that Henrietta was awake, too, and after a while he felt her hand on his shoulder, and he turned his head on the pillow and looked at her. "It's awful to have to lie here quietly like this, knowing that they're hungry," she whispered. There was very little light in the room but he could see that while she spoke she lay perfectly relaxed, with her eyes closed. "I'd give anything if there were some way they could go on and have their breakfast," she continued, still in a whisper. "Yet to get up and offer to fix it myself, or even to suggest they fix it for themselves, would only make them more uncomfortable, considering how they are . . . What do you think?"

"I just don't know," Edmund said, trying to sound less awake than he was.

Finally at seven o'clock they heard Cousin Johnny creep down the steps to fetch the morning *Tennessean* and then creep back up to the guest room again. (He wouldn't for the world have made so free as to sit down in the living room to read the morning paper—not without being expressly asked. It was a wonder Cousin Annie would let him go down and get the paper at all.) Edmund knew, from yesterday, that from this point on the buzz of voices would be only intermittent until the time should come for the first sounds of activity down in the kitchen. Then the buzz would begin again and remain constant until someone knocked on the guest-room door and announced breakfast. And that was the way it happened. Everything went just the way he knew it would until they were all four seated at the breakfast table and he had popped the question to Cousin Johnny. From then on everything was different.

Cousin Johnny had gone up to put on his other suit and his good tie, and Cousin Annie had gone with him. Presently Edmund, thinking he heard Cousin Johnny coming down the stairs, rose from the table and went round and kissed Henrietta's cheek. He meant to join Cousin Johnny in the hall and to take him directly to the car, which had already been brought up to the side door. But when he went out into the big front hall, it was Cousin Annie he saw. She had already come three quarters of the way down the stairs, and when she saw Edmund she stopped there, with her hand on the railing. Even before she spoke, Edmund felt his heartbeat quicken. "It's a pity you've had to wait around," she said. "He's so changeable." Edmund said nothing. Cousin Annie descended the rest of the flight. At the foot of the stairs she said, "He had already changed to his good clothes. But he doesn't, after all, want to miss the sights Henrietta and I will be seeing. He's getting back into his other things now."

Henrietta, hearing Cousin Annie's voice, had come to the dining-room door. "Cousin Johnny's all right, isn't he?" she asked.

"Of course he's all right," said the old lady with a shade of resentment in her voice. "It's that he doesn't want to miss that Presbyterian church or Bellemeade Plantation." Then she made her way into the dining room where she had left her coffee to cool.

Edmund went off in the other direction, making *his* way across the hall and into the dark corridor that led to the side entrance. He knew that Henrietta was following him, but he couldn't trust himself to discuss the situation. He hoped to reach the outside door before she caught up with him and merely to wave to her from the car. But he had forgotten his hat and coat. When he was at the entry door he heard a coat hanger drop on the floor of the cloak closet, which opened off the corridor, and he knew that Henrietta was fetching his things for him. He had to wait there and submit to her helping him on with his coat. Still he would have left without saying anything had she not at the last minute put her hand on his arm and said, "Darling, you mustn't mind."

"I think I really *hate* that woman," he said.

"Oh, Edmund," Henrietta whispered, "it may really have been

Cousin Johnny's decision. And what difference does it make? Why else do we have them here except to let them do whatever they will enjoy most?"

"Yes, why do we?" he said angrily.

Henrietta removed her hand from his arm and stepped back, away from him. With her eyes lowered she said, "We've been over that." Then she looked up at him accusingly: he wasn't seeing her through.

They had been over it, certainly, some two or three years before this. And he had thought, as she had, that he would never ask this question again. As he raced along the corridor, he had known he would ask it if he let her overtake him. That's why he had made such a dash for the car. He might have reached into the closet and grabbed his hat—to hell with the coat!—but he hadn't had his wits about him. And for that you always had to pay.

Finally, though, he kissed Henrietta goodbye again, and he waved to her from the car.

All the way to town this morning, he went over and over the foolish business. It had never been so complicated before. She had always managed to involve him in her good works among the relatives—having discovered his weakness there, she had abandoned most of her other good works—but this time he was involved in a way or in a sense that Henrietta didn't dream of. Or maybe she did. He shouldn't underestimate her. Was it really only a difference in degree this time? In some degree he was always affected by these country visitors as though it were something more than a visit from relatives. With them he had often felt there ought to be more to say to each other than there ever seemed to be. But never about anyone, before Cousin Johnny, had he felt: Here is such a person as I might have been, and I am such a one as he might have been.

Now he could not resist going back to what he considered the real beginning. It was Henrietta who had urged him to leave Ewingsburg, the county seat where they had grown up and where he first practiced law. He hadn't wanted to leave and had argued against it, and, despite the fine opportunities offered him by firms in Nashville, she hadn't begun urging him to go until they had been married for five years and had learned pretty definitely that there would never be any children. When he used to come home for lunch in Ewingsburg and would be lingering over his second cup of coffee, it got so he would catch Henrietta sometimes stealing furtive glances at him. She suspected him of being bored with his life. And yet when he talked of buying up more farm land and joining Uncle Alex and Uncle Nat in their lespedeza venture—aiming for the seed market— Henrietta thought he would be frittering away his life. He ought to be in a big place, she told him, where he could have a real career and be fully occupied.

And so they had gone to Nashville. And Edmund *was* fully occupied. And perhaps that was the trouble. Who could say . . . Not that Henrietta wasn't occupied, too. She was an enthusiastic joiner of clubs and circles and committees. Why not? What better way of getting to know people? Edmund was entirely sympathetic. But she was never satisfied until she had tried to draw Edmund into each activity, and, since she always failed, she was seldom satisfied with the activity afterward. In the early days, she was always finding something new to interest her—and him. Edmund wondered if there would have been a Nashville for the likes of Cousin Johnny and Cousin Annie to see if Henrietta hadn't been so active in the work of preserving landmarks and setting up monuments. (Even his refusal to help iron out the inevitable legal snarls of that work had never completely destroyed her interest in it. Recently she had had a hand in preserving the First Presbyterian Church from the vandals who wanted to pull it down.) For a time she took a great interest in the home for delinquent girls. Her reports of the individual cases had interested him hugely, but not enough to make him consent to join her as a board member. He came very near to being drawn into her juvenile court work, but somehow he even escaped involvement there.

Then, after a number of years, she began bringing in those nieces for the debutante season. Two of the girls were from his side of the family, one from hers. But that didn't matter. They were all of them kinfolks from out home—the nieces, the nephews, the invalids, and finally, after so many years, the nearly contemporary old couples. They were his responsibility, his involvement as much as hers. There was no getting around it—not in Edmund's mind. And so they came, and they came, and they came. Finally, he began to wonder if he and Henrietta weren't more alike than he had ever imagined. It occurred to him that she was really fonder of these visitors and of the people she went out to the country to "see about" than she was of the friends she had gone to such lengths to make in Nashville.

One day he spoke to her about it. And he suggested that perhaps they should think of moving back to Ewingsburg when the time came for him to retire from his practice. Henrietta had laughed at the idea. Why, she asked him, should they plan to bury themselves alive in their old age?

Well, then, he had another idea. (He was only trying to please her, wasn't he?) Why didn't they invite one of her favorites from among their not too affluent relatives, or maybe two of her favorites —"It's the kind of thing people used often to do," he said—to come and live with them on a permanent basis? Wouldn't that give her an even deeper satisfaction than doing only a little for this one and that one? (He didn't say: And then the house would always seem itself.) But in reply Henrietta expressed an astonishment just short of outrage. How could he imagine that this would be the case!

"But why not?" Edmund asked impatiently.

Henrietta shook her head bitterly. To think that he understood so little about what her life was like, she said. And then for the first time in years she mentioned her disappointment at not being able to have children. Edmund was confused. Could there possibly be any connection? Was she merely trying to play on his sympathy? He felt his cheeks growing warm, and could tell from the expression in her eyes that she saw his color rising. But looking deeper into her eyes he saw that she, too, was utterly confused. If there was any connection, then she was as confused about it as he was. She knew no better than he what it meant or why she had dragged it in. And he was sure that, whatever it was, they would never understand it now and that, having discovered it so late, they need not do so. Their course together was set, and he had no intention of trying to change it. But he felt a renewed interest in seeing to what strange places it might yet bring them.

Before he reached his office that second morning of the visit, he saw how salutary it had been for him to go over the whole story in his mind again. It was going to allow him to pass the remainder of the visit in comparative equanimity. From then on, it was as if he was an impartial witness to the contest between Henrietta and Cousin Annie. If, afterward, he had had to testify in court and explain why he did not intervene between them, he would have had to say that he thought it only a kind of game they were playing, and that he had had no idea of how deadly serious they were.

There was no telephone call from Henrietta that day. Edmund tried to reach her just after noon but learned from the maid that she and "the company" hadn't been at home for lunch. The maid happened to know the restaurant out on Hillsboro Pike where they had gone and happened to have the telephone number handy. Edmund could not help smiling as he jotted down the number. Henrietta knew he would be expecting a call from her, and knew that if it didn't come *he* would call—not because he would be afraid she was pouting or because he would feel a need to apologize. She was not a woman who pouted, and she always knew how sorry he was when they had had any kind of tiff. She was wonderful, really. He would find her tonight in the best of spirits. There would be no reference made to their exchange at the side door this morning. It was past, and she had already forgotten it. She was a wonderful woman, and nothing about her was more wonderful than her serenity and the way she was certain to have another suggestion to make to him today or tonight. The only trouble was that he knew what *this* suggestion would be, and it was important that he give her the opportunity of making it as soon as possible. He telephoned the restaurant, but the hostess said that Mrs. Harper and her party had just left.

Not infrequently Edmund stayed home from his office for one day of a visit that wasn't going too well. It was usually the last day. But his staying was by no means a pattern. He could never be certain it was the thing Henrietta wanted, and he always waited for her suggestion. Tomorrow would be the last day for Cousin Johnny and Cousin Annie, and though this was a case in which Henrietta was almost sure to suggest it, it wasn't going to be possible for him to stay. When he came in the house that night, Henrietta was still upstairs dressing. He considered this a stroke of good luck, because it would give her the opportunity he had in mind. Perhaps even it was for this that she happened still to be up there.

Henrietta's dressing for dinner, like Edmund's, consisted not of getting into more formal attire but of putting on something more comfortable and something more youthful than she ever wore away from home. When he came into her room, she was fresh from her bath, still moving about the room in her knee-length slip and her high-heeled mules. And right away she was bubbling with talk about the day's events, proving that she bore him no grudge, even saying the kind of things about Cousin Johnny and Cousin Annie that she had refused to say last night. "Once in the car when we were on our way out to Traveler's Rest—they were enchanted by Traveler's Rest and didn't care for Bellemeade or even the Hermitage—once I said—it was when we were talking about people from Ewingsburg who live here (and whom Cousin Annie has *refused* to let entertain them or even to see)—I said Bob Coppinger has gotten to look exactly like Laurence Olivier. 'Like who?' said Cousin Johnny from the back seat. Cousin Annie was sitting in the front seat with me and she turned around and said to him with the utmost contempt for my allusion, 'Some moving picture star, I think, Mr. Kincaid.' (Yes, she has continued to call him Mr. Kincaid all day today.) It was as if the old dear had read my mind. I had been thinking that even though she disapproves so of TV, we might be able to get them out to see a Western movie tonight—something real old-fashioned, like a movie. But after her remark I knew there was no chance, and that it had been silly of me to think there might be. I even marvel that she knows who Olivier is. But she knows things. She knows things you'd never in the world suppose she did. Let me tell you—Here, give me a hand with these buttons, won't you?"

While she talked she had gone to her closet and pulled out the dress she was going to wear. Edmund was marveling more at the pretty print of the dress material and at the mysterious row of buttons down the back than at Cousin Annie Kincaid's knowledge of movie stars. He realized that the buttons seemed mysterious because they were at once so unnecessary, so numerous and so large—each the size of a silver dollar—and yet were so carefully camouflaged, being covered with the same print the dress was made of. He found it most absorbing, and intriguing, and endearing. And suddenly he recognized the similarity of the whole fashioning of this dress to that of dresses Henrietta had worn when he was courting her. As he stood behind her, buttoning those buttons that began at the very low waistline and continued up to the rounded neckline, he could not resist, midway, leaning forward and kissing her on the back of her neck. Henrietta began to give him the day's itinerary: the First Presbyterian Church, the plantation houses of Andrew Jackson, John Overton, the Harding family.

"Every place we went," she said, "I had a time making them get out and see the very thing they had come to see. But what I was going to tell you was that when we were on our way downtown to see the church, Cousin Annie asked me to point out the James K. Polk Apartments and Vaux Hall! Could you have imagined she would have heard of either or remembered the names? When I told her both buildings had been torn down, she only said, 'I'm not surprised.' . . . What I think is that those were places where friends of hers who came to Nashville a million years ago must have had apartments . . . We might have lived there ourselves if we had come ten or fifteen years before we did. Do you remember when the Braxtons lived there—at Vaux Hall?"

But now it was time for Edmund to rush off into his room and dress. "Well, do make it snappy, dear," Henrietta said. "Remember I've had them all day. You must have noticed I'm quite hoarse from doing all the talking."

At dinner, Edmund made a special point of carrying his full share of the conversation. Cousin Johnny, on the other hand, was completely silent tonight and ate absolutely nothing. Cousin Annie was kept busy eating two portions of everything so that nothing would be wasted on *their* account. It was the first time Cousin Annie had done this, but then it was the first time Cousin Johnny had gone without food altogether. Edmund wondered silently if the old man wasn't hungry and if they couldn't find him something in the kitchen he could eat. Yet he couldn't ask. He began speculating on how many other discomforts the old man might have suffered in the past two days. He noticed that he had come to the table tonight without his vest. And at some moment last night he had noticed how the old man's clothes seemed to hang on him and how he seemed thinner than when he first arrived. The answer was that he had left off his long underwear. It was the central heat in the house! *They* weren't used to it. And now Edmund recalled the scene in the living room when he came into the house this afternoon. Having been detained at the office to make last-minute revisions of his brief for the shoe company case, Edmund had come home a little later than usual, but the houseboy was lighting the log fire in the living room at the usual hour. Edmund had, at the time, been scarcely conscious of one detail in the scene, but subconsciously he had made a note of it. At the moment of his entrance, the houseboy was on his knees fanning the flames of the fire, and across the room, seated beside Cousin Johnny and with him watching silently the houseboy's efforts, Cousin Annie was fanning herself with a little picture postcard of the Hermitage.

Until these details began to pile up in his mind, at the dinner table, Edmund had thought of Cousin Annie as waging a merely defensive war against Henrietta. Now he saw it wasn't so. She had had the offensive from the beginning and she was winning battle after battle. Every discomfort that Cousin Johnny suffered in silence, every dish he did without, every custom he had to conform to that was "bad for him" was a victory over Henrietta, and gave the old lady the deeper satisfaction just because Henrietta might not be aware of it.

But Edmund had no premonition of how far she might be prepared to go—or perhaps already had gone—until after dinner, when Cousin Johnny and Cousin Annie were going up the stairs together. They ascended very slowly, and Edmund realized that her footsteps were every bit as heavy as Cousin Johnny's. He recalled having mistaken her for the old man on the stair this morning. Very likely it had been she, after all, who had come down to fetch the paper each morning. Was climbing the stairs perhaps bad for Cousin Johnny?—the stairs in this house and in all the landmarks he had been taken to see? And when he went upstairs this morning, had it really been that he *couldn't* come back down and go with Edmund to the office? Suddenly Edmund could visualize the old fellow lying on his back in the bed, or even on the floor, before the old lady helped him onto the bed and made him comfortable and then came downstairs to say that he had changed his mind.

When their guests had gone upstairs for the night and Edmund was setting up the card table in the living room, Henrietta still hadn't mentioned tomorrow and the possibility of his staying at home. But after they had arranged their cards and had begun to play, the suggestion wasn't long in coming. By now, however, his concern for Cousin Johnny had driven that problem out of Edmund's mind, and, because of this, his reply to Henrietta was more abrupt than it might otherwise have been.

"There's one thing I do hope," she had said with considerable force, "and that is that you are going to be able to stay at home tomorrow."

"I can't possibly." That was all he said. For a minute they sat looking at each other across the card table.

"But I've told them you'd be here," she said.

"I wish you had asked me earlier," he said, in a softer tone now.

Her voice was still full of confidence. "I *had* counted on it," she said. "And they have gone up to bed thinking you'll be here."

"Tomorrow is Friday," he said, as if speaking to a child. "I'll have to be in court all day. It's the shoe company case. There's no chance."

"Oh," said Henrietta. She knew that this meant there really was no chance.

"I'm truly sorry, Henrietta," he said. "Fortunately, there will be no court on Saturday. I'll be able to go with you to take them home. But there's nothing I can do about tomorrow."

"Of course there's not. I understand that," she said, smiling at him. She was already recovering from her disappointment. Quietly they began playing out their game of cards. During the rest of the time they sat there, it seemed to Edmund that Henrietta played her cards as though she were performing some magic that was going to change everything—in her favor. And he couldn't bring himself to tell her about the sudden insight he had had at the dinner table, or about the ridiculous but genuine and quite black apprehension that he wasn't able to rid himself of.

At some hour in the night he heard the old woman's voice distinctly. He tried to think he had only dreamed it and that some other noise had waked him. But then he heard her again and heard Cousin Johnny. The familiar, funereal tones were unmistakable. He only managed to get back to sleep by assuring himself that it meant it must be nearly morning, by reminding himself that he had to have his sleep if he was to have his wits about him in court today.

The next time he woke, he put on the light and looked at his watch. He was sleeping alone in his own room. The two previous nights he had been with Henrietta in her room, but tonight she hadn't suggested it. His pocket watch was lying on his bedside table, with the gold chain coiled about it. It had been his father's watch and had the circumference and the thickness of a doorknob. Before he fastened his eyes on the Roman numerals to which the filigreed hands pointed, he remembered noticing that Cousin Johnny's watch, which the old man took out and wound before going up to bed each night, was almost identical with this one of his father's. It occurred to him that Cousin Johnny's would be resting now on the bedside table in the guest room with its chain coiled around it. This neat coiling of the chain about the watch was a habit Edmund had picked up from his father and one that his father had no doubt picked up from his own father. When finally Edmund focused his attention on the face of the watch, he found the very hour of the

night itself alarming. It was half past three. From that moment, he
didn't hear Cousin Johnny's voice again; it was only the old lady he
heard. He was certain now that the old man was really very sick.
He waited, sitting on the side of the bed with the light on. There
were silences, broken always and only by Cousin Annie's voice. At
last he got up and switched off the light and felt his way through
the bathroom into Henrietta's room.

"Do you suppose something is really wrong?" Henrietta said
from her bed. He was hardly through the doorway, and the room
was pitch dark. Something in the way she said it made him answer,
"I suppose not."

"The light's been on in their room for some time. You can see it
on the garage roof. Do you think you might just go and make
sure—or I could."

"What good would it do? It would only make matters worse,
considering how they are."

"Well, what do you think?" she said, meaning, Then why are you
here?

"I couldn't sleep."

"Is it that case today?"

"No, but I thought I might sleep better in here." He was sitting
on the side of her bed now. "Do you mind?" He didn't know what
he would do if she said, yes, she minded. He knew only that he
couldn't go back to his own room and bed before morning. He felt
that it hadn't, after all, been the voices that waked him, and that
there *had* been a dream—the kind of dream that could never be
remembered afterward.

"Of course I don't mind, silly," she said. She sounded wide awake.
"I've had a wonderfully funny thought," she said as he lay down
beside her. "You might just go to their door and tell Cousin Annie
that you won't be able to stay home today. Then maybe she would
let *him* get some sleep."

"Can she be that awful?" Edmund said. "You don't suppose it's anything more than just that?"

"I suppose not," she answered, putting her arm around him. "You know what an evil influence you are on people." The touch of her arm was all he had needed. Once again he believed it was the voices that had waked him, and remembered that he must have his wits about him tomorrow.

At seven o'clock nobody went downstairs to fetch the paper. Edmund had left his watch in his room, but neighborhood noises and a distant whistle told him the time. He slept again, and next time he waked he knew it was the unnatural silence in the house that had waked him. He slipped out of bed and went into his room to dress. It was seven-thirty by his watch. He dressed hurriedly, but when he went to look in on Henrietta before going downstairs, he found her also fully dressed and standing with her hand on the knob to the hall door. She had put on lipstick but no other make-up. She looked pale and frightened. He crossed over to her and they went out into the hall together.

The door to the guest room was standing open but the blinds were still drawn and the room was in complete darkness. Presently Cousin Annie appeared out of the darkness, wearing the black dress she had worn on the trip in from the country and clutching some object in her hand. Edmund and Henrietta moved quickly toward her. As they drew near, Edmund saw it was Cousin Johnny's watch she held. When they stood before her in the doorway, Cousin Annie said, "He's gone."

"Gone?" Edmund echoed, and he almost added, "Where?" But in time he remembered the euphemism. She spoke as though they had all been waiting together through the night for the old man to be released from his mortal pain.

He felt Henrietta lean against him. He put his arms about her, and when she turned and hid her face on his shirtfront, he had to support her to keep her from crumbling to the floor.

"You mustn't," said Cousin Annie. "I did everything anyone could have done. We had known for some time he hadn't long."

Henrietta's strength returned. She drew herself away from him and faced Cousin Annie. "But why—how could you let him come if—"

Edmund felt himself blushing. Was his wife really so shameless?

But the old lady seemed to think the question quite in order. She even completed the question for Henrietta. "If it was unwise for him? Because he wanted so much to come, to see what it was like here . . . Like all of us, he was foolish about some things."

The two women stood a moment looking at each other. Without being blind to the genuine grief in Cousin Annie's countenance, Edmund detected the glint of victory in the last glance she gave Henrietta before turning back into the dark room.

Poor Cousin Johnny, Edmund thought to himself . . . Now Henrietta was following Cousin Annie in there, and now he heard the old lady's first sobs and knew that she had given way, as she had to, and was letting Henrietta see after her. The battle was over, really . . . But poor Cousin Johnny, he kept thinking. Poor old fellow . . . Presently Henrietta led Cousin Annie out into the hall again, and as the two women moved toward the door to Henrietta's room, Henrietta gave him a look that recalled him to his senses and reminded him of his obligations. Already it was time for him to begin making the arrangements. He would be at home after all today. The court would grant a postponement under the circumstances. Cousin Johnny was gone, but *he* was still here to see Henrietta through and make the arrangements.

For a moment Edmund stood there staring into the dead man's room. The door should be shut, he supposed. And when he had done this, he would have to go and telephone a doctor. Cousin

Annie didn't realize you couldn't die without a doctor nowadays. While he waited for the doctor to arrive, he would call an undertaker. No, he was being as bad as Cousin Annie. It wouldn't do to call an undertaker before a doctor had been there. He stepped forward and placed his hand on the doorknob. And then, as though it was what he had intended all along, he went inside the room and closed the door behind him.

He waited just inside the door till his eyes got used to the dark. Then he went over to the foot of the bed where she had the old man laid out. At last they were alone—he and Cousin Johnny. There was only just enough light for him to make out that she had him completely dressed, and with something that must be a handkerchief covering his face. No doubt he was wearing the very clothes— his other suit and good tie—that he would have worn to lunch at Jackson's Stable. And would she have put him in his long underwear? Edmund speculated, not idly, and not, certainly, with humor. And the vest? And the lisle socks and the elastic supporters? Yes, she would have. That was how Cousin Johnny would be taken back to Ewingsburg for burial, was how he would be taken away from Edmund's house where he had died. Suddenly, at the thought of it, Edmund was seized with a dreadful terror of their taking the old man away. Wasn't there some way he could postpone it? But postponing it wouldn't be enough. What if he should lock the door to the guest room and refuse to let them have the body! He had heard of cases in which grief had driven people to such madness, and surely his present anguish was grief—if not exactly grief for Cousin Johnny. What if he should refuse to let them have the old man's body!

He stood peering through the darkness at the white handkerchief over the old man's face, the face whose features he already found it hard to remember distinctly. And he was wondering at his own simplicity—indulging in such a fantasy, giving way to such unnatural and morbid feelings! And at such a time. Soon Henrietta or Cousin Annie—or the two of them, even—might come and discover him there. That wasn't likely, but soon he would have to go back to them and he must begin preparing himself for his return. He knew that the first step must be to begin thinking of Cousin Johnny more realistically, not as a part of himself that was being taken away forever but once again as a visitor from the country who had died in his guest room. And, all at once, it seemed to Edmund the most natural thing in the world for him to speak to his dead house guest.

"Well, Cousin Johnny, you're gone," he said. That was all he said aloud. But, placing his two hands on the smooth footrail of the bed as though it were the familiar rail of a jury box, he went on silently: "What was it we were going to talk about, Cousin Johnny, in that talk of ours? Was it our wives and their wars within wars and what made them that way . . . We certainly ought to have got round to that. But it wasn't our wives who divided us. It was somehow our both being from the country that did it. You had done one thing about being from the country and I had done another. You buried yourself alive on that farm of yours, I buried myself in my work here. But something in the life out there didn't satisfy you the way it should. The country wasn't itself any more. And something was wrong for me here. By 'country' we mean the old world, don't we, Cousin Johnny—the old ways, the old life, where people had real grandfathers and real children, and where love was something that could endure the light of day—something real, not merely a hand one holds in the dark so that sleep will come. Our trouble was, Cousin Johnny, we were lost without our old realities. We couldn't discover what it is people keep alive for without them. Surely there must be something. Other people seem to know some reason why it is better to be alive than dead this April morning. I will have to find it out. There must be something."

Heads of Houses

I. The Foreign Parts and the Forget-Me-Nots

Kitty's old bachelor brother gave Dwight a hand with the baggage as far as the car, but Dwight would accept no more help than that. He had his own method of fitting everything into the trunk. His Olivetti and his portable record player went on the inside, where they would be most protected. The overnight bag and the children's box of playthings went on the outside, where they would be handy in case of an overnight stop. It was very neat the way he did it. And he had long since learned how to hoist the two heaviest pieces into the rack on top of the car with almost no effort, and knew how to wedge them in up there so that they hardly needed the elastic straps he had bought in Italy last summer. He was a big, lanky man, with a lean jaw that listed to one side, and normally his movements were so deliberate, and yet so faltering, that anyone who did not mistake him for a sleepwalker recognized him at once for a college professor. But he never appeared less professorial, and never felt less so, than when he was loading the baggage on top of his little car. As he worked at it now, he was proud of his speed and effi- ciency, and was not at all unhappy to have his father-in-law watching from the porch of the big summer cottage.

From the porch, Kitty's father watched Dwight's packing activ- ities with a cold and critical eye. Only gypsies, Judge Parker felt, rode about the country with their possessions tied all over the outside of their cars. Such baggage this was, too! His son-in-law seemed purposely to have chosen the two most disreputable-looking pieces to exhibit to the public eye. Perhaps he had selected these two because they had more of the European stickers on them than any of the other bags—not to mention the number of steamship stickers proclaiming that the Dwight Clarks always traveled tourist class!

Yet the exposed baggage was not half so irritating to Judge Parker as the little foreign car itself. The car would have been bad enough if it had been one of the showy, sporty models, but Dwight's car had a practical-foreign look to it that told the mountain people, over in the village, as well as the summer people from Nashville and Memphis, over in the resort grounds and at the hotel, how com- mitted Dwight was to whatever it was he thought he was com- mitted to. The trouble was, it was a *big* little car. At first glance, you couldn't quite tell what was wrong with it. Yet it was little enough to have to have a baggage rack on top; and inside it there was too little room for Dwight and Kitty to take along even the one basket of fruit that Kitty's mother had bought for them yesterday. Judge Parker pushed himself as far back in his rocker as he safely could. For a moment he managed to put the banister railing between his eyes and the car. He meant *not* to be irritated. He had been warned by his wife to be careful about what he said to his son-in-law this morning. After all, the long summer visit from the children was nearly over now.

Busy at work, Dwight was conscious of having more audience than just Dad Parker—an unseen, and unseeing, audience inside the cottage. Certain noises he made, he knew, telegraphed his progress to Kitty. She was upstairs—in the half story, that is, where everybody but Dad and Mother Parker slept—making sure both children used the bathroom before breakfast. (She knew he would not allow them time for the bathroom after breakfast.) And the same noises— the slamming down of the trunk lid, for instance, and even the scraping of the heavy bags over the little railing to the rack (the *galerie,* Dwight called it fondly)—would reach the ears of brother Henry, now stationed inside the screen door, considerately keeping hands off another man's work. The ears of Mother Parker would be reached, too, all the way back in the kitchen. Or, since breakfast must be about ready now, Mother Parker might be on the back porch, where the table was laid, waiting ever so patiently. Perhaps she was rearranging the fruit in the handmade basket, which she had bought at the arts-crafts shop, and which she was sure she could find space for in the car after everything else was in . . . Everybody, in short, was keeping out of the way and being very patient and considerate. It really seemed to Dwight Clark that he and his little family might make their getaway, on this September morning, without harsh words from any quarter. He counted it almost a miracle that such a summer could be concluded without an open quarrel of any kind. Along toward the end of July, midway in the visit, he had thought it certain Kitty would not last. But now it was nearly over.

When the last strap over the bags was in place, Dwight stepped away from the car and admired his work. He even paused long enough to give a loving glance to the little black car itself, his English Ford, bought in France two summers ago. Such a sensible car it was, for a man who wanted other things out of life than just a car. No fins, no chromium, no high-test gasoline for him! And soon now he and Kitty would be settled inside it, and they would be on their way again, with just their own children, and headed back toward their own life: to the life at the university, to life in their sensible little prefab, with their own pictures and their own make-shift furniture (he could hardly wait for the sight of his books on the brick-and-board shelves!), to their plans for scrimping through another winter in order to go abroad again next summer—their life. Suddenly, he had a vision of them in Spain next summer, speeding along through Castile in the little black automobile, with the baggage piled high and casting its shadow on the hot roadside. He stepped toward the car again, with one long arm extended as if he were going to caress it. Instead, he gave the elastic straps—his Italian straps, he liked to call them—their final testing, snapping them against the bags with satisfaction, knowing that Kitty would hear, knowing that, for once, she would welcome this signal that he was all set.

He turned away from the car, half expecting to see Kitty and the children already on the porch. But they were still upstairs, of course; and breakfast had to be eaten yet. Even Dad Parker seemed to have disappeared from the porch. But, no, there he was, hiding behind the banisters. What was he up to? Usually the old gentleman kept his dignity, no matter what. It didn't matter, though. Dwight would pretend not to notice. He dropped his eyes to the ground . . . As he advanced toward the house, he resolved that this one time he was not going to be impatient with Kitty about setting out. He would keep quiet at the breakfast table. One impatient word from any-body, at this point, might set off fireworks between Kitty and her mother, between Kitty and her father. (He glanced up, and, lo, Dad Parker had popped up in a normal position again.) Between Kitty and her ineffectual old bachelor brother, even. (He wished Henry would either get away from that door or come on outside where he could be seen.) And if she got into it with them, Dwight knew he could not resist joining her. It would be too bad, here at last, but their impositions upon Kitty this summer had been quite beyond the pale—not to mention their general lack of appreciation of all she and he had undertaken to do for them, which, of course, he didn't mind for *himself,* and not to mention their show of resentment against *him,* toward the last, merely because he was taking Kitty away from them ten days earlier than the plans had originally called for. The truth was that they had no respect for his profession; they resented the fact that his department chairman could summon him back two weeks before classes would begin . . . For a moment, he forgot that, in fact, the chairman had not summoned him back.

As Dwight approached the porch, in his slow, lumbering gait, Judge Parker suddenly rocked forward in his chair. Stretching his long torso still farther forward, he rested the elbows of his white shirtsleeves on the banister railing. Dwight, out there in the morning sun, seemed actually to be walking with his eyes closed. Perhaps he was only looking down but, anyway, he came shambling across the lawn as though he didn't know where he was going. Judge Parker had noticed, before this, that when his son-in-law was let loose in a big open space, or even in a big room, he seemed to wander without any direction. The fellow was incapable of moving in a straight line from one point to another. He was the same way in an argument. Right now, no doubt, he had a theory about where the porch steps were, and he would blunder along till he arrived at the foot of them. But what a way of doing things, especially for a man who was always talking about the scientific approach. It had been, this summer, like having a great clumsy farm animal as a house guest. It had been hardest, the judge reflected, on his wife, Jane. Poor old girl. Why, between the fellow's typewriter and record player, she had hardly had one good afternoon nap out. And, oh, the ashtrays and the glasses that had been broken, and even furniture. For a son-in-law they had the kind of man who couldn't sit in a straight chair without trying to balance himself on its back legs. . . . Out-of-doors he was worse, if anything. He had rented a power mower and cut the grass himself, instead of letting them hire some mountain white to do it, as they had in recent years. He had insisted, too, on helping the judge weed and work his flower beds. As a result, Judge Parker's flowers had been trampled until he could hardly bear to look at some of the beds. A stray horse or cow couldn't have done more damage. All at once, he realized that there was an immediate danger of Dwight's stumbling into his rock garden, beside the porch steps, and crushing one of his ferns—his *Dryopteris spinulosa.* Somehow, he must wake the boy up. He must *say* something to him. He cleared his throat and began to speak. As he spoke, he allowed his big, well-manicured hands to drape themselves elegantly over the porch banisters.

"Professor Clark," he began, not knowing what he was going to say, but using his most affectionate form of address for Dwight. "Is it," he said, casting about for something amiable, "is it thirty-eight miles to the gallon you get?"

Dwight stopped, and looked up with a startled expression. He might really have been a man waked from sleepwalking. But gradually a suspicious, crooked smile appeared, twisting his chin still farther out of any normal alignment. "*Twenty*-eight to the gallon, Dad Parker," he said.

"Oh, yes, that's what I meant to say!"

What could have made him say *thirty,* he wondered. Not that he knew or cared anything about car mileage. It always annoyed him that people found it such an absorbing topic. Even Jane knew more about his Buick than he did, and whenever anyone asked him, he had to ask her what mileage they got.

But he couldn't let the exchange stop there. Dwight would think his slip was intentional. Worse still, his son Henry, behind the screen door, would be making *his* mental notes on how ill the summer had gone. The judge had to make his interest seem genuine. "That does make it cheap to operate," he ventured. "And it has a four-cylinder motor. Think of that!"

"Six cylinders," said Dwight, no longer smiling.

The judge made one more try. "Of course, of course. Yours is an Ambassador. It's the Consul that has four."

"Mine is called a Zephyr," Dwight said.

There was nothing left for Judge Parker to do but throw back his head and try to laugh it off. At any rate, he had saved his fern.

At the steps to the porch, a porch that encompassed the cottage on three sides and that was set very high, with dark green latticework underneath, and with the one steep flight of steps under the cupola, at the southwest corner—at the foot of the steps Dwight stopped and turned to look along the west side of the house. Dad Parker's lilac bushes grew there. Wood ashes were heaped about their roots. Beyond the lilacs was the rock pump house, and just beyond that Dwight had a view of Dad Parker's bed of forget-me-nots mixed with delphiniums. Or was it bachelor's-buttons mixed with ager-atum? He was trying to get hold of himself after the judge's sarcasm about the car. In effect, he was counting to a hundred, as Kitty had told him he must do this morning.

For the peace must be kept this morning, at any price—for Kitty's sake. For her and the children's sake he had to control himself through one more meal. And the only way he could was to convince himself that Dad Parker's mistakes about the car were real ones. With anybody but Judge Nathan Parker it would have been impossible. But in the case of the judge it *was* possible. The man knew less than any Zulu about the workings of cars, to say nothing of models of foreign makes. This father-in-law of his most assuredly had some deep neurosis about anything vaguely mechanical. Even the innocent little Italian typewriter had offended him. And instead of coming right out and saying that Dwight's typing got on his nerves, he had had to ask his rhetorical questions, before the whole family, about whether Dwight thought good prose could be composed on "a machine." "I always found it necessary to write my briefs and decisions in longhand," he said, "if they were to sound like much." And the record player, too. The judge *despised* canned music; he preferred the music he made himself, on his violoncello, which instrument he frequently brought out of the closet after dinner at night, strumming it along with whatever popular stuff came over the radio . . . There was not even a telephone in the cottage. That seemed to Dwight the *purest* affectation. Dad and Mother Parker were forever penning little notes to people over in the resort grounds, or at the hotel. They carried on a voluminous correspondence with their friends back in Nashville. During the week, they wrote notes to brother Henry, who had to keep at his job at the courthouse in Nashville all summer long, and only came up to the mountain for weekends. In fact, three weeks ago, when the generator on Dwight's car went dead, Dad Parker had insisted upon writing brother Henry about it. The garage in the mountain village could not furnish brushes and armatures for an English Ford, of course, but from the telephone office Dwight might have called some garage in Nashville, or even in Chattanooga, which was nearer. Instead, he had had to tell Dad Parker what was needed and let Henry attend to it. Henry did attend to it, and very promptly. The parts arrived in the mail just two days later. When the judge returned from the village post office that morning, he handed Dwight the two little packages, saying, "Well, Herr Professor, here are your 'foreign parts.'" Everybody had laughed—even Kitty, for a moment. But Dwight hadn't laughed. He had only stood examining the two little brown packages, which were neatly and securely wrapped, as only an old bachelor could have wrapped them, and addressed to him in Henry's old-fashioned, clerkish-looking longhand.

At the foot of the porch steps, Dwight was listening hopefully for the sound of Kitty's footsteps on the stairs inside. He remained there for perhaps two or three minutes, with his eyes fixed in a trancelike gaze upon the mass of broad-leaved forget-me-nots. (They *were* forget-me-nots, he had decided.) Presently he saw out of the corner of his eye, without really looking, that Dad Parker had produced the morning paper from somewhere and was offering him half of it, holding it out toward him without saying a word. At the same moment, out in the rock pump house, the pump's electric motor came on with a wheeze and a whine. Someone had flushed the toilet upstairs. It was the first flush since Dwight came downstairs, and so he knew that Kitty and the children would not be along for some minutes yet. There would have to be one more flush.

As he went up to the porch to receive a section of the paper, the pump continued to run, making a noise like a muffled siren. That was its *good* sound. It *wasn't* thumping, which was its bad sound and meant trouble. Probably the low ebb in understanding between Kitty and her mother this summer had been during the second dry spell in July. Kitty had come to the mountain with the intention of relieving her mother of the laundry, as well as of all cooking and dishwashing. Those were the things that Mother Parker had hated about the mountain when Kitty was growing up. She had missed her good colored servants in Nashville and couldn't stand the mountain "help" that was available. But it seemed that Kitty didn't understand how to operate her mother's new washing machine economically—with reference to water, that is. During that dry spell, Mother Parker took to hiding the table linen and bedsheets, and the old lady would rise in the morning before Kitty did, and run them through the washer herself. No real water crisis ever developed, but, realizing that Dad Parker would be helpless to deal with it if it did, Dwight got hold of the old manual that had come with the pump, when it was installed a dozen years before, and believed that he understood how to prime it, or even to "pull the pipe" in an emergency. Having learned from the manual that every flush of the toilet used five gallons of water, he estimated that during a dry spell it wasn't safe to flush it more than three times in one day. And as a result of this knowledge it became necessary for him to put a padlock on the bathroom door so as to prevent Dwight, Jr., aged four, from sneaking upstairs and flushing the toilet just for kicks.

It seemed that the pump, like everybody else, was trying to make only its polite noises this morning. But just as Dwight was accepting his half of the newspaper, the pump gave one ominous, threatening thump. Dwight went tense all over. There had been no rain for nearly three weeks. There might yet be a crisis with the pump. In such case, brother Henry would be no more help than Dad Parker. It could, conceivably, delay Dwight's departure a whole day. If that happened, it might entail his pretending to get off a telegram to the chairman of his department. Moreover, he would have to do this before the eyes of brother Henry, in whom Kitty, in a weak moment, had confided the desperate measure they had taken to bring the summer visit to an end. It was Henry, lurking there in the shadows, who really depressed him. It seemed to him that Henry had come up for weekends this summer just to lurk in the shadows. Had he joined in one single game of croquet? He had not. And each time Dwight produced his miniature chess set, Henry had made excuses and put him off.

Dwight looked into Dad Parker's eyes to see if the thump had registered with him. But of course it *hadn't* registered. And when the motor went off peacefully, and when everything was all right again, that of course didn't register, either. To Dwight's searching look Dad Parker responded merely by knitting his shaggy brows and putting one hand up to his polka-dot bow tie to make out if anything was wrong there. Everything was fine with the judge's tie, as it always was. He gave Dwight a baffled, pitying glance and then disappeared behind his half of the morning paper.

II. The Garden House

Dwight sat down on a little cane-bottomed chair and tilted it on its back legs. He opened his half of the paper. His was the second section, with the sports and the funnies. He had learned early in the summer to pretend he preferred to read that section first. Dad Parker had been delighted with this, naturally, but even so he hadn't been able to conceal his astonishment—to put it mildly—that a grown man could have such a preference. To the judge it seemed the duty of all educated, responsible gentlemen to read the national and international news before breakfast every morning. He liked to have something important—and controversial, if possible—for the talk at the breakfast table.

Dwight, tilting back in his chair and hiding behind his paper, was listening for the pump to come on again. He felt positively panicky at the prospect of staying another day, or half day. One more flush of the toilet and he would be free. To think that five gallons of water *might* stand between him and his return to his own way of life! He found that he could not concentrate on the baseball scores, and he didn't even try to read "Pogo." Then, at last, the pump did come on, and it was all right. And again it went off with a single thump, which, as a matter of fact, it nearly always went off with.

Dwight sat wondering at his own keyed-up foolishness, but still he found it irksome that Dad Parker could sit over there calmly reading the paper, unaware even that there was such a thing as an electric pump on the place. It seemed that once the pump had been installed, the judge had deafened his ears to it and put it forever out of his mind. This was just the way he had behaved during the worst dry spell. But Dwight understood fully why no water shortage could ever be a problem for Dad Parker. To begin with, he watered his flowers only with rain water that he brought in a bucket from the old cistern—water that was no longer considered safe for drinking. And Dad Parker, personally, still used the garden house.

The garden house! Dwight was alarmed again. The garden house? Was there any reason for the thought of it to disturb him? There must be. His subconscious mind had sent up a warning. The garden house was connected with some imminent threat to his well-being, possibly even to his departure this morning. Quickly, he began trying to trace it down, forming a mental image of the edifice itself, which was located a hundred yards to the east of the cottage, along the ridge of the mountain. This structure was, without question, the sturdiest and most imposing on the Parkers' summer property. "Large, light, and airy, it is most commodious"—that was how Dad Parker had described the building to Dwight when he and Kitty were first married and before Dwight had yet seen the family's summer place. And Dwight had never since heard him speak of the building except in similar lyrical terms. Like the pump house, it was built of native rock, quarried on the mountainside just three or four miles away; but it had been built a half century back, when masonry work done on the mountain was of a good deal higher order than it was nowadays. Family tradition had it that one spring soon after Kitty's grandfather had had their cottage built, the men of a local mountain family had constructed the garden house for the grandfather free of charge and entirely on their own initiative. It was standing there to surprise "the Old Judge," as the grandfather was still remembered and spoken of locally, when he and the family came up to the mountain that July. The Old Judge had not actually been a judge at all, but an unusually influential and a tolerably rich lawyer, at Nashville, and he had befriended this mountain family sometime previously by representing them in a court action brought against one of their number for disturbing the peace. They had repaid him by constructing a garden house that was unique in the whole region. Its spacious interior was lighted by rows of transom windows, set high in three of the four walls. Below these windows, at comfortable intervals, were accommodations for eight persons, and underneath was a seemingly bottomless pit. Best of all, the building was so situated that when the door was not closed, its open doorway commanded a view of the valley that was unmatched anywhere on the mountain . . . It was there that Dad Parker usually went to read the first section of the paper, before breakfast every morning. And frequently he read the second section there, after breakfast. Suddenly a bell rang in Dwight's conscious mind, and the message came through. Dad Parker had, this morning, already read the first section of the paper once! From the east dormer window, half an hour before, Dwight had seen him returning from the garden house, paper in hand. It was extremely odd, to say the least, for him to sit there poring over the news a second time. Usually, when he had read the paper once, he knew it by heart and never needed to glance at it again—not even to prove a point in an argument. What was he up to? First he had hidden behind the banisters, now behind the paper.

Involuntarily, almost, Dwight tilted his chair still farther back, to get a look at Dad Parker's face. The chair creaked under his weight. Remembering he had already broken one of these chairs this summer, he quickly brought it back to all fours. Another broken chair might somehow delay their getting off! The chair wasn't damaged this time, but the glimpse Dwight had had of Dad Parker left him stunned. The old gentleman's face was as red as a beet, and he was reading something in the paper, something that made his eyes, normally set deep in their sockets, seem about to pop out of his head.

By the time the front legs of Dwight's chair hit the floor, the judge had already closed the paper and begun folding it. As he tucked it safely under his arm, he looked at Dwight and gave him a grin that was clearly sheepish—guilty, even.

But deep in the old man's eyes was a look of firm resolve. A resolve, Dwight felt certain, that *he,* Dwight, should not under any circumstances see the front section of the paper before setting off this morning. Dwight couldn't imagine what the article might be. He had but one clue. He had observed, without thinking about it, that the judge had had the paper open to the inside of the last page. That was where society news was printed, and it was one page that the judge seldom read. Dwight realized now that Dad Parker had given him the second section as a kind of peace offering. And while going through the first section again he had stumbled on something awful.

From inside the cottage there came the sound of Kitty's and the children's footsteps on the stairs.

III. An Old Bachelor Brother

Henry Parker, just inside the screen door, heard Kitty and her children start downstairs. He pushed the door open and went out on the porch. Through the screen he had been watching his father and his brother-in-law, hiding from each other behind their papers. He believed he knew precisely what thoughts were troubling the two men. He had refrained from joining them because ever since he arrived from Nashville last night he had sensed that his own presence only aggravated their present suffering. Each of them was suffering from an acute awareness that he was practicing a stupid deception upon the other, as well as from a fear that he might be discovered. His brother-in-law was leaving the mountain under the pretense that he had been called back to his university. The judge was concealing the fact that there was a party of house guests expected to arrive from Nashville this very day—almost as soon as the Clarks were out of the house—and that an elaborate garden party was planned for Monday, which would be Labor Day. Each man knew that Henry knew about his deception, and each wished, with Henry, that Henry could have stayed on in Nashville this one weekend. Henry couldn't stay in Nashville, however—for good and sufficient reasons—and just now he couldn't remain inside the screen door any longer. Kitty was on the stairs, and his mother was coming up the hall from the kitchen. His lingering there would be interpreted by them as peculiar.

Just as Henry made his appearance on the porch, Dwight and the judge came to their feet. They, too, had heard the footsteps of the women and children. It was time for breakfast. Henry walked over to his father and said casually, "Wonder if I could have a glance at the paper?" The judge glared at him as though his simple request were a personal insult.

"The paper," Henry repeated, reaching out a hand toward the newspaper, which the judge now clutched under his upper arm. The judge continued to glare, and Henry continued to hold out his hand. Henry's hands were of the same graceful and manly proportions as his father's, but, unlike the judge, he didn't "use" his hands and make them "speak." He also had his father's same deep-set eyes, and the same high forehead—even higher, since his hair, unlike his father's was beginning to recede. He glared back at his father, half in fun, supposing the refusal to be some kind of joke. Finally, he took hold of the paper and tried to pull it free. But the judge held on.

"May I just glance at the headlines?" Henry said sharply, dropping his hand.

"No, you may not," said the judge. "We are all going in to breakfast now."

Dwight stepped forward, smiling, and silently offered his section of the paper to Henry. Henry accepted it, but his heart sank when he looked into Dwight's face. Dwight's face, this morning, was the face of an appeaser. Only now did Henry realize that both men imagined he might, out of malice or stupidity, spill their beans at the breakfast table. The judge, it seemed, meant to bluff and badger him into silence; Dwight intended to appease him.

Henry took the paper over to the edge of the porch, leaned against the banister, and lit a cigarette. His mother and sister were standing together in the doorway now, and his father had set out in their direction.

"Breakfast, everybody," said his mother. By "everybody," he knew, she meant him, because he was the only one who had ignored her appearance there. He glanced up from the paper, smiled at her and nodded, then returned his eyes to the paper, which he held carelessly on his knee.

"Henry has taken a notion to read the newspaper at this point," he heard his father say just before he marched inside the cottage.

His brother-in-law lingered a moment. There seemed to be something Dwight wanted to say to Henry. But Henry didn't look up; he couldn't bear to. Dwight moved off toward the doorway without speaking.

"Don't be difficult, Henry," his sister Kitty said cheerfully. Then she and her mother went inside, with Dwight following them.

Henry heard them go back through the cottage to the screened porch in the rear. He knew he would have to join them there presently. He supposed that, whether they knew it or not, they needed him. They were so weary of their own differences that any addition to their company would be welcome, even someone who knew too much.

And how much too much *he* knew!—about them, about himself, about everybody. That was the trouble with him, of course. *He* could have told them beforehand how this summer would turn out.

But they had known, really, how it would turn out, and had gone ahead with it anyway; and that was the difference between him and them, and that was the story of his bachelorhood, the story of his life. He flicked his cigarette out onto the lawn and folded the paper neatly over the banister. No, it wasn't quite so simple as that, he thought—the real difference, the real story wasn't. But he had learned to think of himself sometimes as others thought of him, and to play the role he was assigned. It was an easy way to avoid thinking of how things really were with him. Here he was, so it appeared, an old-fashioned old bachelor son, without any other life of his own, pouting because his father had been rude to him on the veranda of their summer cottage on a bright September morning. Henry Parker was a man capable even of thinking inside this role assigned him, and not, for the time being, as a man whose other life was so much more real and so much more complicated that there were certain moments in his summer weekends at this familiar cottage when he had to remind himself who these people about him were. For thirteen years, "life" to him had meant his life with Nora McLarnen, his love affair with a woman tied to another man through her children, tied to a husband who, like her, was a Roman Catholic and who, though they had been separated all those years, would not give her a divorce except on the most humiliating terms. Henry had learned how to think, on certain occasions with the family, as the fond old bachelor son. And he knew that presently he, the old bachelor, must get over his peeve and begin to have generous thoughts again about his father, and about the others, too.

It *had* been a wretched summer for all four of them, and they had got into the mess merely because they wanted to keep up the family ties. His mother was to be pitied most. His mother had finally arranged her summers at the cottage so that they were not all drudgery for her, the way they used to be when she had two small children, or even two big children, in the days when their cottage was not even wired for electricity and when, of course, she had no electric stove or refrigerator or washing machine and dryer. But in making their plans for this visit Dwight and Kitty had completely failed to understand this. Kitty had moved in and taken over where no taking over was needed. Not only that. Because Dwight had to do his writing—for ten years now they had been hearing about that book of his—and because Dwight and Kitty so disdained the social life that Mother and Dad had with the other summer residents, she had forgone almost all summer social life. Henry had it from his mother that the party on Monday was supposed to make it up to Dad's and her friends for their peculiar behavior this summer, and was not really intended as a celebration of their daughter's departure. To have concealed their plans was silly of them, but Mother had been afraid of how it might sound to Dwight and Kitty.

Kitty had to be a sympathetic figure, too, in the old bachelor's eyes. Kitty had written her mother beforehand that they would come to the mountain only if she could be allowed to take over the housekeeping. Yet her mother had "frustrated" her at every turn. She wouldn't keep out of the kitchen, she wouldn't let Kitty do the washing. Further, Henry agreed with his sister that the cottage had suffered at their mother's hands, that it had none of the charm it had had when they were growing up. It was no longer a summer place, properly speaking. It was Nashville moved to the mountain. There was no longer the lighting of kerosene lamps at twilight, no more chopping of wood for the stove, no more fetching of water from the cistern. The interior of the house had been utterly transformed. Rugs covered the floors everywhere—the splintery pine floors that Mother so deplored. The iron bedsteads had disappeared from the bedrooms; the living room rockers were now used on the porch. Nowadays, cherry and maple antiques set the tone of the house. The dining room even ran to mahogany. And, for the living room, an oil portrait of the Old Judge had been brought up from the house in Nashville to hang above the new mantelpiece, with its broken ogee and fluted side columns. With such furnishings, Kitty complained, children had to be watched every minute, and could not have the run of the house the way they did when she and Henry and their visiting cousins were growing up. It was all changed.

As for the lot of the two men this summer—well, he should worry about them. When thinking of *them,* he couldn't quite keep it up as the sympathetic old bachelor who took other people's problems to heart. What was one summer, more or less, of not having things just as you wanted them? Next summer, or even tomorrow, or an hour from now, each of them would have it all his way again. And by any reasonable view of things that was what a man must do. A man couldn't afford to get lost in a labyrinth of self-doubts. And a man must be the head of his house. They were the heads of their houses, certainly, and they knew what they wanted, and they had their "values." Both of them knew, for instance, that they hated lying about small domestic matters, and tomorrow, or the next hour, would likely find them both berating their wives for having involved them in something that was "against their principles." Henry sighed audibly, took out another cigarette, then put it back in the package. If they but knew how practiced *he* was—without a wife— at lying about small domestic matters! If they knew his skill in that art, they wouldn't be worrying lest he make some *faux pas* at the breakfast table.

Finally, Henry bestirred himself. He crossed the porch and opened the screen door. Passing from the light of out-of-doors into the long, dark hall, which ran straight through the cottage to the back porch, he was reminded of something that had caught his attention when he was leaving Nashville, yesterday afternoon. As he was entering a railroad underpass, he glanced up and saw that there was something scrawled in large black letters high above the entrance. He had driven through this same tunnel countless times in the past, but the writing had never caught his attention before. It was the simple question *Have you had yours*—with the question mark left off. Perhaps it had been put there recently, or it might have been there for years. Some sort of black paint, or perhaps tar, had been used. And it was placed so high on the cement casement and was so crudely lettered that the author must have leaned over from above to do his work. Somehow, as he drove on through the tunnel, Henry had felt tempted to turn around at the other end and go back and read the inscription again, to make sure he had read it correctly. He hadn't turned around, of course, but during the eighty-mile drive to the mountain the words had kept coming back to him. He thought of the trouble and time the author had taken to place his question there. He supposed the author's intention was obscene, that the question referred to fornication. And he had the vague feeling now that the question had turned up in his dreams last night; but he was seldom able to remember his dreams very distinctly. At any rate, the meaning of the question for him seemed very clear when it came back to him now, and it did not refer to fornication. The answer seemed clear, too: *He* had not had *his*. He had not had his what? Why, he had not had his Certainty. That was what the two men had. Neither of the two seemed ideally suited to the variety of it he had got; each of them, early in life, had merely begun acquiring whatever brand of Certainty was most available; and, apparently, if you didn't take that, you took none at all. Professor Dwight Clark was forever depending upon manuals and instruction books. (He even had an instruction book for his little Ford, and with the aid of it could install a new generator.) And Professor Clark had to keep going back to Europe, had literally to see every inch of it in order to believe in it enough to teach his history classes and do his writing. And the judge's garden, while it contained only flowers and combinations of flowers that might have been found in any ante-bellum garden, was so symmetrically, so regularly laid out and so precisely and meticulously cared for that you felt the gardener must surely be some sweet-natured Frankenstein monster. And the decisions that the judge handed down from the bench were famous for their regard for the letter of the law. Lawyers seldom referred to him as "Judge Parker." By his friends he was spoken of as "Mr. Law." Amongst his enemies he was known as "Solomon's Baby." . . . But what was Henry Parker known as? Well, he wasn't much known. He was assistant to the registrar of deeds. He was Judge Parker's son; he was a Democrat, more or less. At the courthouse he was thought awfully well informed—about county government, for one thing. People came to him for information, and took it away with them, thinking it was something Henry Parker would never find any use for. He had passed a variety of civil-service examinations with the highest rating on record, but he had taken the examinations only to see what they were like and what was in them. He did his quiet, pleasant work in his comfortable office on the second floor of the courthouse. The building was well heated in the winter and cool in the summer. Two doors down the corridor from him, Nora McLarnen was usually at her typewriter in the license bureau. Their summers, his and Nora's, were all that made life tolerable. With *his* parents at the mountain, and *her* two sons away at camp, they could go around together with no worry about embarrassing anyone that mattered to them. Their future was a question, a problem they had always vaguely hoped would somehow solve itself. That is, until this summer.

During past summers, Henry had come to the mountain on weekends for the sake of his parents, or for the sake of making sure his mother had no reason to come down to Nashville on an errand or to see about him. But this summer he had come mostly for Nora's sake. Her older boy was now sixteen and had not wanted to go to camp. He had been at home, with a job as lifeguard at one of the public swimming pools. Nora had wanted to devote her weekends to Jimmy. And by now, of course, the younger boy had returned from camp. For Labor Day, Nora had agreed to attend a picnic with the boys and their father—a picnic given by the insurance company for which John McLarnen was a salesman. All summer it had been on Nora's mind that the boys' growing up was going to change things. In the years just ahead they would need her perhaps more than before, and they would become sensitive to her relationship with Henry. She was thinking of quitting her job, she was thinking of letting her husband support her again, she was wondering if she mightn't yet manage to forgive John McLarnen's unfaithfulness to her when she was the mother of two small children, if she hadn't as a younger woman been too intolerant of his coarse nature. She would not, of course, go back to her husband without Henry's consent. But with his consent Henry felt now pretty certain that she would go back to him. They had discussed the possibility several times, very rationally and objectively. They had not quarreled about it, but they seemed to have quarreled about almost everything else this summer. He thought he saw what was ahead.

He was so absorbed in his thoughts as he went down the hall that when he passed the open door to his parents' bedroom he at first gave no thought to the glimpse he had of his father in there. It was only when he was well past the door that he stopped dead still, realizing that his father was on his knees beside the bed. He was not praying, either. He was stuffing something under the mattress. And Henry did not have to look again to know that it was the newspaper he was hiding. He hurried on back to the screened porch, and, somehow, the sight of Dwight, bent over his grapefruit, wearing his traveling clothes—his Dacron suit, his nylon tie, his wash-and-wear shirt—told Henry what it was the judge had to conceal. There would be an article on the society page—something chatty in a column, probably—about those two couples who were driving up to visit the Nathan Parkers, and even a mention of the garden party on Monday.

IV. The Apples of Accord

Kitty was determined that the two children should eat a good breakfast this morning, and she saw to it that they did. Mrs. Parker, who had insisted upon preparing and serving breakfast unassisted, was "up and down" all through the meal. The two women were kept so busy—or kept themselves so busy—that they seemed for the most part unmindful of the men. They took no notice of how long the judge delayed coming to the table, or even that Henry actually appeared before his father did. When everybody had finished his grapefruit, and the men began making conversation amongst themselves, the two wives seemed even not to notice the extraordinarily amiable tone of their husbands' voices or the agreeable nature of their every remark. The only sign Kitty gave of following the conversation was to give a bemused smile or to nod her dark head sometimes when Dwight expressed agreement with her father. And sometimes when the judge responded favorably to an opinion of Dwight's, Mrs. Parker would lift her eyebrows and tilt her head gracefully, as though listening to distant music.

Henry's first impression was that there had not, after all, been a crying need for his presence. His father and his brother-in-law, who a few minutes before had been hiding behind their papers to avoid talking to each other, were now bent upon keeping up a lively and friendly exchange. The judge was seated at his end of the table, with Henry at his left and with Dwight on the other side of Henry at Mrs. Parker's right. Across the table from Henry and Dwight, Kitty sat between the two children.

The first topic, introduced by Dwight, was that of the routing to be followed on his trip. Dwight thought it best to go over to Nashville and then up through Louisville.

"You're absolutely right, Professor," the judge agreed. "When heading for the Midwest, there is no avoiding Kentucky. But keep *off* Kentucky's back roads!"

Henry joined in, suggesting that the Knoxville-Middleboro-Lexington route was "not too bad" nowadays.

"I find the mountain driving more tiring," Dwight said politely, thus disposing of Henry's suggestion.

"And, incidentally, it is exactly a hundred and fifty miles out of your way to go by Knoxville and Middleboro," the judge added, addressing Dwight.

Then, rather quickly, Dwight launched into a description of a rainstorm he had been caught in near Middleboro once. When he had finished, the judge said he supposed there was nothing like being caught in a downpour in the mountains.

But the mention of Knoxville reminded the judge of something he had come across in the morning paper, and his amnesia with regard to his hogging and hiding the first section was so thoroughgoing that he didn't hesitate to speak of what he had read. "There's an editorial today on that agitator up in East Tennessee," he said. "Looks as though they've finally settled his hash, thank God."

"I'm certainly glad," said Dwight. It was the case of the Yankee segregationist who had stirred up so much trouble. Dwight and the judge by no means saw eye to eye on segregation, but here was one development in that controversy that they could agree on. "That judge at Knoxville has shown considerable courage," Dwight said.

"I suppose so. Yes, it's taken courage," said Judge Parker, grudgingly, yet pleased, as always, to hear any favorable comment on the judiciary. "But it is the law of the land. I don't see he had any alternative."

Henry opened his mouth, intending to say that the judge in

question was known to be a man of principle, and if it had gone against his principle, Henry was sure that he would have . . . But he wasn't allowed to finish his thought, even, much less put it into words and speak it.

"Still and all, still and all," his father began again, in the way he had of beginning a sentence before he knew what he was going to say. "Still and all, he's a good man and knows the law. He was a Democrat, you know." His use of "was" indicated only that it was a federal judge they were referring to, and that he was therefore as good as dead—politically, of course.

"No, I didn't know he was a Democrat," Dwight said, hugely gratified.

Here was another topic, indeed. Dwight and the judge were both Democrats, and it didn't matter at the moment that they belonged to different wings of the party. But Dwight postponed for a little the felicity they would enjoy in that area. He had thought of something else that mustn't be passed up. "I understand," he said, pushing the last of his bacon into his mouth and chewing on it rather playfully, "I understand, Judge, that the Catholics have gotten the jump on everybody in Nashville."

The judge closed his eyes, then opened them wide, suppressing a smile—or pretending to. "They've integrated, you mean?"

The machinations of the Catholic Church was a subject they never failed to agree on. "Not only in Nashville," Dwight said. "Everywhere."

"Very altruistic," said the judge.

"Ah, yes. Very."

"If the *other* political parties were as much on their toes as that one, politics in this country would still be interesting."

Henry felt annoyed by this line they always took about the Catholic Church. Perhaps *he* should become a Catholic. That would give him his Certainty, all right. He grimaced inwardly, thinking of the suffering Nora's being a Catholic had brought the two of them. He realized that he resented the slur on the Church merely because the Church was something he associated with Nora. Silly as it seemed, Nora still came in the category of "Nashville Catholics." She was still a communicant, he supposed, and yet this proved that you could be a Catholic without developing the Certainty he had in mind . . . But he didn't try to contribute anything on this subject. He had already seen that contributions from him were not necessary. Perhaps his father and his brother-in-law were no longer consciously trying to keep him silent, but they were in such high spirits over their forthcoming release from each other's company that each now had ears only for the other's voice. And, without knowing it, they seemed to be competing to see who could introduce the most felicitous subject.

From the subject of Nashville Catholics it was such an easy and natural step to Senator Kennedy, and so to national politics, that Henry was hardly aware when the shift came. Everybody had finished eating now. The men had pushed their chairs back a little way from the table. Dwight, in his exuberance, was happily tilting his, though presently Kitty gave him a sign and he stopped. Neither the judge nor Dwight was sure of how good a candidate Kennedy would make. They both really wished that Truman—good old Truman—could head the ticket again. They both admired that man—not for the same reasons, but no matter.

Meanwhile, Kitty and her mother, having finished their own breakfasts and feeling quite comfortable about the way things were going with the men, began a private conversation at their corner of the table. It was about the basket of fruit, which Mrs. Parker still hoped they would find room for in the car. In order to make themselves heard above the men's talk and above the children, who were picking at each other across their mother's plate, it was necessary for them to raise their voices somewhat. Presently, this mere female chatter interfered with the conversation of the men. Judge Parker had just embarked on an account of the Democratic convention of 1928, which he had attended. He meant to draw a parallel between it and the 1960 convention-to-be. But the women's voices distracted him. He stopped his story, leaned forward and took a last sip of his coffee, and said very quietly, "Mother, Dwight and I are having some difficulty understanding each other."

Mrs. Parker blushed. She had thought things were going so well between the two men! How could *she* help them understand each other?

"Is the question of the basket of fruit really so important?" the judge clarified.

Mrs. Parker tried to laugh. Kitty rallied to her support. "It's pretty important," she said good-naturedly.

Henry hated seeing his mother embarrassed. "I imagine it's as important as any other subject," he said.

The judge's eyes blazed. He let his mouth fall open. "Can you please tell me in what sense it is as important as any *other* subject?"

Dwight Clark laughed aloud. Then he looked at Henry and said, unsmiling, "Politics is mere child's play, eh, Henry?" And, tossing his rumpled napkin beside his plate, he said, "Oh, well, we must get going."

"No," said the judge. "Wait. I want to hear Henry's answer to my question."

"I do, too," said Dwight, and he snatched his napkin from the table again as if to prove it.

"We're waiting," said the judge.

"At least theirs is a question that *can* be settled," Henry said, lamely.

"Oh," Dwight rejoined in his most ringing professorial voice, "since we can't, as individuals, settle the problems of the world, we'd best turn ostrich and bury our heads in the sand."

"That won't do, Henry," said Judge Parker. "We're still waiting."

So they *had* needed him, after all, Henry reflected. A common enemy was better than a peacemaker. He understood now that his own meek and mild behavior on the front porch had assured both men that he was not going to spill their beans. And in their eyes, now, he saw that they somehow hated him for it. But, he wondered, why had they thought he might do it, to begin with? Why in the world *should* he? Because he was an old bachelor with no life of his own? He knew that both the men, and the women, too, were bound to have known for years about his love affair with Nora McLarnen. But to themselves, of course, they lied willingly about such a large and unpleasant domestic matter . . . He was an old bachelor without any life of his own! Oh, God, he thought, the realization sweeping over him suddenly that that's how it really would be soon, when he told Nora that she had his consent to go back to John McLarnen. He thought of his office in the courthouse and how it would seem when Nora was no longer behind her typewriter down the corridor. And he realized that the rest of his life with her, the part that had been supposed to mean the most, didn't matter to him at all. He couldn't remember that it *once* had mattered, that *once* the summer nights, when his parents and her children didn't have to be considered, had been all that mattered to him. He couldn't, because the time had come when he couldn't afford to remember it. All along, then, they had been right about him. All his hesitations and discriminations about what one could and could not do with one's life had been mere weakness. What else could it be? He was a bloodless old bachelor. It seemed that all his adult life the blood had been slowly draining out of him, and now the last drop was drained. John McLarnen, who could sell a quarter of a million dollars' worth of life insurance in one year, and whose wife could damned well take him or leave him as he was, was the better man.

While Dwight and the judge waited for him to speak up, Henry sat with a vague smile on his lips, staring at the basket of fruit, which was placed on a little cherry washstand at the far end of the porch. He saw the two children, Susie and her little brother, slip out of their chairs and go over to the washstand. He heard his sister tell them not to finger the fruit. Suddenly he imagined he was seeing the fruit, the peaches and apples and pears, through little Dwight's eyes. How very real it looked.

"The basket of fruit," he said at last, "is a petty, ignoble, woman-ish consideration. And we men must not waste our minds on such." Intuitively, he had chosen the thing to say that would give them their golden opportunity. But before either of the men could speak, he heard his mother say, "Now, Henry," in an exasperated tone, and under her breath.

V. The Juggler

Judge Parker rested his two great white hands limply, incredu-lously on the table. "Henry," he said, "are you attempting to instruct your brother-in-law and me in our domestic relations?" He gazed a moment through the wire screening out into his flower garden. He was thinking that Henry always left himself wide open in an argument. Even Dwight could handle him.

"If that isn't an old bachelor for you," Dwight said, rising from his chair. He wished Henry would wipe the foolish grin off his face. He supposed it was there to hide his disappointment. He had ob-served Henry, all during the meal, trying to work up some antago-nism between his father-in-law and himself—about the roads, about religion, about politics.

The judge was getting up from the table now, too, but he had more to say. "While we discussed all manner of things that you might be expected to know something about, you maintained a profound silence. And then you felt compelled to speak on a subject of which you are profoundly ignorant."

" 'Our universities are riddled with them,' " Dwight said, savoring his joke, feeling that nobody else but Kitty would get it. "Old bachelors who will tell you how you can live on university pay and how to raise your children. I know one, even, that teaches a marriage course."

"*You* might try that, Henry," said the judge. And then he said, "We're only joking, you know. No hard feelings?" He had thought, suddenly, of the extra liquor that Henry was supposed to have brought up from Nashville for the party. Then he remembered that Jane had already asked Henry. It was locked in the trunk of his old coupé.

"Henry knows we're kidding," Dwight said.

Kitty was helping her mother clear the table. Mrs. Parker was protesting, saying that she had nothing else to do all day. Presently, she said to Henry, "Henry, would you take the famous basket of fruit out front? I haven't given up." She *hadn't* given up. How really wonderful it was, Henry thought. And Kitty, too. She could so easily have agreed to take the whole basketful along, could so easily have thrown the whole thing out once they got down the mountain. But it wouldn't have occurred to her.

"Will you gentlemen excuse me?" he said to the two men, smiling at them. And the two men smiled back at him. They felt very good.

When they were all gathered out on the lawn, beside Dwight's car, Kitty looked at her mother and father and said, "It's been a grand summer for us. Just what we needed."

"It's been grand for *us*," Mother Parker said, "though I'm afraid it's spoilt us a good deal. We shouldn't have let you do so much."

"But we hope you'll do it again," Dad Parker said, "whenever you feel up to it."

"I never dreamed I'd get so much done on my book in one summer," said Dwight, really meaning it, but thinking that nobody believed him. He saw that brother Henry was pulling various little trinkets out of his pockets for the children. He had bought them in Nashville, no doubt, and they would be godsends on the trip. Henry knew so well how to please people when he would. He was squatting down between the two children, and he looked up at Dwight to say, "You're lucky to have work you can take all over the world with you."

"Well, I'm sure it requires great powers of concentration," Mother Parker said. She went on to say that she marveled at the way Dwight kept at it and that they were all proud of how high he stood in his field. As she spoke, she held herself very straight, and she seemed almost as tall as her husband. She had had Henry set the basket of fruit on an ivy-covered stump nearby. It was there to plead its own cause. She would not mention it again.

At breakfast, the children had been so excited about setting out for home that Kitty had had to force them to eat. In fact, even the night before, their eagerness to be on the way had been so apparent that Dwight had had to take them aside and warn them against hurting their grandparents' feelings. Yet now, at the last minute, they seemed genuinely reluctant to go. They clung to their uncle, saying they didn't see why they couldn't stay on a few days longer and let him enjoy the tiny tractor, the bag of marbles, and the sewing kit with them. It seemed to Dwight that their Uncle Henry had done his best to ignore the children during all his weekends at the mountain, but now at the last minute he had filled their hands with treasure. And now it was Uncle Henry who was to have their last hugs and to lift little Dwight bodily into the car. When he turned away from the car, with the two children inside it, Henry took Dwight's hand and said, "I'm sorry we never had that chess game. I guess I was afraid you would beat me." It was as if he had seized Dwight and given him the same kind of hug he had given the children. Probably Henry had really wanted to play chess this summer, and probably he had wanted to be affectionate and attentive with the children. But the old bachelor in him had made him hold back. He could not give himself to people, or to anything—not for a whole season.

When finally they had all made their farewell speeches, had kissed and shaken hands and said again what a fine summer it had been, Dwight and Kitty hopped into the little car, and they drove away as quickly as if they had been running into the village on an errand. As they followed the winding driveway down to the public road, Dwight kept glancing at Kitty. He said, "Let's stop in the village and buy a copy of the morning paper."

"Let's not," she said, keeping her eyes straight ahead.

"All right," he said, "let's not." He thought she looked very sad, and he felt almost as though he were taking her away from home for the first time. But the next time he glanced at her, she smiled at him in a way that it seemed she hadn't smiled at him in more than two months. He realized that this summer he had come to think of her again as "having" her father's forehead, as "having" her mother's handsome head of hair and high cheekbones, and as "sharing" her brother's almost perfect teeth, which they were said to have inherited from their maternal grandmother's people. But now suddenly her features seemed entirely her own, borrowed from no one, the features of Dwight Clark's wife. He found himself pressing down on the accelerator, though he knew he would have to stop at the entrance to the road.

In the mirror he saw his two children, in the back seat, still waving to their grandparents through the rear window. Presently, Susie said, "Mama, look at Uncle Henry! Do you see what he's *doing.*" They had reached the entrance to the road now, and Dwight brought the car to a complete halt. Both he and Kitty looked back.

Mother and Dad Parker had already started back into the cottage, but they had stopped on the porch steps and were still waving. Henry was still standing beside the ivy-covered stump where the basket of fruit rested. He had picked up two of the apples and was listlessly juggling them in the air. Dwight asked the children to get out of the way for a moment, and both of them ducked their heads. He wanted to have a good look, to see if Henry was doing it for the children's benefit . . . Clearly he wasn't. He was staring off into space, in the opposite direction, lost in whatever thoughts such a man lost himself in.

Dwight put the car into motion again and turned out of the gravel driveway onto the macadam road, with Kitty and the children still looking back until they reached the point where the thick growth of sumac at the roadside cut off all view of the cottage, and the sweep of green lawn, and the three relatives they had just said goodbye to for a while.

Mrs. Billingsby's Wine

>>>

Shirley Barnes is waiting in Mrs. Billingsby's living room again. This time she is going to see the woman if it means waiting there all afternoon. Shirley lives in one of the new developments out off Summer Avenue, and it isn't often that she gets in to the old part of Memphis, where such well-fixed people as Mrs. Billingsby live. This is the third time she has summoned up the nerve to visit the woman at home, and this time she has come prepared to wait indefinitely. A neighbor is keeping Shirley's two small children, and the meat loaf for supper is already prepared and ready to be popped in the oven.

What healthy-looking houseplants Mrs. Billingsby has! Shirley just can't help wondering who waters them and who sees to setting them out in the sun on good days. They aren't the usual ferns and philodendron. They are unusual plants, which probably require a lot of attention. She can see that the dirt around the grassy-looking thing on the coffee table is rich and rather loose. "Recently repotted and fertilized," she says aloud, quickly putting her fingers over her lips as if to stop herself from speaking again. Then, peering down among the green stalks in a Chinese urn that is on the marble-top

[471]

end table, she observes that there is a plain earthen pot inside the blue and white urn. "Pots within pots," she whispers through her fingers, and she laughs quietly.

Shirley is beginning to feel rather at home in the room. She even notices that the summer slipcovers have been removed from the chairs since her last call, six weeks ago. (On that occasion, she was allowed to wait for ten or fifteen minutes before being told that Mrs. Billingsby was out of town.) No doubt it would be the butler's duty—the one who admitted her and showed her into the living room just now—to remove the slipcovers on a certain date each fall and to replace them on a date in the spring. No, Shirley decides after considerable thought, that would be the downstairs maid's duty, or whoever the girl is who let her in the last time she came—the one who didn't seem to know that Mrs. Billingsby was out of town. The thought of all Mrs. Billingsby's servants makes Shirley smile to herself. Her own neighbors out there off Summer Avenue would not believe that even people in these huge old houses on Belvedere Street still have servants. How much would you suppose she had to pay them per week? Twenty-five dollars, anyway. Altogether, Shirley reckons, Mrs. Billingsby must pay her servants considerably more than her own Granville clears from his dental practice in a month. Poor Granville, with his eight years of expensive education! Where does Mrs. Billingsby find such servants nowadays, with their efficiency and their polite manners? The only kind of help you can get out there off Summer Avenue aren't worth having. It's better to do your own work and save for the future. Shirley reflects that she has never before really seen such servants—not even in Blackwell, where she and Granville grew up and where both Mr. and Mrs. Billingsby came from originally. That's why Shirley is making this call. She and Mrs. Billingsby are old neighbors, and old neighbors should keep in touch. That's a perfect reason to make a call, no matter what Granville says about it.

She returns to the pleasures of speculation. Would it be the butler or the maid who waters the houseplants? Oh, neither! It would be Mrs. Billingsby herself. Now, all at once, she has a clear image of what Mrs. Billingsby, whom she had only glimpses of as a little girl, is like and what her life is like. She would reserve the watering of her luxuriant houseplants as the one domestic task not to be turned over to her servants. When Mr. Billingsby comes home from his office in the afternoon, that's how he finds her, watering the plants in this room or in the other living room across the hall, or perhaps in the dining room behind the other living room. It is just the reverse of what Shirley does, freshening herself up for Granville's homecoming and sitting in the glider as though she hasn't done a lick of work all day. Mr. Billingsby finds Mrs. Billingsby doing the one useful thing she has done all day, and it gives them both great joy. And that's what it is like to be rich.

Rising from her place on the couch, Shirley strolls across the room toward the wide doorway to the hall. Then she strolls back to the window that overlooks the rose garden. It is really strange how much at home she feels! She positively understands what it is like to be Mrs. Billingsby. Yes, she is standing at the window, which has become her own window, overlooking her rose garden, and she has just this minute come in from a bridge luncheon at the Memphis Country Club. Or perhaps she has come in from lunch at Justine's, with two intimate friends. (But is Justine's open for lunch? It doesn't matter.) And they have stopped by the Helen Shop after lunch, or by Seessel's to pick up some avocados and artichokes. The thought of grocerying so casually at Seessel's evokes a giggle from Shirley. She thinks what it would be like if her children were big now and away in an expensive boarding school—no, one should say "prep school"—or even at an Eastern college. She and Granville are Dr. and Mrs. Granville Barnes, of two hundred and something South Belvedere Street, right next door to the elderly George

Billingsbys, with whom they are intimate friends. She envisions a note in one of the society columns that will tell what close friends the two couples are and how they all four began life in the little country town of Blackwell, and even how Mrs. Barnes's and Mrs. Billingsby's families were next-door neighbors there for generations. But it ends there, the newspaper item does, without telling about the ramshackle old cottage Shirley's family lived in, perched right on the sidewalk, or about Mrs. Billingsby's family's big two-story house set so far back in a grove of willow oaks and tulip poplars that in the summertime the two houses weren't visible to each other. None of Mrs. Billingsby's family has really lived in their house since Shirley was born. They went off long ago to Memphis and St. Louis and even Detroit and made or married stacks of money, or went into politics, or became old-maid schoolteachers in exclusive private schools up in Virginia. So far as that family is concerned, the town of Blackwell, Tennessee, could rot! Anyhow, that's what Shirley's mother always said. That family tried to prevent all progress in the town, tried to prevent their putting in street lights and sidewalks even. Shirley's mother once heard Mrs. Billingsby's own mother say, "The only thing Blackwell has left is its natural beauty, and it ought to hold on to that. Otherwise, it's like some poor country girl decked out in a lot of cheap finery." Shirley's old granddaddy, who was a house painter when he wasn't too drunk to hold a brush, always said Mrs. Billingsby's family had never had an eye for anything but money to fill their pockets with. He used to say, "Ever time they seen a dollar they taken after it and they never stopped a-running till they cotched it."

Shirley's dad once owned a little grocery store, but he gave it up to work at the mill—off and on. In the summertime, he would sit on the front porch with his sock feet on the banister rail, and if the subject of Mrs. Billingsby's family came up (in the summertime, some of them would come and stay over there in their house for a few weeks ("just out of sentiment for the place"), her dad, with his feet on the banister rail, would say of them, "Them that has gits."

At the end of a summer, when Shirley and her big brothers were bored and were dreading the opening of school, they would skin over the fence and sometimes manage to get inside that big empty house next door. They would break the glass on a picture frame or two and pull some of the loose wallpaper off the walls in the hall or in the parlor. Shirley could remember the smashed glass on a picture of two old-fashioned-looking gunboats. The boats seemed to be firing pink powder puffs at each other over a body of pale-green water. One year, she told her brothers she would like to have the large orange butterfly that was mounted on cotton under glass in the hall. But when they handed the beautiful thing to her, it turned to powder in her hands. Another year, her brothers stole half the bricks from the old walk going up to the house and sold them to a man who came through town buying up old bricks.

Shirley thinks about the work that lies ahead of her on this autumn afternoon when she has finally found Mrs. Billingsby at home. Mrs. Billingsby will be cold to her on this their first visit together, but Shirley will pretend not to notice. She will leave one of her gloves under the cushion on the couch, and when she returns for it, the very next day perhaps, she will bring Mrs. Billingsby an exotic potted plant like none she has ever seen before. Pretty soon the Billingsbys invite the Barneses to a cocktail party, where they meet practically *everybody*. Then Mrs. Billingsby tells people that Shirley's family and hers were old friends in Blackwell and lived next door to each other for generations. Later, at dinner parties at the Billingsbys', the four of them spend whole evenings reminiscing about old times in Blackwell, and they apologize to other people for boring them with their reminiscences. Then there is an emergency in the middle of the night! Granville gets up and gets dressed and meets Mr. Billingsby at his clinic. Granville relieves Mr. Billingsby's pain and saves the tooth! Not long after that, the Barneses are invited to join the Memphis Country Club, and *every*body begins having Granville as their dentist . . .

By the window overlooking the rose garden, Shirley still stands with her hands folded before her. Suddenly she decides she doesn't really like so many potted plants in a room. It doesn't suit her taste. She saunters casually over to the marble-top end table beside the couch, and her impulse is to remove the big stalky plant there. But she turns away from it. She sees a cut-glass decanter and four glasses on the coffee table. The decanter is half filled with a very dark wine. Shirley shakes her head and says to herself that she doesn't like wine—or doesn't think she does. She glances critically at the stack of magazines and papers lying beside the decanter on the coffee table. She doesn't like magazines and papers lying around in a living room—that much she *knows*. Looking at the end table again, she actually puts out her hand and edges the Chinese urn a little nearer to the center of the table; she experiences a sudden fear that her sleeve may brush against it and knock it off the table and break it. Just as she withdraws her hand, she hears footsteps on the hall stairway. It is Mrs. Billingsby coming down at last. Shirley quickly plops down on the couch. Before her hostess enters, she removes her gloves and sticks one of them underneath the petit-point cushion beside her.

"Now, let me see," says Mrs. Billingsby, extending her hand as she crosses the room to Shirley. "You were the youngest one, weren't you? The one with the dark curls down to her waist."

Shirley rises and offers her hand across the coffee table.

Mrs. Billingsby clasps the hand between her own hands, smiling cordially and peering into Shirley's face. "Yes, it is you," she says. "I do remember your sweet little face. I thought I would if I saw you. Sit down, sit down." She comes round the coffee table and sits beside Shirley on the couch. "I used to catch glimpses of you playing in your yard in the summer, and with your long curls you looked like such an old-fashioned child, so like a little girl from my own generation, that it made me long more than anything else to come back to Blackwell to live."

Shirley finds herself blushing. Why, she *is* going to talk about Blackwell life as though it was something they shared once, as though they really *were* neighbors in the usual, good sense. And what a lovely-looking woman she is, at once so elegant and so natural. Her beautiful hands, now folded in her lap, express the repose and self-assurance that only an elevated mind and spirit can attain. And her blue, blue eyes. How thoroughly you can trust those eyes to see what is best in people and in the world! No wonder one reads in the paper about all the charitable and cultural organizations she heads, and the garden clubs, too, and about her efforts to save the forest trees on North Parkway and the two ante-bellum houses downtown. There is a freshness and vigor about her that make one long to join her and follow her in all her good works. What a joy it is going to be to know her better and better! Even the freshness of her complexion seems good news to Shirley. Mrs. Billingsby really has been napping and is obviously just out of a bath. She has not been trying to deceive Shirley or to postpone their meeting.

"I must tell you at once," she is saying to Shirley now, "how bad I feel about your having to call on *me*. And you've come twice before, you good person you. You came this summer while I was at High Hampton, and you came in the spring when I was so taken up with some silly matters about our old trees in Memphis that I just let all my personal concerns go." As she speaks she bends toward the coffee table and places one hand on the neck of the wine decanter. "But I was not unmindful that you had been here, I want you to know that. Would you join me in a little glass of sherry, or would you rather have coffee? Even before you called the first time, I was not unaware that you and your little family had moved to Memphis. I keep up with the comings and goings of true Blackwellians. Mr. Salisbury still sends me the *Herald* every week. You see, there's a copy there on the table, under those magazines. So many of the names that appear in it now mean nothing to me." She shakes her head sadly. "But a name like Granville Barnes means something. I can assure you, my dear—you're Shirley, aren't you?—I can assure you, my dear Shirley, that it's only because you're a girl still that I left it for you to call on me, instead of myself calling on you." Now she interrupts herself to fill one of the wineglasses and to ask, "Would you much prefer coffee, my dear? You mustn't hesitate to say so if you would."

Shirley is trying to remember what sherry tastes like. Was it sherry or was it claret she had when she and Granville were on their honeymoon in New Orleans? She would give almost anything for a cup of black coffee just now. She frequently has one at this time of day, when Granville is having a highball. Sometimes she has a highball with him, though she is fond of saying it makes her see double and feel single. But she insists to Mrs. Billingsby that a glass of sherry is just what she would like. She accepts the glass, sips it at once, and says, "Ah!"

Shirley thinks it quite beautiful that Mrs. Billingsby has, within the first five minutes, covered all grounds on which her guest might have felt uneasiness. It is how a lady does things, a lady to the manner born. As Mrs. Billingsby goes on to speak of how cold the weather has turned during the past few days, and of winter clothes and of the new hemline and of the *really* best places to shop (Mrs. Billingsby loves Goldsmith's basement and the first floor of Lowenstein's East; she says that any department of any store is only as good as its buyer), Shirley finds her mind going back to the picture glass her brothers broke in Mrs. Billingsby's homeplace, and the butterfly they took from its mounting to give to her, and the mossy bricks they stole from the walk. Oh, why had they been permitted to do that? Suddenly she throws back her head and tosses off her glass of wine.

"And do you and your husband go back to Blackwell often?" she hears Mrs. Billingsby asking.

"The first weekend in every month," Shirley says. "One month we stay with my family, and the next with yours—with Granville's, I mean." How *could* she have made that senseless slip of the tongue? It is because she is so used to talking with Granville, and with no one else, about Blackwell. Or could it be the wine?

"I find it depressing to go back nowadays," says Mrs. Billingsby. She insists on filling Shirley's glass again.

"That's only because none of your family is still there."

"Yes, I suppose so," Mrs. Billingsby consents, with doubt in her voice. "We've all been gone a long time, and it has changed a great deal. There is no social life there of the sort there once was. When I was a girl, Blackwell was such a very gay little place. Yet no parties, I suppose, ever seem as good to anyone as those one went to as a girl."

"That's certainly true," Shirley says. She feels she has spoken too loud and tries to lower her voice. "Granville and I sometimes talk whole evenings away about parties we went to in Blackwell." She knows she should not keep referring to Granville. Mrs. Billingsby has not made one reference to Mr. Billingsby.

"When I was a girl, young people came from all over West and Middle Tennessee to our parties. During the summer, at the time of the June German, every house was full of young lady house guests and young men, too."

Shirley looks at Mrs. Billingsby, not able to imagine what the June German was. She and Granville can never forget the high-school dances of their era, but there were rarely house guests from other towns. Other towns had their own high-school dances. There never seemed any need to import anybody.

As if in response to something, Mrs. Billingsby says, "No doubt it had all changed by the time you came along."

"The first dance I ever went to," Shirley says with enthusiasm, "was in the New Gym at the high school. The New Gym was built in our freshman year—Granville's and mine. Goodness, we had a grand time!"

"You and your husband were in the same class, then?"

"Oh, yes, we went all through school and college together."

"You can't imagine how strange that sounds to the ears of someone of my generation. Mr. Billingsby is nearly ten years older than I. Though we lived within a mile of each other, I didn't really know him till I came back from my year at Miss Merriwether's School."

In a sudden burst of frankness, Shirley says, "Granville and I both worked our way through college, and I worked while he got through dental school. He tells people that I *put* him through, but of course he exaggerates." She is on the verge of confiding in Mrs. Billingsby how hard those years were. But she bites her tongue and tries to think of something else to say. Nothing she thinks of seems appropriate.

"I envy you girls who went to college," Mrs. Billingsby says humbly. "My mother wished to send me and my sister to college, but Father was afraid of what we just might learn there!"

"Still," says Shirley, wondering if her talk of college might have sounded like boasting, "your boarding schools in those days were much better than our high schools today."

"Ah, far better," Mrs. Billingsby agrees—too quickly, it seems to Shirley. "And I don't complain of not going to college, really. Our education prepared us very well indeed. For life, for the good life as it used to be lived in Blackwell. It makes me heartsick to go back and see how it has all changed there. It was a dear old town, with giant trees meeting over the streets, with handsome lawns and superb flower gardens. Even the public square was a charming place before they built that modernistic courthouse in the thirties and ripped down all the coverings over the sidewalks in front of the stores."

Shirley tries to imagine the square with the old courthouse and the sidewalk covers. She tries in vain. Presently she sips at her wine. Then she empties the glass. The room seems to have grown very warm.

"On the hottest day," continues Mrs. Billingsby, "you could walk in shade under those coverings all around the square. And no man spoke to you unless you spoke to him first. But think what it's like now. It's all sun and noise on a summer afternoon. I was there one day this summer. It was incredible. Young girls and boys racing about the sidewalks shouting to each other. And women my age down there on the square in shorts and halters!" (Shirley manages to whisper, "No!") "You couldn't cross the street without one of the young people in a little foreign car—in Blackwell!—blowing a horn at you. They took down those sidewalk coverings I don't know how many years ago, and now the stores—chain stores all of them, of course—have huge, bright-colored plastic fronts to them. It is a blinding spectacle, the square in Blackwell is today! Really ghastly!"

A powerful wave of nostalgia has suddenly swept over Shirley—a nostalgia for the blinding spectacle of Blackwell's public square. She can only remember it the way Mrs. Billingsby has described it in its latter-day, fallen state. That is the way she must think of it. That is the way, she realizes, she *wants* to think of it. It is *her* home town—hers and Granville's. The other town, the old town Mrs. Billingsby described, never existed for her. It probably never existed for her parents, either, she reflects. Who would recognize any town in which only a few of the girls and boys went to parties, so few that they had to invite girls and boys from other towns in order to make it any fun? In their day—hers and Granville's—nobody cared whether the people who came to a party lived on the Mill Hill or on Church Street, whether you lived in one of the big houses set back amid trees or in a ramshackle little place like her dad's. On a Saturday afternoon, she and a bunch of girls would ride around the square in an open roadster while boys called outrageous things to them from other cars or from the uncovered sidewalks. She *loved* the way the square looked as she knew it, without any trees on the courthouse lawn, without any coverings over the sidewalks, and with the bright false fronts to the old stores. That was girlhood. That was when there had been no scraping together dollars to pay fees at the College of Dentistry. That was when there was no scrimping to make time payments on the furniture for the baby's room.

Now she realizes that Mrs. Billingsby's reflections upon Blackwell have somehow wounded her. She eyes the empty glass in her hand and gently sets it on the coffee table. She knows that she must conceal the hurt she feels. And so she does what she knows Granville would say she ought to do—she changes the subject. And as she does so, without being fully conscious of her purpose, she rises from the couch. She is going to leave.

On her feet, she feels a little dizzy. But her speech is clear and firm, giving no evidence of her physical sensations. "Well," she says, "Blackwell is Blackwell, but Granville and I already like Memphis. In fact, we like it very, very much."

"Even Memphis has changed, though," Mrs. Billingsby replies at once, not rising. "It soon won't be the same city—not the city Mr. Billingsby and I came to forty years ago. They're cutting down our trees to make way for superhighways and pulling down famous old mansions to make way for the high-rise apartments and office buildings."

For a moment Shirley hesitates. She is trying to push out thoughts of the smashed picture glass and the stolen bricks. There is the feel of the dry, powdery butterfly between her fingers. She waits until Mrs. Billingsby has risen and has said "Must you go so soon?" before she speaks. About Memphis she feels perfectly free to take her stand. "Oh, most of the things they're doing we like," she says. "The new buildings they're putting up are beautiful, we think. And Granville says we're away ahead of most cities in planning for traffic. It is an exciting place to live. Memphis is a wonderful city, Mrs. Billingsby."

Mrs. Billingsby has risen from the couch now and she follows Shirley across the room. In the wide doorway to the hall, she stops and says with a smile, "I'm glad you like Memphis. I can't altogether agree with you about it, but I'm glad you like it. Anyway, we both love Blackwell, don't we?" Standing in the doorway, she looks older—an old lady.

"Yes, we both love Blackwell, Mrs. Billingsby," says Shirley.

"I'm sorry you must go so soon. And I'm sorry I kept you waiting so."

"I just wanted to say hello," Shirley says. Then, suddenly blushing, she adds, "But I believe I've dropped one of my gloves."

"Really?" says Mrs. Billingsby. "I didn't . . ."

Shirley hurries across the room and pulls the glove from under the cushion. "It was on the divan," she says, holding it up for Mrs. Billingsby to see.

Je Suis Perdu

***

L'Allegro

The sound of their laughter came to him along the narrow passage that split the apartment in two. It was the laughter of his wife and his little daughter, and he could tell they were laughing at something the baby had done or had tried to say. Shutting off the water in the washbasin, he cracked the door and listened. There was simply no mistaking a certain note in the little girl's giggles. Her naturally deep little voice could never be brought to such a high pitch except by her baby brother's "being funny." And on such a day as this, the day for packing the last suitcases and for setting the furnished apartment in order, the day before the day when they would really pull up stakes in Paris and take the boat train for Cherbourg—on such a day, only the baby could evoke from its mother that resonant, relaxed, almost abandoned kind of laughter . . . *They* were in the dining room just sitting down to breakfast. *He* had eaten when he got up with the baby an hour before, and was now in the *salle de bain* preparing to shave.

[484]

The *salle de bain,* which was at one end of the long central passage, was the only room in the apartment that always went by its French name. For good reason, too: it lacked the one all-important convenience that an American expects of what he will willingly call a bathroom. It possessed a bathtub and a washbasin, and it had a bidet, which was wonderful for washing the baby in. But the missing convenience was in a closet close by the entrance to the apartment, at the very opposite end of the passage from the *salle de bain.* Altogether it was a devilish arrangement. But the separation of conveniences was not itself so devilish as the particular location of each. For instance just now, with only a towel wrapped around his middle and with his face already lathered, he hesitated to throw open the door and take part in a long-distance conversation with the rest of the family, because at any moment he expected to hear the maid's key rattling in the old-fashioned lock of the entry door down the passage. Instead, he had to remain inside the *salle de bain* with his hand on the doorknob and his gaze on the blank washbasin mirror (still misted over from the hot bath he had just got out of); had to stand there and be content merely with hearing the sound of merriment in yonder, not able—no matter how hard he strained—to determine the precise cause of it.

At last, he could resist no longer. He pushed the door half open and called out to them, "What is it? What's the baby up to?"

His daughter's voice piped from the dining room, "Come see, Daddy! Come see him!" And in the next instant she had bounced out of the dining room into the passage, and she continued bouncing up and down there as if she were on a pogo stick. She was a tall little girl for her seven years, and she looked positively lanky in her straight white nightgown and with her yellow hair not yet combed this morning but drawn roughly into a ponytail high on the back of her head.

And then his wife's voice: "It's incredible, honey! You really must come! And quick, before he stops! He's a perfect little monkey!"

But already it was too late. The maid's key rattled noisily in the lock. As he quickly stepped backward into the *salle de bain* and pulled the door to, he called to them in a stage whisper, "Bring me my bathrobe."

Through the door he heard his wife's answer: "You know your bathrobe's packed. You said you wouldn't need it again. Put on your clothes."

His trousers and his shirt and underwear hung on one door hook, beside his pajamas on another. His first impulse was to slip into his clothes and go and see what it was the baby was doing. But on second thought there seemed too many arguments against this. His face was already lathered. He much, much preferred shaving as he now was, wearing only his towel. But still more compelling was the argument that it was to be a very special shave this morning. *This morning the mustache was going to go!*

Months back he had made a secret pact with himself to the effect that if the work he came over here to do was really finished when the year was up, then the mustache he had begun growing the day he arrived would *go* the day he left. From the beginning his wife had pretended to loathe it, though he knew she rather favored the idea as long as they were here, and only dreaded, as he did, the prospect of his going home with that brush on his upper lip. But he had not even mentioned the possibility of shaving the mustache. And as he wiped the mist from the mirror and then slipped a fresh blade into his razor, he smiled in anticipation of the carrying on there would be over its removal.

In the passage now there was the clacking sound of the maid's footsteps. He could hear her taking all her usual steps—putting away the milk and bread that she had picked up on her way to work, crossing to the cloak closet, and placing her worn suede jacket and her silk scarf on a hanger—just as though this were not her last day on the job; or rather, last day with *them* in the apartment, because she was coming the following day, faithful and obliging soul, to wax the floors and hang the clean curtains she herself had washed. Their blessed, hardworking Marie. According to his wife, their having had Marie constituted their greatest luck and their greatest luxury this year. He scarcely ever saw her himself, and sometimes he had passed her down on the boulevard without recognizing her until, belatedly, he realized that it had been her scarf and her jacket, and his baby in the carriage she pushed. But he had gradually assumed his wife's view that their getting hold of Marie had been the real pinnacle of all their good luck about living arrangements. Their apartment was a fourth-floor walkup, over-looking the Boulevard Saint-Michel and just two doors from the rue des Écoles; with its genuine *chauffage central* and its Swedish kitchen, and even a study for him. It was everything they could have wished for. At first they had thought they ought not to afford such an apartment as this one, but because of the children they decided it was worth the price to them. And after his work on the book got off to a good start and he saw that the first draft would almost certainly get finished this year, they decided that it would be a shame not to make the most of the year; that is, not to have some degree of freedom from housekeeping and looking after the children. And so they spoke to the concierge, who recommended Marie to them, saying that she was a mature woman who knew what it was to work but who might have to be forgiven a good deal of ignorance since she had not lived always in Paris. They had found nothing to forgive in Marie. Even her haggard appearance his wife had come to speak of as her "ascetic look." Even her reluctance to try to under-stand a single word of English represented, as did the noisy rattling of the door key, her extreme consideration for their privacy. Every morning at half-past eight, her key rattled in the lock to their door.

She was with them all day, sometimes taking the children to the park, always going out to do more marketing, never off her feet, never idle a moment until she had prepared their evening meal and left them, to ride the Métro across Paris again—almost to Saint-Denis—and prepare another evening meal for her own husband and son.

Yet this maid of theirs was, in his mind, only a symbol of how they had been served this year. It was hard to think of anything that had not worked out in their favor. They had ended by even liking their landlady, who, although she lived but a block away up the Boulevard Saint-Michel, had been no bother to them whatever, and had just yesterday actually returned the full amount of their deposit on the furniture. Their luck had, of course, been phenomenal. After one week in the Hôtel des Saints-Pères, someone there had told them about M. Pavlushkoff, "the honest real-estate agent." They had put their problem in the hands of this splendid White Russian—this amiable, honest, intelligent, efficient man, with his office (to signalize his greatest virtue, his sensibility) in the beautiful Place des Vosges. Once M. Pavlushkoff had found them their apartment they never saw him again, but periodically he would telephone them to inquire if all went well and if he could assist them in any way. And once in a desperate hour—near midnight—they telephoned him, to ask for the name of a doctor. In less than half an hour M. Pavlushkoff had sent dear old Dr. Marceau to them.

And Dr. Marceau himself had been another of their angels. The concierge had fetched round another doctor for them the previous afternoon, and he had made the little girl's ailment out to be something very grave and mysterious. He had prescribed some kind of febrifuge and the burning of eucalyptus leaves in her room. But Dr. Marceau immediately diagnosed measles (which they had believed it to be all along, with half her class at L'École Père Castor already out of school with it). Next day, Dr. Marceau had returned to give the baby an injection that made the little fellow's case a light one; and later on he saw them through the children's siege of chicken pox. Both the children were completely charmed by the old doctor. Even on that first visit, when the little girl had not yet taken possession of the French language, she found the doctor irresistible. He had bent over her and listened to her heart not through a stethoscope but with only a piece of Kleenex spread out between her bare chest and his big pink ear. As he listened, sticking the top of his bald head directly in her face, he quite unintentionally tickled her nose with the pretty ruffle of white hair that ringed his pate. Instantly the little girl's eyes met her mother's. From her sickbed she burst into giggles and came near to causing her mother to do the same. After that, whenever the doctor came to see her, or to see her little brother, she would insist upon his listening to her heart. It would be hard to say whether Dr. Marceau was ever aware of why the little girl giggled, but he always said in French that she had the heart of a lioness, and he always stopped and kissed her on the forehead when he was leaving.

That's what the whole year had been like. There was *that,* and there had been the project—the work on his book, which was about certain Confederate statesmen and agents who, with their families, were in Paris at the end of the Civil War, and who had to decide whether to go home and live under the new regime or remain permanently in Europe.

As far as his research was concerned, he had soon found that there was nothing to be got hold of at the Bibliothèque Nationale or anywhere else in Paris that was not available at home. And yet how stimulating to his imagination it was just to walk along the rue de l'Université in the late afternoon, or along the rue de Varenne, or over on the other side of the Seine along the rue de Rivoli and the rue Saint-Antoine, hunting out the old addresses of the people he was writing about. And of course how stimulating to his work it was just being in Paris, no matter what his subject. Certain of his cronies back home at the university had accused him of selecting his subject merely as an excuse to come to Paris . . . He couldn't be sure himself what part that had played in it. But it didn't matter. *He had had the idea, and he had done the work.*

With his face smoothly shaven, and dressed in his clean clothes, he was in such gay spirits that he was tempted to go into the dining room and announce that he was dedicating this book to M. Pavlushkoff, to Dr. Marceau, to Marie, to all his French collaborators.

He found the family in the dining room, still lingering over breakfast, the little girl still in her nightgown, his wife in her nylon housecoat. At sight of his naked upper lip his wife's face lit up. Without rising from her chair, she threw out her arms, saying, *"I must have the first kiss! How beautiful you are!"*

The little girl burst into laughter again. "Mama!" she exclaimed. "Don't *say* that! *Men* aren't beautiful, *are* they, Daddy?" She still had not noticed that the mustache was gone.

It was only a token kiss he got from his wife. She was afraid that Marie might come in at any moment to take their breakfast dishes. Keeping her eyes on the door to the passage, she began pushing him away almost before their lips met. And so he turned to his daughter, trying to give her a kiss. Still she hadn't grasped what had brought on her parents' foolishness, and she wriggled away from him and out of her chair, laughing and fairly shrieking out, "What's the matter with him, Mama?"

"Just look!" whispered his wife; and at first he thought of course she meant look at him. "Look at the baby, for heaven's sake," she said.

The baby was in his playpen in the corner of the dining room. With his hands clasped on the top of his head and his fat little legs stuck out before him, he was using his heels to turn himself round and round, pivoting on his bottom.

"How remarkable!" the baby's daddy now heard himself saying.

"Watch his eyes," said the mother. "Watch how he rolls them."

"Why, he *is* rolling them! How really remarkable!" He glanced joyfully at his wife.

"That's only the half of it," she said. "In a minute he'll begin going around the other way and rolling his eyes in the other direction."

"It's amazing," he said, speaking very earnestly and staring at the baby. "He already has better coordination than I've *ever* had or ever *hope* to have. I've noticed it in other things he's done recently. What a lucky break!"

And presently the baby, having made three complete turns to the right, did begin revolving the other way round and rolling his eyes in the other direction. The two parents and the little girl were laughing together now and exchanging intermittent glances in order to share the moment fully. The most comical aspect of it was the serious expression on the baby's face, particularly at the moment when, facing them and stopping quite still, he shifted the direction of his eye rolling. At this moment the little girl's voice moved up at least one octave. She never showed any natural jealousy of her baby brother, but at such times as this she often seemed to be determined to outdo her parents in their amusement and in their admiration of the baby. Just now she was so convulsed with laughter that she staggered back to her chair and threw herself into it and leaned against the table. As she did so, one of her flailing hands struck her milk glass, which was still half full. The milk poured out over the placemat and then traced little white rivulets over the dark surface of the table.

Both parents pounced upon the child at once: "Honey! Honey! Watch out! Watch what you're doing!"

The little girl crimsoned. Her lips trembled as she said under her breath, *"Je regrette."*

"If you had drunk your milk this wouldn't have happened," said the mother, dabbing at the milk with a paper napkin.

"Regardless of that," said the father with unusual severity in his voice, "she has no business throwing herself about so and going into such paroxysms over nothing." But he knew, really, that it was not the threshing about that irritated him so much as it was the lapse into French. And it was almost as though his wife understood this and wished to point it out. For, discovering that a few drops of milk had trickled down one table leg and onto the carpet, she turned and herself called out in French to the maid to come and bring a cloth. His own mastery of French speech, he reflected, was the thing that *hadn't* gone well this year. After all, as he was in the habit of telling himself, *he* hadn't had the opportunity to converse with Marie a large part of each day, or to attend a primary school where the teacher and the other pupils spoke no English, and he hadn't—with his responsibilities to his work and his family—been able to hang about the cafés like some student. It was a consoling thought. Righteously, he put aside his irritation.

But now his little daughter, sitting erect in her chair, repeated aloud: *"Je regrette. Je regrette."* This time it affected him differently. It was impossible to tell whether she was using the French phrase deliberately or whether she wasn't even aware of doing so. But whether deliberate or not, it had its effect on her father. For a time it caused him to stare at his daughter with the same kind of interest that he had watched his son with a few moments before. And all the while his mind was busily tying the present incident to one that had occurred several weeks before. He had taken the little girl to see an old Charlie Chaplin film one afternoon at a little movie theater around the corner from them on the rue des Écoles. They had stayed on after the feature to see the newsreel, and then after the newsreel, along with a fairly large proportion of the audience, they had risen in the dark to make their way out. The ushers at the rear of the theater were not able to restrain the crowd that was waiting for seats; and so there was the inevitable melee in the aisles. When finally he came out into the lighted lobby he assumed that his little girl was still sticking close behind him, and he began getting into his mackinaw without even looking back to see that she was there. Yes, it was thoughtless of him, all right; but it was what he had done. As he tugged at the belt of the bulky mackinaw, he became aware of a small voice crying out above the noise of the canned music back in the theater. What interested him first was merely the fact that he did understand the cry: *"Je suis perdu! Je suis perdu!"* Actually he didn't recognize it as his daughter's voice until rather casually and quite by chance he glanced behind him and saw that she was not there. He threw himself against the crowd that was still emerging from the exit, all the while mumbling apologies to them in his Tennessee French which he was sure they would not understand (though himself understanding perfectly their oaths and expletives) and still hearing from the darkness ahead her repeated cry: *"Je suis perdu!"* When he found her she was standing against the side wall of the theater, perfectly rigid. Reaching down in the darkness to take her hand he found her hand made into a tight little fist. By the time he got her out into the light of the lobby her hand in his felt quite relaxed. Along the way she had begun to cry a little, but already she was smiling at him through her tears. "I thought I was lost, Daddy," she said to him. He had been so relieved at finding her and at seeing her smiling so soon that he had not even tried to explain how it had happened, much less describe the chilling sensations that had been his at that moment when he realized it was the voice of his own child calling out to him, in French, that she was lost.

Now, in the dining room of their apartment, he was looking into the same flushed little face and suddenly he saw that the eyelashes were wet with tears. He was overcome with shame.

His wife must have discovered the tears at the same moment. He glanced at her and saw that she, too, was now filled with pity for the child and was probably thinking, as he was, that they were all of them keyed up this morning of their last day before starting home.

"Oh, it's all right, sweetie," said his wife, putting her hand on the top of the blond little head and pointing out the milk to Marie. "Accidents will happen."

Squatting down beside his daughter, he said, "Don't you notice anything different?" And he stuck his forefinger across his upper lip.

"Oh, Mama, it's gone!" she squealed. Placing her two little hands on his shoulders, she bent forward and kissed him on the mouth. "Mama, you're right," she exclaimed. "He *is* beautiful!"

After that, the spilled milk and the baby's gyrations were events of ancient history—dismissed and utterly forgotten.

A few minutes later, the little girl and Marie were beside the playpen chattering to the baby in French. His wife had wandered off into the bedroom, where she would dress and then throw herself into a final fury of packing. She had already asked him to make himself scarce this day, to keep out of the way of women's work. *His* duties, she had said, would begin when it came time to leave for the boat train tomorrow morning. Now he followed her into the bedroom to put on a tie and a jacket before setting out on his day's expedition.

She had taken off her housecoat and was standing in her slip before the big armoire, searching there among the few dresses that hadn't already been packed for something she might wear today. He stopped in front of the mirror above the chest of drawers and began slipping a tie into his collar. He was thinking of just how he would spend his last day. Not, certainly, with any of his acquaintances. He had said goodbye to everyone he wanted to say goodbye to. No, he would enjoy the luxury of being by himself, of buying a paper and reading it over coffee somewhere, of wandering perhaps one more time through the Luxembourg Gardens—the wonderful luxury of walking in Paris on a June day without purpose or direction.

When he had finished with his tie, he discovered that his wife was now watching his face in the mirror. She was smiling, and as their eyes met she said, "I'm glad you shaved it but I shall miss it a little, along with everything else." And before she began pulling her dress over her head she blew him a kiss.

Il Penseroso

The feeling came over him in the Luxembourg Gardens at the very moment he was passing the Medici Grotto at the end of its little lagoon. He simply could not imagine what it was that had been able to depress his spirits so devastatingly on a day that had begun so well. Looking back at the grotto, he wanted to think that his depression had been induced by the ugliness and the triteness of the sculpture about the fountain there, but he knew that the fountain had nothing to do with it. He was so eager to dispel this sudden gloom and return to his earlier mood, however, that he turned to walk back to the spot and see what else might have struck his eye. Above all, it was important for it to be something outside himself that had crushed his fine spirits this way, and that was thus threatening to spoil his day.

He didn't actually return to the spot, but he did linger a moment by the corner of the palace, beside a flower bed where two workmen—surreptitiously, it seemed to him—were sinking little clay pots of already blooming geranium plants into the black soil, trying to make it look as though the plants honestly grew and bloomed there. From here he eyed other strollers along the path and beside the lagoon, hoping to discover in one of them something tragic or pathetic which he might hold responsible for the change he had felt come over him. He would have much preferred finding an object, something not human, to pin it on, but, that failing, he was now willing to settle for any unhappy or unpleasant-looking person—a stranger, of course, someone who had no claim of any kind on him. But every child and its nurse, each shabby student with satchel and notebooks, every old gentleman or old lady waiting for his terrier or her poodle to perform in the center of the footpath appeared relatively happy (in their limited French way, of course, he found himself thinking)—as happy, almost, as he must have appeared not five minutes earlier. He even tried looking farther back on the path toward the gate into the rue de Vaugirard, but it availed him nothing. Then his thoughts took him beyond the gate, and he remembered the miserable twenty minutes he had just been forced to spend trying to read his paper and enjoy his coffee in the Café Tournon, while a bearded fellow American explained to him what was wrong with their country and why Americans were "universally unpopular" abroad.

But even this wouldn't do. For he was as used to the ubiquitous bearded American and his café explanations of everything as he was to the ugly Italian grotto; and he disliked them to just the same degree and found them equally incapable of disturbing him in this way. He gave up the search now, and as he strode out into the brightness of the big sunken garden he quietly conceded the truth of the matter: the feeling was not evoked by his surroundings at all but had sprung from something inside himself. Further, it was not worth all this searching; it wasn't important; it would pass soon. Why, as soon as it had run its course with him he would not even remember the feeling again until . . . until it would come upon him again in the same unreasonable way, perhaps in six months, or in a few days, or in a year. When the mood was not on him, he could never believe in it. For instance, while he had been shaving this morning he truly did not know or, rather, he *knew not* that he was ever in his life subject to such fits of melancholy and gloom . . . But still the mood *was* on him now. And actually he understood the source well enough.

It sprang from the same thing his earlier cheerful mood had come from—his own consciousness of how well everything had gone for him this year, and last year, and always, really. It was precisely this, he told himself, that depressed him. At the present moment he could almost wish that he hadn't finished the work on his book. He was able to wish this (or almost wish it) because he knew it was so typical of him to have accomplished just precisely what he had come to accomplish—and so American of him. Generally speaking, he didn't dislike being himself or being American, but to recognize that he was so definitely the man he was, so definitely the combination he was, and that certain experiences and accomplishments were now typical of him was to recognize how he was getting along in the world and how the time was moving by. He was only thirty-eight. But the bad thought was that he was no longer *going to be* this or that. He *was.* It was a matter of *being.* And to *be* meant, or seemed to mean at such a moment, to *be over with.* Yet this, too, was a tiresome, recurrent thought of his—very literary, he considered it, and a platitude.

He went on with his walk. The Jardin du Luxembourg was perfection this morning, with its own special kind of sky and air and its wall of flat-topped chestnuts with their own delicate shade of green foliage, and he tried to feel guilty about his wife's being stuck back there in the apartment, packing their possessions, trying to fit everything that had not gone into the foot lockers and the duffel-bags into six small pieces of luggage. But the guiltiness he tried for wouldn't materialize. Instead, he had a nasty little feeling of envy at her packing. And so he had to return to his efforts at delighting in the singular charm of the park on a day like this. "There is nothing else like it in Paris," he said, moving his lips, "which is to say there is nothing else like it in the world." And this pleased him just as long as it took for his lips to form the words.

It wasn't yet midmorning, but the little boys—both the ragged and the absurdly over-dressed-up ones—had already formed their circle about the boat basin in the center, and, balancing themselves on the masonry there, were sending their sailboats out over the bright water. This was almost a cheering sight to him. But not quite. For it was, after all, a regular seasonal feature of the place, like the puppet shows and the potted palm trees, and it was hardly less artificial in its effect.

He was rounding the lower garden of the park now; had passed the steps that led up toward the Boulevard Saint-Michel entrance and toward that overpowering monster the Panthéon. (There were monsters and monstrous things everywhere he turned now.) He was walking just below the clumsy balustrade of the upper garden; and now, across the boat basin, across the potted flower beds and the potted palms, above the heads of the fun-loving, freedom-loving, stiff-necked, and pallid-faced Parisians, he saw the façade of the old palace itself. It also loomed large and menacing. There was no look of fun or freedom about it. It did not smile down upon the garden. Rather, out of that pile of ponderous, dirty stone, all speckled with pigeon droppings, twenty eyes glared at him over the iron fencing, which seemed surely to have been put there to protect the people from the monster—not the monster from the people. It was those vast, terrible, blank windows, like the whitened eyes of a blind horse, that made the building hideous. How could anyone ever have found it a thing of beauty? How could . . . Then suddenly: "Oh, do stop it!" he said to himself. But he couldn't stop it. Wasn't it

from one of those awful windows that the great David, as a prisoner
of the Revolution, had painted his only landscape? That unpleasant
man David, that future emperor of art, that personification of the
final dead end to a long-dying tradition! "Oh, do stop it!" he said
again to himself. "Can't you stop it?"

But still he couldn't. The palace *was* a tomb. The park was a
formal cemetery. He was where everything was finished and over
with. Too much had already happened here, and whatever else
might come would be only anticlimactic. And nothing could be so
anticlimactic as an American living on the left bank of the Seine
and taking a morning walk in the Jardin du Luxembourg. He
remembered two novels whose first chapters took for their setting
this very spot. Nothing was so deadening to a place as literature!
And wasn't it true, after all, that their year in that fourth-floor
walkup had been a dismal, lonely one? Regardless of his having got
his work done, of his having had his afternoons free to wander not
only through the streets where his heroes had once lived but also
through the Louvre and the Musée Cluny and through the old
crumbling *hôtels* of the Marais? Regardless of the friends they had
made and even of the occasional gay evening on the town. Wasn't it
really so that he had just not been willing to admit this truth until
this moment? Wasn't it so, really, that he had come to Paris too
late? That this was a city for the very young and the very rich, and
that he, being neither, might as well not have come? What was he
but a poor plodding fellow approaching middle age, doing all right,
getting along with his work well enough, providing for his family;
and the years were moving by . . .

Suddenly he turned his back on the boat basin and the palace, and
started at a brisk pace up the ramp that leads toward the great
gilded south gate. And immediately he saw his daughter in the
crowd! She was moving toward him, walking under the trees.

He saw her before she saw him. This gave him time to gather his wits, and to recall that his wife, as soon as she got *him* out of the apartment, was determined to get *them* out, too, so that there would be no one to interfere with her packing. And now, during the moment that *she* did not see him, he managed to find something that he could be cross with her about. She was ambling along, absent-mindedly leaning on the baby's carriage—that *awful* habit of hers—and making it all but impossible for Marie to push the carriage. She had come out from under the trees now, and as she skipped and danced along, her two bouncing blond ponytails, which Marie had fixed, one directly above each ear, were literally dazzling in the sunlight. "Daddy," she said, as she came within his shadow on the gravel path. Her eyes were just exactly the color of the park's own blue heaven. His wife's mother had said it didn't seem quite normal for a girl to have such "positive blue" eyes. And her long little face with the chin just a tiny bit crooked, like his own!

He took her hand, and they went down the ramp toward the row of chairs on their left. "If we sit down, you'll have to pay," she warned him.

"That's all right," he said.

"I'll sit on your lap if you'll give me the ten francs for the extra chair."

"And if I won't?"

"Oh, I'll sit on your lap anyway, since you've shaved that mustache."

The old woman who collected for chairs was hot on their heels. He paid for the single chair and tipped her the price of another.

"I saw how much you gave her," his daughter said reproachfully. "But it's all right. She's one of the nice ones."

"Oh, they're all nice when you get to know them," he said, laughing.

She nodded. "And isn't it a lovely park, Daddy? I think it is."

"It's too bad we're going home so soon, isn't it?" he said.

"Daddy, we just *got* here!" she protested.

"I mean going back to America, silly," he said.

"I thought you meant to the apartment . . . But we're *not* going back to America *today*."

"No, but tomorrow."

"Well, what difference does *that* make?"

He saw Marie approaching with the carriage. "Let's give our chair to Marie, since I have to be on my way," he said.

"Then you have to leave now?" she asked forlornly.

He gave her a big squeeze with his arms and held her a moment longer on his knee. He was wondering where his dark mood had gone. It was not just gone. He felt it had never been. And why had he lied to himself about this year? It *had* been a fine year. But still he kept thinking also of how she had interrupted his mood. And as soon as she was off his knee, he began to feel resentful again of the interruption and of the mysterious power she had over him. He found that he wanted the mood of despondency to return, and he knew it wouldn't for a long while. It was something she had taken from him, something she had taken from him before and would take from him again and again—she and the little fellow in the carriage there, and their mother, too, even before they were born. They would never allow him to have it for days and days at a time, as he once did. He felt he had been cheated. But this was not a mood, it was only a thought. He felt a great loss—except he didn't really feel it, he only thought of it. And he felt, he *knew* that he had after all gotten to Paris too late . . . after he had already established steady habits of work . . . after he had acknowledged claims that others had on him . . . after there were ideas and truths and work and people that he loved better even than himself.

Miss Leonora When Last Seen

▼▼▼▼▼▼▼▼▼▼▼▼▼▼▼▼▼▼▼▼

I

Here in Thomasville we are all concerned over the whereabouts of Miss Leonora Logan. She has been missing for two weeks, and though a half dozen postcards have been received from her, stating that she is in good health and that no anxiety should be felt for her safety, still the whole town can talk of nothing else. She was last seen in Thomasville heading south on Logan Lane, which is the narrow little street that runs alongside her family property. At four-thirty on Wednesday afternoon—Wednesday before last, that is to say—she turned out of the dirt driveway that comes down from her house and drove south on the lane toward its intersection with the bypass of the Memphis-Chattanooga highway. She has not been seen since. Officially, she is away from home on a little trip. Unofficially, in the minds of the townspeople, she is a missing person, and because of events leading up to her departure none of us will rest easy until we know that the old lady is safe at home again.

Miss Leonora's half dozen postcards have come to us from points in as many states: Alabama, Georgia, North Carolina, West Virginia, Kentucky—in that order. It is considered a fair guess that her next card will come from Missouri or Arkansas, and that the one after that will be from Mississippi or Louisiana. She seems to be orbiting her native state of Tennessee. But, on the other hand, there is no proof that she has not crossed the state, back and forth, a number of times during the past two weeks. She is quite an old lady, and is driving a 1942 Dodge convertible. Anyone traveling in the region indicated should watch out for two characteristics of her driving. First, she hates to be overtaken and passed by other vehicles—especially by trucks. The threat of such is apt to make her bear down on the accelerator and try to outdistance the would-be passer. Or, if passed, she can be counted on to try to overtake and pass the offender at first chance. The second characteristic is: when driving after dark, she invariably refuses to dim her lights unless an approaching car has dimmed its own while at least five hundred feet away. She is a good judge of distances, and she is not herself blinded by bright lights on the highway. And one ought to add that, out of long habit and for reasons best known to herself, Miss Leonora nearly always drives by night.

Some description will be due, presently, of this lady's person and of how she will be dressed while traveling. But that had better wait a while. It might seem prejudicial and even misleading with reference to her soundness of mind. And any question of that sort, no matter what the rest of the world may think, has no bearing upon the general consternation that her going away has created here.

Wherever Miss Leonora Logan is today, she knows in her heart that in the legal action recently taken against her in Thomasville there was no malice directed toward her personally. She knows this, and would say so. At this very moment she may be telling some newfound friend the history of the case—because I happen to know that when she is away from home she talks to people about herself and her forebears as she would never do to anyone here. And chances are she is giving a completely unbiased version of what has happened, since that is her way.

The cause of all our present tribulation is this: The Logan property, which Miss Leonora inherited from one of her paternal great-uncles and which normally upon her death would have gone to distant relatives of hers in Chicago, has been chosen as the site for our county's new consolidated high school. A year and a half ago, Miss Leonora was offered a fair price for the three-acre tract and the old house, and she refused it. This summer, condemnation proceedings were begun, and two weeks ago the county court granted the writ. This will seem to you a bad thing for the town to have done, especially in view of the fact that Miss Leonora has given long years of service to our school system. She retired ten years ago after teaching for twenty-five years in the old high school. To be sure, four of us who are known hereabouts as Miss Leonora Logan's favorites among the male citizenry refused to have any part in the action. Two of us even preferred to resign from the school board. But still, times do change, and the interests of one individual cannot be allowed to hinder the progress of a whole community. Miss Leonora understands that. And she knows that her going away can only delay matters for a few weeks at most. Nevertheless, she is making it look very bad for Thomasville, and we want Miss Leonora to come home.

The kind of jaunt that she has gone off on isn't anything new for the old lady. During the ten years since her retirement she has been setting out on similar excursions rather consistently every month or so, and never, I believe, with a specific itinerary or destination in mind. Until she went away this time, people had ceased to bother themselves with the question of her whereabouts while she was gone or to be concerned about any harm that might come to her. We have been more inclined to think of the practical value her trips have for us. In the past, you see, she was never away for more than a week or ten days, and on her return she would gladly give anyone a full and accurate account of places visited and of the condition of roads traveled. It has, in fact, become the custom when you are planning an automobile trip to address yourself to Miss Leonora on the public square one day and ask her advice on the best route to take. She is our authority not only on the main highways north, south, east, and west of here, in a radius of six or eight hundred miles, but even on the secondary and unimproved roads in places as remote as Brown County, Indiana, and the Outer Banks of North Carolina. Her advice is often very detailed, and will include warnings against "single-lane bridges" or "soft shoulders" or even "cops patrolling in unmarked cars."

It is only the facts she gives you, though. She doesn't express appreciation for the beauty of the countryside or her opinion of the character of towns she passes through. The most she is likely to say is that such-and-such a road is "regarded" as the scenic route, or that a certain town has a "well-worked-out traffic system." No one can doubt that while driving, Miss Leonora keeps her eyes and mind on the road. And that may be the reason why we have never worried about her. But one asks oneself, What pleasure can she ever have derived from these excursions? She declares that she hates the actual driving. And when giving advice on the roads somewhere she will always say that it is a dull and tedious trip and that the traveler will wish himself home in Thomasville a thousand times before he gets to wherever he is going.

Miss Leonora's motivation for taking these trips was always, until the present instance, something that it seemed pointless even to speculate on. It just seemed that the mood came on her and she was off and away. But if anything happens to her now, all the world will blame *us* and say we *sent* her on this journey, sent her out alone and possibly in a dangerous frame of mind. In particular, the blame will fall on the four timid male citizens who were the last to see her in Thomasville (for I do not honestly believe we will ever see her alive here again) and who, as old friends and former pupils of hers at the high school, ought to have prevented her going away. As a matter of fact, I am the one who opened the car door for the old lady that afternoon and politely assisted her into the driver's seat—and without even saying I thought it unwise of her to go. I *thought* it unwise, but at the moment it was as if I were still her favorite pupil twenty years before, and as if I feared she might reprove me for any small failure of courtesy like not opening the car door.

That's how the old lady is—or was. Whatever your first relation to her might have been, she would never allow it to change, and some people even say that that is why she discourages us so about the trips we plan. She cannot bear to think of us away from Thomasville. She thinks this is where all of us belong. I remember one day at school when some boy said to her that he wished he lived in a place like Memphis or Chattanooga. She gave him the look she usually reserved for the people she caught cheating. I was seated in the first row of the class that day, and I saw the angry patches of red appear on her broad, flat cheeks and on her forehead. She paused a moment to rearrange the combs in her hair and to give the stern yank to her corset that was a sure sign she was awfully mad. (We used to say that, with her spare figure, she only wore a corset for the sake of that expressive gesture.) The class was silent, waiting. Miss Leonora looked out the window for a moment, squinting up her eyes as if she could actually make out the Memphis or even the Chattanooga skyline on the horizon. Then, turning back to the unfortunate boy, she said, grinding out her words to him through clenched teeth, "I wish I could *throw* you there!"

But it is ten years now since Miss Leonora retired, and, strange as it may sound, the fact of her having once taught in our school system was never introduced into the deliberations of the school board last

spring—their deliberations upon whether or not they ought to sue
for condemnation of the Logan home place. No doubt it was right
that they didn't let this influence their decision. But what really
seems to have happened is that nobody even recalled that the old
lady had once been a teacher—or nobody but a very few, who did
not want to remind the others.

What they remembered, to the exclusion of everything else, and
what they always remember is that Miss Leonora is the last of the
Logan family in Thomasville, a family that for a hundred years and
more did all it could to impede the growth and progress of our
town. It was a Logan, for instance, who kept the railroad from
coming through town; it was another Logan who prevented the
cotton mill and the snuff factory from locating here. They even kept
us from getting the county seat moved here, until after the Civil
War, when finally it became clear that nobody was ever going to
buy lots up at Logan City, where they had put the first courthouse.
Their one idea was always to keep the town unspoiled, unspoiled by
railroads or factories or even county politics. Perhaps they should
not be blamed for wanting to keep the town unspoiled. Yet I am not
quite sure about that. It is a question that even Miss Leonora doesn't
feel sure about. Otherwise, why does she always go into that
question with the people she meets away from home?

I must tell you about the kind of lodging Miss Leonora takes
when she stops for rest, and about the kind of people she finds to
talk to. She wouldn't talk to you or me, and she wouldn't put up at
a hotel like mine, here on the square, or even at a first-class motel like
one of those out on the Memphis-Chattanooga bypass. I have asked
her very direct questions about this, pleading a professional interest,
and I have filled in with other material furnished by her friends of
the road who have from time to time stopped in here at my place.

On a pretty autumn day like today, she will have picked a
farmhouse that has one of those little home-lettered signs out by the

mailbox saying "Clean Rooms for Tourists—Modern Conveniences."
(She will, that is, unless she has changed her ways and taken to a
different life, which is the possibility that I do not like to think of.)
She stops only at places that are more or less in that category—old-
fashioned tourist homes run by retired farm couples or, if the place
is in town, by two old-maid sisters. Such an establishment usually
takes its name from whatever kind of trees happen to grow in the
yard—Maple Lawn or Elmwood or The Oaks. Or when there is a
boxwood plant, it will be called Boxwood Manor. If the place is in
the country, like the one today, it may be called Oak Crest.

You can just imagine how modern the modern conveniences at
Oak Crest are. But it is cheap, which is a consideration for Miss
Leonora. And the proprietors are probably good listeners, which is
another consideration. She generally stops in the daytime, but since
even in the daytime she can't sleep for long, she is apt to be found
helping out with the chores. Underneath the Oak Crest "Clean
Rooms for Tourists" sign there may be one that says "Sterile Day-
Old Eggs" or, during the present season, "Delicious Apples and
Ripe Tomatoes." It wouldn't surprise me if you found Miss Leonora
today out by the roadside assisting with the sale of Oak Crest's
garden produce. And if that's the case she is happy in the knowledge that any passer-by will mistake her for the proprietress's
mother or old-maid sister, and never suppose she is a paying guest.
In her carefully got-up costume she sits there talking to her new
friend. Or else she is in the house or in the chicken yard, talking
away while she helps out with the chores . . . It is Miss Leonora's
way of killing time—killing time until night falls and she can take
to the road again.

Miss Leonora is an intellectual woman, and at the same time she
is an extremely practical and simple kind of person. This makes it
hard for any two people to agree on what she is really like. It is hard
even for those of us who were her favorites when we went to school

to her. For, in the end, we didn't really know her any better than anybody else did. Sometimes she would have one of us up to her house for coffee and cookies on a winter afternoon, but it was hardly a social occasion. We went up there strictly as her students. We never saw any of the house except the little front room that she called her "office" and that was furnished with a roll-top desk, oak bookcases, and three or four of the hardest chairs you ever sat in. It looked more like a schoolroom than her own classroom did, over at the high school. While you sat drinking coffee with her, she was still your English teacher or your history teacher or your Latin teacher, whichever she happened to be at the time, and you were supposed to make conversation with her about *Silas Marner* or Tom Paine or Cicero. If it was a good session and you had shown a little enthusiasm, then she would talk to you some about your future and say you ought to begin thinking about college—because she was always going to turn her favorites into professional men. That was how she was going to populate the town with the sort of people she thought it ought to have. She never got but one of us to college, however, and he came back home as a certified druggist instead of the doctor she had wanted him to be. (Our doctors are always men who have moved in here from somewhere else, and our lawyers are people Miss Leonora wouldn't pay any attention to when they were in school.) . . . I used to love to hear Miss Leonora talk, and I went along with her and did pretty well till toward the end of my last year, when I decided that college wasn't for me. I ought to have gone to college, and I had no better reason for deciding against it than any of the others did. It was just that during all the years when Miss Leonora was talking to you about making something of yourself and making Thomasville a more civilized place to live in, you were hearing at home and everywhere else about what the Logans had done to the town and how they held themselves above everybody else. I got to feeling ashamed of being known as her protégé.

As I said, Miss Leonora is an intellectual woman. She seldom comes out of the post office without a book under her arm that she has specially ordered or that has come to her from one of the national book clubs she belongs to; and she also reads all the cheapest kind of trash that's to be had at the drugstore. She is just a natural-born reader, and enjoys reading the way other people enjoy eating or sleeping. It used to be that she would bedevil all the preachers we got here, trying to talk theology with them, and worry the life out of the lawyers with talk about Hamilton and Jefferson and her theories about men like Henry Clay and John Marshall. But about the time she quit teaching she gave up all that, too.

Aside from the drugstore trash, nobody knows what she reads any more, though probably it is the same as always. We sometimes doubt that she knows herself what she reads nowadays. Her reading seems to mean no more to her than her driving about the country does, and one wonders why she goes on with it, and what she gets out of it. Every night, the light in her office burns almost all night, and when she comes out of the post office with a new book, she has the wrappings off before she is halfway across the square and is turning the pages and reading away—a mile a minute, so it seems— as she strolls through the square and then heads up High Street toward Logana, which is what the Logans have always called their old house. If someone speaks to her, she pretends not to hear the first time. If it is important, if you want some information about the roads somewhere, you have to call her name a second time. The first sign that she is going to give you her attention comes when she begins moving her lips, hurriedly finishing off a page or a paragraph. Then she slams the book closed, as though she is through with it for all time, and before you can phrase your question she begins asking you how you and all your family are. Nobody can give a warmer greeting and make you feel he is gladder to see you than she can. She stands there beating the new book against her thigh, as though the book were some worthless object that she would just as soon throw away, and when she has asked you about yourself and your family she is ready then to talk about any subject under the sun—anything, I ought to add, except herself. If she makes a reference to the book in her hand, it is only to comment on the binding or the print or the quality of the paper. Or she may say that the price of books had gotten all out of bounds and that the postal rate for books is too high. It's always something that any field hand could understand and is a far cry from the way she used to talk about books when we were in school.

I am reminded of one day six or eight years ago when I saw Miss Leonora stopped on the square by an old colored man named Hominy Atkinson. Or his name may really be Harmony Atkinson. I once asked him which it was, and at first he merely grinned and shrugged his shoulders. But then he said thoughtfully, as though it hadn't ever occurred to him before, "Some does call me the one, I s'pose, and some the other." He is a dirty old ignoramus, and the other Negroes say that in the summertime he has his own private swarm of flies that follows him around. His flies were with him that day when he stopped Miss Leonora. He was in his wagon, the way you always see him, and he managed to block the old lady's path when she stepped down off the curb and began to cross the street in front of the post office and had cut diagonally across the courthouse lawn. It was the street over there on the other side of the square that she was about to cross. I was standing nearby with a group of men, under the willow oak trees beside the goldfish pool. Twice before Miss Leonora looked up, Hominy Atkinson lifted a knobby hand to shoo the flies away from his head. In the wagon he was seated on a squat split-bottom chair; and on another chair beside him was his little son Albert. Albert was eight or nine years old at the time, a plump little fellow dressed up in an old-fashioned Buster Brown outfit as tidy and clean as his daddy's rags were dirty.

This Albert is the son of Hominy and the young wife that Hominy took after he was already an old man. The three of them live on a worn-out piece of land three or four miles from town. Albert is a half-grown boy now, and there is nothing very remarkable about him except that they say he still goes to school more regularly than some of the other colored children do. But when he was a little fellow his daddy and mama spoiled and pampered him till, sitting up there in the wagon that day, he had the look of a fat little priss. The fact is, from the time he could sit up in a chair Hominy used never to go anywhere without him—he was so proud of the little pickaninny, and he was so mortally afraid something might happen to him when he was out of his sight. Somebody once asked Hominy why he didn't leave the child home with his mama, and Hominy replied that her hands were kept busy just washing and ironing and sewing for the boy. "It's no easy matter to raise up a clean child," he pronounced. Somebody else asked Hominy one time if he thought it right to take the boy to the square on First Monday, where he would be exposed to some pretty rough talk, or to the fairgrounds during Fair Week. Hominy replied, "What ain't fittin' for him to hear ain't fittin' for me." And it was true that you seldom saw Hominy on that corner of the square where the Negro men congregated or in the stable yard at the fairgrounds.

Before Miss Leonora looked up at Hominy that morning, he sat with his old rag of a hat in his lap, smiling down at her. Finally, she slammed her book shut and lifted her eyes. But Hominy didn't try to ask his question until she had satisfied herself that he, his young wife, and Albert there beside him were in good health, and several other of his relatives whose names she knew. Then he asked it.

"What does you need today, Miss Leonora?" he said. "Me, *I* needs a dollar bill."

She replied without hesitating, "I don't need anything I'd pay *you* a dollar for, Hominy." Hominy didn't bat an eye, only sat there gazing down at her while she spoke. "I have a full herd of your kind up at Logana, Hominy, who'll fetch and go for me without any dollar bill. You know that."

She was referring to the Negro families who live in the outbuildings up at her place. People say that some of them live right in the house with her, but when I used to go up there as a boy she kept them all out of sight. There was not even a sound of them on the place. She didn't even let her cook bring in the coffee things, and it gave you the queer feeling that either she was protecting you from them or them from you.

"What do you think you need a dollar for, Hominy?" she asked presently.

"I needs to buy the boy a book," he said.

"What book?" It was summertime, and she knew the boy wouldn't be in school.

"Why, most any book," said Hominy. "I jist can't seem to keep him in reading."

Miss Leonora peered around Hominy at Albert, who sat looking down at his own fat little washed-up hands, as if he might be ashamed of his daddy's begging. Then Miss Leonora glanced down at the book she had got in the mail. "Here, give him this," she said, handing the brand-new book up to that old tatterdemalion. It was as if she agreed with the old ignoramus that it didn't matter what kind of book the boy got so long as it was a book.

And now Albert himself couldn't resist raising his eyes to see the book that was coming his way. He gave Miss Leonora a big smile, showing a mouthful of teeth as white as his starched shirt collar. "Miss Leonora, you oughtn't to do—" he began in an airy little voice.

But his daddy put a stop to it. "Hush your mouth, honey. Miss

Leonora knows what she's doing. Don't worry about that none." He handed the book over to Albert, hardly looking at it himself. Those of us over by the goldfish pool were never able to make out what the book was.

"I certainly thank you, Miss Leonora," Albert piped.

And Hominy said solemnly, "Yes'm, we are much obliged to you."

"Then move this conveyance of yours and let me pass," said Miss Leonora.

Hominy flipped the reins sharply on the rump of his mule and said, "Giddap, Bridesmaid." The old mule flattened its ears back on its head and pulled away with an angry jerk.

But even when the wagon was out of her way Miss Leonora continued to stand there for a minute or so, watching the receding figure of Albert perched on his chair in the wagon bed and bent over his book examining it the way any ordinary child would have examined a new toy. As long as she stood there the old lady kept her eyes on the little black boy. And before she finally set out across the street, we heard her say aloud and almost as if for our benefit, "It may be . . . It may be . . . I suppose, yes, it may be."

II

School integration is not yet a burning issue in Thomasville. But some men in town were at first opposed to consolidation of our county high schools until it could be seen what kind of pressures are going to be put on us. In the past eighteen months, however, those men have more or less reversed their position. And they do not deny that their change of mind was influenced by the possibility that Logana might be acquired for the site of the new school. Nor do they pretend that it is because they think Logana such an ideal location. They have agreed to go along with the plan, so they say, because it is the only way of getting rid of the little colony of Negroes who have always lived up there and who would make a serious problem for us if it became a question of zoning the town, in some way, as a last barrier against integration. What they say sounds very logical, and any stranger would be apt to accept the explanation at face value. But the truth of the matter is that there are people here who dislike the memory of the Logans even more than they do the prospect of integration. They are willing to risk integration in order to see that last Logan dispossessed of his last piece of real estate in Thomasville. With them it is a matter of superstition almost that until this happens Thomasville will not begin to realize its immemorial aspirations to grow and become a citified place.

So that you will better understand this dislike of the Logan name, I will give you a few more details of their history here. In the beginning, and for a long while, the Logan family didn't seem to want to spoil Thomasville with their own presence even. General Logan laid out the town in 1816, naming it after a little son of his who died in infancy. But during the first generation the Logan wives stayed mostly over in Middle Tennessee, where they felt there were more people of their own kind. And the men came and went only as their interest in the cotton crops required. In those years, Logana was occupied by a succession of slave-driving overseers, as was also the Logans' other house, which used to stand five miles below here at Logan's Landing.

Now, we might have done without the Logan women and without the county seat, which the women didn't want here, but when the Logans kept the railroad out everybody saw the handwriting on the wall. The general's grandson did that. He was Harwell Logan, for many years chief justice of the state, and a man so powerful that in one breath, so to speak, he could deny the railroad company a right of way through town and demand that it give the name Logan Station to our nearest flag stop . . . And what was it the chief justice's son did? Why, it was he who prevented the cotton mill and snuff factory from locating here. The snuff factory would have polluted the air. And the cotton mill would have drawn in the riffraff from all over the county . . . Along about the turn of the century it looked as though we were going to get the insane asylum for West Tennessee, but one of the Logans was governor of the state; he arranged for it to go to Bolivar instead. Even by then, none of the Logan men was coming back here very much except to hunt birds in the fall. They had already scattered out and were living in the big cities where there was plenty of industry and railroads for them to invest their money in; and they had already sold off most of their land to get the money to invest. But they didn't forget Thomasville. No matter how far up in the world a Logan may advance, he seems to go on having sweet dreams about Thomasville. Even though he has never actually lived here himself, Thomasville is the one place he doesn't want spoiled.

Just after the First World War, there was talk of our getting the new veterans' hospital. During the Depression, we heard about a CCC camp. At the beginning of the Second World War, people came down from Washington and took option on big tracts of land for "Camp Logan." Very mysteriously all of those projects failed to materialize. Like everything else, they would have spoiled the town. But what else is there, I ask you, for a town to have except the things that tend to spoil it? What else is there to give it life? We used to have a boys' academy here, and a girls' institute, which is where Miss Leonora did her first teaching. They were boarding schools, and boys and girls came here from everywhere, and spent their money on the public square. It wasn't much, but it was *something*.

The boys' academy closed down before I was born even, and there isn't a trace left of it. The Thomasville Female Institute burned in

1922, and nothing is left of it, either, except the crumbling shells of the old brick buildings. All we have now that you don't see on the square is the cotton gin and the flour mill and the ice plant. We claim a population of eighteen hundred, counting white and colored, which is about five hundred short of what we claimed in the year 1880. It has been suggested that in the next census we count the trees in Thomasville instead of the people. They outnumber us considerably and they have more influence, too. It was to save the willow oaks on the public square and the giant sycamores along High Street that someone arranged to have the Memphis-Chattanooga bypass built in 1952 instead of bringing the new highway through town. It was some Logan who arranged that, you may be sure, and no doubt it gladdens his heart to see the new motels that have gone up out there and to know that the old hotel on the square is never overcrowded by a lot of silly tourists.

To my mind, Miss Leonora Logan is a very beautiful woman. But to think she is beautiful nowadays perhaps you would have to have first seen her as I did when I was not yet five years old. And perhaps you would have to have seen her under the same circumstances exactly.

I don't remember what the occasion was. We were on a picnic of some kind at Bennett's Wood, and it seems to me that half the town was there. Probably it was the Fourth of July, though I don't remember any flags or speeches. A band was playing in the bandstand, and as I walked along between my mother and father I noticed that the trunks of the walnut trees had been freshly whitewashed. The bare earth at the roots of the trees was still dappled with the droppings from the lime buckets. My father pointed out a row of beehives on the far edge of the grove and said he hoped to God nobody would stir the bees up today as some bad boys had once done when there was an outing at Bennett's Wood. My father smiled at Mother when he said this, and my guess is that he had been amongst the boys who did it. My mother smiled, too, and we continued our walk.

It was just before dusk. My impression is that the actual picnicking and the main events of the day were already over. I was holding my mother's hand as we came out from under the trees and into the clearing where Bennett's Pond is. Several groups were out on the pond in rowboats, drifting about among the lily pads. One boat had just drawn up to the grassy bank on the side where we were. My mother leaned toward my father and said in a quiet voice, "Look at Miss Leonora Logan. Isn't she beautiful!"

She was dressed all in white. She had stood up in the boat the moment it touched shore, and it seemed to me that she had risen out of the water itself and were about to step from one of the lily pads onto the bank. I was aware of her being taller than most women whose beauty I had heard admired, and I knew that she was already spoken of as an old maid—that she was older than my mother even; but when she placed the pointed toe of her white shoe on the green sod beside the pond, it was as if that lovely white point had pierced my soul and awakened me to a beauty I had not dreamed of. Her every movement was all lightness and grace, and her head of yellow hair dazzled.

The last rays of the sun were at that moment coming directly toward me across the pond, and presently I had to turn my face away from its glare. But I had the feeling that it was Miss Leonora's eyes and the burning beauty of her countenance that had suddenly blinded me, and when my mother asked me fretfully what was the matter and why I hung back so, I was ashamed. I imagined that Mother could read the thoughts in my head. I imagined also that my mother, who was a plain woman and who as the wife of the hotelkeeper made no pretension to elegance—I imagined that she was now jealous of my admiration for Miss Leonora. With my face still averted, I silently reproached her for having herself suggested the thoughts to me by her remark to my father. I was very angry, and my anger and shame must have brought a deep blush to my whole face and neck. I felt my mother's two fingers thrust under the collar of my middy, and then I was soothed by her sympathetic voice saying "Why, child, you're feverish. We'd better get you home."

I must have had many a glimpse of Miss Leonora when I was a small boy playing on the hotel porch. But the next profound impression she made on me was when I was nine years old. One of the boarding students at the Institute had been stealing the other girls' things. It fell to Miss Leonora to apprehend the thief, who proved to be none other than a member of the Logan clan itself—a sad-faced, unattractive girl, according to all reports, but from a very rich branch of the family. She had been sent back to Thomasville to school all the way from Omaha, Nebraska.

Several hours after Miss Leonora had obtained unmistakable evidence of the girl's guilt and had told her she was to be sent home, it was discovered that the girl had disappeared. Word got out in the town that they were dragging the moat around the old windmill on the Institute grounds for the girl's body. Soon a crowd of towns-people gathered on the lawn before the Institute, near to where the windmill stood. This windmill was no longer used to pump the school's water—the school had town water by then—and there was not even a shaft or any vanes in evidence. But the old brick tower had been left standing. With its moat of stagnant, mossy water around it, it was thought to be picturesque.

The crowd assembled on the lawn some fifty or sixty feet away from the tower, and from there we watched the two Negro men at their work in the moat. The moat was fed by a sluggish wet-weather spring. It was about twenty feet wide and was estimated to be from ten to fifteen feet deep. And so the two men had had to bring in a boat to do their work from. On the very edge of the moat stood Miss Leonora, alongside Dr. Perkins, the chancellor of the Institute, and with them were several other teachers in their dark-blue uniforms. They all kept staring up at the windows of the old brick residence hall, as if to make sure that none of the girls was peering out at the distressing scene.

Presently we heard one of the Negro men say something to the other and heard the other mumble something in reply. We couldn't make out what they said, but we knew that they had found the girl's body. In a matter of two or three minutes they were hauling it up, and all of the women teachers except Miss Leonora buried their faces in their hands. From where we were, the slimy object was hardly recognizable as anything human, but despite this, or because of it, the crowd sent up a chorus of gasps and groans.

Hearing our chorus, Miss Leonora whirled about. She glared at us across the stretch of lawn for a moment, and then she came striding toward us, waving both hands in the air and ordering us to leave. "Go away! Go away!" she called out. "What business have you coming here with your wailing and moaning? A lot you care about that dead girl!" As she drew nearer, I could see her glancing at the ground now and then as if looking for a stick to drive us away with. "Go away!" she cried. "Take your curious eyes away. What right have you to be curious about *our* dead?"

A general retreat began, down the lawn and through the open gateway in the spiked iron fence. I hurried along with the others, but I kept looking back at Miss Leonora, who now stood on the brow of the terraced lawn, watching the retreat with a proud, bemused expression, seeming for the moment to have forgotten the dead young woman in the moat.

How handsome she was standing there, with her high color and her thick yellow hair that seemed about to come loose on her head and fall down on the shoulders of her blue shirtwaist.

Beyond her I had glimpses of the two Negro men lifting the dead body out of the water. They moved slowly and cautiously, but after they had got the girl into the boat and were trying to move her out of the boat onto the lawn, I saw the girl's head fall back. Her wet hair hung down like Spanish moss beneath her, and when the winter sunlight struck it, all at once it looked as green as seaweed. It was very beautiful, and yet, of course, I didn't feel right in thinking it was. It is something I have never been able to forget.

One day when we were in high school, a girl in the class asked Miss Leonora to tell us about "the Institute girl who did away with herself"—because Miss Leonora did sometimes tell us about the old days at the Institute. She stood looking out the classroom window, and seemed to be going over the incident in her mind and trying to decide whether or not it was something we ought to know more about. Finally she said, "No, we'll go on with the lesson now."

But the class, having observed her moment of indecision, began to beg. "Please tell us, Miss Leonora. Please." I don't know how many of the others had been in the crowd that day when they pulled the girl out of the moat. I was not the only one, I'm sure. I think that everybody knew most of the details and only wanted to see if she would refer to the way it ended with her driving the crowd away. But Miss Leonora wouldn't have cared at all, even if she had thought that was our motive. She would have given us her version if she had wanted to.

"Open your books," she said.

But still we persisted, and I was bold enough to ask, "Why not?"

"I'll just tell you why not," she said, suddenly blazing out at me. "Because there is nothing instructive in the story for you."

After that day, I realized, as never before, that though she often seemed to wander from the subject in class, it was never really so. She was eternally instructing us. If only once she had let up on the instruction, we might have learned something—or I might have. I used to watch her for a sign—any sign—of her caring about what we thought of her, or of her *not* caring about her mission among us, if that's what it was. More and more it came to seem incredible to me that she was the same woman I had gone feverish over at Bennett's Wood that time, which was probably before Miss Leonora had perceived her mission. And yet I have the feeling she was the same woman still. Looking back on those high-school days, I know that all along she was watching me and others like me for some kind of sign from us—any sign—that would make us seem worthy of knowing what we wanted to know about her.

I suppose that what we wanted to know, beyond any doubt, was that the old lady had suffered for being just what she was—for being born with her cold, rigid, intellectual nature, and for being born to represent something that had never taken root in Thomasville and that would surely die with her. But not knowing that that was what we wanted to know, we looked for other, smaller things. She didn't, for instance, have lunch in the lunchroom with the other teachers, and she didn't go home for lunch. She had a Negro woman bring her lunch to her on a tray all the way from Logana, on the other side of town. Generally she ate alone in her classroom. Sometimes we made excuses to go back to the room during lunch hour, and when we came out we pretended to the others that we had had a great revelation—that we had caught Miss Leonora Logan eating peas with her knife or sopping her plate with a biscuit. We never caught her doing anything so improper, of course, but it gave us a wonderful pleasure to imagine it.

It was while I was in high school that Miss Leonora inherited Logana. She had already been living in the house most of her life— all of it except for the years when she taught and lived at the Institute—but the house had really belonged to her grandfather's brother in St. Louis. The morning we heard she had inherited the place, we thought surely she would be in high spirits about her good fortune, and before she came into the room that morning one of the girls said she was going to ask her how it felt to be an heiress. It was a question that never got asked, however, because when our teacher finally appeared before us she was dressed in black. She had inherited the house where she had lived most of her life as a poor relation, but she was also in mourning for the dead great-uncle away off in St. Louis. For us it was impossible to detect either the joy over the one event or grief over the other. Perhaps she felt neither, or perhaps she had to hide her feelings because she felt that it was really the great-uncle's death in St. Louis she had inherited and the house in Thomasville she had lost. Our lessons went on that day as though nothing at all had happened.

But before I ever started going to the high school, and before Miss Leonora went there to teach, I had seen her on yet another memorable occasion up at the Institute—the most memorable and dramatic of all, because it was the night that the place burned down. I remember the events of that night very clearly. It was a February night in 1922. The temperature was in the low twenties, and no doubt they had thrown open the drafts in every one of the coal-burning heaters up at the Institute.

The fire broke out in the refectory and spread very rapidly to the residence hall and the classrooms building. Like any big fire, it quickly drew the whole town to the scene. Before most of us got there it was already out of hand. All over town the sky looked like Judgment Day. On the way to the fire, we could hear the floors of the old buildings caving in, one after the other; and so from the beginning there was not much anybody could do. The town waterworks couldn't get enough pressure up there to be of any real use, and after that girl drowned herself they had filled in the old moat around the windmill.

The first thing that happened after I got in sight of the place was that the gingerbread porches, which were already on fire, began to fall away from the buildings. There were porches on the second and third floors of the residence hall, and suddenly they fell away like flaming ladders that somebody had given a kick to. The banisters and posts and rafters fell out into the evergreen shrubbery, and pretty soon the smell of burning hemlock and cedar filled the air . . . The teachers had got all the girls out safely, and the first men to arrive even saved some of the furniture and the books, but beyond that there was nothing to be done except to stand and watch the flames devour the innards of the buildings. This was very fascinating to everybody, and the crowd shifted from one point to another, always trying to get a better view and to see into which room or down which corridor the flames would move next.

Miss Leonora was as fascinated as any of the rest of us, and it was this about her that impressed me that night. It was not till later that I heard about how she behaved during the first phase of the fire. She had dashed about from building to building screaming orders to everyone, even to the fire brigade when it arrived. She would not believe it when the firemen told her that the water pressure could not be increased. She threw a bucket of water in one man's face when he refused to take that bucket and climb up a second-story porch with it.

I didn't see any of that. When I arrived, Miss Leonora was already resigned to the total loss that was inevitable. On a little knob of earth on the north side of the lawn, which people used to call the Indian Mound, she had taken her position all alone and isolated from the general crowd. The other teachers had been sent off with the Institute girls to the hotel, where my mother was waiting to receive them. But wrapped in a black fur cape—it was bearskin, I think, and must have been a hand-me-down from some relative— Miss Leonora was seated on one of the iron benches that were grouped over there on the mound. Her only companions were two iron deer that stood nearby, one with its head lowered as if grazing, the other with its iron antlers lifted and its blank iron eyes fixed on the burning buildings.

She sat there very erect, looking straight ahead. It was hard to tell whether she was watching the flames or watching the people watch the flames. Perhaps she was fascinated equally by both. It was all over for her. She knew that practically nothing was going to be saved, but still she wanted to see how it would go. Now and then a shaft of flame would shoot up into the overcast sky, lighting up the mixture of cloud and smoke above us, and also lighting up the figure of Miss Leonora over on the mound. Some of the women whispered amongst themselves, "Poor Miss Leonora! The school was her life." But if you caught a glimpse of her in one of those moments when the brightest light was on her, it wasn't self-pity or despair you saw written on her face. You saw her awareness of what was going on around her, and a kind of curiosity about it all that seemed almost inhuman and that even a child was bound to resent somewhat. She looked dead herself, but at the same time very much alive to what was going on around her.

III

When Miss Leonora's house was condemned two weeks ago, *somebody* had to break the news to her. They couldn't just send the clerk up there with the notice, or, worse still, let her read it in the newspaper. The old lady had to be warned of how matters had gone . . . We left the courthouse at four o'clock that afternoon, and set out for the Logan place on foot. None of us wanted to go, but who else would go if we didn't? That was how Judge Potter had put it to us. I suppose we elected to go on foot merely because it would take longer to get up there that way.

It was while we walked along under the sycamores on High Street that I let the others talk me into doing the job alone. They said that I had, after all, been her very favorite—by which they meant only that I was her first favorite—and that if we went in a group she might take it as a sign of cowardice, might even tell us it was that to our faces. It was a funny business, and we laughed about it a little amongst ourselves, though not much. Finally, I agreed that the other three men should wait behind the sumac and elderberry down in the lane, while I went up to see Miss Leonora alone.

Once this was settled, the other three men turned to reminiscing about their experiences with Miss Leonora when they were in high school. But I couldn't concentrate on what they said. It may have been because I knew their stories so well. Or maybe it wasn't that. At any rate, when we had walked two blocks up High Street I realized that I was out of cigarettes, and I told the others to wait a minute while I stepped into the filling station, on the corner there, to buy a package. When I paid for the cigarettes, Buck Wallace, who operates the station, looked at me and said, "Well, how did it go? Do we condemn?"

I nodded and said, "We're on the way up there to tell her, Buck."

"I guessed you were," he said. He glanced out the window at the others, and I looked out at them, too. For a second it seemed that I was seeing them through Buck Wallace's eyes—them and myself. And the next second it seemed, for some reason, that I was seeing them through Miss Leonora's eyes—them and myself. We all had on our business suits, our lightweight topcoats, our gray fedoras; we were the innkeeper, the druggist, a bank clerk, and the rewrite man from the weekly paper. Our ages range from thirty to fifty—with me at the top—but we were every one of us decked out to look like the same kind of thing. We might have just that minute walked out of the Friday-noon meeting of the Exchange Club. In Buck Wallace's eyes, however, we were certainly not the cream of the Exchange Club crop—*not* the men who were going to get Thomasville its due. And in Miss Leonora's eyes we were a cut above the

Exchange Club's ringleaders, though not enough above them to matter very much. To both her and Buck we were merely the go-betweens. It just happened that we were the last people left in town that the old lady would speak to, and so now we—or, rather, I—was going up to Logana and tell her she would have to accept the town's terms of unconditional surrender.

"You may be too late," Buck added as I was turning away. I looked back at him with lifted eyebrows. "She was in here a while ago," he went on to report, "getting her car gassed up. She said how she was about to take off on one of her trips. She said she might wait till she heard from the courthouse this afternoon and again she might not . . . She was got up kind of peculiar."

When I rejoined the other men outside, I didn't tell them what Buck had said. Suddenly I mistrusted them, and I didn't trust myself. Or rather I knew I *could* trust myself to let *them* have their way if they thought Miss Leonora was about to leave town. I was pretty sure she wouldn't leave without hearing from us, and I was pretty sure they would want to head us back to the courthouse immediately and send official word up there before she could get away. It would have been the wise thing to do, but I didn't let it happen.

In the filling station Buck Wallace had said to me that she was "got up kind of peculiar," and that meant, to my understanding, that Miss Leonora was dressed in one of two ways. Neither was a way that I had ever seen her dressed, and I wanted to see for myself. It meant either that she was got up in a lot of outmoded finery or she was wearing her dungarees! Because that is how, for ten years now, the old lady has been turning up at the tourist homes where she stops, and that is how, if you wanted to recognize her on the road, you would have to watch out for her. Either she would be in her finery—with the fox fur piece, and the diamond earrings, and the high-crowned velvet hat, and the kind of lace choker that even old ladies don't generally go in for any more and that Miss Leonora has never been seen to wear in Thomasville except by a very few— or she would be in her dungarees! The dungarees are the hardest to imagine, of course. With them she wears a home-knit, knee-length cardigan sweater. And for headgear she pulls on a big poke bonnet she has resurrected from somewhere, or sometimes she stuffs her long hair up under a man's hunting cap or an old broad-brimmed straw hat. A queer sight she must present riding about the country-side these autumn nights; and if she rides with the top of her con-vertible put back, as I've heard of her doing in the dead of winter even, why, it's enough to scare any children who may see her and some grown people, too . . . Here in Thomasville, only Buck Wal-lace and a few others have seen her so garbed, and they only rarely, only sometimes when she was setting out on a trip. They say she looks like some inmate who has broken out of the asylum over at Bolivar.

But that's how she turns up at the tourist homes. If she is with the two old maids at Boxwood Manor or Maple Lawn, she affects the choker and the diamond earrings. She sits down in their parlor and removes the high-crowned velvet, and she talks about how the traditions and institutions of our country have been corrupted and says that soon not one stone will be left upon another. And, still using such terms and phrases, she will at last get round to telling them the story of her life and the history of the Logan family in Thomasville. She tells it all in the third person, pretending it is some friend of hers she has in mind, and the family of that friend. But the old maids know right along that it is herself she is speaking of, and they say she seems to know they know it and seems not to care . . . And if she is with the farm couple at Oak Crest, then she's in her dungarees. She at once sets about helping with the chores, if they will let her. She talks religion to them and says there is no religion left amongst the people in the towns, says that they have forsaken the fountain of living waters and hewed them out broken cisterns that can hold no water—or something like that. And finally she gets round to telling *them* her story, again pretending that it is some friend of hers she is speaking of, and again with her listeners knowing it is herself. The farm couple won't like seeing an old woman wearing dungarees, but they will catch the spirit of her get-up, and they understand what it means. For they have known other old women there in the country who, thrown entirely on their own, living alone and in desperate circumstances, have gotten so they dress in some such outrageous way. And the two old maids probably still have some eye for fashion and they find Miss Leonora pretty ridiculous. But they remember other old ladies who did once dress like that, and it seems somehow credible that there might still be one somewhere.

When Miss Leonora is at home in Thomasville, it is hard to believe she ever dresses herself up so. Here we are used to seeing her always in the most schoolteacherish, ready-made-looking clothes. After the Institute burned, she changed from the uniform that the Institute teachers wore to what amounts to a uniform for our high-school teachers—the drab kind of street dresses that can be got through the mail-order catalogues. Right up till two weeks ago, that's how we were still seeing the old lady dressed. It was hard to realize that in her old age she had had a change of heart and was wishing that either she had played the role of the spinster great lady the way it is usually played or that she had married some dirt farmer and spent her life working alongside him in the fields.

I even used to think that perhaps Miss Leonora didn't really want to go off masquerading around the country—that it was a kind of madness and meant something that would be much more difficult to explain, and that all the time she was at home she was dreading her next seizure. Recently, however, I've come to realize that that wasn't the case. For years, her only satisfaction in life has been her periodic escapes into a reality that is scattered in bits and pieces along the highways and back roads of the country she travels. And what I hope above all else is that Miss Leonora *is* stopping today at Oak Crest or Boxwood Manor and *does* have on her dungarees or lace choker.

But now I must tell what makes me doubt that she is, after all, staying at one of those tourist homes she likes, and what makes me afraid that we may never see her here again.

I left the other men down at the corner of the lane and went up the dirt driveway to Logana alone. Her car was parked at the foot of the porch steps, and so there was no question about her being there. I saw her first through one of the sidelights at the front door and wasn't sure it was she. Then she opened the door, saying, "Dear boy, come in." I laughed, it was so unlike her to call me that. That was not her line at all. She laughed, too, but it was a kind of laugh that was supposed to put me at my ease rather than to criticize or commend me, which would have been very much more in her line . . . I saw at a glance that this wasn't the Miss Leonora I had known, and wasn't one that I had heard about from her tourist-home friends, either.

She had done an awful thing to her hair. Her splendid white mane, with its faded yellow streaks and its look of being kept up on her head only by the two tortoise-shell combs at the back, was no more. She had cut it off, thinned it, and set it in little waves close to her head, and, worse still, she must have washed it in a solution of indigo bluing. She had powdered the shine off her nose, seemed almost to have powdered its sharpness and longness away. She may have applied a little rouge and lipstick, though hardly enough to be noticeable, only enough to make you realize it wasn't the natural coloring of an old lady and enough to make you *think* how old she was. And the dress she had on was exactly right with the hair and the face, though at first I couldn't tell why.

As I walked beside her from the center hall into her "office," her skirt made an unpleasant swishing sound that seemed out of place in Miss Leonora's house and that made me observe more closely what the dress was really like. It was of a dark silk stuff, very stiff, with a sort of middy-blouse collar, and sleeves that stopped a couple of inches above the wrists, and a little piece of belt in back, fastened on with two big buttons—very stylish, I think. For a minute I couldn't remember where it was I had seen this very woman before. Then it came to me. All that was lacking was a pair of pixie glasses with rhinestone rims, and a half dozen bracelets on her wrists. She was one of those old women who come out here from Memphis looking for antiques and country hams and who tell you how delighted they are to find a Southern town that is truly unchanged.

Even so, I half expected Miss Leonora to begin by asking me about my family and then about what kind of summer I had had. "Now, I know you have had a fine summer—all summers are fine to a boy your age," she would say. "So don't tell me what you have been doing. Tell me what you have been *thinking*, what you have been *reading*." It was the room that made me imagine she would still go on that way. Because the room was the same as it used to be. Even the same coffee cups and blue china coffeepot were set out on the little octagonal oak table, beside the plate of butter cookies. And for a moment I had the same guilty feeling I used always to have; because, of course, I hadn't been reading anything and hadn't been thinking anything she would want to hear about.

What she actually said was much kinder and was what anybody might have said under the circumstances. "I've felt so bad about your having to come here like this. I knew they would put it off on you. Even you must have dreaded coming, and you must hate me for putting you in such a position."

"Why, no. I wanted to come, Miss Leonora," I lied. "And I hope you have understood that I had no part in the proceedings." It was what, for months, I had known I would say, and it came out very easily.

"I do understand that," she said. "And we don't even need to talk about any of it."

But I said, "The county court has granted the writ condemning your property. They will send a notice up to you tomorrow morning. You ought to have had a lawyer represent you, and you ought to have come yourself."

I had said what I had promised Judge Potter I would say; she had her warning. And now I was on my own. She motioned me to sit down in a chair near the table where the coffee things were. When she poured out the coffee into our two cups, it was steaming hot. It smelled the way it used to smell in that room on winter afternoons, as fresh as if it were still brewing on the stove. I knew she hadn't made it herself, but, as in the old days, too, the Negro woman who had made it didn't appear or make a sound in the kitchen. You wouldn't have thought there was one of them on the place. There didn't seem to be another soul in the house but just herself and me. But *I* knew that the house was full of them, really. And there was still the feeling that either she was protecting me from them or them from me. I experienced the old uneasiness in addition to something new. And as for Miss Leonora, she seemed to sense from the start that the other three men were waiting down the lane—the three who had been even less willing than I to come, and who were that much nearer to the rest of the town in their feelings. Several times she referred to them, giving a little nod of her head in the direction of the very spot where I had left them waiting.

"When I think of the old days, the days when I used to have you up here—you and the others, too—I realize I was too hard on you. I asked too much of my pupils. I know that now."

It was nothing like the things the real Miss Leonora used to say. It was something anybody might have said.

And a little later: "I was unrealistic. I tried to be to you children what I thought you needed to have somebody be. That's a mistake, always. One has to try to be with people what they want one to be. Each of *you* tried to be that for me, to an admirable degree. Tim Hadley tried hardest—he went to college—but he didn't have your natural endowments." Then she took pains to say something good and something forgiving about each of the four. And, unless I imagined it, for each of those that hadn't come up with me she gave another nod in the direction of the elderberry and sumac thicket down at the corner.

"We were a dumb bunch, all along the line," I said, not meaning it—or not meaning it about myself.

"Nonsense. You were all fine boys, and *you* were my brightest hope," she said, with an empty cheerfulness.

"But you can't make a silk purse out of—" I began.

"Nonsense," she said again. "It was neither you nor I that failed." But she didn't care enough to make any further denial or explanation. She set her cup down on the table and rose from her chair. "It's been like old times, hasn't it," she said with a vague smile.

I looked away from her and sat gazing about the office, still holding my empty cup in my hand. It hadn't been like old times at all, of course. The room and the silence of the house were the same, but Miss Leonora was already gone, and without her the house was nothing but a heap of junk. I thought to myself that the best thing that could happen would be for them to begin moving out the furniture and moving out the Negroes and tearing the place down as soon as possible. Suddenly, I spied her black leather traveling bag over beside the doorway, and she must have seen my eyes light upon it. "I'm about to get off on a little trip," she said.

I set my cup down on the table and looked up at her. I could see she was expecting me to protest. "Will it be long?" I asked, not protesting.

"I don't know, dear boy. You know how I am."

I glanced at the traveling bag again, and this time I noticed her new cloth coat lying on the straight chair beside the bag. I got up and went over and picked up the coat and held it for her.

On the way out to the car, I kept reminding myself that this was really Miss Leonora Logan and that she was going away before receiving any official notice of the jury's verdict. Finally, when we were standing beside her car and she was waiting for me to put the bag, which I was carrying, inside the car, I looked squarely into her eyes. And there is no denying it; the eyes were still the same as always, not just their hazel color but their expression, their look of awareness—awareness of you, the individual before her, a very flattering awareness until presently you realized it was merely of you as an individual in her scheme of things for Thomasville. She was still looking at me as though I were one of the village children that she would like so much to make something of. I opened the car door. I tossed the bag into the space behind the driver's seat. I even made sure I did the thing to her satisfaction by putting one hand out to her elbow as she slipped stiffly in under the steering wheel.

Neither of us made any pretense of saying goodbye. I stood there and watched the car as it bumped along down the driveway, raising a little cloud of dust in the autumn air. The last I saw of her was a glimpse of her bluinged head through the rear window of her convertible. When she turned out into the lane and headed away from town toward the bypass, I knew that the other three men would be watching. But they wouldn't be able to see how she was got up, and I knew they would hardly believe me when I told them.

I have told nearly everybody in town about it, and I think nobody really believes me. I have almost come to doubt it myself. And, anyway, I like to think that in her traveling bag she had the lace-choker outfit that she could change into along the way, and the dungarees, too; and that she is stopping at her usual kind of place today and is talking to the proprietors about Thomasville. Otherwise, there is no use in anyone's keeping an eye out for her. She will look too much like a thousand others, and no doubt will be driving on the highway the way everybody else does, letting other people pass her, dimming her lights for everyone. Maybe she even drives in the daytime, and maybe when she stops for the night it is at a big, modern motel with air conditioning and television in every room. The postcards she sends us indicate nothing about how she is dressed, of course, or about where and in what kind of places she is stopping. She says only that she is in good health, that it is wonderful weather for driving about the country, and that the roads have been improved everywhere. She says nothing about when we can expect her to come home.